THE IMMORTAL LOVE SERIES
BOOK 1

ANNA SANTOS

Copyright © 2016 Anna Santos
Extended Edition
Copyright© 2021 Anna Santos
All rights reserved.
**Inquiries about additional permissions should
be directed to:**authorannasantos@gmail.com

Cover Design by Cristal Designs
Edited by Marcy Anderson
Proofread by Nancy Zee

*This is a work of fiction. Names, characters,
places, brands, media, and incidents are either
the product of the author's imagination or are
used fictitiously. Any resemblance to similarly
named places or to persons living or deceased
is unintentional.*

DEDICATION

To the ones who dream with their eyes open.

CURRENTLY AVAILABLE

Soulmate – Book 1
The Witch and the Vampire King– Book 2
Spellbound – Book 3
Shattered – Book 4
Sacrifice—Book5
Claimed—Book 6

For an updated list of books, and to have access to my upcoming releases, check my **website**:

http://www.annasantosauthor.com

Or Facebook:
https://www.facebook.com/AnnaSantosAuthor

CHAPTER ONE

SHANE

SHE WAS A VISION in black leather pants and a sexy white top. With dazzling, big, blue eyes and a doll-like face with red pouty lips, she moved with the grace and prowess of a feline. All eyes followed her—both male and female—as she walked toward the counter and took a seat on a stool. Brushing back her long black hair away from her face, her skin gave off a gentle glow, looking softer than silk.

I couldn't help but feel drawn to her like a June bug to a porch light. *Can she be the most beautiful woman I've ever seen?* I'd lived for more than two mortal lives. Never in that time had I ever wanted to get to know a woman as badly as I wanted this one. It was as if she had a magnetic pull and the ability to make me forget about everything around me. All but her turned into a blur as my senses focused on her presence.

The pull I felt served as a reason to approach her. With no control over my body, I walked to the counter, sat next to her, and flashed my sexiest smile.

God! Her scent is an addiction, completely intoxicating. She smelled like a bouquet of roses, orchids, poppies, Heaven, vanilla, and candy. What a feast for my senses! She was the personification of lust, temptation, and dreams come true. I couldn't believe it. I had long since lost faith in finding her, but there she was, after all this time: *my soulmate.*

"I'm not interested," she replied to my smile before I'd had the opportunity of opening my mouth. "You're not my type," she added as an afterthought.

That caught me off guard. *What's that even supposed to mean?*

Stupidly, I asked, "And what is your type?" I'm not usually that pathetic with words, but I'm not often rejected, either. Come to think of it, I've never been rejected before.

The downside of your soulmate being a human—she doesn't recognize you as *hers*.

The stunning creature didn't answer my stupid question, thankfully. She just took a good look at me as if I were an annoyance, averted her eyes, and called for a drink from the bartender. He had a smile on his face before looking over and giving me a mocking expression as if to call me a loser. Sam was probably gloating at the fact that I'd been rejected, but he didn't know I wasn't going to give up on her that easily. After all, she was my other half.

My eyes wandered down her figure, intrigued by her choice of clothes. She was so sexy, my heart hurt. Yet, that wasn't the safest night for her to enter this place. There was a gang of dangerous predators lurking in a dark corner of the bar. Their eyes were riveted on her. I could sense their heads turning, smelling the air to catch her intoxicating scent.

She was too irresistible to be true, and I was utterly dazzled by her. I couldn't even believe that she was here. It was like a dream, and if it truly was one, I dearly hoped I never awoke from it.

"Can I buy you a drink?" I asked, trying to make conversation.

Sparing me a look, she requested, "Could you just leave?" Her tone was soft but not impolite—far from it. She had a sexy, girly voice, and I swear I could detect a hint of concern. Like being far away from her was the best option for me.

The problem was that she was mine. At least, I would do anything to make her mine. Leaving her there to be a vampire's snack was out of the question. It was out of the question before I smelled her. Now, it was a death sentence to anyone who dared to touch her.

"Are you new in town?" I was curious and wouldn't be driven away anytime soon.

"Yes," she answered, throwing back more of her drink.

I noticed that she was looking at the mirrors on the wall. Her eyes were on the dark figures not far from us. I almost sighed with impatience. Humans were inclined to get themselves in danger. They were drawn to evil creatures like moths to flames. She couldn't possibly be serious.

That dark 'emo' look attracts her?

They weren't even the best-looking specimens of their race. They were newborn, pale, and skinny. The vampires had arrived an hour ago, and I had only seen them two or three times before. They weren't from my town. Still, they knew who I was, and they hadn't caused any trouble—yet. Even if they looked hungry, in a bar filled with werewolves and shapeshifters, they wouldn't get lucky. If they knew what was good for them, they would leave and stop staring at the girl.

Moments after, as if they had read my thoughts, the vampires got up and glided out of the bar. My eyes followed them, my hand ready on the gun resting at my hip, so they would get the message. She was under my protection, and if they dared to make her an unwilling blood donor, they would feel my wrath. I was the law in this town, and they would do well to remember it.

But as the vamps left, she got up, paid for her drink, and walked toward the exit. For a moment, I must confess, I was hooked on her luxurious curves until I realized that she was leaving. I didn't know her name or her phone number, and the vampires would smell her arrival into the dark of the night.

I grabbed my coat and headed outside, only to encounter my enticing soulmate zipping up a leather jacket and sitting on a killer-looking bike that would make any biker's dreams come true, such as my own.

I thought I was hallucinating because it was farfetched that my dream girl rode a bike, and she had such impeccable taste.

That's so damn hot!

Putting a backpack on her back, she reached for the helmet. That was when the vampires came out of the dark and passed her, joking and pushing each other as if drunk. I knew better. The temptation was too much for them to resist. Even the possibility of dealing with me wasn't enough to deter them from backing off.

The young woman must have sensed that something was amiss because she put her helmet down and took her backpack off, looking from me to them as if intrigued. They were closer to her, and they were incredibly fast when they needed or wanted to be. I'm also fast at shooting, and I'm strong and deadly when I have to be. No blood-sucking monster would lay a hand on her precious head, especially not when she was meant to be mine.

The vampires seemed to reconsider when they saw my eyes narrowing and my hand falling to the revolver that would shoot special wooden and silver bullets. I was prepared, and they knew that. I had killed others who didn't respect the laws of this town. I would kill again without hesitation, and they knew that as well. So, they had to have known that it would be smarter to back off and leave. I guess they were feeling foolish because two sped over to attack me, and one jumped on her.

She screamed, but before she could do much more, the vampires were already exploding into ashes while my revolver smoked from the three precise and quick bullets I'd shot. After checking that there weren't any more vampires in sight to harm my soulmate, I re-holstered my gun.

When I looked at her, she stood blinking at the falling ashes. Then her eyes widened as she looked at me, surely confused by the disappearance of the three supposed men. Humans naturally assume they are hallucinating and try to forget all things supernatural, as they are impossible to be true. Vampires vanishing into wisps of ash only happens in movies.

I wanted to say something to reassure her, but before I could open my mouth, she was falling to the ground. I rushed to her in time to stop her from hitting the dusty pavement. She fainted into my arms.

"Miss?" I felt stupid calling her that, but I didn't know her name. I caught her against my chest, and her scent hit me only to soothe my soul as my body tensed, and my wolf softly growled in my mind. We were both awestruck.

My arms around her felt right. We were made for each other, and I didn't know if it was the mate bond acting out, but everything about her seemed perfect. I never wanted to let her go.

Meanwhile, no one came outside. They knew better than that, except for Sam. He came to see if I was still alive and brought me back to reality.

"Problem solved?" he asked, not making a fuss about it. It wasn't anything that hadn't happened before.

"Yeah," I grumbled in reply, more concentrated on the human than on him. "Take care of her bike, will you?" I shouted over my shoulder.

"Right," he answered, giving me the thumbs up in reassurance.

I carried her, sat her on the front seat of my car, and drove home. It was a waste of time to take her to see a doctor. She would eventually wake up, and a cup of tea would be enough to calm her down. Besides, once she woke up and properly thanked me for saving her life, I was hoping I could convince her to stay and give me a chance. After all, we were meant to be together.

I needed to find out who she was and why she was traveling with only a backpack. She looked young and delicate. It could have been my protective instinct kicking in, but I wanted to take care of her. Not to mention that I wanted to know *everything* about her.

While I was driving, it was hard to concentrate on the road.

The woman was lovely. Even though my heart had almost stopped beating with the possibility of losing her minutes after finding her, now that the danger was gone, her scent relaxed me, and her presence ignited a spark of hope in my heart.

I had found her.

Her mouth was enticing. Just thinking about a kiss from those lips had me trembling. The sexual attraction was overwhelming. I wondered how it would be to have her husky voice in my ear, begging me for more kisses while moaning in pleasure...

I'm losing it! I should probably stop having those fantasies due to the growing tightness in the front of my pants. It would look bad if I had a raging hard-on when she woke up in my home.

I needed to control my urges, even if she was a gorgeous temptation. My sex fantasies were out of the question for the time being. I was more interested in taking care of her and making sure she was okay. She wasn't some hot woman to have a good time with. She was going to be my whole world, and I was hell-bent on making her realize that she couldn't live without me, either.

CHAPTER TWO
ANNABEL

WITH SHORT BROWN HAIR, dazzling blue eyes, high cheekbones, and plump, heart-shaped lips, this guy was the hottest I've seen in a while. In fact, his face should be immortalized in photos or paintings of how handsome it was.

The one-week stubble made him even sexier as he smiled at me. For a moment, I forgot the purpose of being in that forsaken place in the middle of nowhere. Saying that he was dreamy was not enough, but I lacked the proper adjectives to describe how breathtaking and distracting he was.

I'd followed every curve made by his shirt and jeans when I first noticed him at the back of the bar. Even with so many guys there, it was like my senses were drawn to him and only him. I could not deny that he was hot. He would be quite gorgeous in his birthday suit. He was a real temptation on legs, but one I couldn't afford at that moment. Still, one I had difficulty resisting after listening to his deep, sexy voice as he tried to make conversation. I never expected him to come to me. I'd hoped to go to him. The weird pulling attraction to him was messing up my purpose for being there. But having him coming to me wasn't on my plans. It was a damn distraction.

I tried to dissuade him and make him leave me alone. I got nervous when I noticed that he had a revolver hidden under his shirt. From the corner of my eye, though, I understood why all the men went back to their seats and stopped giving me the same attention as when I'd entered. No one would dare try to pick me up with him next to me. Not even the dark figures I had tracked here. This dude was dripping with power and had respect among the others.

And he had an amazing smile. I almost smiled back, but I

couldn't drop my guard. Besides, it wasn't his species that I was interested in. I wanted to make acquaintance with the three vampires in the darkest corner, surrounded by werewolves and shapeshifters but, to my surprise, no humans. I needed information about their creator.

Apparently, the gods had some twisted sense of humor and put that gorgeous, breathtaking man in my way.

The gods could suck it! I wasn't looking for a playmate.

Waking up, I sighed deeply, inhaling the freshness and warmth of the cozy place where I lay. The memories of the previous night were still fresh on my mind.

Then, it hit me. I had no clue where I was or how I got here. I was comfortable, though. Nevertheless, I couldn't understand why the sun was so warm on my face. I felt safe. As if I were ten years old again and still living at home. I had never felt safe since the attack. It had been eight long years of running, chasing, and hiding. Sleeping the whole night without waking up covered in sweat with a racing heart was also something new.

How did I get here, anyway? It was all a bit foggy.

I remembered going outside, seeing the vampires, and watching the gorgeous man shoot them down. I was surprised and disappointed at the same time because I wanted to talk with at least one of them.

Once they were gone and my plans frustrated, I did what any normal human would do after encountering dangerous creatures.

I fainted.

At least, I pretended to. I couldn't blow my cover. I let him play the savior part.

Before I hit the ground, I was held in strong and careful arms. My savior smelled even better up close. I had to restrain myself from the temptation of wrapping my arms around him and letting a moan of pleasure escape my lips.

He talked to someone before taking me in his arms and placing me in his car. I had seen the badge over his belt, next to the gun. He was the authority in that town—a supernatural enforcer and not a hunter like me. As a werewolf, he knew what those things were and what they wanted to do to me.

If the werewolf hadn't intervened, I'd have defended myself. Luckily, the guy was fast enough to deal with the vampires on his own, and I didn't want to draw attention to the fact that I was a hybrid.

My kind wasn't welcome in many places. We were still seen as aberrations. Soulless beings that should have been put to death before they were even born.

I was sure the guy wouldn't even bother protecting me if he knew what I was.

Fisting my hands, I sighed deeply. I needed to focus now that my marks were gone.

What happened once I was inside of his car?

Did I fall asleep?

It had been three long days of following those vampires around, hoping they would take me to their master. My decision to enter the bar cost me my only lead.

Nevertheless, how was I stupid enough to drop my guard and fall asleep in the seat of a stranger's car?

I opened my eyes in alarm, realizing I had no idea where I was.

All I saw was the ceiling made of dark wood. All I felt was the softness of the sheets against my body. My head felt heavy when I inhaled deeply and dared to move one hand and explore the rest of the bed before having a panic attack like any woman who wakes up in a strange bed with a strange man in a strange place after the strangest night.

"Hi," a male voice said from next to the bed and reassuringly outside of it.

I turned my head to stare at him and blinked at the sight of his gorgeous and shirtless persona. The most distracting thing about him was his amazing smile, though.

Is it possible for him to be even more gorgeous in the sunlight? Apparently yes. *And why is he shirtless?*

"Hungry?" He crouched next to the bed, and his eyes sparkled. "Do you remember what happened last night?"

"No." My throat felt sore, and my voice came out raspy. My heartbeat increased with the notion that I probably looked like crap with my messy hair and wake-up face.

Seriously! *Am I crazy?* I was thinking about how I looked when I was in an unfamiliar house, in the bed of a man whose name I didn't even know.

"You fainted outside the bar. I brought you to my house," he explained.

Sitting up and taming down my hair, I kept my eyes on his happy face. I didn't share his joy since I was assessing if I was safe or not. I was also self-conscious about having been carried around by him and not even waking up.

I should have known better than to let my guard down. How did that even happen?

Clearing my throat, I asked, "Where are my things?"

"There." He pointed at a chair. "You're safe, and I didn't touch anything. Or you."

I frowned at him. The smile was gone from his lips, but there was a glint of hope in his eyes that confused me. My eyes zoomed in on his perfect lips, and I gulped at the urge to taste them.

I am losing it. No doubt.

He stood up. "Do you need clean clothes? I can lend you one of my t-shirts and sweatpants if you want to take a shower before joining me for breakfast in the kitchen."

"I have clothes in my backpack."

His fingers ran through his hair before he nodded. "The bathroom is that way."

I looked to where he was pointing. Inhaling sharply, I assessed the space I was in. It was spacious and rustic. Too big to be a guest room. Probably his bedroom.

He brought me to his home, removed my leather jacket, and let me sleep in his comfy bedroom. My body began to relax as I realized that worse things could have happened the night before.

Having a sexy Greek god bringing me to his home and putting me in his bed wasn't one of them. It was actually nice of him—a strange kind of nice. Then I remembered: *he had a badge.*

My shoulders straightened, and my jaw tensed. He'd probably have a lot of questions about who I was. Maybe he just thought that he might get lucky if he saved me since he had tried to pick me up at the bar.

Nevertheless, he had been respectful enough and helped me. I couldn't be ungrateful to him. But where had he slept? And why was he shirtless, showing off his perfect abs and breathtaking chest? It was getting hard to concentrate and speak.

"Do you remember what happened outside the bar before you fainted?"

He wanted to know if I remembered the mean vampires that tried to attack me and suck my blood. If I remembered them bursting into flames. It was normal for his kind to fear being discovered. Especially since I expected him to think that I was human and didn't know anything about supernatural beings.

I had to play the naïve card. I couldn't blow my cover.

"Everything is blurry. How much did I drink?" I fisted my hands to the comforter and closed my eyes for a few seconds. "My head hurts."

"We'll talk about that later," he said in a soft and kind voice. I glanced at him and saw the concern in his gaze.

Brushing my hair down once again to make sure that I didn't look awful, I looked around to distract myself from the fact that blood rushed to my cheeks every time our eyes met. The strange pull from last night made my stomach clench, and my arms tingled with the need to get close to him.

The bedroom was stunning and made entirely of wood. I needed to evaluate where I was in case I needed to run away, fast. By the look of it, we were probably in some kind of cottage or a spacious modernized mountain bungalow because I could see the enormous balcony and outstanding view. We were in a high place with privileged views over the forest and surrounding mountains. It felt like paradise. I'd always dreamt of living somewhere peaceful, where no one could harm me or hunt me down. Where I could feel safe. But I'd understood rather quickly that nowhere was safe, not for someone like me.

His question brought me back to reality. "Do you like it?"

I gave him my attention. "What?"

"The view."

"It's amazing…"

He smiled as if pleased with the answer.

"How far are we from civilization?" I asked.

He probably thought I was scared of my whereabouts because his smile faded, and he looked at me with concern.

"I have no intention of harming you," he clarified, and I believed him. "I just didn't know where you lived, so I brought you to my home."

"I understand," I assured him.

He loosened up and smiled again. "I'll be in the kitchen making us breakfast. Meet me there when you're ready," he said before leaving the bedroom and closing the door.

Getting up, I snooped around, assessing that there was no

feminine touch in the bedroom. The bathroom was spotless, too, with no women's objects or accessories of any kind that girlfriends tend to leave behind to mark territory. Maybe he wasn't the type of guy who liked to have flings longer than they should be. It seemed like he was single and unattached, which briefly made me thrilled before I pushed aside such a girly thought.

I had no time or intention of pursuing any kind of intimacy with him. No. I had to get dressed, get my things, and leave. I had a job interview today and an important mission in his town. I had to stop swooning over how gorgeous and attractive he was, but it seemed that he had left his smile imprinted in my mind.

I took more time than I'd intended in the bathroom because my body was sore, and the hot water was relaxing and soothing. Also, monologues tended to take a bit of time to get resolved, and my mind was a mess of doubts and regret. I couldn't ease the feeling that my hard work had blown up in ashes. My three leads were dead, and I was back at square one.

I dressed in my casual clothes, the ones that said I was a good girl and not a *femme fatale* in leather pants and a sexy top. Then I entered the kitchen that was located just outside the door. The scent of cinnamon and freshly made coffee filled the air, making the place feel incredibly cozy.

The space was divided into a kitchen and a living room. He definitely liked big windows and large rooms. He also had a simple taste in decor.

I liked that.

My eyes met his. He was at the counter with a cup of coffee in hand. He looked at me from head to toe, and I couldn't help but feel a little clumsy in my jeans, t-shirt, and wet hair. I was almost tempted to ask him if he would like to borrow one of my t-shirts, but I said nothing because I was enjoying the view. I shouldn't be ungrateful for his reluctance to wear clothes when it pleased me so much to stare at his abs.

Also, he smiled at me. That made me smile back and lower my defenses. I didn't understand why I beamed back at him, but he seemed so nice that I couldn't help but feel a warm and fuzzy feeling taking over my stomach.

Approaching the kitchen, I sat on a stool in front of the counter. He served me breakfast like it was the most natural thing in the world between two strangers who didn't even know each other's names. I couldn't say no to those delicious pancakes served with blueberry syrup and strong black coffee. The smell was tantalizing and made me realize how hungry I was.

He sat down next to me after serving, not across from me on the opposite side of the counter. He was right there, invading my senses and looking utterly relaxed while I couldn't breathe. His presence affected me in a way that I wasn't used to. I almost didn't dare to make eye contact with him since I shivered every time our eyes met.

His eyes followed my every move. It was as if I was an exotic animal of some sort, and he was studying me. Maybe I was overreacting, and he was acting normal, but it seemed as if he looked at me in a peculiar way—not bad, but a way that made me feel analyzed.

Usually, I wasn't affected by having men's eyes on me. I was sure of myself and knew I was pretty. I knew I could steal the attention of a room only by walking in, dressed to impress, and ready to seduce my prey. But my undeniable attraction to him was making me shy and totally breathless. I was coming down with a case of utter attraction to him. I was normally good at ignoring men and didn't really give a damn about their looks or sexual interest in me.

So why am I so fascinated by this one?

The intensity of his gaze ignited the crazy butterflies inside my stomach. My body reacted with tingling sensations on my neck and palms. Every time I looked at his face, I felt the undeniable allure.

"What's your name?" he asked as I ate. I endured his gaze, unsure if I should answer or not. "You didn't have any kind of identification on you. Do you need to call your parents to tell them where you are?"

I frowned at him, almost choking on my pancake. *How old does he think I am?*

"I live by myself, and my ID is in my bike."

"So—what's your name?" he asked again, forcing me to answer once and for all.

"Annabel. But you can call me Anna."

He beamed. "I'm Shane."

My blood raced straight to my cheeks.

God! He was so undeniably handsome and had such an amazing smile, I didn't even notice he had his hand out in greeting. When I finally saw, his smile had faded away, and he rested his hand on his leg again.

"Where do you live?"

He was curious. I felt trapped.

"I've just arrived in town."

"You moved here?" he exclaimed in a tone that didn't hide his excitement. I felt the butterflies in my stomach fluttering once more. His enthusiasm thrilled me. "Where are you staying?"

"In the motel."

"That crappy place?"

I shrugged. "I didn't have time to look for a place yet."

"I've never seen you before. Do you have family here?"

"No. I came here to work."

"Where?" He seemed staggered.

I was beginning to think I was answering too many questions. It would look suspicious if I didn't, but it was also intriguing that he was astounded about new arrivals to town. Maybe they weren't used to having new people here.

I indulged his curiosity. "I'm a substitute teacher at the high school. I teach English Literature."

"You're a teacher." He truly seemed amazed now or maybe shocked.

"Yes," I confirmed with a polite smile.

"Don't get me wrong." He chuckled at my reaction. "It's just that you look so young, and you really don't dress like a teacher. At least, not at night."

"And how should a teacher dress?" I asked, getting upset by the prejudice.

"Hmm." He got up and simply didn't answer as if he had known the conversation was taking an unwelcome turn.

Apparently, he didn't want to argue with the stranger female he had kindly taken home and given his bed to while he slept on the couch. He'd even made me breakfast, so I shouldn't feel offended. He sure knew how to make pancakes and coffee. I could get used to this.

"When do you start working?" he inquired as he began to clean the kitchen.

"Next Monday, but I have to speak to the principal today."

"I'll go with you and show you the town and the school."

"I don't want to impose. You must have better things to do."

Jesus! He wanted to show me the town. What's next? Dinner and a movie? I wasn't looking for a playmate or a boyfriend or whatever men called a relationship these days.

He held his hands on the countertop. "It's not a problem, and you wouldn't be imposing. I've nothing better to do. Besides, I know the principal, and you would be stuck going on foot."

"My bike is at the bar, isn't it?"

"Yes. And I still need to check your identity and papers."

"Why?" I asked as I got up and gave him the empty cup and plate, which he took and washed.

"I'm the sheriff," he said.

I arched an eyebrow. "You're the sheriff? Aren't you a bit young for that?"

"I'll take that as a compliment." He grinned, making me lose all will to tease him or even breathe.

CHAPTER THREE

ANNABEL

THINGS WEREN'T HAPPENING as I had planned. The hot sheriff seemed to want everything except to leave me alone. Ever since we'd left his house, he had taken it upon himself to be my personal driver. I would have to wait with him until late afternoon, when the bar opened, before I could get my papers and, ultimately, my bike.

Even when I showed him my car, which was parked outside of my motel room, Shane found another excuse to follow me everywhere. Including but not limited to my room, where I dressed adequately—in the bathroom—to meet the school principal.

I guess he liked how I dressed for my meeting, because he gave me a smile of approval when I came out wearing a black skirt and white shirt that had 'professional' written all over them. For the finishing touches, I had straightened my hair and put on glasses.

After he walked a circle around me, he whispered in my ear, "I like that naughty library look."

His warm and electrifying hand touched my back, making me shiver and almost sigh with pleasure. He smelled like a mixture of heaven and hell, he looked irresistible, and I had to admit that I hadn't experienced a man's hand on me in a long time.

At least, not a man's hand that made me feel aroused and safe at the same time.

I expected him to take it further, like lowering his lips to my ear as I closed my eyes with desire. I'd thought maybe he would then pull me into his arms and kiss me, finally showing me what those dreamy lips tasted like. But, sadly, he didn't.

He asked, "Have you ever met the principal?"

"N-No."

"Well, James is a bit of a player, so be careful."

I was counting on him being a player, or else I wouldn't be able to get the information about an original vampire that I needed. James was a vampire. Shane should know that, I figured. It was probably why he was warning me in the first place. He was getting oddly protective.

Things were getting complicated.

How would I go on with my plan if Shane was in the equation?

Then again, was he really? Nothing had happened yet, and I wasn't exactly counting on anything to happen. However, the problem was that my body didn't agree with my rationality. If my body had its way, it would be touched by Shane and his lips, his hands, his everything, and drowned in his amazing scent. I was feeling a severe infatuation for the guy. It didn't help that he was the nicest person I'd met in a while. Shane also made me smile. It had been forever since I'd smiled so willingly and freely. And even longer since I'd found a guy interesting enough to spend time with.

"I'll try to remember that," I said, accepting his warning as his hand moved up my back, making my skin burn like fire.

"We should have dinner tonight," he whispered alluringly as he leaned into my ear.

"Okay," I sighed.

Slowly, he pressed his lips against my earlobe as his hands closed around my arms. Then he pulled me until my back was pressed against his chest. My whole body was trapped by a severe desire for him. I was shamelessly surrendering myself to his touch and his alluring voice in my ear. That was so—*wait!*

What was I saying? Dinner? A date? No. No dates. No men. No complications. I didn't want to create ties with anyone. No one should know me well enough to be put in danger. I couldn't give in so easily to a man.

Even with that in mind, I wondered *why breathing was so tricky, and why was it a struggle to simply open my eyes?* I was thoroughly aroused by his touch. I was incapable of coherent speech, but I found that I didn't want to be coherent, or even rational, for that matter. Who cared about rationality when he was this close to me, smelling like heaven and promising me paradise with his sexy voice?

"Dinner at my place. I'll cook," he added, burying his head in the crook of my neck and inhaling as if he wanted to become inebriated by my scent, too.

His tongue flicked out, licking my neck. Words became impossible to form once he touched me. I don't think that it was a question but more an affirmation on his part about what was going to happen.

"And now…" he spoke into my ear gently, tormenting me once more.

By then, my whole body was awake with desire. I couldn't control myself. I didn't want to. I wanted to melt against his body and taste his lips.

"Now I'm going to kiss you," he breathed and turned me to him, snaking my arms around his neck without any resistance on my part.

At least, I wasn't the only one burning up with need. I could feel his tense body and his desire growing inside his pants against my stomach. That aroused me. I felt my nipples getting hard as breathing was once again a challenge. I focused on closing my eyes, pressing my fingers on his back and waiting patiently to feel his mouth against mine. Tilting my head back, I offered my lips for the taking.

His lips finally touched mine, and everything became quiet around me. The touch of our lips felt like silk falling over silk. My mouth opened when he pressed harder and deepened our kiss. Irrationality took over me, making me feel wobbly and needy. A strong and deadly feeling of longing swept me off my feet. I had to hold on tighter to him because my legs lost the strength to support me.

How can a kiss feel so sizzling?

His arms wrapped around my waist and prevented me from falling. To be this close to him, in his arms, lips moving against lips—it was like nothing I had ever experienced. He was gentle, and I couldn't stop myself from letting go, giving in to the passion and to him.

For the first time in my life, I gave up control and let my emotions take over me. My whole body shivered and ached with desire when our mouths parted and our tongues tangled. If heaven existed, it surely had to be against his lips, feeling his kisses, and with his arms around me. His kisses were tender, sweet, breathtaking, and too good to be true! Time ceased to exist. Gravity was a vague idea in my mind. I couldn't let him go. I wanted more. I wanted his tongue and my tongue playing together, discovering and making me feel alive and blissful. I wanted our lips sealed together, his arms around me, pulling me tight against his solid and warm body. I wanted to melt and merge with him. They weren't normal kisses. They were mind-blowing experiences!

CHAPTER FOUR

ANNABEL

SHANE WAS OUTSIDE the principal's office while I talked to Mr. Gilmore, a vampire who looked like he had been at least forty years old when he was turned. He seemed impressed by my résumé yet intrigued by my choice to teach English Literature in the middle of nowhere.

The lack of people aspiring to teach at Affinity had been crucial for my acceptance. The death of an old vampire teacher, this one a whopping sixty years old when he had been turned, was the reason for the vacancy. I wasn't the one who had killed the old vamp, but I would have loved to finish him off, given a chance. He was killed because he partook in an all-you-can-eat buffet of blonde girls and young boys in Las Vegas.

I spent most of the interview distracted. I was still aroused by Shane's kisses back at the motel. Even while one-hundred-and-forty-two-year-old James Ward was quite attractive for a blood-sucking vampire, Shane had something else—a force that pulled me to him and made me feel like a powerful, sexy woman.

I wanted him badly. I had already come to terms with that fact. Besides, Shane was a good friend of James Ward's, so my initial intention to seduce James was out of the question as soon as he saw Shane's hand on my shoulder, marking his territory. I didn't mind. I only had eyes for Shane at that point. It was like he had cast a spell on me, so I didn't care about James or my plan to flirt with him. I would get the information I needed some other way.

When the interview ended, James and Shane walked down the corridor, having a friendly conversation. Shane's hand didn't leave mine, which rendered me more confused and distracted than ever before. We looked so much like a couple, I didn't even recognize myself or my behavior. I was not the type of girl to give her hand to a boy and be mushy and clingy, but it felt nice and normal.

I was losing it. I needed to ditch him and start thinking straight.

"You better stop doing that, or I can't be held responsible for what I'll do next."

"Doing what?" I asked, puzzled by Shane's words.

We were outside the school entry. James had said his goodbyes and disappeared around the corner. Meanwhile, I was trying to find an excuse to be left alone for a while. I needed enough time to call Jason and explain to him my lack of success in finding clues to the vampire's domain.

"Biting your lip."

"I'm not—" I broke off, catching myself biting down again as I thought over his answer. There it was: my teeth on my bottom lip, wreaking havoc on it in response to my frayed nerves.

"Is something wrong?" he asked, obviously puzzled by my hesitation.

Typically, I was alone and, in turn, didn't speak much. I really only had Jason to talk to, and that was on the phone. In my line of work, I couldn't make new friends. I also had Jessica, who was a witch and supernatural hunter like me. I was naturally quiet and didn't have the social skills necessary to make small talk or even make up a good excuse as to why I needed to be left alone for a minute.

"Nothing's wrong," I said, but I made a mistake. I didn't look him in the eye to reassure him, so he didn't believe me. Instead, he put his hands on my arms, making me face him and lose my senses again.

He had stunning, concerned blue eyes. I couldn't help it, so I kissed him as I fell into his embrace. That's right. *I kissed him.* I couldn't get our kisses in the motel room out of my mind since we'd left for my interview. I just had to kiss him again. Everything seemed to fall into place when our lips molded together. It even explained why I'd been reacting so senselessly to him since the first minute we'd met.

"Let's go to my place," he whispered, his voice sending shivers of lust down my spine.

"Yes." I gasped.

Kissing him was a rush of adrenaline that had the power to make me forget everything and want to, instead, strip my clothes and jump right in bed with him.

"I mean..." I was able to clear my head and pull back. "I need to go to the bank and find a phone to call my cousin."

"Don't you have a cell phone?"

"It's in my bike." I gave him a look that said 'it's-all-your-fault.' Then I asked, "Don't you have to be at the police station?"

"I already called ahead to warn them that I wasn't going to be in today."

I stared at him, stunned for a moment.

Shane had taken the day off to be with me. If I was a normal person, that would've been very endearing. But I wasn't a normal person.

His presence was overwhelming, and I had to silence my overly excited thoughts for a moment and try to be reasonable. I had to prioritize.

"I really need to call my cousin, Jason. He must be worried sick," I mumbled. I needed to be left alone, so I could collect my thoughts and stop acting so irrationally when this man was around. I had to admit that he was hot, but I also had crucial things to solve. My life was already too complicated as it was. It would be too much to let him haunt my mind with sexual desires.

"Why would your cousin be worried?" He frowned as if he didn't believe what I was saying.

I folded my arms across my chest and eyed him. "I'm not going to call up a boyfriend or a long-lost lover or whatever you think I have. My cousin is the only family I have since…"

"Since?" he encouraged me to continue.

I instantly regretted explaining myself to him. He had nothing to do with my life, and I didn't want to get into this very personal matter with him. But, amazingly, I did.

"Since my parents died." I almost choked and broke into tears from admitting it out loud. It was still painful after all those years.

Shane noticed my pain. He reached out and brought me into his arms. Magically, my defenses crumbled, and I felt safe, shielded against all the unhappiness as his hand stroked my hair.

Damn! I must have hit my head somewhere and didn't remember doing so because I was not normally fragile and needy. Usually, I didn't feel safe in a man's arms. I rarely let them get that close in the first place. There was definitely something wrong with the way I was reacting to Shane.

"Do you normally take stray orphan women home?" I asked as he clutched me to his chest, feeling too mystified to keep my thoughts quiet but thankful for his attention.

"No, you were the first," he answered. Smiling, he leaned down and took over my lips, kissing me so sweetly that my legs turned to jelly.

I tried to tease him to fight the attraction. "What about young women who faint after being attacked by vampires?"

"No. You were also my first. I normally don't pick up girls at bars."

"They pick you up instead?" I dared to ask.

"Sometimes," he answered in an amused tone. "Are you trying to ask me if I'm single?"

"Yes," I confirmed, looking him in the eye and noticing his

cocky smile. Damn, he was just so gorgeous, and he was completely aware of it.

"I was single…" he began to say, which made me start to pull away from him, my heart in my mouth. "But now, I think I'm taken. She's accepted a date with me tonight and hasn't turned down any of my kisses yet."

Cocky, without a doubt, charming, and entirely too persistent.

"Slow down, cowboy. It's only a date," I said, not sure whether to laugh or feel concerned about the road Shane wanted to take with our relationship.

He couldn't be serious. Men weren't usually that keen on jumping into a relationship.

"I regret to inform you but judging by the number of people who have passed here in the last ten minutes, I'm confident in saying that the whole town believes that we are a couple," he said with a smile and an easy tone that made me freeze in panic.

There went my purpose of passing through the town without bringing attention to myself. In a place like this one, this kind of news was probably worthy of a newspaper article.

"You look like you're going to run and never come back," Shane said. This time, he wasn't smiling. He seemed concerned.

He couldn't be more right. *Is he a mind reader now?*

I bluntly asked, "Are you some kind of stalker?"

"No."

"Are you sure? I just met you—last night."

"I like you."

Just like that, I was left with nothing to say to that revelation. Direct and persistent: those were two must-haves on my 'perfect man' list. Intelligent and breathtaking were also included. I should've just written Shane to save myself some time.

I was really losing it. Because, even while I was thinking he was perfect, I knew he had to have some kind of flaw.

"And I want to know you better," he added.

Still nothing to say. My head was spinning. He had come into my life at such a bad time.

Then again, when would be a good time for me?

He placed two fingers under my chin. "After we know each other better, you can decide if you want me in your life or not. If you don't want me, I'll go back to my boring life and never bother you again."

With what I hoped to be a relaxed shrug, I grabbed his hand and mumbled, "Okay."

His lips curled up as he let out what sounded like a relieved sigh.

His interest in me was flattering enough, so I decided I was going to let things happen on their own. Besides, we had already kissed, and it was beyond perfect. I couldn't help but want to kiss him again. He wouldn't leave me alone anyway, and I was…enjoying the company. It hit me then that I didn't want to be left alone. It was odd, but the idea of being apart from him made my heart hurt.

Sighing, I looked around, taking note of all of the people who were staring at us as if we were a pair of tigers in a circus act.

That was when it hit me like a ton of bricks. The whole town was crawling with werewolves and vampires. They were in couples, walking around like mere mortals. I couldn't even imagine that kind of thing existing. *My God!* They were pretending to be humans in a town of supernatural beings, living in supposed harmony. Vampires greeted werewolves when passing by on the street. Little kids played with each other and laughed: kids who were werewolf cubs and some who were probably even hybrids, like me. I had never seen anything like that.

"What's wrong?" Shane asked, placing his hand on my

shoulder as my eyes studied the citizens of the town.

"Nothing." I gave him my attention, trying to cope with the fact that Shane himself was a werewolf. I couldn't deny myself that crucial fact anymore.

Werewolves and my kind didn't mingle. Werewolves were territorial and protective of their pack. Hybrids weren't normally welcome in their groups. Shane being the sheriff in a town like that meant that the others respected him.

Why would he want to socialize with me?

Shane had no idea what I was.

But why would he even want to be seen with a supposed human in a town of supernatural beings?

I pleased him. That was clear every time he kissed me. But still, *would he talk to me if he knew what I truly was?*

I had nothing against his kind. They were loyal, and the majority wanted to be left alone, living in harmony in some countryside community. He seemed to be a nice guy. I should tell him what I was. But why should I?

Does it matter?

CHAPTER FIVE
ANNABEL

"SO—VAMPIRES?" SHANE ASKED while we were walking down the street on our way for a late lunch at the local diner.

"What?" I was completely spaced out.

"You think you were attacked by vampires. That was what you said back there, before I almost made you think I was crazy."

"So what were they if not vampires? They simply disappeared when you shot them."

"They ran. I gave a warning shot, and they took off."

"And the dust?"

Now I was just being cheeky to see what excuse he was going to give me. He wasn't going to tell me what he was or what the people in this town were. He wouldn't tell their secrets to a human.

Shane had no idea that I wasn't a human. Hybrids smelled like humans. It was our way of staying safe from human hunters and supernatural radicals who wanted our heads.

Being a hybrid wasn't easy. We could at least hide among humans and tell only the ones we trusted precisely what we are. Shane could be hot and apparently harmless, but he hadn't yet earned my trust. I hadn't survived for so long by willingly trusting someone I'd just met.

His fingers brushed a strand of hair out of my face. "It was dry last night. Sometimes the wind blows and carries dust along with it."

"*Hmm.*"

"Vampires don't exist," Shane said, grinning as he held my hand. "You must have bumped your head when you fainted."

"Probably," I replied, knowing perfectly well that he took me in his arms long before I could fall to the floor with my fake faint.

I stared at our hands together and felt warm inside. My muscles relaxed as I looked around at the seemingly friendly community with its cozy little shops and charming buildings.

We walked in silence until he spoke again. "You can't actually believe that I killed vampires."

Maybe he wanted to know if I was convinced by his explanation.

"You did save me from those guys. Vampires or not," I replied.

Playing the damsel in distress was a funny thing for me, and I almost chuckled, but I didn't want to hurt his feelings. Even though I could protect myself, it was nice to be saved for once. He cared enough to come outside and protect a stranger from vampires.

"We don't like those types of people in this town. I didn't like the way they were looking at you," he confessed, making my heart speed up. He was, without a doubt, a good guy. "Besides, they were warned to behave when they got here a few days ago—but seemed to forget about that."

"So they weren't from this town?" I asked, gathering information.

"No, they were outsiders. We don't mind outsiders as long as they play by our rules," Shane stated. I stared at him, intrigued by his words.

His gaze softened. "What were you doing in the bar that late?"

"That's kind of a sexist question. Can't a girl go out for a late drink?"

"I didn't mean to sound sexist." His face became pale at my accusation. Apparently, he didn't want to seem judgmental. It was interesting how much he wanted to please me.

"I can take care of myself." I smiled, so I wouldn't hurt his feelings. "But I appreciate you coming out to check on me, even if I think you were hitting on me at the bar."

"I was definitely hitting on you," he confessed, making my silly heart jump inside my chest. "And I'm very interested in knowing how you're planning to thank me," he added in a relaxed tone, throwing in a naughty smile that made me laugh.

"I'll let you pay for my lunch since my wallet is in my bike."

"Yes, I'm kind of guilty of that situation, but I'll gladly pay for your lunch and drive you to Sam's Bar, so you can get your bike back. I just couldn't leave you outside the bar."

"You're quite the gentleman, even if you took me to your home and put me in your bed while I was unconscious."

"I tried to wake you up," he clarified. "I didn't take advantage of you, and I didn't know where you were staying."

"I believe you," I said to reassure him.

His eyes beamed once more, and I felt warm inside.

Moving closer, he inquired, "So, is the bike actually yours? Or did you steal it from a former boyfriend?"

"Do you like it?" I asked, fully aware that he was trying to gather information about my life.

"Yes, it's gorgeous and expensive," he added.

"Don't worry, I didn't steal it. It was my brother's."

"You said you had no family besides your cousin," he reminded me.

"I don't. He's…" I lost my voice before I could finish that sentence.

A lump formed in my throat, and the pit of my stomach burned. I didn't like to talk about it. *Why did he have to be so nosy about my life?* It wasn't his fault, though. My life was messed up.

I stopped walking and stared at the ground to conceal my emotions.

Shane drew near me. "I swear that I'm not trying to make you sad, but we should talk about that another day."

"About what?"

"About what happened to your family."

"I don't like to talk about it."

"You can tell me when you're ready," he whispered, voice laced with honey.

On any other occasion, his tender voice and closeness would have made me feel good, but I was reinforcing my defenses, and I had no intention of telling him anything else about me.

"I don't like to talk about it," I repeated, pursing my lips, so he would leave me alone.

I let go of his hand and walked away. He followed after me.

"Annabel," he called, and I knew he wasn't going to drop the subject. "You will eventually have to trust someone."

I stopped walking, turned around, and stared at him, annoyed by his words and perplexed by the way he could read me so well.

Is my inability to trust that clear?

The real question, though, was why did he care about that? *What could my life, my past, my feelings, and dreams possibly mean to him?* We had only just met. We weren't friends, just acquaintances with a good steamy dose of sexual attraction.

"Shane, do you want to take me to bed or cure my trust issues?"

"Both," he answered, not shocked at all by my bluntness. "Besides, we must talk about ourselves and our lives if we want to get to know each other."

"That is such—"

"What?" He dared me to end that sentence.

"Bullshit," I finished, letting the word roll out of my mouth with full force.

"I guess we should work on a way for you to trust me first," he said casually as he rubbed his arm.

Shane didn't seem angered by my words, just concerned about changing my mind. He puzzled me. He should be running away from me right now. Most guys would.

"Whatever," I replied, trying to seem emotionally unattached by his words, even though they had me wishing they would come true.

He looked saddened by my chilly answer. Making him sad was something I realized I didn't like to do. It physically hurt, and not only in my heart. My stomach felt cramped.

I was definitely falling for him in the few hours I'd been with him. *That could not be good…*

Then I said what I had promised myself never to tell a man. But I knew it would make him feel happier—or, at least, I expected it to. "Shane…I like you, too."

"I know," he answered, grinning, obviously pleased by my words. "Your heart beats faster when we get closer, and when we kiss…"

"What?" I dared him to finish his sentence with my arms folded and narrowed eyes. I felt irritated at him for being so cocky about my feelings for him.

"Nothing." He ran a hand through his hair in the very first nervous impulse I'd caught him doing.

I laughed. I was probably losing my mind, but I felt like a teenager with her first crush.

He furrowed his brows. "What?"

I stopped laughing, shrugged my shoulders, and gazed at the floor, watching the pavement. A disturbing thought caught my attention. "You probably have a lot of girls in town chasing you around," I said out loud.

"Not all," he replied.

He was definitely cocky and not reassuring at all! Panic washed over me.

He must have read my mind.

"But I only have eyes for you," he said, holding my hands before I could run away.

"You're probably just tired of the girls here." I immediately regretted saying that and bit my lip.

"You're so cute, being jealous for nothing," he replied with a grin that made me shiver with lust and fury.

Damn it, I shouldn't be reacting like a silly girl, but I couldn't help it.

"I'm not jealous!" I tried to defend myself, but being flustered didn't help my case.

He simply chuckled, and I glared at him haughtily, waiting for him to stop. Nothing I said seemed to affect him negatively. *How could he be so cheerful and optimistic all the time?*

"You need to learn how to relax," he said while gently rubbing my shoulders, making me lose all will to fight.

My body got electric and shaky with his closeness and touch. "You are so…"

"Handsome and sexy?"

"Full of yourself."

"Hum…realistic, you mean? Come on, honey, relax and stop trying to pick a fight with me. You won't get rid of me that easily."

I stood quietly, not sure whether to be more surprised by his deduction or by the fact that he'd called me "honey" with a sexy and placating voice that could melt ice on the top of the highest mountain.

And I guess his kiss just melted stone to magma because the sizzling kiss he gave me next was enough for me to act adorable and cute the entire meal we had at the local diner.

I almost didn't recognize myself as I laughed with real happiness and talked to strangers who were being friendly to the sheriff's girl. Everyone was so lovely that I felt immediately at ease.

CHAPTER SIX

SHANE

IT WAS ALMOST eight o'clock. I had everything ready, and I looked myself over in the mirror for the hundredth time.

A romantic dinner wasn't a thing I would typically do. Not for a woman with who I only used to pass the time. However, Annabel was different. She was the woman I wanted to spend the rest of my life with. Anna was my amazing and breathtaking soulmate. She was also mysterious and full of surprises, which left me feeling impressed and intrigued. She was growing on me. Destiny or not, that goddess was everything I'd ever dreamed of in my soulmate.

Though, I needed to fix the loneliness and sadness that was making her close her heart to me. I wanted to protect her and keep her safe from the world, but I had to take things slow to not scare her away. The problem was that I couldn't take my hands off her. I just wanted to hold her, smell her, and get lost in her silky and plump lips.

The food was ready, the wine was opened to breathe, and the scented candles were burning in orange and yellow. The fireplace was warming the room. I even had on soft music for background noise. In turn, the full moon was beautiful that night, and the view from the balcony was perfect to watch the stars.

I had a million questions for her. I wanted to know everything. On the other hand, I just wanted to eat, drink, kiss her, and take her to bed, so I could spend all night making her mine. She would be so loved that she wouldn't be able to leave me or sleep with another man.

I wanted her, and I sure made that clear all over town today.

I'd noticed James's surprised eyes when he saw me with her. I had touched and held her hand, so he understood she was taken.

That school teacher was mine and off-limits to him. I knew what
a sick bastard he was, seducing human teachers who went there
to work. He had probably chosen Annabel because of her looks.

I had a stunning and intelligent soulmate. No matter how she
looked, I would think that she was hot and sexy. We were born to
be together. We matched. She laughed at my silly jokes. That was
always a good sign. I was still mesmerized by the fact that I had
found her.

My heart was threatening to stop beating if, for some reason,
I were to lose her or scare her away. The pressure was real, and
being apart from her was already making me feel lonely and sad.

It was eight o'clock, and I fixed my collar again. I was dressed
to impress with a white Boss shirt and dark suit pants. I'd even
shaved. I wanted that night to be perfect, but I was anxious
because Annabel insisted on being left alone in her motel room
before coming to my home at eight. The road could be tricky,
and she could get lost. She could simply run away, and I would
never see her again.

I was beginning to get paranoid.

The doorbell rang, and I went flying to open the door. And
there she was. I almost stopped breathing when I saw her in that
beautiful red dress that hugged her perfect curves, with a sexy
heart-shaped neckline. She had stunning breasts and beautiful
long hair that was elegantly curled. Her makeup was soft but
appealing, highlighting her lips and eyes. I had a serious
fascination with her red lips. Her mouth was made for me to kiss.
It also pleased me the way her eyes lit up at the sight of me.

As for me, I was shaking like a schoolboy on his prom night.
I remembered all my dates. All of those women weren't nearly as
hot and beautiful as Annabel was to me.

"You look amazing." That was all I could manage to say after
what seemed like ages staring at her in silence.

"You look very sharp and—"

I arched an eyebrow. "And?"

"Different." She smiled, her gaze aimed at the floor. Looking up, she added, "You look gorgeous, too."

I grinned, flattered by the compliment made in her sexy, sweet voice. I loved everything about her. I was doomed to worship her for life. Not doomed, no—I was blessed. The gods had blessed me with her.

"Come on in," I told her, aware that it was freezing outside, and she was in a sleeveless dress.

Annabel entered but halted, amazed by the décor, her eyes lingering on the table's scented candles. "How could you possibly have had the time to do all this?"

I closed the door and joined her. "Do you like it?"

"It's amazing," she whispered, sounding surprised. "And it smells delicious."

"I hope you like meat. I mean red meat. Some women don't."

She looked at me with narrowed eyes, obviously wondering how many women I had dated and prepared romantic dinners for.

Aware of my mistake, I tried to explain to her piercing eyes, "I mean...I mean many women, in general, don't like meat or don't eat it at all. I don't really do this often, rarely even. In fact, this is the first time I've done something like this."

Her perfectly shaped lips curled into a smile, apparently amused by my babbling.

Placing a hand on her lower back to guide her to the table, I asked, "Do you want some wine?" I wanted to change the subject.

"Yes, please."

While I served the wine, she stared at the fireplace and walked past the table, touching the roses with her fingertips. She walked with the elegance of a cat and the alluring light of a goddess. She was so beautiful that I almost spilled the wine on myself because I couldn't stop looking at her. I was clumsy around her. I tried to act cool and calm, but I was always nervous and unsure of what to do to make her look at me the way I looked at her.

"The wine is delicious and sweet," she said after a while of confusing silence as we stared at each other and sipped the wine.

It hit me that I hadn't kissed her at the door. *I should have kissed her.* But then I probably wouldn't have been able to stop, and the night would've been ruined. Not ruined, but it would have been a failure that I didn't want to regret. I wanted us to have a romantic dinner. I wanted to talk to her and learn things about her.

"I'm glad you like it. Are you hungry?"

"What's your plan?" she asked, running her finger along the rim of the glass. She wet her fingertip and sucked it off with her lips, making me swallow hard.

She was being naughty on purpose.

"My plan for what?"

"For tonight."

"Dinner, talking, and perhaps a massage, so you'll stop being so tense all the time," I replied.

She pursed her lips together and then grinned. "Weren't you planning on taking me to bed?"

She was so blunt sometimes, I didn't know how to react. I wasn't sure if she was testing me or trying to find a reason to get rid of me. Was she searching for some kind of an excuse like some women used to lose interest in a guy, like him being too much of a player or not romantic enough, or just wanting to jump into their pants and leave them afterwards?

"Annabel," I whispered in her ear, making sure not to touch

her. Her heartbeat accelerated, goosebumps erupted, and her pupils dilated, not to mention how delicious she smelled and how her excitement only increased the sweetness of her scent. My own body got tense and aroused. "Let your guard down and trust me. Nothing will happen that you don't want to happen. I'm not trying to get you drunk or trick you. I want to get to know you better."

"Shane," she replied with her alluring voice that sent spirals of lust down my spine. "I have nothing against sleeping with you. I'm fully dressed for that."

I couldn't help looking at her cleavage, noticing her perky breasts and luxurious, soft skin. Under that dress would be some kind of sexy lingerie that I almost couldn't wait to see and take off to get between her legs.

Thoughts like those only made me aroused and impatient.

"I'm not easy to take to bed. You'll have to work for it," I said softly, catching her off guard.

She looked at me and shook her head like she thought I was unbelievable.

"And don't think for a moment that I won't punish you if you try to ruin this night with your irony and inability to take me seriously," I warned her. "Just trust me for a while tonight." I ran the tip of my index along her cheek. I wanted our night to be perfect, to make her enjoy herself and fall in love with me.

"Okay, Shane. I'll stop being sarcastic and trust you," she whispered as her breath feathered across my mouth.

I smiled, pleased because it was clear by the way she'd reacted to me and looked around attentively that she didn't trust anything or anyone. She was always vigilant, as if she expected to be surprised at any second by an unknown fear. It intrigued me, and I wanted to make sure she felt safe with me. I was there for her now; nothing would harm her again.

"Anna." I sighed, brushing her lips with mine. "Why do you have to test me all the time?"

"I don't," she refuted, shivering in my arms.

With narrowed eyes, she leaned her head back, so she could stare into my eyes. We were burning; we always burned together and reacted perfectly to the desire that our touch created. It was irrationality with insanity as if the whole world would stop turning, the stars would fall from the skies, and we would burst into a supernova.

Touching my face, she said, "I wanted you to know that I want to sleep with you." Her lips touched mine before she added, "You don't need all this to take me to bed."

I held her face between my hands. "But I want all this. You deserve all this. I want to have dinner with you, talk to you for a while, dance with you under the moon, and then take you to bed."

She stared at me quietly with her big, beautiful, blue eyes. My breathing halted as I waited for her reaction.

"I'll try to be patient then," she finally said.

I took possession of her mouth.

"And Shane," she called to me, making me open my eyes. "I do like meat."

"Good. Let's eat then."

CHAPTER SEVEN
ANNABEL

DINNER WAS PERFECT. The wine was slightly sweet and velvety to the palate. The candles and roses were, at first sight, a bit cliché. But as time passed by, I thought they were the most romantic thing.

I'd never had a man do this for me. Neither had I had a man refuse to be intimidated by the way I could make any romantic act seem like a joke. Shane didn't seem like a man who could be frightened by my cynicism. He seemed to look past it and understand my fears.

The night was so perfect and relaxing that I indulged myself in being a woman, a normal woman in the arms of a man who was gorgeous, sexy, and charming. A woman who wanted to be swept off her feet by him, who smiled and giggled like a fool at his silly jokes and lame attempts to teach me coin tricks. We even danced while staring at the moon and stars. I let myself go and enjoyed everything. Shane was amazing and captivating.

The most surprising thing was that he didn't seem too eager to take me to bed and finish the night with some fast sex to end all the sexual tension between us. In fact, we ended up on the balcony, sitting on the cypress-wood loveseat swing. He had my legs on his lap, hovering close to my face as he told me about some funny stories that had happened to him on duty. He was a good storyteller, and he made me laugh. The sexy werewolf inflamed my being with mindless and irrational happiness, while his tenderness only made me hunger for him more.

My mind often drifted away to hot fantasies. I would imagine his hands climbing my legs, touching and caressing them, while his lips kissed my inner thighs and tamed the fire that was devouring me. I don't remember ever being so aroused for a guy.

Not even in the time of the year that I was in heat, controlled by my panther side.

"Are you tired?" he asked, holding my hands and kissing them.

I followed his movements. My breath hitched as I enjoyed the soft pleasure of his lips on my skin.

"No." *Tired? No. Aroused? Yes!*

His lips curled into a smile, and I hoped he was done talking. I think he read my mind. "Come and sit on my lap. I want to kiss you."

I obeyed promptly, sitting on his lap and wrapping my arms around his neck while staring at his gorgeous baby-blue eyes. His scent intoxicated me, and I could barely control myself and keep my fangs hidden.

He softly nibbled on my lower lip and then left small kisses on my mouth, taunting me repeatedly.

"Are you cold?" he asked, caressing my shoulders and picking me up in his arms like I weighed nothing at all.

"No." I deepened the kiss, making it hard for him to move forward because he couldn't see where he was going. I had my hands over his face, holding it tight. I could barely breathe as desire consumed me.

My feet touched the ground, and Shane's hands held my waist. I walked back only to be pinned against the glass of the balcony door.

Lifting me up, he snaked my legs around his waist. I moaned when I felt how aroused he was. His arousal ignited more fire, and my nipples stiffened until they hurt. I wanted to engulf him and undress him. I was impatient, but he kept kissing me and grinding me against him until I felt that I was going to lose my mind if he didn't do anything else.

The need was overwhelming, and it crippled my rationality. I needed him. *Now.*

"Not here, honey," he whispered, out of breath, when I began to unbutton his shirt with impatient hands.

"Why not?" I complained.

Shane grinned, but it wasn't an amused grin. He seemed to smile as though he was pleased by my sulking face and impatient voice.

"Inside," he whispered in my ear with his husky and promising voice as he let my feet land on the ground.

We entered, and he turned to close the balcony door.

I didn't waste any time. I unzipped my dress, slowly taking it down to reveal my black corset with red lace overlay, my G-string, and stockings. The dress fell on the floor.

Shane's lips curled into a smile as his eyes roamed up and down my body.

As soon as he recuperated from the sight of me, he brought me back into his warm embrace and ripped body. His mouth took possession of mine. His arms circled my waist, and his hands trailed down my derriere, so he could lift me up and sit me on the kitchen's counter. His lips flooded my neck and cleavage with kisses.

Giggling, I enjoyed the wildness of our kisses and the nibbling sensation of his teeth on my skin as all his caresses created havoc in my lower stomach and rippled tidal waves of frissons down my back and arms.

"This definitely beats your other clothes," he whispered between kisses.

His fingers touched the back of the corset. It was laced with a red satin ribbon, but it didn't seem challenging for him. Apparently, it wasn't the first time he had to unwrap a woman from a corset.

His mouth on the mount of my breasts made it difficult for

me to think about his ability to take off corsets. I moaned and shivered, mussing his hair and holding his head in that perfect spot.

Arching my back, I offered my breasts to his mouth, longing for him to suck and kiss them because my nipples were so hard they hurt against the fabric. So, when he finally was able to free one and take it to his mouth, I sighed with relief and moaned. His hands cupped my breasts still inside the corset. He kept squeezing them gently as his tongue circled around my nipple. I was utterly lost to lust by then, so I let him do whatever he wanted.

Shane took his time kissing, suckling, and gently nibbling as he took me to heaven and back. My mind lost the ability to reason about the place or the time. It was as if sweet oblivion had found me and indulged me with its bliss. I never thought I could be so sensitive and feel so much pleasure from someone playing with and kissing my breasts. But the fact was that any place he touched, my skin reacted, and my brain received so much pleasure that I knew it would converge into the most perfect orgasm I'd ever had.

I had experienced pleasure before, but nothing like I was expecting to experience that night. He didn't even have to get inside me. Although I wanted him to so badly that I was ready to beg him. I was betting that if he ran his fingers softly over my sex or kept descending with his mouth, I would come. I would, without a single doubt, come. But it seemed he liked to tease me to desperation.

CHAPTER EIGHT

SHANE

HER AROUSAL WAS SO CLEAR, sweet, and delightfully touchable that I found it challenging to continue to be patient and keep the foreplay going. I had carefully planned to be self-controlled, to give the most of myself before giving up to the desire, passion, and wild, primal need of getting inside her. Annabel's moans were like the most beautiful, sexy poems ever written.

Still, I wanted her to understand that we were made for one another and that anything, any kind of sexual or emotional relationship she'd had before, was nothing compared to what we had together.

I wanted to kiss, lick, and taste each part of her to memorize her inside my head, skin, soul, and wolf. She was *mine*, and I never wanted that moment to end, so I wouldn't be alone ever again. I didn't fully realize how lonely I'd been and what a senseless life I'd had until I saw her, smelled her, kissed her, talked to her, and heard her laugh, moan, and breathe. I felt the void in my chest and soul being filled by her.

So…this was *Love*. No wonder everybody wanted to feel it.

"Shane, I swear I'll bite you senseless if you don't take me to bed right now," Annabel warned, waking me up from my over-romantic thoughts.

I laughed against her breasts. She spoke her mind, and she was impatient and demanding. My soulmate was going to make my life extremely interesting. I liked that about her.

"Kinky," was all I said.

Before she could protest, I kissed her and took her in my arms to head to my bedroom.

As I laid Annabel in my king-size bed, her hair fell down like a wave of darkness across the striped blue and white comforter. Her body molded perfectly against the bedding, still wrapped in the sexy black silken corset.

My mate was so beautiful that I stopped breathing momentarily, placing a vision of her in my memory. Her cheeks were soft red, her lips were a bit swollen because of my kisses, and her breasts were almost fully showing, with little red marks from sucking on them. She was beyond beautiful. She was the reason I'd lived for so long.

Annabel could never understand it, but all the pain and loneliness I'd endured for the last two centuries were gladly accepted if it meant finding her in this timeline, in this form, existing. She was human, but she could be half-alien for all I cared—she was perfect. She was mine, she…was *mine*.

I thought I would never say that in my life. I had finally found *my soulmate*.

"What's wrong?" Annabel asked, caressing my thigh with her foot and most likely finding my fixated gaze and smile peculiar.

"Nothing," I replied, taking her foot in my hand and kissing it. Her legs, covered with those silky black stockings, looked incredibly sexy. I could just kneel down and spend the rest of the hour, kissing them until I reached her G-string and pulled it off with my teeth.

"I'm getting cold," she complained in a husky voice that made me harder as if that was even possible. I wanted her so badly that it was insane how I was just sitting there, staring at her.

I was being a bit of a masochist for delaying and remaining so patient.

She was not so patient. Annabel sat on the bed, making her hair fall into disarray over her heart-shaped face. Then she knelt and took my shirt off, trailing her mouth on my chest and abdominal muscles. Her lips were soft and teasing. Her teeth on my nipples made me gasp and pull her away, moaning in protest. She chuckled, pulling me against her, her breasts pinned against my chest, her mouth near my mouth, my hands holding her wrists.

"I want you," she whispered, eyes narrow with desire.

"Do you?" I asked, teasing her and putting her arms behind her back as her mouth looked for mine. She didn't do anything to try to get free. On the contrary, she opened her lips to let my tongue in. We devoured each other in another steamy, deep kiss.

My wolf's evil side wanted to dominate her. It wanted to make her beg for my touch. And even if my good side wanted to do everything to please her, I knew I had to take control, make her want me more than once, make her dream about me for days, years, or an eternity, if I had to. And, amazingly enough, all my parts had agreed not to mark her until she wanted it. A mark could be protection, a bond, but it also could mean her death. Other supernatural creatures would know she belonged to a wolf, and they could want to play with her and even kill her for fun, just because they could. I couldn't bear the thought of losing her.

She freed her hands at some point during our kiss, and I didn't even notice. I was holding her waist firmly, almost bruising her skin. I kept her against my aching erection. Being against her hot and soft sex made me ease a bit; it was satisfying. My pants and her underwear were between us. Her hand had already unzipped my pants and was slipping them open. When her hand touched my boxers, finding my hard cock, I bit her lip, making her gasp. Her hand on my hard shaft, caressing it gently, almost made me come.

She whimpered with lust when I grabbed and molded her butt with both hands—it was perfectly shaped. I enjoyed feeling it in my hands. I felt how hot she was in her thong when I lowered my hands to the back of her thighs and spread her legs to make them wrap around my waist. Her hips balanced against my hand when two of my fingers circled her entrance as gently as I could. Then I sank them inside as she panted for air.

Her lips were on mine, more biting than actually kissing. We were too busy gasping from our mutual masturbation. But when her hands dropped alongside her waist, and she began to moan repetitively, I knew she was almost coming. Her nipples were hard against my chest, she swayed faster under my hand, but I wasn't going to give her the satisfaction that easily. *Oh, no! She would have to wait a bit longer.* I wanted her to come with me inside her.

"Do you want me inside you?" I asked in her ear, slowing even more, almost stopping, so she could open her eyes and face me.

She was pleasantly flustered by desire, her eyes big and confused when she opened them. She blinked several times, adjusting to the light.

"Tell me, Annabel, do you want me inside you?" I teased her, slipping my fingers out and rejoicing with her moan of complaint.

"Yes," she begged, moving her hand faster over my sex and making it pulsate even more. It was obvious it liked her hand as her teasing fingers caressed and wrapped around to rub it.

"How do you want me?" I asked, and she blushed even more, to my surprise.

I liked her blushing. However, I wasn't expecting what she said next. It left me flustered with increased lust and wandering thoughts. My heart started to beat faster.

"I want you in my mouth," she teased, lowering her mouth, trailing kisses along the way, and stopping just under my belly button. She licked the tip, making me growl with pleasure. She was about to go lower when I pulled her up.

"Where else do you want me?" I asked near her mouth,

engulfing her lower lip and playing with the strings of her reduced panties. "You are so wet," I breathed out, almost losing my patience. Her wicked smirk made me also grin.

"Take the rest of my clothes off. I don't want anything but you against me," she demanded, gasping as she put her arms up, so I could take her corset off.

I loosened the straps on the corset and pulled it up. Then I gently laid her on the bed, taking her stockings off one by one while kissing her exposed skin. She was enjoying that. It was tickling her, and soon she had on just the thong.

My hands were trembling so badly it was absurd. I was trying to get rid of my pants, but I couldn't stop staring at her almost naked body. It was delicious, and I nearly fell to the floor as I jumped on one leg to take off my pants. She found it amusing.

I have to admit it was a bit comical. But I shouldn't have been so nervous about making love to her. It was just that the expectation of it and the pressure of making it perfect were getting to me.

When I was in my boxers, she rose and pulled me to her, making me fall on the bed. We wrapped around each other, kissing as if the world was ending. As if breathing depended on it. I tried to give her a new round of foreplay, kissing her all over from head to toe. Finding the exact spots she liked to be kissed and touched, where she was ticklish and where she would sigh with yearning and giggle with pleasure. She would most definitely have love bites on her the next day. I hoped she would. I wanted her to look at them and blush every time she recalled what we had done.

"Please, please," she whispered, begging me to stop when it tickled her or sighing when she was enjoying it.

"Please, what?" I asked, a wicked smile on my lips. She was getting tired and maybe even sleepy. It was a long foreplay. "Tell me, Annabel, please what?"

"Please do it again," she said, making me chuckle. She was funny. I had to give her credit. I was tormenting her with tickles, and she knew I would do it again if she asked me to stop.

"Maybe I'll stop completely," I provoked close to her mouth.

"Don't you dare," she warned, throwing a pillow at me and narrowing her eyes.

I growled, pretending to be upset, and grabbed her and tickled her, making her scream as she tried to move off the bed to run away from me. She wasn't making a lot of effort to get out of my arms, though. We were playing, even if each time our skin touched it was like the ringing bells of Christmas were shouting in my ears.

Grabbing her, I made her fall over the pillows and wrap her legs around me. Then I watched her as I let her calm down, lingering my stare on her breasts and on her mouth. She was gorgeous beyond words, and her laughter was music to my ears. I could spend my eternity staring at her.

"Ask me," I told her near her mouth, not letting my weight crush her. She was fragile, and I was still heavy. I wanted her to surrender to me. If she would put it in words, maybe her soul would recognize and accept me as hers and hers only.

"What do you want me to ask you?"

"To make love to you."

"No," she denied, playing with her hair.

I was surprised by her answer, but I noticed she was smiling mischievously when she said it. She was teasing me like I was teasing her. I smirked at her, pulling her body to mine until she felt my need against her own wet, hot center.

"You are teasing me again," she complained, not believing that I was serious.

The thong had small laces on the sides of it. Grinning, I

undid them with two fingers.

She looked surprised by my actions, but then she smirked at me and pulled me down for a kiss. She rolled me over and placed me under her, sitting naked over my protuberance. I felt the warmth and humidity coming from her as she rubbed herself against me. I almost lost my calm. My wolf was howling like mad inside my head. He wanted to submit and take her in that exact moment, but I wasn't going to let him ruin everything savagely.

"Now *you* beg," she whispered in my ear, trailing kisses on my neck.

I caressed her thighs. I could submit some other night, but not tonight. Our first time would be like I wanted: her under me. She could do whatever she wanted the next time. At that moment, she would have to enjoy it and let me lead. So I pulled her up and wrapped my lips around her nipple, sucking it and making her shiver and sway harder and faster. Holding her under her arms, I made her fall under me again.

"No one will beg then," I whispered, taking my boxers off with one hand as my cock throbbed impatiently.

She tensed and then relaxed when I suckled on her nipples and gently spread her legs. I trailed kisses down her stomach, feathering her sex with my breath. She closed her eyes, raising her waist and sighing in pleasure when I began thrusting my finger in and out. I had my other hand free at that moment, and my cock was ready to take her.

Anna slid down the bed, her legs lacing around my waist, her feet trying to pull me nearer. She wanted our waists to lock. I wanted that too, so I gently nudged the tip of my cock against her folds. The touch made me gasp, and her hips swayed, asking for more. I entered her in a smooth thrust, instantly exhaling in bliss. Annabel was wet and tight, making me quiver with how hot and perfect it was to be wrapped inside her.

When I was finally all in, relief hit me like a tsunami. Until yearning burned through me, asking for more, urging me for movement and a lot more pleasure. Her hands, clenching my back, told me that she was comfortable enough and wanted more. So, I thrust, synchronizing my movement to her hips' balance, her craving matching my own. Each thrust was more and more mind-blowing. It was paradise each time I slid inside her, buried deep, and locked at our waists. Every time, my whole body trembled with desire and pleasure.

I wasn't going to endure much longer before climaxing. It wasn't just our movements, but also the sexy moans that were leaving her throat. Everything about us making love was stimulating beyond words. I found myself opening my eyes, watching how her face frowned in pleasure, her breathing left her parted lips, and her breasts swayed to the beat of our moving hips. She was gorgeous! Her breasts were full and beautiful. Her skin was soft, making my own skin tingle and shiver. I thrust deeper, harder, wanting us to melt together.

I trailed my fingers between her breasts, caressing and feeling her chest go up and down. Analyzing the loud sound of our beating hearts, I stared at her fisted hands as they grabbed the comforter. I noticed how her head leaned back on the pillow. Her loose hair fell wildly on the bed. It was a rush of adrenaline each time she moved her pelvis against mine, pulling me deeper inside her, moaning because of the pleasure, and making me groan in reply. I was fascinated by her. Totally enthralled by our mating ritual and losing my mind with each gasp and movement of her lips.

I drowned my mouth in her mouth, fighting and sucking her tongue, grinding our hips together and making her jerk with pleasure. I couldn't take it any longer. I would eventually come and release inside her, turn her on her back and start all over again. She was tight and hot, almost coming by the way she was gasping for air. But I wanted to kiss her deep and hard, grind my body against her, feel her skin against my skin and her heart beating against my chest. I wanted to space out inside my mind, hypnotized by her breathing, her moaning, and the urgency of her body for release.

My tongue played with her tongue as my fingers pressed against her back. I thrust faster and pressed every single nerve in her molten core until she couldn't take it anymore. Her muscles contracted in spasms, and she screamed in pleasure inside my mouth. Her hands moved to my hair, pulling it roughly. Her legs held me tighter, stopping me from moving and preventing me from breathing. Her teeth bit my lower lip, and I grinned in victory, satisfied by her orgasms.

I couldn't endure, and I didn't need to anymore. So, I gave in to pleasure and groaned in bliss, molding her butt in my hands and slightly raising her off the bed. I let the wave of pleasure wash over my body and soul, making me tingle and quiver in satisfaction. She liked that, because her body jerked again, and she lost her breath, gasping my name in my ear with a warm exhalation.

I grinned against the hollow of her neck, reluctant to let her go of my embrace, holding her possessively. I didn't want that moment ever to end. It was perfection wrapped in bliss. Having her in my arms, still pressed against my body, feeling the shivers of pleasure running down my spine, and listening to her satisfied breathing was more than perfection—it was nirvana.

"Are you okay?" she asked, cuddling my head while calming herself down from the savage state she'd been in while experiencing pleasure.

I simply nodded and nibbled her ear, glimpsing the smile of happiness she wore. Her eyes were open, beaming with satisfaction. I couldn't help but feel like she was the most beautiful thing I had ever seen in my whole existence. I could've stayed like that forever. I smiled back at her, hopelessly in love.

"Are you okay?" I asked, realizing that I might have exaggerated my use of strength.

Anna nodded, playing with her index finger over my nose, drawing lines across my face, extremely concentrated on staring at me. I couldn't stop smiling at her, fascinated by her, curious about everything she was feeling, and worried about her well-being.

"Are you tired?" I questioned, paying attention to her heartbeat. I was letting her catch her breath, but I was still aroused. The way her hair covered the pillow like a veil made her look like a sensual and exotic angel. It was impossible not to feel stirred by that goddess.

"I'm not tired," she assured.

I would've given anything to know what she was thinking right then and there. She looked caught inside her thoughts and, at the same time, fascinated by what we were doing.

She placed her finger on my lower lip, pulling it down and biting down on her own. "I'm not tired at all," she whispered, raising her head to meet my mouth. She kissed me, watching my reaction. "And you aren't tired either," she mumbled, no doubt feeling my aroused cock against her core.

I hadn't moved since the first time. I could have continued what I was doing moments after it was over—that was how much she made me hard. But I wanted her to catch her breath.

"Do it again," she breathed in my ear, moving her hips, so I entered her, accepting me once again inside the hotness of her walls.

My muscles tensed, my heart pounded, my hips thrust forward while I closed my eyes, embracing the darkness and focusing on her needs. Her body relaxed under mine, surrendering to my thrusts. Her hand moved down my spine to my butt cheek, encouraging me to keep moving.

I said nothing, too inebriated on my own yearning, the softness of her skin, and the scent of our bodies together as we moved at the same pace, dancing to the rhythm of our desire. We took things slow, enjoying the shivers of pleasure, the waves of electricity running throughout our bodies, every single contraction of our muscles, and the soft laughter that left her mouth and mine.

The bed was spinning under our bodies. Every inch of my skin was bursting with fire, ready to fly away to paradise again. When I felt her hugging me tighter and exhaling against my ear, I understood that she was experiencing another row of orgasms. Her walls tightened around my cock and made me lose my ground, skyrocketing into a perfect orgasm that made my entire body quiver and shatter in pleasure. I was so high that I might have lost consciousness for a moment.

Annabel's fingers stroked the back of my neck until my heart rate calmed down, letting my face rest against her breasts. I could have rolled over and slept, but instead of letting her go, I loosened my weight on her and trailed kisses on her neck and breasts. Her nipples puckered under my lips and tongue. Her body quivered with my small love bites. I had no idea if we were taking too long or not with foreplay and making love because I was more interested in kissing her and making her ticklish under my mouth, ignoring the existence of time and life outside those walls.

She was addictive. She was my world and the cure for all my loneliness and doubts. We were in my bed, away from everything, and I had no intention of letting her go until my heart stopped aching, and we both fell asleep, exhausted.

CHAPTER NINE

ANNABEL

IT WAS LATE in the morning. I was in the middle of the bedroom, wearing nothing but his shirt and staring at Shane, who slept half-covered by the sheets. He was gorgeous. He was breathtakingly sexy, and I was having a hard time deciding to leave his house while he was sleeping and never appear in his life again.

Sometime around dawn, I fell asleep in his arms. We had both been exhausted by the physical effort. Maybe 'drained' was the better word because we seemed incapable of letting go of each other.

It was insane! I wanted him even more each time we made love. And each time we did, it was better. I don't even remember how we were able to stop. I just knew I didn't sleep much, and when I woke up, I felt a roller coaster of feelings.

My initial plan—the one I had made the previous day—was to wake up before he did, get out of the bed, grab my things, and sneak out. That was exactly what I did, until the sneaking out part, because there I stood in the middle of the room with very little determination to leave.

How could I leave after the night we had? After all we talked about: music, books, films, and his job? *After that fantastic long night of sex?*

"Anna," he whispered, scaring me out of my thoughts. "Come back to bed, honey." He rolled over and opened his eyes. "It's still early."

"I…" I choked. I had no excuse to give him.

"You've been there for at least ten minutes, deciding if you should leave or not."

Damn! Busted! Guess werewolves are tireless at making love and are light sleepers.

So I crawled back in bed and into his arms. He kissed me gently on my neck, closing his eyes and resting his head against my shoulder.

I sighed in pleasure. Desire ignited my body just by lying next to him, touching his skin, and feeling the brush of his lips. I blushed, realizing that I was becoming a sex addict. Besides, I was sore, so how could I possibly think about doing it *again*?

"You'll not get rid of me that easily," he sighed, making me sulk and forget all about sex. At least for the moment.

I did feel guilty about being so sneaky. He didn't deserve it. The night between us was perfect, from the dinner to the bed.

I liked his next words. "It's Saturday, sweetie, so relax and spend the day with me."

"I wanted to go home and change clothes," I said, finally remembering an excuse.

"You won't need clothes for the time being."

He wasn't helping me forget about sex with those words! Lust coiled inside my stomach.

"Aren't you tired?" he probed.

"I've already slept." That was the truth. "I don't sleep much."

He snapped his eyes open. "Okay. Let's get up then. Have a shower together. I'll make breakfast again."

"Pancakes?" I asked immediately with a hopeful voice.

"Whatever you want, honey." He smiled at me, making me melt with desire.

"Okay."

"And we can watch a movie later. I have an amazing collection of classics."

"I don't have clothes. I only brought the dress."

"I'll let you wear some of mine. After all, my shirts seem to look better on you." His compliment made me giggle. I was feeling extremely comfortable inside his shirt, smelling his cologne.

"Annabel," he whispered close to my lips, "I hope you aren't too hungry because it may take a while to shower."

"How come?" I asked, amused by his mischievous grin and raised eyebrows.

"I may feel the need to kiss you from head to toe while washing you."

I gulped, closing my legs as I remembered how meticulous he was with the foreplay. "I'm not that hungry," I assured, making him chuckle. He seemed pleased as he brushed his lips against mine and grabbed me in his arms to take me to the bathroom.

Just like that, I stayed and had the best day of my life.

We saw old funny movies that made us laugh until we cried. We talked, ate, listened to music, and talked some more. Shane was curious about what I liked to eat and watch on TV, what I read, and the music I listened to. The sexy werewolf was fascinating and incredibly funny. He even sat me on his lap in front of the fireplace and read me poetry that made me feel like someone else, someone who had an ordinary life and a normal relationship. He was easy to be around. He didn't judge or make fun of my tastes. He simply wanted to know why I liked something, and then he would share what he liked with me. It was easy to be 'me' next to him.

When the night came, we made love again. This time, we started on the couch, ended on the floor in front of the fireplace, and did it again in the bedroom. It was so mindblowing every time that I had no plans to leave the next morning. The idea of leaving that place to go back to my cold, ugly motel room wasn't appealing anymore. I wanted to be with Shane, to hear him laugh, to listen to him talk with that deep, husky voice, and to share my thoughts with him. Reality could wait a bit longer. I deserved a break from cruelty, death, and loneliness.

"Are you scared?" he asked me on Sunday night while we were seated on the couch, watching the news.

"Of what?" I asked, intrigued as I leaned my head back to stare at him.

I was paying little to no attention to the TV, enjoying the bliss of being quiet in his arms, relaxing and forgetting all my problems.

"You start classes tomorrow."

"I have forgotten about that."

"Where did you teach before coming here?"

"Let's not talk about that," I told him, sighing deeply and closing my eyes. But I was no longer relaxed because I felt the weight of reality sneaking in and tainting my serenity.

"Can't I know anything about your life?" he asked, his voice laced with disappointment.

"What do you want to know exactly?" I demanded, leaving his arms and sitting to face him.

I couldn't forget that he was the sheriff, and even if my undercover identity was bulletproof, he could call the places where I'd worked before and find strange coincidences with some vampires' killings. There was only a limited amount of time I could pretend to be normal. Apparently, it had run out because Shane wanted to know more about me. I couldn't show him that part of me.

Besides, I still didn't know what side he was on. *Was he one of the good guys, or did he work for some of the evil vampire lords that take over a city and plant their cubs in high places to get blood, money, and power?* He wasn't a vampire, but there were packs of wolves working for vampires. The organization I worked for wanted to remain secret to the supernatural community for a good reason.

"How old are you?" he asked after a moment of silence.

I found the question odd. "Twenty-three."

He smirked most strangely. "Do you know how old I am?"

I suspected that, by that smile, he wasn't twenty-eight, like he appeared to be. However, I really didn't have any idea how long a werewolf could live. My teammates and I had found, on our paths, some really old ones who looked like teens but who were extremely strong. They weren't a race to ignore and joke about.

Shane smelled strong; his presence felt strong. He was without a doubt an important member of that community, or they wouldn't give him the post of sheriff. I shivered, thinking about what bad things he could have done.

He seemed like a really nice guy. He was intelligent, charming, and gentle. The town looked pretty cozy and peaceful, too.

I didn't want to think about it. I didn't need to think about it. Shane and that supernatural town weren't a problem to my organization; I was there for a *personal* reason.

"Do you give up?" Shane asked, bringing me out of my thoughts.

"Yes, you're too old for me," I joked.

Shane didn't smile. "I wondered how old you were when you finished college. That's all. I don't want you to be upset by the question. It's just you are so…" He paused.

"I got my doctorate when I was twenty," I said, shrugging it off. "Is it a crime to be smart?"

I was not lying. I had entered college when I was fifteen. I was a child prodigy. A doctorate in literature wasn't the hardest thing to achieve while living a double life. However, facing the murder of my parents and being recruited by a secret organization of humans and hybrids that fought supernatural beings who didn't obey the rules was.

"No. I like the fact you're smart," he said softly, apparently not wanting to upset me again.

I didn't know why I was even upset for being questioned

about my age. Maybe because I was sure that he was older, much older, than me. I could feel it. He acted like it. He wasn't immature, and I liked that. But maybe my age could be a problem for him.

I wasn't going to get any older, but he didn't know that. My aging process had slowed down. My last exams showed it. My vampire side was kicking in. Soon enough, I would have to feed more often on blood. The idea didn't please me much, but my panther side also liked to eat raw meat. *It had blood in it, so why start being picky?* I simply had to hunt an animal and eat more often.

"I think it's time for me to go." I got up, uncomfortable with the sudden silence.

Not that we hadn't been silent before, but, at that moment, I wasn't comfortable there anymore. He seemed to want to ask questions that I couldn't answer, or, at least, couldn't answer with the truth. I didn't want to lie to him. I felt guilty, as if it wasn't right to lie to him. Being around him seemed way too familiar and relaxing, but I couldn't open up, and I didn't want to feel the pain of lying.

"Don't be silly, Anna," he said, catching my hand and making me sit down next to him. "I'm not judging you. I couldn't care less about your age. I mean, unless you're a minor. Are you a minor?" He smiled in a lame attempt to make me smile back, and he almost achieved it, but I was able to maintain my annoyed-by-the-questions face. "You never showed me your ID. Why couldn't I know your age?"

"If you wanted to know my age, why were you so surprised when I told you?"

"I thought you were older. Even if you don't look older, you sound older. You are intelligent, and you know a lot of things. We have smart conversations. Plus, you are a teacher."

I eyed him, mentally rebuilding my walls to keep him outside and protect myself from feeling vulnerable. I wasn't quite sure why I was still there. I had meticulously planned to leave the previous morning and never see him again.

It hurt to think about leaving. It shouldn't hurt. I should be smarter and not fall for the guy's sweet talk, with his dreamy blue eyes and lips that gave amazing kisses. I had let him in, and I was beginning to regret it. It was time to put an end to that weekend and come back to reality.

"Anna," he called, probably guessing that I was plotting a way to run from him again. It shouldn't bother me so much if I never saw him again. "What are you thinking?" He pulled me closer.

I avoided his gaze, dwelling on the idea that I had let things go too far, and I needed to get rid of him. I wanted to leave without any drama. It had been fun, but the weekend was over, and so were we.

"I need to get dressed and…"

"What are you talking about?" he asked, his voice laced with panic.

I raised my eyes to look at him. "The weekend is over," I explained, trying not to sound sad about it. "I should leave."

"No," he said with a serious face. "I don't want you to leave."

"Shane, this was fun, but I…" He put the tip of his fingers over my lips, shutting me up.

My silly heart rejoiced with the fact that he didn't want me gone.

Shane's eyes seemed sad when he spoke, "I don't want you to leave. I want you to tell me what you were thinking. You were really quiet."

"I wasn't thinking about anything."

"It's your first day at work. I thought that you may be worried about that."

"No."

He seemed to be memorizing my face. It was impossible to ignore the intensity of his eyes on mine, and the softness of his hand caressing my skin.

"Do you want to know what I was thinking?"

"Yes," I answered, raising my hand to touch his face.

"I was worried."

"About what?"

"I don't want you to go back to that motel room to sleep tomorrow," he said.

I frowned. "Tomorrow?"

"Tonight, you will sleep here with me," he stated, smirking as if I didn't have any other choice.

Okay, I wasn't planning to leave anyway—that night, that is. No, actually, I was too mesmerized by him to even think about the future—the next day, the hour, the minute we would eventually be apart. It was like he had put a spell on me.

I tried to follow his next words.

"But I guess tomorrow you'll be reluctant to come back here since you have to wake up early, and we seem to…well, not sleep during the night." He smirked mischievously, and I kept frowning at his words. I might have been smiling if I wasn't so confused about his statement.

"Do you want me to come back here tomorrow?" I asked, my heart rate rising from the happiness I felt.

He was implying that he wanted to see me again. The butterflies went wild inside my stomach; my lips almost drew up in a smile.

I looked down and tried to control my excitement. Things were getting out of hand… Whatever had happened between us needed to end. I had other priorities, and he was a distraction.

"I really don't want you living alone in that motel," he whispered, raising my chin, so I could stare at him.

I blinked several times at his sweet, worried, and intriguing words. "I can take care of myself."

"Still, it's not a nice place to live."

"I haven't had the time to look for somewhere else."

"You don't need to look. You can move in with me."

He said that. For real! My mouth almost opened wide in disbelief. And he had such a straight face while saying it.

"*What?*"

I got up, alarmed. *Move in with him? Things were escalating quickly. Was he crazy?* We had just met. We didn't even date. I was just passing by. I wasn't looking for a…

"I have an extra room," he added.

I sat again, more confused than ever.

"Do you want me to rent a bedroom?" I asked, trying to understand the purpose of his words. Maybe he was trying to make extra money, but it would be weird to have him as a roommate.

"*Hell no!* I want you to move in with me. You aren't sleeping in another bedroom. You can put your stuff in the other bedroom to have your privacy. I don't know. Whatever you want to do there, but…" He pulled me onto his lap, speaking near my mouth. "You belong in my bed."

If he was trying to seduce me, it didn't work. It only scared me and made me avoid his mouth.

"Shane, we had lots of fun this weekend, but I think you are rushing things." I pushed him away, trying to release his hold, so I could get up and get the hell out of there.

"Anna," he called, hurt by my evasive maneuvers. He let me go, and I got up.

"Don't do that," I complained, trying to ignore his pleading eyes.

"You don't need to fear me. I would never hurt you," he whispered in a tender voice that made me gulp.

Deep inside of me, I felt that he was telling the truth, but my rationality knew better than to trust his words.

"Please, baby. Just relax. Come back to my arms, and we'll talk about this."

"About what?" I asked, moving back and not falling into his trap. The physical attraction would always get the best of me. When we touched, he had control over me.

"Annabel," he called, offering me his hand, so I would draw near him.

I reluctantly gave him my hand.

He held and caressed it with his thumb while using his blue eyes to hypnotize and shatter my defenses. "I want you to move in with me to keep you safe. Anna…there are many things in the world that you don't know about. Scary things. This town isn't what it seems. It can be dangerous at night. It can even be dangerous during the day."

His reasons to convince me to move in with him left me even more baffled. Not only did he want to see me again, but he was also concerned about my safety.

But I wouldn't be moved by his gesture. It was still odd for him to be that keen on convincing me to move in with him. *We had just met!*

"God, Shane, I've lived in big cities, and I was fine! How can this place possibly be worse than a big city?" I asked, pretending to be ignorant of the fact that I knew he was right.

A town full of vampires, werewolves, witches, shifters, and hybrids was eventually dangerous to a human, especially a pretty young woman. But moving into his house would ruin my chances of hunting and doing my thing without having to lie more than necessary.

What was I saying? Had I really thought about the possibility of actually *moving in with him?* I was becoming insane. It was already crazy that he wanted me to move in with him to protect me! That was kind of nice of him, I think, or just eerie. Things were fuzzy. My mind was spinning, and my heart was clenching inside my chest, making me feel vulnerable.

"Promise you'll think about it this week," he pleaded before I could say anything else.

"There's nothing to think about. I don't make plans for the future. I won't move in with you. We've only known each other for a few days. Besides, the school year ends in two months. My contract will be up, and I'll no longer need to stay in town." I tried to reason with him. I was logical and coherent and felt quite pleased about that. Maybe I was getting my sanity back.

"James can hire you to stay longer. They'll need someone next year."

"We just slept together!" I snapped, upset by his solutions and insistence.

Why was he making plans for us? Was he completely crazy? He was a werewolf, and, as far as he knew, I was a human. There was no future for us. He would eventually find his soulmate and never remember me again. *Didn't he know that?* So why play that game when I was the only one with something to lose?

He had a soulmate. I didn't. Hybrids don't have soulmates. We are doomed to be alone.

The way he looked at me when I said those four words. It seemed like I had hurt him deeply.

"Anna, we didn't just sleep together," he said slowly, trying not to seem angry, but he definitely was. His voice was trembling, and I felt terrible for being so coldhearted. "We talked, we laughed, we made love, we saw movies, we danced under the moon and the stars, and we bonded."

"Shane, do you understand how crazy you sound?" I asked, mystified by his words.

He was giving too much importance to our affair. It was true, we were good together. He was amazing. I had lots of fun and good memories. I could even spend more time with him—eventually. But, all that talk about bonding—it sounded deranged. It sounded like...

"I told you, Annabel. I won't let you run from me," he added, killing my line of thought.

What the hell was he saying?

"Seriously? Are you crazy? Do you normally stalk every girl you sleep with?"

"No! Of course not! I didn't want it to sound like that."

"How the hell did you want it to sound then?" I shouted.

"Romantic," he whispered, making me shut up. He rubbed the back of his neck. "Did I frighten you?"

I was still trying to understand if I was really in the middle of a conversation like that one. I shook my head, even if I didn't know if it had frightened me or not. For the moment, it made me feel weird and confused. Was he obsessed with me?

"I'm sorry. I didn't want to sound like a psychopath," he said, still looking at me to see if I was relaxing and believing him.

I was blaming myself for letting my guard down.

"I think I should leave," I mumbled, but I didn't move. It was as if my body was stuck and didn't want to obey. I knew I should run the hell out of there. *So why was I not doing it?* The word he used, 'psychopath,' was surely one that could describe him by the previous speech of wanting me to move in with him and not letting me run from him. The problem was that he was the most gorgeous psychopath I knew. He had such dreamy eyes, and he made me shiver each time we touched. I almost wanted him to be obsessed with me.

Okay, fine, that was not too sane of me, either. Not proud of it! At least, we would be perfect for one another, both loony. But let's face it, in my line of work—the killing of evil supernatural beings' stuff—it was not hard to meet psychos. However, they didn't act like Shane or weren't as nice as him.

Analyzing my reactions, it seemed that my vampire side wanted to be adopted by him. Which was quite ironic, since wolves and vampires don't have the best of relationships. My panther side didn't care. It was too busy wanting to run the hell out of there, so it wouldn't be caught in a relationship. But me, I, Annabel was scared like hell of what I was beginning to feel for Shane.

"Please stay," he pleaded, putting his hands over mine. "I wanted you to know that I want to keep seeing you. But you seem too eager to get rid of me."

I looked at our hands. That made sense. "Dating?"

"Yes. Dating you. Don't you want to date me?"

"I don't have much free time..." I said, trying not to look in his eyes as I sucked on my lower lip.

I also tried hard to breathe and not to cry my heart out. I was getting emotional. *Why was I getting emotional?* My heart was beating fast. *I didn't want to say no to him.* That was why I was feeling like that. I was getting emotional because I wanted to hear that from him. I wanted to see him again, to date him.

Holy crazy bunch of gods that are worthless and don't do anything right! I didn't date werewolves or vampires or any other supernatural beings, for that matter. *They* have a freaking soulmate! *Hybrids* don't! Hybrids are incomplete and inferior to them because we are anomalies. We weren't created by the gods. They didn't give us a soulmate.

We are doomed to stay lonely forever.

It was supposed to be a one-night stand! Now he wanted to date me, and I...wanted to date him. I could slap myself and call myself stupid a bunch of times. I was getting myself into a mess, knowingly and willingly.

"Don't you want to see me again?" he asked with a heartbreaking voice.

I looked up at him and swallowed hard. I felt so much like cursing. Puppy eyes were like cheating at cards. *So unfair!*

I nodded.

"Not just for sex, Anna."

I looked at him sideways. "You didn't complain before."

Did he think I was that shallow? I blushed, realizing that I had jumped into that with an expiration date. But he couldn't blame me if he knew that I knew that he had a soulmate. I caved because he was too irresistible, and I was just human, sort of. I had...needs.

"What are you thinking?" he asked.

"You're extremely clingy for a..."

He furrowed his eyebrows.

"For a guy," I specified before making the mistake of ending with 'werewolf'.

"Guys have feelings, too," he declared as if he had the truth on his side.

"Sure. Let's just agree to disagree."

He arched an eyebrow. "You're doing it again."

"Doing what?"

"Using sarcasm to shut me out and...conceal your fears."

I frowned and folded my arms.

"Please take me seriously." He moved closer and caressed my face. "What will it take for you to tell me, yes?"

I seriously pondered his question, with my heart beating fast and my body trembling. He unfolded my arms, kissing my temples and making me close my eyes.

"I'm not going to stay for long," I explained, trying to make him realize that sooner or later, I would leave. I couldn't stay. He shouldn't make plans.

Why is he making plans?

"Then you have nothing to lose in giving us a try," he reasoned.

I knew he was trying to manipulate me into accepting him.

The amount of kisses he was leaving on my face was another way of trying to convince me. I had to give him credit: he was persistent. I must please him a lot. It was actually flattering, having him wanting to date me. He was captivating and breathtaking. Surely there must be a lot of women who wouldn't have had a second thought about dating him.

If only my life was simple enough to date and have fun, without a care in the world! The last thing I needed was a controlling and possessive werewolf boyfriend. He would drive me insane. But damn, I was so into him! And he didn't seem to be a controlling jerk. If anything, he was sweet and romantic, nicely protective, and extremely passionate in bed. Outside of it, too. Shane made me happy. He made me feel safe and made me laugh.

He was too perfect to be true!

"If I say yes," I whispered, "I don't want to talk about my past."

It seemed like a condition. I felt like it was a condition that I needed to fully be with Shane and not have to lie to him. I didn't like to lie. I was good at it, but I didn't want to fabricate things about my past, especially to someone I liked. Because I *did* like him. But I would eventually disappear from his life, and he would never see me again. However, I still had a couple of months there. I could take some time off and teach and date and be happy, like a normal person.

We didn't have any future together. I knew that. He would know that, too.

So why not risk it?

The passion would eventually fade away, and I would grow to be annoyed by him and his habits. I was sure of that. I was good at finding flaws in others. He would get tired of me, too. I could be annoying and strange. I liked my space and my silent moments. Besides, we were not meant to be, so what could go wrong, right?

For the moment, I could enjoy what we were feeling for one another. I could have fun and have sex. However, as I stared deep into his eyes, I felt weirdly caught in them and unnaturally anxious. *Could I fall for him?*

"We don't need to talk about our pasts if you don't want to," he agreed. "Is that what it takes for you to date me?"

"Yes," I whispered, noticing his lips were inching closer to mine.

"Good…but I have to warn you," he said before putting his lips over mine.

I stared at him, annoyed that he was still talking.

His next words made me giggle against his chest, baffled by his nerve. "If you keep dating me, you will most probably be the one to stalk me. That is how addictive I am."

CHAPTER TEN

ANNA

I HAD TONS of delayed school papers to grade. While missing a literature teacher, the department had assigned an essay on a book that the students had read, and the end result was a stack of papers scattered across the unstable round table of my motel room.

I had already gone for a run, taken a bath, and eaten something I'd stored in the small fridge. I was preparing myself to face a long, late night. At least, I could take solace in the fact that I didn't have classes in the morning, so I could sleep in. Besides, I was a nocturnal person by nature; my real job included long, sleepless nights.

The problem with my good intentions to get some work done was that my mind was too occupied with Shane. I'd thought about him all day long ever since leaving his home that morning to face my first day at school. What was supposed to be a one-night stand became a whole weekend. I had to confess, it had been an amazing and unforgettable weekend with him. Just thinking about it made me feel lonely and terribly aroused all over when I recalled his kisses, his adventurous hands, and my mouth trailing across his skin.

I couldn't concentrate, and I couldn't get any work done. I missed him and wanted to go to him. We hadn't spoken since that morning. He had said he would call, but he hadn't, and I was going out of my mind.

I needed to do something to get my mind off him. Since hunting was out of the question, I thought that maybe I could go to a bar. Well, the only bar in town was the one where Shane was probably hanging out.

He must be picking up some other naïve girl. I started to feel incredibly stupid. *How could I be such an idiot?* It was an affair. I couldn't have an actual boyfriend. *Am I going crazy?* He was the sheriff of this supernatural town while I was a hunter and a nomad. I couldn't trust anyone with the secret of who I truly was, and I would eventually have to leave.

But he said that we were dating and that he wanted to keep seeing me.

Why hadn't he called or texted?

I had to face the hard truth. He had fooled me. All his talk about trusting him and his witty charm made me fall for him. I should have left Saturday morning and forgotten all about him.

I should go to his place and see what he is doing. I should ask him why he didn't call.

Maybe I was being paranoid, and he was too busy to call. I needed a distraction.

I sat in front of my laptop with pursed lips while twirling a strand of hair around my finger. I could always call Jessica, my bestie, and ask her what she was doing. Maybe write down my report about what had happened with the three vampires that were now gone. Perhaps Jason had found a new lead about where we could find a pureblooded vampire. That meant that I wouldn't need to stay here for much longer. I could leave and forget all about Shane and our sexy time together.

My heart hurt at the thought of leaving. *Stupid heart!*

Sighing deeply, I leaned back on the sofa and looked at the ceiling. "I'm going nuts."

Someone knocked on my door, interrupting my obsessive thoughts. I wasn't expecting anyone, so I opened the door with caution and found Shane on the other side.

I didn't know how to react. *Should I be happy, or should I be mad?*

I settled on suspicious. *What is he doing here at this time of night?*

"Good evening," he said with a boyish grin. "Are you okay?"

He leaned closer with squinted eyes.

I nodded. "Why wouldn't I be okay?"

He pursed his lips. "Are you busy?"

I shook my head and clenched the doorknob harder with my hand. "No. Why?" I tried to play it cool, but my heart was skyrocketing with his presence while I was doing my best to look poise.

He smiled again, making my insides turn up and down with overjoy. "Can I come in?"

Stepping back, I opened the door.

His enticing scent hit my nostrils and swirled around my body once he passed the threshold. He looked around the space as if looking for something.

To my dismay, I realized that I had given up too quickly by letting him in. He might see that as permission to spend the rest of the night with me.

Why else would he be coming here?

He hadn't called all day. I wasn't going to let that slide so easily.

Closing the door, he stepped in front of me and leaned down.

His sudden closeness made me step back.

He frowned. "What's wrong?"

I wanted to lash out, but I was aware that questioning him about his lack of contact wouldn't help since I didn't call him either.

"I-I…" Shrugging, I bit the inside of my lip. "Just tired."

His hand circled around my wrist, and he pulled me closer.

Glancing up, I gulped the moment our bodies collided and his arms laced around my waist. His mouth covered mine in a long, slow, and all-consuming kiss that dissipated my lousy mood like magic. My body melted into his embrace, and my lips surrendered against his.

I can't possibly give in to him so easily.

My body, however, had little to no intention of rejecting him. I yearned for him, and I didn't need foreplay. I was already aroused. But that was a long and tender kiss, and he seemed to have no intentions of taking my clothes off and throwing me on the bed.

Pulling away after nibbling on my lip as if he was punishing me, he asked, "Why haven't you replied to my text messages and picked up the phone?"

He leaned his forehead against mine. I opened my eyes, still processing his words as he waited for an answer.

I blinked. "What text messages?" I had nothing. I'd checked my phone all day, hoping for something.

"I know you had a busy day, but have you checked your phone today?"

"Yes. What number did I give you?" I suddenly understood how silly I had been. I'd never checked my other phone, my real phone, the one whose number I shouldn't have told him about.

I left his arms and looked around. *Where did I put it? Oh, damn!* It was in my bag, my slayer bag—the one Shane should never see.

He followed my aimless stroll to the table where I'd left my purse before asking, "How many numbers have you got?"

I opened my purse and fumbled for the phone. "Two."

"Why?"

"One for work and the other for my personal life." I took my phone and placed it on the table.

Shane had his arms folded in front of his chest and his brows knitted together when I turned around. "Which one did you give me?"

He seemed troubled by this, as if I wasn't taking him seriously. The problem was that I was. So seriously that I had given him my real, permanent phone number.

"My personal one. I had my work phone with me all day," I answered, feeling guilty. "I think I left the other in the car."

Unfolding his arms, he narrowed the distance between us and pulled me back into his embrace. "Don't you ever do that to me again!" His voice was low and raspy as he placed my hair behind my ears. Cupping my face between his hands, he confessed, "I was worried sick about you!"

"I'm fine. I had a lot of things to do."

"I've missed you."

My heartbeat skyrocketed. He was so undeniably sweet and upfront. I liked that. It was refreshing.

"I've missed you, too." I grabbed my hand to his shirt, feeling silly because I realized that I was becoming sentimental and foolish. I shouldn't expose my feelings so openly. It was worth it, just to see the smile he gave me with that soppy declaration.

Is he for real?

His lips softly pecked mine, and he hugged me tightly before grabbing my hand and taking me to the couch where we sat next to each other.

Turning to me, he placed his hand behind my back and caressed a few curls away from my eyes. "How was your day? Did you like your new students?"

"I haven't met them all, but they seem polite and hardworking. A few were intrigued about my age, but—" I stopped talking and frowned at him. "Do you really want to know?"

"Of course." He brushed his fingers against my cheek and smiled. With a whisper, he added, "I want to know everything about you."

Grinning, I asked him. "And how was your day? Did you have a lot to do?"

He shrugged. "Uneventful. I wanted to have lunch with you,

but you didn't reply to my texts."

I grabbed his hand and entwined our fingers together, moving closer to rest my head on his shoulder. "I had lunch with another teacher. She seems nice."

"Do you want to have lunch with me tomorrow?"

"Sure. But I don't have classes in the morning."

He kissed the top of my head. "Does that mean that I can spend the night here?"

I giggled. "Maybe, though I have a lot of work to catch up."

"I'll play nice."

I looked up at him, watching how gorgeous he was. "Not too nice, I hope."

His lips curled up, and his eyes glinted. Grabbing my chin, he whispered, "Maybe we can be bad now, and I'll let you work in the morning."

"No more talking?"

"I'll do whatever you want to do."

Nibbling on my lower lip, I reached up and whispered against his lips, "I want to kiss you and make love to you."

He looked me deeply for a moment before closing his eyes and locking his lips with mine.

Our bodies together felt like perfection. I couldn't get enough of his mouth and how good it felt to be touched and touch him. His skin was addictive, and I enjoyed listening to his heartbeat increasing with the foreplay.

My hands circled his neck, and my fingers traveled up his head and found the way to his soft hair. Deepening our kiss, I felt his fingers clutching my hips.

He tilted his head back, allowing me to explore his neck and his collarbone with kisses. My breathing was narrowed by desire, and I was more impatient about taking his clothes off than I should. The crazy attraction between us shattered any self-control

I had over my libido.

"I shouldn't be this compliant since you ignored me the entire day," he whispered.

"I promise I won't ignore you tomorrow."

"You have no idea how precious you are for me," he mumbled, searching my mouth to kiss. He looked at me for a moment as his hand cupped my face. "Not knowing that you were okay on your first day at your new school put me in a foul mood."

"The principal has been most accommodating, and my colleagues seem very nice. You have no reason to worry about me."

Shane sneered. "Don't trust the principal so easily. He's…"

I covered his mouth with a finger. "A player. I know."

"And we are…"

"Dating," I finished his sentence with a smile.

He nodded and kissed me with a demanding grip that stirred back the need for further contact between us.

The way his lips touched me, and he wrapped me in his arms with so much caution and concern were nothing like I had ever experienced before. His kisses made me lose all sense of gravity. His plump, soft lips made it difficult to stop touching them. My hands enjoyed unbuttoning his shirt while I touched his shapely torso.

My breasts were hard with yearning. I felt impatient when he slowly started to unbutton my shirt while kissing my neck and my shoulders. Once the shirt was out of the way, he cupped my breasts. Seconds later, his mouth fell on one of my nipples. His tongue swirled, and his lips nipped at my breasts, giving equal attention to each.

By then, I was lying against the couch with a cushion behind my back. My fingers ran through his hair as my back arched with

need. I was continually gasping, feeling my stomach swirl with
lust. His hands touching me and his mouth on my breasts were
enough to make me lose myself, but I was missing him inside me.
It was tormenting how much I needed to make love to him, to
ease my mind and body. I didn't want to wait any longer.

I grabbed his belt and unbuckled it with impatience. I did the
same to his pants. My hand plunged inside, caressing his already
hard shaft. Feeling it pulsate between my hand made me even
more impatient as I listened to him moan and gasp for air.

Shane took over. He grabbed my hands and pulled me up, so
he could take my shirt off, removing his own after. I lay on the
couch as he ripped my shorts off my legs, pausing to look at my
almost-naked body. I was left with my panties on. I didn't care. I
wanted him to climb on top of me, so I could feel the touch of
his skin and kiss him senseless while we made love.

Instead, his mouth pressed against the fabric of my panties,
and I almost came right there. I swayed under his mouth while
his hands grabbed the panties and took them off. Then he gently
spread my legs and nestled his head between my thighs. His lips
feathered my pussy before he plunged in his tongue and licked
me until I couldn't do anything else but moan and tense under his
skilled tongue.

It didn't take long for me to climax over and over again, until
I couldn't take anymore, and my throat was sore from moaning
and voicing for the divinity. I was a firm believer that one
wouldn't call for god while having sex. Until I met Shane. Now, I
couldn't stop myself from screaming and moaning in pleasure
while blaspheming without restraint or control.

The sexual attraction between us was insane. The sexual
release made me the happiest I've been for years. Despite the
circumstances of my arrival to that town and my pressing task,
Shane was what I needed to feel sane and focused. He might be a

distraction, but he relaxes me and soothes the helplessness I feel inside—all the time.

When I stopped convulsing from the orgasm, Shane raised his head to watch me with shiny eyes and a mischievous smile.

Regaining my breath, I watched him as he got up and turned me onto my stomach. He grabbed the back of my neck and parted my legs to kneel. His lips brushed down my spine and moved up. He took his time nibbling on my neck while pressing his hardness against my butt.

With closed eyes, I lost myself in the bliss of his touch. My body quivered, and my limbs felt weightless. His hand and mouth consumed all my attention. It was only when his hips moved against me that I realized we had leaned forward, and his cock was thrusting inside me, effortlessly. Swallowing a moan, I moved my hips to let him go deeper. One hand cupped my breast, the other grabbed my hip, and he thrust in and out before filling me up and pressing harder and faster until all we could do was moan and gasp with the overwhelming pleasure.

I whimpered in yearning each time he moved forward before finishing with a good stroke that sent ripples of pleasure throughout my body. It was driving me over the hedge again. He wasn't doing it fast but taking his time. Each stroke was perfect and mind-blowing, as if we were becoming one. He mastered all my movements, making all the effort.

I didn't want it ever to end, but I came again, as I felt his spasms inside me, doubling the pleasure and making me urgently gasp for air and feel my claws grow and clench the couch.

It wasn't just my claws. My vampire teeth also came out, scaring me for losing control. I didn't want to attack him, but I couldn't control the happiness and the pleasure that my little monsters felt because of Shane.

That's what I call the creatures that take over my shape when

I let my fangs out or shift to my panther's form. But it was a loving term because I loved my vampire and panther. They were the reason for my strength and immortality. Besides, they were my parents' legacy. They made me with all their love. I could never forget that. I was made out of love because a vampire and a panther shifter refused to obey the stupid rules.

I had the better of two races, and I refused to believe that I was a genetic anomaly. If the gods gave soulmates to other races, then it would be because it was okay to mingle. They just forgot that their progeny would lack something. But humans couldn't identify their soulmates, either, even if some believed they had one. Maybe we had to look harder to find ours, even if the other races claimed that we didn't have a soulmate and insisted that we were aberrations that shouldn't exist.

I refused to believe I was a mistake since the ability to conceive between two different races was possible. The theories were aplenty, and none pleased me. I disagreed with the ancient laws and was glad that mentalities were changing, even if many creatures still saw it as wrong to mingle. Nevertheless, the world was not perfect. There were bad and good people and some in between. Therefore, some people were liberal about interspecies mating and the existence of hybrids, and there were ones who were not. I, for one, was glad to find a community where all seemed happy living together. But I was letting my thoughts run wild again.

I calmed my heartbeat and took control of my body, hiding my teeth and claws. Shane was holding me in a tight hug, grinding his chest against my back. I could hear his heartbeat slowing down. We were still on the couch, but I was not touching it. I was floating above it inside his arms, wrapped in a cocoon of bliss. I could have stayed like that forever.

"Are you okay, Shane?" I asked.

His breath was extremely heavy. I was not good at guessing,
but I thought maybe he was also trying to control his wolf. It
reminded me that I'd love to see his wolf form. I was sure it was
beautiful, but I cast the thought away. Shane wasn't mine to be
romantic about. I had no right to see his wolf. His wolf couldn't
care less about me. I was not his mate but the entertainment until
he found his soulmate.

Thinking stuff like that while we make love only sadden me
and ruins my mood. I don't want to be ruin what's happening
between us. I'd been lonely and sad for the past eight years. I
wanted to enjoy life with Shane as long as I could so the
memories of us together would have a special place in my heart
once I had to leave.

"I'm okay… So, can we talk now?" he asked, trying to be
funny.

We laughed, and he loosened his grip on me.

I turned to face him, staring at his beautiful eyes as I stroke
the hair near his forehead. His eyes never shifted before me—he
had tremendous control over his wolf. How would his wolf look
like?

"I should work before bed," I mumbled, caught in his gaze.

There was no conviction in my voice because I didn't have
any willpower to leave his arms after that memorable sex on the
couch.

"You'll have time for that. Now you're going to give me your
other phone number, have a shower with me, and then we're
going to bed. That is if you don't mind me staying the night here
with you."

"Do you still want to spend the night here?" I didn't expect
him to want to stay after satisfying our hunger for each other.

"Don't you want me to stay?" He seemed disappointed, as if
I had hurt his feelings.

My question was careless and I felt like kicking myself. The last thing I wanted was for him to have that gloomy look in his eyes: It made me feel like crap. But I was not used to having a relationship like this, *whatever this was.* I was certainly not used to having someone like Shane. He was caring and romantic. Probably a mind-reader too. Shane was incredible.

My dad was sweet like that with my mom. They were mates, and they spent their time together, sharing everything, being romantic. Tears welled up in my eyes for remembering them at that precise moment.

He cupped my face with a startled expression. "What's wrong, Anna?"

I tried to look away and squint my eyes to control my emotions, but I was still in his arms, and he had no intention of letting me go.

"Honey, did I do something wrong?"

He could probably listen to my heartbeat increase and feel the quivering of my body. I tried to think about something else instead of ending up sobbing like a helpless child.

I loved them so much, I couldn't help but feel emotional.

"You did nothing." I held him closer, placing my head on his shoulder and taking in his scent and the peace his arms gave my soul.

Why can't he be mine? Why does he have to have a mate?

I was so jealous of her. I wanted to belong to someone.

To him.

I thought he was perfect. Shane always said the right words and was sweet and kind. His mate will be extremely lucky when they find each other.

Why was I feeling all that need and a sudden desire for a soulmate? I had never been interested in finding a man and settling down to have a family and act how the society expects women to act. My life was messy and dangerous. My mission and real work were all I needed until that moment. Until Shane came into my life.

I needed to be rational, but, at the same time, I was feeling everything except rational. I was feeling sad, needy, and lonely. I needed to be in his arms and hold him tightly. It was the only thing that had calmed me down over the past few days.

Why can't he be mine?

I knew my parents loved me, but why did they make me if they knew that I would never have something like they had—a soulmate?

If only I knew how to get to them, those gods who play dice with our lives, I would beat them senseless!

"I'll go if you want me to leave," he said as if he had come to terms with that.

I opened my eyes, coming out of my troubled stormy world of thoughts. "No. I don't want you to leave." I held him tighter. "Sometimes, I can be an idiot. But I'll do whatever you want. If you still want to stay with me."

Maybe I had scared him away for almost breaking down in tears.

"Whatever I want?" he asked, his voice caressing my shoulder as his hand pressed against my lower back.

I giggled, the teasing in his voice enflaming my happiness again. "Whatever you want."

"I just want to be next to you. Even if you have to work."

Apparently, he was easy to please. I almost laughed at that thought, even if I was confused as to why he wanted to spend so much time with me.

Suddenly, I was taken from the uncomfortable couch and stood in front of his naked body, fully aware that I was also naked. I couldn't help but stare at him as my body shivered, not from sadness but from lust. I was getting aroused again, and I realized that I had never liked sex so much. It used to be a controllable thing, a hormonal problem to fix during some months of the year. I would generally lose interest after a couple of times. I'd had some good-looking lovers before, but no one like Shane. He made my blood boil, and he woke up every single part of my undiscovered desires, yearnings, and fantasies. I felt my whole being glow with happiness because of spending time with him. It was utterly bizarre and perfect at the same time.

"How big is the shower in this place?" he asked, bringing me to his arms and making our naked bodies touch.

"Not big enough," I sighed, standing on my tiptoes to get near his mouth and kiss him.

I knew we weren't going to stop kissing because he held on to me and lifted me up to carry me to the bathroom.

I had to confess, I loved to be treated like a woman. I liked him carrying me around as if it was the most natural thing to do. It felt good being pampered and have someone concerned about my well-being.

CHAPTER ELEVEN
ANNABEL

I DON'T KNOW how he did it, but I spent more time at his place in the two weeks that followed than I did at my motel room. The sex was *amazing*. That was one of the reasons I stayed at Shane's place and left my mark all over his bedroom and bathroom. He didn't seem to mind. It wasn't just about the sex, though. Shane was captivating. He made me laugh and feel happy. He was affectionate and supportive when I had homework to correct and papers to grade. And he gave wonderful massages. Basically, he was too good to be true.

One of the highlights of my day was to have lunch with Shane at the town diner, Mama Bear's Diner. We met there because it was next to our workplaces. The other was to finish the day in his house, talking while we cooked. *Haven't I already said that the sex was amazing?* We were always touching when we were together, and it was hard to keep our clothes on when we got to his place at night for dinner. He looked hot in a uniform, even if he normally preferred to wear normal, casual clothes.

Who am I kidding? He looked *hot* in any kind of clothes or out of them.

At school, things were going well, even if the other teachers acted strangely. It was probably because they thought I was the only human among them and didn't know what was going on. Nevertheless, they were all nice enough, and I made some friends among the other teachers, like the drama teacher and the cute vampire girl who taught math and had eaten lunch with me on my first day at school.

The whole town was friendly and peaceful. It was as though no one was supernatural at all. But I knew better than to trust first impressions, so I never truly let my guard down.

The teenagers seemed, at first sight, normal and lazy. There were the jocks, the emos, the popular kids, the outcasts, the geeks, and other types I could not classify. Of course, then we had to divide the groups into wolves, vampires, witches, succubi, other shifters, and the hybrids. There were also a lot of human students from nearby villages because, even if the school was private, they had scholarships, and let's face it, humans were like a plague. They existed everywhere, despite the village's intention to remain free of them or, at least, keep the supernatural knowledge safe from them.

Regarding the teenage hybrids, they were stronger and almost invulnerable, which was what made them respected and, most of the time, feared by other species. Even with the differences, all the students were accepted by their peers. For me, it was truly mind-blowing how well everybody got along. It was clearly an open-minded community, and it was growing on me.

As for the principal, James Ward, he was extremely nice to me, even while I was pretending not to understand his kind gestures as seduction. He was a charming man, but I was not falling for his twisted game. He was a *manwhore* since he also flirted with the other teachers, especially the good-looking ones. He was most likely having sex with some of them, but he was not having any luck with me. I was with Shane, and I would be faithful to him. No matter what others would say about my panther side, I wasn't going to cheat on my boyfriend. Yes, *my boyfriend*. In Shane's words, we were dating and we were exclusive. It may have taken me a while to get used to the word girlfriend. Yet, I eventually got used to the idea of having a boyfriend as sweet and caring as Shane.

Let me clear up any confusion about feline shifters. They are known for being unfaithful to their mates. They mate for life like werewolves and vampires or other shifters, but they like to fool around. I was not like that, yet I knew many that were. Jason was one of them. My cousin didn't have a mate because he was a hybrid, but he couldn't be faithful to a girlfriend—not that he actually knew what the meaning of the word girlfriend was. He had a lot of girlfriends scattered around the country. I was sure of that, even if he had a mate, he wouldn't be true to her or him. But I had no intentions of being unfaithful to Shane while we were dating. Besides, I couldn't care less about Mr. Ward or any other guy in town, for that matter. My whole world revolved around that sexy werewolf.

Sometimes, I wondered if Shane was like Jason. But the hot werewolf only had eyes for me, and I was clever enough to realize that fact and be amazed by it. While Jason was always on the lookout for the next girl to seduce, sleep with, and dump, Shane was not. There were a lot of good-looking women in town, and he never seemed to be aware of them.

I was letting my guard down because Shane was unlike any other guy I'd dated before. Everybody loved him. They respected him. Even the girls I taught seemed to be jealous of me because most of them had a crush on him. The ones who were werewolves seemed more jealous than the others as if they knew something I didn't. Sometimes, I would catch pieces of their conversation. Normally, it was about how gorgeous and sexy Shane was and how they couldn't understand why he dated a human. Humans were weak, narrow-minded, and breakable. They weren't good enough to be trusted, and Shane would eventually have his heart broken. Then they would argue about who would mend his bleeding heart after I left him.

I would roll my eyes, annoyed about my private love life being the subject of conversation at school, and even more annoyed by the fact that the werewolves thought I could hurt Shane. As if I could really hurt him when they were the lucky ones who had a predestinated soulmate. They all had a soulmate. He had a soulmate, too, whom he would eventually find. I didn't.

Slowly, every day, that thought whispered darkly inside my mind, becoming louder and louder, until it began ruining my happiness.

My feelings for him were getting stronger every day. I became possessive as I didn't want to lose him to another woman. But nothing could make Shane stay with me if he found his mate. It didn't matter how she looked or how old she was—he was hers, and she was his. They were part of one another, and I was the one who would end up with my heartbroken, stepped on, and ground into dust. That was why I always dated hybrids or humans. Or until I met Shane and had my feet swept right out from under me.

CHAPTER TWELVE
ANNABEL

"SQUAD LEADER, CAN you hear me?" the voice reached me as if I was underwater and my transmitter signal was weak. But I was simply distracted as I recalled how sad Shane had become for not being able to spend the weekend with me. Again.

"Can we breach the premises," a male voice asked, waiting for orders.

Tapping my transmitter, I turned on my coms. "The Watchtower hasn't cleared us yet."

"We have all the intel that we need. Why are we still waiting?" the male voice grumped on the other side.

A female voice joined the conversation. "Calm down, Oliver."

"The drones aren't in position yet," I reminded the werewolf. "Why are you so impatient today?"

"My wolf is restless. I don't know what's going on, but I want to enter the compound and free all the prisoners the soonest as possible," Oliver replied.

"We're almost done scanning the building," the watchtower's female voice said on the other side. "You know they always boobytrap their buildings so they can escape faster in case of a breach."

"Just hurry up, Selene," the werewolf muttered.

"Is that the way to talk to your girlfriend?" Jason's cheerful voice teased on the coms.

"Jason, what are you doing here?" I asked, not expecting my cousin to show up. "I thought you were in Las Vegas."

"I was called back to help Jessica with a vampire nest in Boston. I heard you were here and came to offer assistance since I've nothing else better to do tonight."

"This is just a routine op. There was no need," I mumbled as I looked at my tablet and read the last intel about the compound we were attacking. "Everybody received the layout of the building and the location of the traps?"

A few muttered yeses were the answer to my question.

"According to the sensors, there are forty vampires, two werewolves, and what we assume to be ten kidnapped human victims," Selene said. "How do you want to proceed, squad leader?"

"Jason, how many are in your team?"

"I'm a one-person team," he answered.

"You're joining Delta Team then. They are in the back of the compound. Once they cut the power, secure the backdoor exits, and don't let anyone escape."

"What about us?" Oliver, the impatient one, asked.

"Once the snippers disable the guards at the front entrance, my team will move upstairs to where the vampires seem to be concentrated. There are only four vampires in the basement, next to the humans. Beta Team will take care of them and protect the humans while we deal with the enemy. Delta Team should cover the staircases and meet us upstairs if we need backup."

"Who will be watching the rooftop if they try to escape by there?" Jason asked.

"The snippers will use WS50 caliber bullets if anyone tries to escape. We are authorized to neutralize or eliminate the targets if needed," I replied.

"Uh! We aren't kidding tonight. What did they do? Besides feeding on humans and kidnapping them?"

"They are sex traffickers. They are selling human slaves to whoever pays them. All their targets are underaged. The youngest, the better for them."

"Bastards," Jason growled. "I'll kill them slowly, then."

"As far as we know, this is where the leader behind this operation is located. We just need to make sure that their computers aren't harmed because we want to hack into their system and track down their buyers," Selene disclosed.

"Yes, yes. Kill the enemy, leave the electronic alone," Oliver grumbled.

"Dude, what's wrong with you?" Jason questioned with a mocking voice. "Is Selene leaving you dry?"

"Shut up, Jason," Selene warned.

"Everybody chill and get ready," I ordered. "You can act like teenagers once this mission is over and the victims are saved."

No one dared to speak.

I checked my submachine gun, made sure that I had the daggers placed in my vest to throw if needed, and counted the extra clips. "Snippers one and two, do you have a clear shot of the guards?"

"Target acquired," the snipers informed.

"The drones are positioned," Selene warned. "We have images of the compound's surrounding area."

Moving my arm up, I signaled my team to stealthily move between the parked trucks and empty shipping containers. We advanced in line formation, the closest possible to the front entrance.

"S1 and S2, engage," I ordered the snipers.

The two first shots killed the two vampires patrolling. Before the guy at the front gate could react, another hit put him down. Shots to the head would neutralize vampires but didn't kill them for good.

In a blink of an eye, we dashed to the gate door. Two of my men stabbed the enemy in the middle of their chest with a silver stake. It was a technique to render them immobile once they healed. Severing the head and stabbing the heart killed most of the supernaturals. Bullets to their head, not so much unless they were laced with wood and silver—WS bullets.

"Delta Team, cut the power," I ordered.

The alarm sounds went off, creating the necessary noise for us to breach

"Two minutes for the backup generator to turn on," Selene warned. "Sensors show two targets coming your way."

"Moving to intercepted," I said, signaling two of my men to move forward and start clearing the path.

Even if everything was dark, supernaturals have good night vision. Cutting the power was necessary to prevent them from destroying the disks and to disable the security measures. In turn, the alarms would go off, creating enough noise to confuse their enhanced senses. Our targets were blind and partly deft for the time being.

Danny and Stephan moved forward, aiming their submachine gun with laser scope at the vampires' heads that sped down to check what was happening. Once the first wave was dealt with, they swiftly moved to the side of the entrance and protected themselves.

"The rooms down the corridor have sensor heat signatures. They are standing up and moving to the doors," the watchtower informed.

I closed my fist in the air. "Let them come and shoot on sight."

The other four members and I received the new wave of enemies with a round of fire. The four vampires were neutralized before reaching for their guns.

Danny and Stephan followed down the corridor and threw stun grenades inside the rooms as they opened the door. The ones that stayed behind me stabbed the vampires and followed me to the staircase.

"Tabby, take position near the elevator and shoot the ones that come down," I ordered. "Danny and Stephan will cover your six once they clear the rooms." I looked back. "Oliver, your team will descend to the basement and free the prisoners."

"This is Watchtower. Jason is on the roof," Selene warned.

"Jason, what are you doing on the roof?"

"I got bored waiting. I want to take part in the action."

"The enemies are moving to the stairs," the watchtower informed.

"Change to blades to engage the enemy coming down the stairs. Activate speed and acrobatic mode," I ordered.

"Roger that," my team replied, knowing what they had to do.

Shouldering my submachine gun, I reached for my sword and sped up the stairs. I cut the distance by walking over the ledge and jumping over the steps. The first vampire descended, and I sliced his neck before he realized that he wasn't alone. He burst into flames when his head detached from his body. The teammates behind me dashed to the next vampires and did the same.

We killed ten vampires before reaching the top level and stop in front of the door that gave access to the next rooms.

"Someone quiet the damn alarm!" a male voice shouted from afar. "Do I have to do it myself?" He kept ranting, "Where the fuck are Brad and Johnny?"

"Watchtower, what's their status? Are we clear to enter the room?" I whispered to my coms.

The alarm stopped. I heard the white static of the radio before a voice shouted, "We're under attack. Someone is shooting at us. We need help."

I heard the sound of chairs being dragged and the magazines on guns being pulled.

"Watchtower?"

"They are coming your way. We have a problem with Oliver's team."

"Shit," I muttered and looked back at my three companions. "Use your side guns and aim to the head."

"I'm going to help," Selene warned.

"No!" I growled, aware that I couldn't shout. They already knew we were here, but we had to open that door and neutralize them. "Selene? Watchtower? Are you there?"

No answer. She disobeyed me and left her post. I was sure of it.

My attention focused on the submachines discharged downstairs. A second later, guns fired upstairs. And we didn't have a watchtower to tell us what was going on.

Just great!

"Should we wait for them to open the door?" one of my teammates asked.

Focusing on the task at hand, I ordered, "Move from the door. They are most likely to shoot at it. We'll break the windows on the corridor and throw stun grenades. Group of two and watch your six when you enter the room. Cameron, you're with me. Use the carousel method when moving across the room."

Without wasting time, we ducked and rushed to the windows on each side of the office's entrance. We broke them just when bullets pierced through the door.

I crashed the window with the back of my gun, and Cameron threw two stun grenades. He ducked, and I aimed at the two shooters turning the door into Swiss cheese.

The stun grenades forced the other vampires to duck. We jumped inside the room and circled around, rotating the shooting.

Even if we were cautious not to shoot the computers, the vampires weren't that careful.

At this point, it was all about survival. Nevertheless, I was going to have a serious talk with Selene once we were out of the wood.

Cameron and I sheltered behind a desk to replace our clips.

"This is not going great," Cameron mumbled as he caught his breath.

I glimpsed at the other team not far from us. Touching my coms, I whispered. "Time for plan B. S1 and S2, aim at the windows on the top floor and take out the enemy. Permission to use SW bullets."

Once I issued the order, the glasses exploded as the snippers began shooting at the ones taking cover behind the furniture and close to the windows.

The noise was deafening, but I needed to know what was going on. "Jason, what's your location? What's happening downstairs?"

"I found another way to the basement. They have a hostage situation, and I'm going to catch them by surprise."

"Good luck, then."

"Stop, stop. We surrender," a voice said from inside the room. "Do you hear me? Tell your men to stand down. We surrender."

That was fast. "S1 and 2, stand down. Do you copy?"

The shooting stopped.

I shouted, "Throw your weapons on the floor and raise your hands in the air."

"Do as she said," the guy ordered.

The sound of metal clashing against the floor echoed inside the room.

"Don't shoot. We are unarmed and walking towards the door," he informed.

"S1, can you confirm what they are saying?"

"Affirmative, Squad Leader. Five men are standing up with their hands in the air. I have their leader in my sight."

"You know what to do if they reach for a weapon," I whispered to the snippers. "The rest of you, grab your stakes."

My teammates nodded and removed the stakes from their utility belts.

"We are moving towards the door," the guy informed.

I focused on their footsteps smashing the glass and signaled my men to stab the ones closest to them. I showed them three fingers. When the last finger dropped, they swiftly moved from their location and pierced the stake in the middle of the enemy's chest.

Wisps of ashes from the snippers' targets still swirled around the space as their leader stood still, shaking in fear with his fingers entwined behind his head.

His lips trembled when I faced him with a stake in my hand. "Y-you don't need t-to k-kill us. We surrender."

I smirked at him. "You won't die. It's just easier to neutralize you like this." With that said, I carved the stake into his chest, and he froze with dread in his eyes, falling back like a slab.

Turning around, I looked at my teammates. "We should go downstairs and help."

CHAPTER THIRTEEN
ANNABEL

ONCE THE SITUATION upstairs was under control, my team and I rushed to get to the basement and help with whatever was happening. As we sped down the stairs, I heard two of my team members shouting at each other.

When I stepped into the corridor, Oliver walked past me with a scared girl in his arms, clutching to his neck as if life depended on it.

Selene stood at the end of the corridor, bawling her eyes out. "Don't walk away from me!"

Oliver paused. I noticed the bullet wounds on his back. Some had hit the bulletproof vest, but he had two on his shoulder that bled and should be hurting him.

"Don't I mean anything to you?" Selene screamed, clearly upset and in pain.

"I told you, we're over. Don't try to stop me from leaving, or I'll hurt you," Oliver muttered.

"More?" Her hands closed into fists. "Bastard!"

Danny held Selene before she ran and jumped on Oliver.

Ignoring her screams, the werewolf continued his way to the exit with the scared girl shivering and sobbing in his arms.

"What the hell is going on?" I asked, facing Danny, Stephan, and Selene. "We are here to work, not to wash dirty laundry in public."

Stephan rubbed the back of his neck with wide eyes while Danny had his work cut out by trying to calm down Selene, who was sobbing and focusing her rage on him.

A hand covered my shoulder, and I glimpsed Jason standing behind me. "Walk with me, cousin."

"What happened? Did anyone get hurt? Why are they

fighting?" I questioned him. His hand moved to my lower back, and he escorted me outside. "Are the prisoners okay? Where's Oliver going with that girl?"

Jason sighed and looked at the moon in the dark sky. The cold wind swirled around us. I filled my lungs with the fresh air, allowing myself to relax for a second.

Glancing at him, I reminded him, "I have things to take care of inside the compound. I have no time for a stroll on the parking lot."

"Oliver had a reason to be impatient tonight."

I frowned at him, waiting for him to proceed with the explanation.

He wetted his lips before adding, "It seems that he found his soulmate. Oliver broke formation and went on a rampage when he sniffed her. The enemy began shooting aimlessly. He shielded her with his body to protect her from the bullets. We eventually killed the vampires, but a few of the prisoners were wounded. No one died," he quickly added as if that excused Oliver's conduct.

Jason's words sank on me. "Oliver found his mate. That was why Selene... They were dating for three years now. He just... dropped her like that?"

Jason nodded. "That's why Selene's crying and upset. Still, she should've known better. Hybrids shouldn't date purebloods. It never ends well. Now, she's left with a broken heart, and Oliver couldn't care less about her because he found his other half." Jason stopped walking and groaned. "He should be reprimanded for his reckless attitude. Mate or not, there were other prisoners to save. Everything could have ended in tragedy. Luckily his other teammates pulled their weight, and the vamps were taken out before they could hurt more prisoners or escape."

Even if I had heard Jason's recount of the events, there was only a sentence echoing inside my mind. *Oliver found his mate.*

Jason grabbed my arm. "Are you okay? Do you think you should be running ops after coming from the hospital?"

I looked at my cousin and blinked to dissipate the fog that had taken over my mind. "I'm fine."

"How's everything at the hospital? Any change in his condition?"

"My blood transfusions are helping to keep him steady, but he's still in a coma. The doctors are sure that only the blood of a pure vampire can heal him."

Straightening his shoulders, he clenched his jaw. "And we aren't any closer to finding one."

I ignored the defeated speech. "You should visit Kevin and talk to him."

"I'm planning to go there tomorrow." Smiling as if he wanted to lift my spirits, he placed his hand on the top of my head and rubbed it. "Cheer up. I'm going back to Detroit to follow another lead."

I brushed his hand away, annoyed by him treating me like a child.

He leaned closer. "How are things going on in Affinity? Did you find any useful lead about where the family of purebloods lives?"

"There are a lot of supernaturals living in that town. Plenty of hybrids too."

"I read your report. You seem to be enjoying spending your time there."

I kept a straight face. "The security is strict, and I'm still trying to blend in. There isn't a lot going on in the school, and the community is still an enigma. They seem friendly enough, and crime is almost inexistent. They don't trust me enough to tell me about their problems since they assume that I'm a human."

He frowned. "Revealing that you're a hybrid is dangerous.

Even in a community that seems to accept us amidst them."
Jason sighed. "You have no idea what deranged stuff might happen inside the walls of their homes."

I snickered. "Don't be absurd."

He frowned. "That doesn't sound like you. You're always extra careful and mistrust everyone and everything. Have they brainwashed you? Are you compromised?"

My eyebrows knitted together. "Are you serious?"

He blinked a few times as if choosing his next words. "You wouldn't put your brother's life at risk."

I nodded. "Still, there isn't much going on in the school. If there was a bad apple, you killed it at Las Vegas. Even the principal seems to play by the rules."

Jason folded his arms and arched an eyebrow. "What rules are those?"

"No feeding and killing humans. Don't harass students. You know, the usual."

His posture relaxed, but his forehead was still wrinkled in thought.

"What do you want to say?" I questioned him.

He shrugged. "It's your call if you want to continue to stay there or not."

"There's still a lot that I haven't investigated. Though the principal isn't the pureblood we were looking for, I'm sure I'll eventually hear something useful. I'll try to bypass the security measures. They are hiding something in the forest."

He kept staring at me.

"I've been running in the forest. Last Friday, I tried to cut past the marked path, and there was a patrol of werewolves and vampires stopping anyone from going there."

"That is suspicious," Jason claimed.

"I agree."

He rubbed his chin. "Do you think they are some sort of militia, protecting a secret compound?"

"Not a militia, but they are adamant about protecting their own and stopping outsiders from snooping around. Maybe the royal family lives there."

"Hum. And the town? Did you spot a royal vampire walking around?"

"It's not like they stand out," I muttered.

"If they are that important, they will have extra security around them and display wealth," Jason reasoned.

I shook my head. "Even if our intel says that there's a royal family pulling strings, I found no evidence of that. The mayor is human. The majority of the police force is shapeshifters who answer to an alpha. I believe he serves someone else, though."

"The fact that a family of vampires is able to command several races that generally don't mingle, it's impressive and troublesome."

"It only means that they aren't purists and might be future allies to our cause," I argued.

"Maybe you should cut your losses and return home," he countered.

"I-I...the school year is almost over. I can't abandon my students like that."

Jason smirked. "Is that town growing on you, or did you find something there that you like?"

I felt my cheeks burn despite the cold surrounding us. "D-Don't be absurd."

Jason shrugged. "Weren't you planning on seducing the principal? Jessica said that he was a handsome fellow. Maybe you fancy him and want to fool around for a bit. No one will blame you if that's the case. You need to...loosen up."

His teasing smirk and glinting eyes annoyed me. Pushing him

back, I muttered, "He's not my type."

* * *

Once the enemy was secured and locked, and the medical teams arrived to take care of the wounded, I returned to Affinity.

It was well past midnight when I parked my bike in front of Shane's cabin and removed my helmet.

I should have gone to my motel bedroom. Being there was a mistake. But I needed to see him.

My eyes were on the front door when the lights turned on, and the door opened. Shane stepped outside wearing sweatpants and a t-shirt. His hair was ruffled as if he had been asleep, and I'd woken him up.

"How did you know I was here?" I asked him.

"I heard the bike." He marched towards me.

"Shane, it's freezing. You shouldn't…" His arms were around me, and he pulled me closer to his warm body.

"Did you miss me? Is that why you returned early?"

"Did I wake you?" I deflected.

His lips covered mine for a few seconds before he helped me remove my backpack and reached for my hand to guide me inside his home. "Honey, you shouldn't be driving in this cold. There's ice and the roads are dangerous."

He abandoned my backpack over a table and walked us to the couch. Turning around, he removed my leather coat and reached for a wool sweater left on the sofa. I moved my arms up, and he slid it over my head and my arms. Once that was done, he kissed me again, deeper and sweeter.

Being next to Shane made my body relax, and I realized how tired I was.

He made me feel safe.

Cupping my face, he stared at me with caring eyes. "Are you okay? Are you hungry?"

"Just tired." I leaned closer. "And a bit cold." I snaked my arms around him and hid my face against his chest. He smelled like safety and bliss. I inhaled deeply. "I'm exhausted. Can I sleep here with you?"

His hand rubbed my head. "Of course, you can sleep here with me. This is your home, too."

My heart constricted with his answer. I knew it was a lie, but I wanted it to be true. I wanted him to be my home. For the second time that night, I realized that I had to let go of him. Even if that hurt like hell and I'd go back to be alone.

My thoughts dissipated when he took me in his arms. "Let's get you to bed. We'll talk in the morning."

"I need to take my clothes off," I mumbled, too fatigued to open my eyes.

He sat me on the bed. "I'll help you with that, and then I'll cuddle you to sleep."

I smiled and nodded. I kept my eyes closed so he didn't notice that tears welled up and threatened to fall down my cheeks.

He took off my boots and fumbled with my belt. Suddenly, his hands were cupping my face. "Is something wrong?"

I was too fragile, and the tears were falling down. Opening my eyes, I faced him. "I'm just really tired."

"You don't want to talk about it?"

I shook my head and wiped the tears with the back of my hands.

His fingers brushed against my cheeks, smearing the remaining tears until they disappeared. "Nothing bad happened to you, right? You're not hurt or…Just tell me the truth."

"I'm fine." I nibbled on my bottom lip. "Nothing hurt me. I

just had a hard day."

It took him a few seconds to nod and get up. "I'm going to fetch you a glass of water. Change into your pajama and slip into bed. I'll be right back."

I nodded and did as he told me.

When he came back, I heard him talk on the phone.

"Can you handle things without me?" he said to whoever was on the other side. "Yes, just keep them in a cell until the morning, then call their parents. I have a personal matter to take care of." He chuckled softly. "Yes, it does involve my girlfriend."

I sat up in the bed. "Is something wrong? Do you need to leave?"

"Some kids started a fight at Sam's bar. Nothing worth my full attention." He offered me the glass of water. "I put sugar in it. You look pale."

I drank, my hands slightly trembling, which didn't go unnoticed by Shane. "I'm just a bit cold."

He took his place in bed next to me, and I placed the empty glass on the nightstand.

Opening his arms, he invited, "Come here, baby."

I snuggled in his arms and relaxed against the warmth of his body. It was easier to fall asleep when I was with Shane. His presence quieted my thoughts and soothed my soul.

One moment I was thinking how nice it was to be in Shane's arms, and the next, I was waking up with the sun on my face.

Stretching, I blinked a few times before opening my eyes and realizing that Shane was dressing up in front of the mirror. "Morning."

He looked at me and beamed. "Did I wake you? I tried not to make any noise."

I sat up and shook my head. "Are you going somewhere?"

He buttoned up his shirt. "I'm going to have brunch with

a...friend. He's also a superior, so I can't take you with me. We have businesses to take care of." He fixed his hair. "I'm not going to take long, but you'll have to eat breakfast on your own. Do you mind?"

I shook my head. "It's okay. You had no idea that I was coming here. I'm sure you had plans that didn't include me."

He frowned and glanced at me. "Are you mad?"

"No. I swear." I smiled to prove my point. "I can take care of myself. I'll get dressed and go back to my motel room."

"Don't be silly." Narrowing the distance between us, he leaned down and brushed his lips against mine. "Stay here, get dressed, we'll go out for lunch when I return."

"Are you sure that you don't mind that I stay?"

He grinned and kissed me again.

I pushed him back slightly. "Morning breath."

He smirked and gave me a last peck before leaning back and walking to the mirror. "Just don't wander off into the forest and get lost again."

I perked up. "What? What do you mean by that?"

"My deputies told me that you got lost Friday morning on your jog. You should be more careful. There are wild animals in the forest, and the paths are there for a reason."

"Oh." I pouted, feeling guilty for getting caught. Did he suspect anything?

"If you want to explore the forest, we can go together. I know the most beautiful places there. But you can't go on your own and without a weapon."

I nodded while nibbling on my bottom lip.

"I'm not mad," he assured me. "Just preoccupied." He put a leather jacket on. Smiling, he added, "Have I told how happy I am for you to be back sooner?"

I smiled back at him, feeling crazy butterflies in my stomach.

He was undeniably charming. How could a place like that with such a thoughtful sheriff have a dark and twisted secret?

I blinked when I felt his lips against mine. "If you keep staring at me like that, I'm going to miss my appointment."

"How am I staring at you?" I whispered against his lips.

"I'm not going to tell you, or you'll stop. I'm very fond of that stare and want to see it more often."

I giggled like an infatuated teen, which was very close to the truth.

His hand cupped my cheek. "Anna, I... I have a lot about me that I want to share with you."

I gulped, caught off guard.

He continued, "But you need to trust me and understand that I'd never let anyone hurt you. Being alone is hard, and you mistrust people. I get that. But you're no longer alone. You have me."

I frowned at his words. "Is this because I cried yesterday?"

He shook his head. "No. It's because you should know by now that I'm serious about you. This isn't just a fling."

As serious as a werewolf with a soulmate can be. I faked a smile. "You're going to be late if you don't hurry up and leave."

His lips became a straight line. "Just don't run away while I'm gone."

I nodded.

His face was still serious when he spoke. "Promise."

"I promise," I whispered, smiling so he relaxed. "I'm not going anywhere. Even if I'd left, you know where I'd go."

"I have no idea where you go when you leave town."

The sadness lacing his voice hit me hard.

Before I could say anything else, Shane turned his back on me and grabbed his cellphone from the dresser. It took everything in me not to stand up and rush to him so I could hold him and promise him that I wouldn't let him go.

But that would be a lie.

"Text me if you feel lonely," Shane mumbled before walking to the door and opening it.

I watched his jaw tense before he glanced over his shoulder.

"I'll be here," I assured him.

His gaze softened, but he still looked troubled.

The urge to reassure him surfaced again. "L…Later."

For a moment, my mind went back in time, and I recalled how Kevin said his goodbyes. *Love you, sis.*

Telling Shane that I loved him would be madness. A tragedy waiting to happen. I love only three living people with all my heart: Kevin, Jessica, and Jason.

When did that include Shane?

"Later," he said before closing the door behind him and leaving me to my solitude.

CHAPTER FOURTEEN
ANNABEL

SATURDAY NIGHT'S EVENTS were Monday's favorite topic to gossip about. My students seemed overly excited about it as I eavesdropped on their murmured conversation, relying on the fact that they thought I couldn't hear them.

"They say Cameron is still in jail, and his father hasn't come to get him," one of the students, Janice, said while using the book she should be reading to cover her mouth.

"Serves him right," her friend, Sally, muttered. "He's a bully and has been stalking Alicia since her wolf surfaced."

Her friend's eyes widened. "Do you think the rumor is true?"

Sally leaned closer. "What rumor?"

"That she's his mate."

Sally rolled her eyes. "I doubt it. Alicia loves Mason. They're the perfect couple."

"Being the perfect couple doesn't make it right. If they aren't mates, they aren't meant to be together."

"It could take decades before one finds their mate."

"Or never find it," another girl pinched in.

"We need to finish this group assignment. More work and less gossip," Sally reminded them.

"I'm hungry," another complained.

"We still have ten more minutes of class. We should take notes."

Once the muttered conversation stopped, I scribbled a few questions on my notebook and made a mental note to text Shane and make sure everything was okay with him.

When the class was over, I went to the teachers' lounge.

"Annabel, I am so glad you're here," the Math teacher, Evelyn, jumped to her feet and rushed to me before I could close the door.

"Is everything okay?"

"I just didn't want to eat alone today." She pouted.

I blinked and browsed around the room. I only found the cute sports coach in a corner, looking at a manual and taking notes.

"Sebastien is here," she huffed, "but he's too busy to come and eat with me." Grabbing my arm, she guided me to the chairs.

"I thought you wanted to eat."

"We still have time." She sat down and forced me to sit. Grinning, she batted her eyelashes at me. "I thought you might want to catch up about the latest school drama."

I arched an eyebrow "What school drama?"

"Haven't you heard? Our students from 12 B were in a fight with a class from another school," she gossiped. "Since your boyfriend is the Sheriff…" She shrugged.

"We don't talk about our works."

She smirked. "I'm sure you have better things to do with him. I know I would if he was mine."

I frowned, but before I could reproach her about her insinuation, the door opened, and the Drama teacher came in.

"Hi!" she greeted, dropping her books on the table and grinning at us. "Annabel, I'm glad I've found you here. I need to talk to you about the school play." She glanced at her watch. "But I only have half an hour to eat. Can we talk later in the day? Do you mind coming to the Drama room once your classes are over?"

"Sure."

She smiled, grabbed her purse, and left.

"How rude!" Eve complained.

I stared at her. "Why?"

"She didn't even say hi to me." She leaned closer. "You and I need to stick together since we're the only two outsiders."

"Haven't you been here for almost two years?"

"Yes, but they still see me as an outsider. They don't invite me to their secret weekend meetings." She squinted. "I guess you don't have that problem."

"Why? Are you saying that because I don't spend my weekends here?"

She shook her head. "You're the sheriff's girlfriend. I'm sure he tells you everything."

I shook my head with a shrug. "I don't care about other people's lives. Whatever Shane does with his friends during the weekends is his problem."

Her eyebrows knitted together in a pensive stare. "I guess he wouldn't tell you everything since you're still new here and have no idea of what's going on." She crossed her legs and grinned. "You need to tell me how you were able to score the town's hottie. Where did you meet? Did you come here to be with him?"

"You're extremely curious."

Her hand closed around my arm, and she shook me with a childlike moan of complaint. "Come on. We're friends. Friends share stuff about their private lives. I can tell you who I'm fond of." She glanced over her shoulder to Sebastien, who seemed oblivious to our presence and conversation.

I giggled. "Forget it. You don't need to tell me. It's all over your face."

She blushed slightly.

The door opened, and the principal peeked in. "Miss Winters." He smiled when his gaze locked with Eve's. "I was looking for you."

Looking at me, he greeted me from afar with a short nod, "Miss Donovan."

Eve got up with an eager expression. "Do you need anything, Principal?"

"We need to speak in private. Could you follow me to my office?"

Eve's smile widened. "I'll be right there." She looked at me and fixed her hair. "We'll talk some other time. Maybe we could go for a coffee after classes tomorrow evening."

"Sure."

She grabbed her purse and rushed to the door, leaving with the principal.

I looked at my phone and pondered about contacting Shane. "Sebastien, I guess I can't convince you to join me for lunch."

He raised his head and smiled. "I already deal with screaming teenagers when I train the team. The school canteen is madness at this hour."

"You're right." I got up. "I still have two hours before my next class. I think I'm going to eat outside the school premises."

He waved with a smile. "Have fun and say hi to Shane."

I giggled at how perceptive he was.

A few minutes later, I was heading to the front gate when I noticed the group of unknown young boys perched against a wall and observing the students exit the school.

I wouldn't have taken a second look if I didn't hear their obnoxious comments about the girls.

"The teachers are getting hotter and hotter," one of them commented. "Look at that beauty." He elbowed his companion.

"Smells like a human. Probably hybrid trash," his friend on his right spat.

"Hybrid or human, I'd tapped her," the previous one said.

"We aren't here to check their whores," another dude said. "Sooner or later, that scum will have to leave school, and we'll make him pay for his disrespect."

"Yeah," his colleagues groaned.

"Cameron is in jail because of him," another muttered.

"She didn't even look at us. I'm sure she is human," one of the guys said when I passed by without acknowledging their presence. "I might follow her and see where she lives. Maybe I'll pay her a visit."

"And do what?" his friend asked.

"Hey, sweetheart, look at me. I have something worth your attention!"

I ignored his catcalls because I was sure he was making some obscene gesture.

"Hey, bitch! I'm talking to you."

I paused and was about to turn around and give them a piece of my mind when arms snaked around mine, and the sweet sound of two of my students' voices made me relax.

"Where are you going, Miss Donovan?" one of them asked, forcing me to keep walking.

"Are you going to see your hot boyfriend, the Sheriff?" the other one questioned, projecting her voice for them to hear.

"Yes." I smiled at them, almost sure that they came to my rescue. It was sweet of them to take care of someone who was being harassed. "I'm heading to the Police Station. And you, don't you have classes in the afternoon?"

"We do. But we are going to the coffee shop."

"You don't need to walk me there."

Samantha whispered in my ear. "Those guys aren't from our town. They're just looking for trouble. They won't dare to do anything if we are together."

"They're just kids pretending to be grownups."

"They can be annoying," Sam muttered.

"And dangerous," Jennifer added. "We're worried about Mason. They're waiting for him, but he doesn't want to call his dad. Someone should warn the sheriff that they are here."

I frowned. "Are they the same ones that were arrested last Saturday?"

"Yes," Samantha replied. "It seems they didn't learn their lesson."

"You see," Jennifer began, "their leader, Cameron, was harassing one of us. Mason told him to stop and be respectful. But they are chauvinistic pigs and think we find that sort of behavior sexy."

"They have plenty of places to go, but they still like to come here to start fights," Sam added.

"I'm sure the principal will handle it if they become violent," I assured them.

* * *

Before I entered the Police Station with Sam and Jennifer, we heard the voice of two men arguing. One of those voices belonged to Shane.

My students seemed to lose their nerve once we stepped across the threshold and saw the guy arguing with Shane.

"What's wrong?" I asked Jennifer.

She bit her lower lip. "That's Cameron's brother, Austin."

Sam pulled at my arm and whispered, "He's hot but an ass."

I smirked at her description, glancing at the guards watching Austin shout at Shane. They were keeping a safe distance. Not that I believed that Shane would need any help to deal with Austin.

"I'm here to take my brother home, and you can't stop me!"

Austin claimed. "Everybody else was released. Why hasn't he?"

"No one from his family came to get him," Shane replied, shoving his hands in his pockets and shrugging with a sneer.

That seemed to rattle Austin even more. "You should have called me in the first place!"

"Cameron didn't want to bother you on your father. He seemed to be happy to stay here."

"That's bullshit, and you know it! You just kept him here because of who he is. Your people have a problem with mine."

"It's not your people," Shane argued. "Your father is still the one calling the shots, and he didn't find a priority to come and free your brother. Do you think I didn't call him?"

Austin snarled. "He did nothing to be arrested!"

Shane sighed deeply, removing his hands from his pockets and rubbing between his eyes. "We've been over that already. He and his friends started a fight and injured several people. Sam's bar is wrecked."

The dude snarled again. "I'll pay for the damages." He stepped closer and glared at Shane. "Now, release my brother."

Shane looked him dead in the eye. "Are you forgetting who you're talking to, boy?"

The testosterone in that place was through the roof. Austin was attempting to intimidate Shane, and he was having none of that.

Shane's voice came out guttural when he leaned closer. "Do I need to teach you who is the one calling the shots here?"

Austin growled but eventually lowered his eyes and then his head. His voice came softer when he spoke. "Release Cameron. I'll take responsibility for what he has done, and I'll pay for the damages."

Shane arched an eyebrow. "And your father?"

"He wanted to teach my brother a lesson. I'm sure Cameron

has gotten the message."

Shane relaxed his gaze and shoulders. "Very well, but I don't want your boys causing problems in my town again. If it happens, they won't be released without facing a judge."

"Sheriff, you might want to tell them that now," Jennifer said, interrupting their conversation.

Shane and Austin glanced at us.

Jennifer stepped closer to the dividing countertop. "Cameron's buddies are outside the school bullying and intimidating the students. They are looking for another fight."

Shane's eyes swept the area before locking on me. A surge of heat took over me.

Sam pitched in. "They were calling us whores and bitches."

"Us?" Shane asked, his eyes squinting.

"They were rude to our teacher, too," Sam clarified. "Jennifer and I protected her."

Shane arched an eyebrow. Clenching his jaw, he glared at Austin. "Do I have to teach them a lesson, so they learn how to respect women?"

Austin shrugged. "I know nothing about it."

"You better hurry before they hurt someone. They were talking a lot of trash," Sam urged.

"You better follow me to the school and control your boys. You won't like what will happen to them if I hear them insulting my woman and the town's girls." Shane growled, clearly losing his temper. Glancing back at his three deputies, he ordered, "Jake, you stay behind. Brad and Lars, come with me."

Marching to the door, Shane stopped in front of me. "I'll take care of this. Stay here and wait for me to come back."

I nodded.

Shane exited.

"Wait. I'm going too." Austin rushed to catch up with Shane.

Jennifer and Sam shared a look.

"Serves them right," Sam muttered.

Jennifer nodded. "They deserve a good whooping for what they were saying." Staring at me, she smiled. "Don't worry, Miss Donovan. Your boyfriend can take care of himself."

"I'm not worried about him, but the boys seem to be in trouble."

"They need to have their mouths washed with soap," Sam grumbled.

Jennifer pushed Sam's shoulder. "Our teacher is safe now. We should go back to school and see what's going to happen."

Sam grinned. "Miss, you stay here. It's safer. We'll go back to school."

Before I could say anything, the girls were rushing outside.

On my own, I looked around and saw Jake staring at me. "Hi, Jake."

"Hi, Annabel. How's your day going?"

I shrugged. "I'm not sure. A bit more unusual than normal, I guess."

He rubbed the back of his head with a shy smile. "I hope that you weren't too scared about what happened. We don't normally have these sorts of things happening. But there's a family rivalry going on."

"I'm sure Shane will handle it."

He nodded. "Did you come here to have lunch with him?"

"Yes."

"If you're hungry, maybe you should go to the diner and eat. It can take a while before he gets back."

I headed to the waiting seats and sat down. "I'll wait. I have time."

"Okay. I'll be here if you need anything."

I smiled and grabbed my phone, texting Jessica about

trivialities while Shane was gone.

Twenty minutes later, the seven wannabe criminals lined up at the door. With their hands tied up with zip ties and lowered heads, they stomped to the front desk. Shane entered, followed by his deputies and Austin. I noticed a few of the boys had bruises on their faces.

Jumping to my feet, I moved to intercept Shane. "What happened?"

Shane shrugged.

"Did you hit them?"

"No. They got into a fight with a few of our boys before we arrived and broke them apart," Shane explained.

Walking behind the boys, Shane slapped each on the back of their heads. "Do you see this woman? She's my girlfriend and our school teacher. You were disrespectful to her. You need to kneel and ask for forgiveness. You'll learn how to be gentlemen and respect all women. Got it?"

The boys exchanged a look before staring at Austin as if waiting for his approval.

"Don't look at Austin. You should fear me," Shane warned.

The boys dropped to their knees in front of me.

Glimpsing at Austin, I noticed the anger in his eyes. He wasn't pleased to see his boys being humiliated like this.

Nevertheless, the sort of behavior displayed by them was taught by their male roles inside their pack. For all I know, Austin was a giant asshole too.

One of the boys spoke first. "We're sorry, Miss. We didn't know you were the sheriff's woman."

I frowned at him. "I'm no one's property. Your behavior was inappropriate. Period."

Shane slapped him on his head. "Apologize for being rude.

Women aren't whores or bitches. Unless you believe that your mothers are that too! Do you think they'd approve of your behavior? Don't you have sisters? Would you like if a guy called your sister a whore?"

The boys muttered. "We're sorry."

Austin intervened, "Now, that's over. Can they get up and wait outside while you free Cameron?"

Shane squinted at him. "I hope they don't do this again."

"Sure." Austin sank his hands in his pockets. "I'll control them. Just give me back my brother, and we'll leave your idyllic town."

Shane groaned before looking at Jake. "Release the kid and make sure his brother signs all the release papers." He stared at the boys. "My men will escort you outside town. You better don't come here looking for trouble again."

They nodded.

Walking to me, Shane held my hand. "I'm going out for lunch with Annabel, Jake."

"See you later, boss," Jake said.

"Who's going to free us?" one of the boys asked.

Shane glanced at his other two officers. "See where they parked their cars and let them loose only when they leave the Police Station."

"Yes, Boss," Lars replied while Brad groaned and nodded.

Shane grabbed my hand and guided me out of there. Once we were on the sidewalk, he circled his arm around my waist and pulled me closer. "Were you scared?"

I shook my head.

"Next time something like this happens, call me."

"Were any of my students hurt?"

"Sam and Jennifer said they escorted you when they heard the guys being rude and making threats."

I nodded. "Yes, it was nice of them to come to my rescue."

"I should have smacked them harder."

Stopping, I starred at him. "I'm safe. You can relax. But I need to know if the kids are okay."

"They're fine." He placed a strand of loose hair behind my ear. "They can take care of themselves. The school security was attempting to break them off when we arrived. But I scolded the security for not taking action sooner. It doesn't matter if they were outside the school. Calling names and bullying is against the law."

I kissed him and stroked his cheek. "I'm hungry. Aren't you?"

"Yes." He puckered his lips in a pensive stare. "Maybe I should get you a taser and teach you a few self-defense moves. What do you think?"

"That's sweet, but I can take care of myself. It was just a bunch of kids wanting to look tough."

"They are stronger than they look." I reached for my purse and showed him my keychain with a small acrylic dagger. "It's for self-defense."

Shane didn't seem convinced. "It's not really sturdy. It barely causes any harm."

"Depends where I stab it."

He grinned and kissed my lips. "Maybe it's best to get you at school from now on."

I laced my arms around his neck and spoke close to his mouth. "You're sweet, but I'm not letting a bunch of bullies stopping me from living my life. I'll call you so you can save me if something like this happens again, but you don't need to be overprotective."

He caressed my cheek. "You're precious to me. I don't want anything bad to happen to you. Nor anyone being disrespectful."

His words made my heart flutter. His eyes were kind and passionate. His actions were always sweet. He was the perfect boyfriend.

It was harder and harder not to acknowledge that I was falling deeper and deeper under his charm. Yet the universe seemed to be conspiring to deliver me a message. Shane had his soulmate, somewhere. Sooner or later, no matter how special I was for him, he was going to stop caring for me. Shane was going to break my heart.

The idea of him leaving me for another terrified me.

It doesn't matter how perfect we are together. We aren't meant to be.

Unaware of the turmoil inside my heart, Shane kissed my forehead. "Let's eat, baby. I'll accompany you to school after."

CHAPTER FIFTEEN
SHANE

ANNABEL'S ATTITUDE HAD CHANGED for the past week. She had been aloof and more brooding than usual. Something was going on, and it hurt me that she didn't want to share what was troubling her with me.

Perhaps, I was overzealous after what had happened in front of the school. Yet, somehow, I sensed that she was trying to push me away and guarding herself against what we felt for one another.

That night, I offered to cook dinner. Anna claimed she was not hungry. I offered to massage her neck. She declined and evaded any attempt of closeness between us. I had to handle it with care, but I couldn't pretend that nothing was wrong. I mused about what I could do for her to open up with me and stop looking as if the world was about to end. Maybe a direct approach worked best.

"What's wrong with you tonight?" I knelt next to her and pressed her hands to my lips. She was on the couch, staring at the TV with absent eyes.

Recoiling in her seat, she mumbled, "Nothing."

"You look sad. Did I do anything to make you unhappy?" *One can never know.*

"No."

"Was it at school? Did something bad happen, or did someone say something that upset you?"

"No. School is fine."

I took a seat by her side and inhaled sharply. "Are you homesick?"

"Homesick?" My heart tightened inside my chest with the look she offered me. "I don't have a home to be homesick for."

Her words resonated inside my head. I'd hoped that she embraced the idea that her home could be here with me. My home was with her, no doubt about it. She had become my whole world. Wasn't I her whole world too?

I took her hand in mine. "You could have a home."

I hadn't talked to her about moving in since the night I'd almost blown it all with my impatience and had made her think I was a psychopath. Nevertheless, we spent all our free time together. We only needed to get all her belongings from the motel to make it official. Anna already slept there at night and ate with me. I loved smelling her in my place and seeing her books, clothes, and beauty products scattered around.

"I think—" She paused and sighed as she removed her hand from mine. "All this is a huge mistake."

I stopped breathing momentarily. Her words felt like a punch in my guts since I believed everything was fine between us. More than fine, actually.

I was head over heels for her. If she intended to kill me with pain, she simply had to say that she didn't want me anymore, and that would be it. Living *without her* wasn't an option. Not when I'd spent two hundred years waiting to meet her, and I'd almost lost my faith in finding her or believing she existed. My mate had only existed for twenty-three years. She was a human and didn't understand what a mate was. She couldn't recognize me as hers and only hers for all eternity. Maybe it was about time I explained to her that we were meant to be and tell her that whatever was bothering her, we could talk about and fix it.

With furrowed eyebrows, I questioned her, "What's a mistake?"

"Us," she whispered as if she was afraid to say it out loud.

She avoided my eyes and moved uncomfortably on the couch. My heart by then had stopped beating.

"Why?"

"It's getting too intense," she explained.

I blinked a few times. "And why is that a problem?"

She was so complicated! I could almost see all her walls become reinforced with concrete or maybe adamantium. Yes, I was a Wolverine fan. Not important right now. What was important was that it was hard to make Anna trust me and open up. It was challenging to understand what she felt for me. Her words were killing me.

Is she already sick and tired of me?

Was I not letting her breathe, not giving her the space she needed to feel happy? I knew she was reluctant about letting someone in her life, but I couldn't help being a hopeless romantic around her.

She was mine.

I could feel my wolf howl inside my head from the pain. I needed to shut him up, so I could listen to what she was saying.

"We should just—break up," she said with a serious face, no trace of feelings for my alarm. She didn't answer my question and simply confessed what was crossing her mind.

For a moment, I was speechless while panicking that she wanted to break up. I only wanted to hold her until she would promise to never leave me. I had to tell her how I felt and understand why she thought we should break up. I had to. Before my wolf went all mad and got self-destructive. *We loved her.*

"I don't want that. I love you!" I almost felt my voice disappearing. Being rejected by my mate was excruciatingly painful.

She fluttered her eyelashes at me as if trying to make sense of my words. "What did you say?"

Licking my lips, I repeated, "I love you."

"You... love me?" She gulped and closed her eyes

momentarily. Her hands shook as she held them tighter. Panic grew in her gaze, and I realized it was probably too soon to confess.

But isn't that what a woman typically wants to hear from a man? I couldn't let her leave me. If she was feeling insecure all of a sudden about my feelings, I had to fix that. However, I didn't expect her to react with panic to my confession. I couldn't understand what made her want to break up with me. We were happy. I made her happy. I was sure of that. *So why did she want to leave me?*

"You heard me. I love you," I asserted.

The harm was done. I'd wanted to tell her every time we made love. Every time she'd smiled at me.

"That's not funny," she claimed with an upset expression, folding her arms in front of her chest.

"It's not supposed to be funny. I'm not kidding," I attested, matching her serious tone and adding a bit of annoyance. I should've been the one feeling offended for being rejected.

"Shit!"

I opened my mouth in surprise. Okay, that wasn't the kind of expression I expected to hear from her in reaction to 'I love you.' I was upset now. "I say *I love you,* and all you have to say is shit?"

"Yes. The world is all messed up!"

"Care to explain that?"

"Since when do men say that without being threatened or forced by a woman? And you tell me that out of the blue? As if I needed that burden on my shoulders!"

I jumped to my feet. "Burden? My love is a burden to you? So, we can have sex, but I can't love you? Is that the fucked-up idea you have of a relationship?"

I was furious. Not just that, I was feeling used, and my heart hurt due to her lack of feelings for me. My heart seemed to want to burst out of my chest or explode. *How could my soulmate say something like that to me? Didn't she feel anything for me? Was I a hobby?*

"Of course not," she replied with a sad voice and shining eyes. She was holding back the tears, to my surprise.

I sat back on the couch. My rage was gone because she seemed miserable.

Her voice came out broken. "It's just that—I realized something and I don't—I didn't—I never thought you could say that to me. And even if you say it," she continued, wiping the tears from her eyes and facing me, "we cannot be together."

I placed my hand on her shoulder, leaning my head to watch her. "Why not, Anna?" I was trying to understand what would make her say something like that while tears ran down her cheeks.

"Shane…" She sounded desperate. "This is a hobby for you, us as a couple. You don't believe we have a future together. I've had a good time with you, but I have to put a stop to this before I get hurt."

"I'd never hurt you. I love you, Annabel."

She shoved my hand away. "Stop saying that!"

It was as if my sweet tone and new confession had upset her. As if my confession had hurt her instead of making her happy. That made no sense at all. Was she insane? Just my damn luck, finding another crazy woman in my life!

"I love you!" And I felt like cursing by adding a 'fucking' in the middle of the words 'I' and 'love.'

I was trying not to be mad, but I was trembling. I was losing it. *Why in the hell wouldn't she believe me?* It was not like I was going around telling every woman I saw that I loved her. I had never said that to anyone before. Only my mate would receive those words. It felt wonderful to finally say them.

Anna got angrier as she got up. "You don't even know me!

You don't understand half of me! You don't know anything about my life, my pain, fears, and wishes! So, don't you dare tell me you love me!"

I straightened up and faced her, frustrated. "I don't need to know anything about your past to love you. And you aren't inside my head, so you don't know what I know about you, what I feel about you. Don't you dare tell me I don't know you! I know you. I care for you! I listen to everything you say to me about yourself, anything you think is safe to tell me. I hold you tight when you sleep to make your bad dreams go away. I love you, this Annabel, who you are to me. Even if you have another side of you, I would love that, too. I even love the crazy one you are showing me right now. I don't understand what you are so afraid of, what makes you want to push me away, but I will not let you go without fighting to make you stay! Do I make myself clear?"

I was breathless when I was done talking, so I sucked in a breath. My words came out angrier than I'd wished them to, but I believe that they some kind of effect because she became quiet, her eyes wide open, attentive to everything I was saying. I think she was holding her breath. All I could think about was that she had the most adorable red mouth, and I wanted to bring her close and kiss her. *I guess madness was a mutual characteristic.*

I waited for her to speak. She seemed to be processing my words or trying to find something to say.

When she said abruptly, "I know you are a werewolf," it was my turn to be astonished.

CHAPTER SIXTEEN

SHANE

IT WAS MY TURN to stare at her for a long time without opening my mouth. She didn't say anything else. She stared back at me with guilt in her eyes. My mind was blank, even if I was intrigued by that affirmation—confession—accusation. *What was it?* How did she know, or how did she find out that I was a werewolf? *And for how long did she know that?*

All good questions.

I tried to be rational. "Are you rejecting me because you found out I'm a werewolf? Who told you that, and why aren't you freaking out?"

"I already knew it from the first time I saw you."

My arms fell to my sides as my eyes widened. "That's why you said I was not your type," I mumbled, while a light turned on inside my head, and my wolf tried to take over my thoughts. I made him shut up. I didn't want to feel cheated, but there was only one way for her to know what I was and for me not to know what she was. "You are a hybrid!" I didn't express the rest of what I was thinking, that she was a sexy, breathtaking, deceitful hybrid. I felt like growling. *Why hide it?*

"Yes." She sighed as if feeling ashamed. "I should have told you sooner."

"Yes, you should have," I whispered, still upset with her deception.

Anna was staring into my eyes, which were probably shifting to black. My wolf was feeling angrier than I was. I was just feeling confused and resentful. "Does James know? Am I the last to know?"

"No, of course not. You are the first to know," she assured.

Knowing that made me calm down. I sat on the couch, and

she folded her hands and released a sigh.

Her voice came out glum. "Shane."

I gazed up as if I was seeing her for the first time. My hand reached for her and pulled her to me as I hid my head against her chest. She was tense, but she placed her hands on my shoulders.

I grumbled, upset as my fingers dug on her waist.

"Are you mad?"

I couldn't answer her question yet. Though, I knew I shouldn't judge her so quickly. Hybrids weren't very keen on sharing their existence with other species. They were—paranoid, solitary, very secretive, and, most of them, powerful. *That explained a lot, actually.*

I couldn't blame her for not trusting me sooner. But it didn't matter to me if she was a hybrid. She was *my mate.* "What species are you?" If only she were half-werewolf, that would make it so much easier for her to understand our bond.

"Does it matter? We don't belong together. You will eventually find your soulmate, and it will not matter at all if I love you or not," she explained, releasing herself from my grasp and avoiding my gaze as she folded her arms and held the tears.

I got up with her words still pounding in my mind as I tried to make sense out of them. Suddenly, my eyes widened as I finally understood. I'm proud to think that I'm a smart guy, but damn, my mind was slow to process that moment. I finally got there, even if my favorite part was that she was in love with me. I almost laughed like a crazy person as my heart raced. I could lose my sanity with her. Still, her heart was beating fast too, and she seemed desperate. The smile on my face vanished as I watched her wiping the tears falling from her eyes.

Was it true, then? Hybrids couldn't recognize their mates. *Could she possibly be immune to our bond? Was I the only one affected by the energy I felt coming from her?*

"Are you feeling jealous of my mate?" I asked after prolonging the silence for far too long.

"What?" she asked, apparently caught off guard by my question.

I was being wicked. I should have told her the truth, but I wanted to know one thing first. *How much did she love me?*

"Annabel." I stepped forward and cleaned her tears with my thumbs. "You said you love me, so why do you want to break up?"

"Are you serious?" she asked, leveling her voice as she stepped back. "You have a soulmate! Do you care so little about her?"

"You knew that before you started dating me."

"I was not planning on falling in love with you," she huffed and pinched her eyes momentarily. Her tone was softer when she resumed speaking. "Besides, I hear them talk. They are all against you dating me. And they expect me to break your heart and leave you." She looked at me since I was quiet. "You know how weird that sounds, me breaking your heart? Is everybody crazy around here, even you?"

I reached out and brought her against me. "Who cares about what they say? Annabel, don't you understand? I love you, and you love me."

Anna splayed her hands on my chest. "Shane, seriously, are you crazy? You're saying that you love me, but you don't. Not really. And I can't continue to love you because I don't want to be a hobby for you while you wait for your soulmate to come along and make you stupidly happy!"

I made the mistake of smiling because I loved her so much, and I was actually stupidly happy with her. Besides, she couldn't help herself from saying that she loved me again. Not just that, Annabel had a serious problem of being jealous of my mate, meaning herself. That was promising. So, when she saw my smile, she misinterpreted. She thought I was mocking her.

"That's not funny! Do you think hybrids like not having a mate? Do you think we don't envy you? How do you think I feel being in love with you and not wanting you to find your mate? Do you know how terrible this sounds for me? How bad it makes me feel? And I'm so mad at you for making me fall in love with you and being sweet and caring and making me feel like this. And all you do is smile as if this is a joke!" She closed her fists, and her body trembled under my palms. "Does making girls fall in love with you make you feel fulfilled?"

"Annabel, do you have any idea how long I've been waiting for my soulmate?" I asked, disturbed by her distress. I cupped her face in my hands and made her look at me.

"Who cares? That is not an excuse! My father waited six hundred years for my mother," she retorted, with shiny eyes as if I was the worst person in the world.

I was stunned by how long her father had waited. He must have been a vampire to live that long, a strong one, too, without a doubt.

"Honey," I explained in an indulging voice, "I've waited two hundred long years for you." I circled my arm around her waist and raised her chin with my hand. She seemed to be trying to understand my words. Her eyes were wide as they looked into mine, and she was barely breathing, though her heart was pounding fast. "Did you understand?"

"I'm not a pure race. I'm not even half-werewolf. So h-how can that be?"

She didn't seem to believe me, but her words piqued my interest. "What species was your mom?"

"Panther," she replied.

I smirked.

That explained so many things!

Felines were suspicious and reluctant to lose their independence. They were also famous for... My eyes must have grown dark with jealousy because she seemed to understand where my thoughts were running.

"I'm not like that. My mother wasn't like that, either. She was always faithful to my dad. I don't—"

"I trust you. Calm down," I demanded, caressing the hair that was falling over her cheeks and smiling to show her how happy I was. I was feeling much lighter after confessing and finally knowing that her feelings for me were similar. She loved me. It was like the rest didn't matter, but she had questions. A lot of questions from the look of it.

"I still don't understand how I can possibly be your mate. You're a pure werewolf. I've never heard of anything like that."

"We're never wrong about this, honey."

I could never be wrong about the fact that she was my mate. The past weeks also had shown that she was unquestionably all I'd ever wished and asked the gods for in a mate. Even that adorable stubbornness about not giving up her freedom.

"I don't know how this works for hybrids, but you have to search inside yourself, listen to your instincts, and see why you love me and are pulled to me. You must feel our connection. One of your sides must want me."

"They both want you, even my wild panther."

That delightful confession made me chuckle. I hugged her tight and buried my face against her neck.

It only took seconds for her to tense and pull me back. "So you don't mind me being a hybrid?"

I shook my head. "Sweetheart, you have no idea how much I love you and how much I wished for you."

"I didn't know I had a mate."

I kissed her lips, enjoying the salty sensation of her tears and hoping it'd calm her down. Then, I stroked her face as I talked sweetly to her. "Like with any relationship, you must understand that our bond can only be completed if you choose to accept me. A couple doesn't work out if there isn't trust and commitment from both parties. You have to want to be my mate like I want you to be mine."

"And you really want to be with me?"

"Anna, I love you. What more can I do or say to make you see that?"

She hugged me and fondled my head as she trembled.

"I found you. You'll never be alone again," I whispered, wanting to reassure her and calm her down. "You can't imagine how happy I have been. I want you to be happy too."

Despite the initial grieving and fear, now that I knew she was a hybrid, I felt better. She could protect herself if someone tried to attack her because of my marking. And I could finally mark her, and our bond would be complete when she drank from me. Her vampire side would be completely surrendered to me. Mate blood was the most powerful thing to vampires. It would also be hot like hell, being bitten by her. Combining both biting and sex, mating would be like nirvana.

I was pulled out of my fantasies by her questions. "So, this means you approached me at the bar because you'd sensed I was your mate?"

She broke the hug to stare into my eyes. She didn't look pleased. *Why?* I had no idea. She should've been pleased that I'd pursued her and didn't let her escape. It was not like I'd kidnapped her and made her stay with me against her will. It was not unusual for that kind of behavior between soulmates, especially among soulmates that were humans and needed a bit of persuading. But I would never do that. Love can't be forced. She had to choose me willingly.

"No, not really." I grinned, trying to explain. She narrowed her eyes. "I just understood you were my mate when I sat down next to you and caught your scent. There were like fifty people in that bar, but I couldn't smell you right when you came in. I sat next to you because you were breathtakingly hot. I had no clue you were my mate. But it was a bit hard not to notice you that night. I was drawn to you, Anna, and when I smelled you— You have no idea how I wanted to grab you and never let you be apart from me again. And you rejected me. That was—traumatic!"

She laughed, which made me smile. It wasn't a mocking laughter. She seemed pleased. Happiness was returning to her state of mind. I wanted her to be happy and stay happy with me.

"Sorry about that. I was…I wasn't looking for a one-night stand. I was there…for the drinks. But if it pleases you, I thought you were irresistible, too."

I furrowed my brow. "Really? It didn't look like it."

"But I did. It's hard to explain," she mumbled and sighed deeply. "I was just being stubborn."

"So—it was because I was a wolf that you rejected me?"

"Not because of that. I was…busy that night and kind of tired."

"Yeah, busy staring at the vampires."

She shrugged and didn't say anything else about that. It intrigued me, though, because now that I knew she was a hybrid, she could have easily handled those weakling vampires. But then again, maybe not. I didn't know how strong she was, and there were three vampires—maybe she was curious about them because she was also half-vampire. It was not uncommon for hybrid vampires to feed on turned vampires.

My attention focused on her as she spoke her next words. "So, your love for me is like… a forced thing?"

It was my turn to frown. Her statement made me want to lower my lips to hers and use my teeth to bite and punish her for saying something like that. "You know that you were made for me, right? It's not a forced thing. You're my other half. Or have your parents never explained that to you?"

"I was being cruel," she said, sighing as she pouted. "You have a cruel soulmate."

"No, I don't. You're perfect." I chuckled when she stared at me with surprise and doubt in her eyes. By the look on her face, she seemed to come to an understanding. "What?"

"I'm going to be stuck with you for all eternity," she uttered. I didn't know how to feel about her choice of adjective to describe our bond and future. "I mean, me and you—you and me—we are mates!"

"Why don't you seem happy about it? You said you love me. Are you—Anna…?"

"Shane…" She kissed me like she understood all my senseless babbling.

I didn't want to lose her. I couldn't bear the thought that she would be able to leave me. I didn't know how strong a bond could be with a hybrid: maybe it was easier for her to let me go.

"You are mine," she said over my lips with a smile. That reassured me a bit. "*Just mine.*"

Now I felt her possessive vampire side talking, or maybe it was all her. However, my wolf repeated those same words in my mind and enjoyed hearing them from his mate.

CHAPTER SEVENTEEN
ANNABEL

MAKING LOVE TO SOMEONE YOU LOVE and who loves you back is amazing. I couldn't get enough of hearing him say that he loved me, and I couldn't stop myself from saying it back. I seemed to be caught in a lame and mushy romantic movie and enjoying every single moment of it.

The following week, we spent our mornings working, our lunchtime making love in his office, and our nights in the bar where we'd met. We talked and played pool or darts, but mostly we spent time with Shane's friends and some of their female mates. They were all friendly and happy for us. I was getting used to feeling like I belonged somewhere. I was feeling at home, maybe because I had found my mate, and he had the power to make me feel happy and forget all about my problems, doubts, and fears.

In the meantime, life felt strangely right, and Shane didn't question my absence on my days off. I kept secrets for his safety because I had to trust him to open up about everything from my past and present. It was one thing to be madly in love and believe in soulmates and another to tell someone about my past and my origins. I still didn't know anything about his past and whom he worked for. That town was anything but ordinary.

It wasn't in my plans to stay there for so long and fall in love, but I realized that Shane probably had the answers to all of my problems. He knew everybody in town, and he also had some strange absences. Sometimes I would hear him talking on the phone, making a report to someone above him. One night, he was called to respond to an emergency that, later in the morning, he told me was to catch some young vampires who were making trouble in a city nearby. Now that he knew I was a hybrid and didn't need to hide that he was a werewolf, things got a little easier. Our conversations were about the town and its daily supernatural events.

However, Shane had his secrets. I wasn't the only one keeping them. The problem was that Shane acted like he had no secrets. I was scared to ask him and then have him realize that my intentions weren't noble. I didn't want to betray him, but I couldn't betray my objective of helping my brother. I needed to find a pureblood vampire to save the only direct family I had.

* * *

SHANE

Old girlfriends are like a grain of sand in one's shoes. Sasha was a good example, yet, in my case, she was an evil thorn in my paw. She came over from time to time to my house to talk and, sometimes, to remember old times. This usually included having sex, and then I'd send her away and tell her for the thousandth time that I didn't want anything serious with her anymore. We weren't soulmates, and she was all but sane. Actually, Sasha was the reason I had stayed away from relationships before I found Annabel and fell hopelessly in love with her.

In my defense, it had been thirty painful years of having a turbulent relationship with Sasha and twenty more years since we were apart. Yes, we had a history together, and Sasha continued to be obsessed with me. She couldn't or didn't want to move on. But being a stubborn vampire princess didn't help my case for making her realize that we were over, and I was sick and tired of her possessive control and relentless insistence.

Things were different this time when she came to my home. I doubted that the visit was cordial like she claimed. James must have told her about Annabel, and she came to see with her own eyes. Thankfully, Annabel was at work, so I invited her to my house to have a final conversation. Yet, she played rough, and I had to be rude and send her away. I had no wish to play her dangerous games or sleep with her. My heart was taken. Sasha could look like a goddess, walk with the elegance of the vampire she was, but her red lips, doll face, tall and apparently fragile figure were like burning ice to me—deadly to the touch. She would have to deal with the fact that I had found my soulmate and that there was no more 'us'.

I had almost succeeded in sending her away when Annabel arrived. My heart raced in my chest. Not from distress because Sasha was there and she could make a scene or attack Anna, but because my soulmate was gorgeous and I loved her more and more each day. Having her next to Sasha confirmed that Anna was fire and love, while Sasha was cold and evil—a remorseful waste of my time. Sasha was a miserable being who had no idea what real love was. She didn't understand what it was to feel completed by another one and to want to spend an eternity making that person happy.

The princess looked at Annabel like she was under a microscope. She examined her from head to toe with a grimace on her face that showed she disapproved of my mate. *But what else was new?* And it was not as if I needed her permission or even wanted her opinion. Anna was more than adequate. All Sasha was feeling was plain stupid jealousy. She could die green for all I cared.

Anna stopped on the porch, staring at us. Then she smiled at me, eyes sparkling, and tried to greet Sasha. The princess didn't even bother to look at Anna's hand. That annoyed me.

"You couldn't get any lower," Sasha spat like venom from a snake. "You are out of your mind if you prefer her to me!"

"Sasha, leave! You are not welcome here anymore," I ordered.

"This can't possibly be your soulmate! You are crazy!"

I said nothing to that statement and glared at her. My wolf was going out of his mind from the insult thrown at my mate by that hateful vampire. Because I was not speaking and was staring at her with black eyes, she knew I was not kidding. My wolf was not in the joking mood, either. I would shove her into her limousine if she said anything else insulting to my mate.

Sasha turned to Anna, spreading a little more of her poison. "Enjoy yourself, honey," she said snidely, with a smirk on her face. "When he gets enough of you, he will come back to me. He always does."

With those silly statement, Sasha walked away and entered her limo, followed by her bodyguards. The limo left shortly after.

Anna blinked with a puzzled expression. And I was left with the problem of explaining myself like Sasha had planned all along. That was why she was stalling. She wanted to meet Annabel and make her jealous. She wanted to spread discord between us.

"What the hell was that?" Annabel asked.

I sighed. "She's annoyed because I've sent her away and because she found out you and I are together."

Frowning, she questioned, "Did you use to date that thing?"

"It was a long time ago," I said, running my fingers through my hair. "It's been twenty years since we've been together. She means nothing."

"Really? It doesn't look like it. It seemed like she didn't want to let you go. As if she thought she owned you!"

"Sasha… It's a complicated story. But she doesn't own me, and we weren't dating when I met you. She just came here to make you jealous. She's territorial."

"Hmm." Anna stared at the dust on the road that the limo

had left behind.

I grew anxious. "You know I love you, don't you? And we're mates. She's no threat to you. Are you mad?"

She shrugged. "No, I was just wondering why you even dated her in the first place."

"She was different then. And we were raised together. It's a long and complicated story. But we aren't together anymore, and you are my life. You are my only love."

The serious look on Anna's face faded. She relaxed her shoulders. "She will eventually find her soulmate and get over you."

"Yes, yes she will." I didn't say anything else about that, so Annabel wouldn't be worried.

Things had ended between Sasha and me because she was mad and cruel. When discovering that her soulmate was a mere human and not a pureblood, she decided to order his death while still an infant. With that decision, she condemned herself to spend her eternity alone. Then, she had the nerve to declare that she had done that because she was in love with me and I should be her soulmate and not a fragile human boy. That vampire was out of her mind, and she would probably try to hurt my beautiful Annabel.

"Sasha is dangerous and jealous," I said, grabbing Anna's arm. "She may try something against you."

"Don't worry. I can take care of myself. That vamp can't hurt me."

"Anna, she's not just a vamp. She is a pureblood."

Hybrids could be strong, but purebloods were another kind of predator and enhanced being. Anna was no match for Sasha if she tried anything. I was hoping that she wasn't bold enough to hurt my mate. But I didn't want Anna to be left in the dark. I didn't want Sasha to provoke her, so she had an excuse to harm her.

Anna's lips curled into a smile. "Really?"

Her smile didn't make any sense to me. Why would she find that information interesting? She should be scared or worried.

"Be careful, and call me if you see her in town or if you suspect someone is following you."

"Honey." She laced her arms around my neck. "That vampire was annoyed because you blew her off, wasn't she?"

"Of course I blew her off! You are my mate, and I love you."

"She's stunning," Anna said, losing her smile and pouting.

"And evil. I don't like evil girls. Just hot and sexy girls who look like you and taste like you," I whispered, stealing a kiss as I grinned.

Anna stepped back. "I don't want her here again."

I arched an eyebrow. "Don't you trust me?"

"Yes, but...she's evil, remember. And...she looks like a movie star! Are you sure?"

"Am I sure of what?"

"That you are over her?"

"Yes, I'm sure. I prefer your gorgeous curves and cherry lips any time to anything she has," I said, grabbing her and kissing her to prove my point. "You are gorgeous and smart and all kinds of perfect. I love you, and you don't need to worry about Sasha."

"How long did you date her?"

"Now you want to know something about my past?" I asked, teasing her. Why was she even feeling jealous of that insipid vampire?

"Is it a secret?" She seemed displeased, but I had the right to keep secrets since she didn't want to talk about her past even after knowing we were soulmates.

"No, it's not a secret. But I will only tell you something about my past if you tell me something about yours."

"Like what?"

"Place of birth, what happened to your parents and brother," I enumerated, hoping for an effort on her part to share a bit of her life with me.

She puckered her lips pensively. "If I tell you something about my past, will you talk about what happened between you and Sasha?"

Anna appeared to reconsider. I guess jealousy was getting the best of her.

I nodded as I said, "Yes."

"Okay! I'll talk about what happened to my parents."

I knew it was painful for her. But I needed to know the extent of the tragedy so that I understood her better. Yet, that day I would have accepted anything she wanted to share. It didn't have to be about her parents' death. I knew it was the hardest thing she had to talk about. However, if she wanted to open up, I wouldn't decline because all that secrecy was worrying me.

"Anna, the mate bond is the strongest bond between two people. I will always do everything to make you happy and protect you, even if I have to—"

"What?" she asked, frowning.

"Even if I have to go against my own kind or my superiors. You will always be first, so whatever you tell me, it will be kept between us. I won't judge or break your trust."

Arching her eyebrow, she probed, "Why are you telling me that?"

I caressed her cheek and said to reassure her, "So you understand that you will never be alone again."

"My parents didn't abandon me. They were taken from me," she whispered, voice laced with sadness. "The problem of having a soulmate, Shane, is that you can also be taken from me, and I couldn't cope with another loss."

"You aren't the only one feeling scared," I assured, touched by her words. "After a while of crazy living, fun, and some failed relationships, all I could think about was finding you. I've traveled the world searching for you. I almost lost faith in finding you. And do you know what happens to supernatural beings who lose the will to live?"

"They grow old and die."

I nodded, placing a kiss on her forehead. "I'm glad you found me. I've never been so happy in my life."

"Not even with Sasha?"

"Ouch, low blow! And no, not even with Sasha. She was a mistake. Sasha is a cold, mean vampire princess, and you're everything I've ever wanted. You're better than I've dreamed and asked for. Anna, you are perfect."

"Keep saying that. You've almost convinced me." She grinned, pleased by my words.

"I can convince you much better inside…" I said with a husky voice.

"I still want to know all about Sasha and you," she said, thinking I was probably using sex to divert the subject.

"Oh, don't worry about that. I'm not planning to hide anything from you if you're willing to share some of your secrets with me. Now let's go inside. It's getting chilly, and we both have a lot of sharing to do," I teased, surrounding her shoulders with my arm and leading her indoors.

CHAPTER EIGHTEEN
ANNA

SHANE ACTED OVERLY PARANOID the days after Sasha's flamboyant appearance in our lives. He also became preoccupied once I told him my parents had died at the hands of a radical group that was against interracial marriages and hybrids' existence.

Hatred killed my parents. Nevertheless, I knew that their love for us was so strong that they protected their children's whereabouts from the enemy. Luckily for us, we weren't home when the enemy invaded it and killed my mom and dad. We were with my Aunt Philippa—Jason's mom.

My father often worried about our safety and had our house filled with surveillance cameras, bodyguards, secret passages, and hideaways. I was too young to understand his paranoia, but he was right to be concerned. After all, my brother and I were hybrids. Even if the world had evolved, many were against our existence. My father knew about the radical groups, like the one that attacked our house, that chased hybrid kids to study them and ultimately kill them. After all, my parents were the co-founders of the organization that I worked for.

I had the surveillance videotape of the invasion. I'd watched it a thousand times, memorizing how they breached into my home, killed the bodyguards, destroyed the cameras one by one, and followed their leader's orders to grab the family and find my brother and me. I watched my mom being used to control my father and stop him from fighting and killing the invaders. Then, they tortured my parents, so they told them where we were. I witness how they tried to use my mom's life to bargain with my father and how my mom begged him to not give in. Each time my mom screamed in pain, the grief and hurt in his eyes was enough to grind my heart into dust. Yet, each time the blade touched her skin, she would beg him to not say a word.

The evil torturer felt pleasure in harming others. That ignoble being, who my father seemed to know, kept brutalizing until he finally killed my mom, which drove my father to scream in unbelievable pain. As much as I cried and shouted the first times that I watched it. My mom's killer laughed at the pain he was causing, and without a shred of empathy, he cut my father's head.

I often wake up with a startle, remembering my father's weeping eyes staring at the hidden video camera, mumbling that he loved us before his head flew away and his lifeless body fell on the ground next to my mom's. For the first years after my parents' death, I'd wake up screaming in panic or simply cried all night, mumbling my parents' murderer's name like a curse.

I knew his name. I knew it because my father screamed it when he killed my mom.

His name was Alaric.

It has been eight years since my parents died, but I can never forget that they gave their lives to protect my brother and me. I had to honor their sacrifice and continue their life work—helping people in need and stopping the radicals from hurting other families and hybrids.

I also made it my objective to hunt down and make that scumbag pay for my parents' death, along with all the other people he killed in the name of some higher good—some misconceived radical idea of racial superiority. He had no right to play God and decide who would live and die.

As I found out, Alaric was an ancient and powerful pureblood vampire who was against breeding between races. He believed vampires were the superior race and that the others should be enslaved by them. Because of that, he targeted varied species couples exclusively. My father being a pureblood vampire was even a bigger crime to Alaric.

Even with the increase of awareness in modern society, his radical group had a large concerning number of followers. It had gained popularity in America, with cells in Europe that did the same: hunted hybrids and killed them. In fact, Alaric's group was responsible for making a hybrid-killing serum. Alaric was responsible for my brother's coma. Kevin was slowly dying, just resisting longer because of our pureblood vampire genes. Pure vampire blood seems to be the cure to a disease that only the purebloods are immune to.

Our scientists believe that they can use blood transfusions to heal my brother and then synthesize an antidote and a vaccine against it. But finding pureblood vampires who are willing to help us and our cause isn't an easy feat. The ones who exist are hidden and well protected. Too scared to go out of their lair, so they live caged in, surrounded by guards, cubs, and human blood donors.

Finding out that Sasha was a pureblood gave me hope. It meant that all the intel I had gathered about Affinity wasn't wrong. Too bad that Sasha wasn't friendly and would rather slice my throat than talk to me. She believed that Shane was her property and that alone was enough for me to dislike her. The stronger you are, the more you think you're above all laws and rules. Sasha bloodline and royal title turned her into a spoiled brat, and it made me wary of the type of family that raised a being like her.

I had to take my time and find out a lot more about the royal family ruling over Affinity. The cruelest people hide behind virtuous deeds and good intentions. They could be using everybody in town to secure their status and their wellbeing. As much as I loved Shane and trusted that he was kind and reliable, I couldn't tell him the real reason why I was in Affinity and request an audience with his superior. If anything, I had to save Shane from this town if the royal family was corrupt.

"What are you thinking?" Shane asked as we ran through the forest.

"Wondering where we are going?" I answered. "You've been testing my resistance for the past three days. We have established that I can run for many miles, and I'm fast. I've told you that I've had basic defense classes. Why are you still paranoid about leaving me alone in the forest?"

Shane stopped running and caught his breath. I stopped beside him and grabbed a bottle of water from my utility belt. After taking a sip, I offered to him.

"No, I'm good. Thanks," he declined and inhaled deeply as his head tilted up and he faced the few sunrays dripping through the trees. "I love how quiet and peaceful this place is."

I looked around, unsure of where we were. "We never entered this deep in the forest before."

"I want to test your reflexes today, so we are going to the boot camp facilities."

"What's that?"

"It's where we train our enforcers and patrolling groups. Not all the protectors use uniforms in this town." He placed a hand on my shoulder. "We are going to train on our own for the first times so I can evaluate your performance and level. Then, you can join a group if that will interest you. Not every supernatural wants to be an enforcer or even enhance their fighting skills."

I folded my arms. "If I prove to you that I can protect myself, will you stop worrying about Sasha?"

He shook his head. "I talked with her uncle about her behavior, and he said he was going to control her and send her abroad."

I arched an eyebrow at him. "Isn't that good news?"

"She can hire someone to harm you."

Unfolding my arms, I leaned closer and smiled softly at him.

He frowned. "Why are you smiling? You should be concerned."

"Because you love me, and you'll protect me."

He snickered and shook his head. "I'd give my life for you, honey." He tucked a loose strand of hair behind my ear. "But I'll feel more reassured if I knew you could shoot a gun and neutralize an opponent long enough for you to run and call for me." Pressing his lips in a straight line, he added, "I'm sorry that my love for you puts you in danger. I wasn't expecting Sasha to come between us."

His words made my body tense. I grabbed my hand to his shirt and pulled him closer. "The fact that we are mates, and I'm a hybrid puts a target on you. There are far more dangerous creatures in the world than Sasha."

His palm cupped my left cheek. "That's why you have to know how to defend yourself if anyone comes for you."

His statement made me feel incredibly proud of having him as my soulmate. As protective as he was, he didn't want me to be a damsel in distress. He saw me as his equal, and that was the best feeling ever.

He brushed his lips against mine. "Now that you've rested let's continue our jogging."

* * *

In our world, being a woman is dangerous but being a hybrid woman is worse. My family made sure I wouldn't be a victim but a warrior and a future defender of the oppressed, just like my mom and dad.

I was four when dad began my training. He taught me all forms of martial arts, sword fights, crossbow tossing, and how to use many types of blade weapons and guns. He'd prepared me as if he'd known that he wouldn't be here anymore to take care of my brother and me. He also prepared my brother, but I had to finish his training since he was only twelve when our parents were gone. Not that I was much older.

Nevertheless, Aunt Philippa took good care of us and we joined the organization when we were old enough. Kevin was going to turn twenty in a few months. I had to save him.

Finding the soulmate that I never knew I had, wasn't on my plans. Especially with Kevin in a coma and needing my blood transfusions every week. Still, allowing Shane to train me with the other enforcers was a way to find out more about how the town was organized. Pretending to be less skilled than I truly was, was a way to conceal what I did with my spare time. Not to mention that no matter how good I was, Shane had years of experience, years of leading troops and defending his master's domains from rivals and rogue attackers. He was a terrific fighter and an amazing teacher. The kids in the lower classes adored him, and the adults respected him. As skilled as I was, I wasn't sure that I could beat him, and I was glad we weren't enemies.

Flirting, tickling, and laughing were a constant in our one-on-one training. I was a sucker for feeling thrilled by the pat on the head he offered me every time I did something right and the encouraging smile when I failed. Spending time with Shane made me happy. It had been a while since I trained without feeling the pressure of being the best so that my teammates wouldn't be put at risk.

Being in that community made me feel safe.

Not only that, being able to be myself in a community of supernaturals was something new to me, but that I was genuinely enjoying. Now that they knew I was a hybrid, people talked about their daily lives around me, and no one paused a conversation

when I entered the teachers' lounge, the bar, or any other place
that was crawling with supernaturals.

I was one of them.

Training with the community was good for me. Since I'd
moved here and met Shane, I wasn't working out as much as I
should. Over the past two weeks, I'd caught up and gotten in
shape again. It had also strengthened my bond with him. I got to
know another aspect of his personality, and it was a massive turn
on. There was something incredibly intimate about sword
fighting and body-to-body combat with your soulmate. But
would he understand my reasons once I told him who I was and
what had brought me to his town? Would he fight with me or
against me?

Each day, I discovered more about how the town worked. Its
inhabitants were extremely organized and concerned with
everybody's security. As I suspected, Shane had a direct link with
the rulers of this place. He received many mysterious phone calls,
which he would answer in private. The calls that he didn't conceal
were about the security plans and perimeter runs. It was his duty
to designate teams during the day in the police station and fix the
schedules if someone couldn't make it.

Even if I was curious, I respected Shane's privacy since he
also respected mine. I hadn't asked Shane directly about the royal
family, but he had made it clear that he would tell me everything
about his job and the town once I was ready to prove my
loyalty—whatever that meant. Shane wanted me to be part of his
life, to have a home with him in Affinity. I was touched by it, and
I was hoping that, in time, I would trust him completely and
make him part of my life, too.

Meanwhile, from what he had shared with me, everybody in
town had an hour or a day in the week to do security patrols in
the woods and along town boundaries. There was also an elite

squad—most of them belonged to the town police force—
formed by the best and strongest warriors, and Shane was their
incontestable leader. Those warriors had the biggest
responsibilities and had to always be ready to be summoned or
ready to fight off anyone who disturbed the order or broke the
law—be they outsiders or townspeople.

The town was extremely well organized to ensure its citizens'
safety, mostly to protect the children. The children were sacred.
There were a lot of hybrids. I empathized with that. I could
understand the concern and severe safety measures. I couldn't
help but feel proud and admire my mate even more. Shane was
all I could ever have dreamed of in a mate. He was perfect and
radiated power and a feeling of protection that made me feel at
home. He was making me feel as if I belonged there, next to him,
forever.

CHAPTER NINETEEN
SHANE

ANNABEL WAS HOLDING BACK. I knew it, but I wouldn't say anything. Maybe she feared hurting me. Maybe she didn't know how strong she was. Perhaps she was doing it on purpose.

The fact was that, when we trained, she always held back her strength, her abilities, and her knowledge, letting me win easily. Therefore, I tried something else. I couldn't train with her the same way I trained my men. I worried about hurting her. For that reason, after one week of training alone with me, I put her in the community training schedule. There were women and other men there to practice with or be taught by. Maybe she would be more open to showing her abilities if I weren't around all the time, asking her if she was okay or if I'd hurt her. I must confess, I go a bit crazy every time she fell or got bruised.

It was Friday night, and we had gone out to dine in a fancy French restaurant. It had been an exhausting week, and I wanted to reward my better half with a romantic night out.

"I'm really proud of you," I whispered, holding her hand over the table.

The restaurant was an elegant place, and Anna looked stunning in her short black dress and silver pumps. Her glossy dark hair was styled in a classy low rolled updo, showing her pretty face and gorgeous neck. I had a fixation with that neck. Then again, I was obsessed with every single part of her, especially her eyes, lips, and neck. I was having withdrawal symptoms from sitting on the other side of the table, unable to wrap her in my arms.

"Is that why we are dining out?" she asked, smiling with her perfect, shiny red lips.

Her eyes shone every time she smiled at me. It made me feel

even more in love with her because I knew I made her happy.

"No, I just wanted to show you off," I said in a playful tone, making her chuckle and touch her necklace. "Besides, Sam's Bar is hardly the place to take you out every night. And the food is better here than in Mama Bear's Diner."

"Oh, I wouldn't bet on that yet. Do you normally come here to eat?" she asked, looking at the surrounding tables with interest.

"I have a good friend who likes to eat here," I said, running my fingers on her palm.

"James?"

"Him, too," I confirmed, turning to the waiter who brought the wine I had chosen and was showing me the bottle.

Releasing Anna's hand, I tasted the wine and approved it. He poured the drink into our glasses and filled Anna's glass of water.

"He's here with the drama teacher," Anna whispered after the waiter left.

"Did he see us?" I asked, talking in the same secretive way.

"He's coming our way," she replied, drinking water and putting on a smile to greet them.

I knew she wasn't too fond of him because he was a player, but she tried to be polite since he was her boss and my friend.

"What a nice coincidence, finding you two here," James said, arriving at our table with the tall, chocolate-skinned drama teacher.

Her name was Natasha if I was not mistaken. He shook my hand and patted my shoulder. Meanwhile, I got up to greet his companion.

"Anna, it's nice to see you here. We haven't seen you that often in school this past week," Natasha said, going over to kiss her.

"Shane has been monopolizing all my free time with the practices and patrolling," Anna replied. Natasha was a vampire, so she was also part of the supernatural community.

"Annabel, it's always a pleasure," James said, pressing Anna's hand against his lips with his trademark sexy grin.

He was pushing his luck, but I wasn't going to make a scene because of it.

"Mr. Ward, your table is ready," the waiter informed.

James released my mate's hand and smiled at the young boy. "I'll leave you to your romantic dinner, but if you want to share a glass of wine with us, feel free to join us at our table," he said, looking at me and then at Anna.

She was talking to Natasha. They seemed friendly enough.

"Annabel, you can come by my office next week, so we can exchange ideas about the school play. The girls are thrilled about it, and I would love your help," Natasha said before following James to their table, which was on the other side of the restaurant.

It wasn't that I didn't like James—I just didn't want him ogling my mate the way he did. He had his own date. Natasha was a beautiful woman, and Anna was mine, so he should act like a good friend and stop flirting every time he saw her.

"What's wrong?" Anna asked me, noticing my pensive stare.

"Is he always like this at work?" I wondered.

"Don't worry, I can handle him."

Her answer didn't reassure me, but I knew she could. I had witnessed her taking down my men, the ones who were stupid enough to lower their guard because she looked like a harmless girl. Anna knew how to take care of herself. Of course, that didn't change my fervent desire to protect her, whether she needed it or not.

"You're my mate, Anna. James needs to back off with his flirting ways."

"You're adorable when you get a bit possessive about me, but you need to calm yourself down and understand that he mostly does that to upset you."

I frowned. "I'm fully aware of that. But it doesn't mean I won't smack his face if he makes you feel uncomfortable at work."

"Does he have a history of harassing other teachers?" she wondered aloud, losing her smile.

"Well, he has the reputation of being a playboy. Any girl who goes out with him knows what to expect from him. He also has the nasty habit of trying to sleep with other people's mates."

She said nothing to my words, simply looked away at her plate and fiddled with the cloth napkin on her lap.

"I'm sorry. I didn't want to ruin our night by talking about James."

Anna gazed at me with a serious expression before asking, "Is it because I'm half panther?"

"Of course not. I trust you."

"It doesn't seem like it when you feel so insecure about James."

I realized that I had exaggerated and given too much importance to James. I didn't want her to feel uncomfortable and think that I didn't trust her.

I sighed, offering her my hand, and she held it. "I'm sorry, baby. It's just that James has been acting like a jerk the past few weeks since he found out that you're my mate and a hybrid."

"He's jealous, Shane," she stated. "People like him hide their insecurities behind a mask of fake happiness and a reckless lifestyle. They're lost in life, without a purpose and someone who cares about them. He's not a threat to you unless you make him one with your insecurities."

I kept my eyes on her, baffled. She was extremely wise for someone her age. She was right. I was acting immature. Anna was a beautiful woman, and I had to get used to having other men staring at her. Nothing in her behavior led me to believe that she wasn't taking our relationship seriously. Since she'd found out that we were mates, things between us had become even better.

"Do you want to go back home?" she asked.

"No, I want to stay right here on this date with my gorgeous girlfriend, eating miniature French food."

She chuckled, happiness returning to her face. She had joked about the portions French restaurants tended to serve. She wasn't sure if I was going to be satisfied because I liked big burgers. As if on cue, the waiter brought the appetizers: figs oozing with goat cheese.

"It looks delicious," Anna said, glancing at my face to see my reaction. She had chosen the appetizers.

"Too bad it doesn't smell better," I joked, stealing another smile from her.

"It's probably the goat cheese, but the honey and the figs smell wonderful."

"I trust your taste." I looked at the plate, unsure if I should ruin the presentation. It was sophisticated. "We should talk about next week," I said after eating a small portion.

"Why? Is something important happening next week?"

"I'm going to assign you for patrolling."

She rested her hand next to the plate. "So soon?"

"You've passed all the tracking and fighting tests with flying colors. Everybody agrees that you seem ready to be part of the tracking and patrolling team."

"That's an important step for being part of your community, isn't it?"

"Yes, it is. Besides, people don't think you can be a spy because you're a hybrid."

"Oh, I guess hybrids are the ones they would least expect to work with the radicals who chase us." She drank water as I nodded.

"Yes, it wouldn't be coherent. But you earned your promotion."

"Am I going to win a badge for that?" she joked.

"You won something a lot better than a badge," I teased her. "You won a date with me."

"I hope that won't be a common reward for other winners," she said, making me chuckle.

"No, this was a custom-made reward for you only."

"Lucky me."

"I'm glad you liked your prize. Since you're my mate, I had to vouch for you."

"To whom?"

"To the king."

"There's actually a king?" Her brow furrowed. "How old-fashioned! I thought there was some sort of committee that ruled over the town and decided on supernatural business."

"There is, but there's also a king."

"A vampire king?"

I nodded.

She pursed her lips. "When can I meet him?"

"When you pledge your allegiance to him."

"Isn't that a bit old-fashioned? Why would I pledge my allegiance to someone I haven't met yet?"

"Because that's how it works," I said.

"Hum." She drank more water.

I stopped eating and drank some wine. After cleaning my mouth, I said gently, "I need you to trust me on this."

She leaned closer and spoke lower, "We live in a republican country. Why do I need to obey a king?"

I smirked, aware that she had a lot to learn about my town's ways and the benefits of living here. "Honey, if you want to take your place by my side in this community, you need to pledge your loyalty to our king. You need to do so for the others to trust you. After that, there won't be any more secrets between us. You'll know everything about me, and I hope you'll tell me everything about you."

Anna sat quietly with absent eyes. Maybe I was moving too fast or pressuring her too soon. But we were mates. I wanted her to be part of my life, and I wanted to be part of hers.

"I'll think about it," she said, continuing to eat.

I thought she would be a lot more excited about my news, but there was something peculiar about her attitude. While I didn't believe that she was a spy, I knew she had a secret. There was more to her parents' death, which made her reserved and suspicious of people in general.

Since Anna told me of how her parents died and about the hard time she had endured after that, my protective instincts grew even stronger. It was as if I couldn't breathe if I wasn't next to her. Furthermore, we had a lot more in common than she realized. There was another issue bothering me; it went by the name of Sasha. The princess hadn't tried anything against Annabel...yet. Her uncle had succeeded in sending her abroad, but I wasn't sure that she wouldn't create trouble or send anyone to hurt Anna.

"Anna," I called, feeling my heart hurt inside my chest. "You don't want to leave me, do you?"

She frowned. "Why would you think that?"

"It's been three weeks since you learned that we are mates. You're still leaving on the weekends... And you seem to come back sadder on Mondays. Why can't you tell your family about us? Why can't I meet your cousin, Jason?" I was fishing with those questions, but I needed something to reassure me about her mysterious trips on the weekends.

"I told you that I must leave for the weekends. We talked about this when we first started to date."

"I know, but I would like to know where you go and what's so important that it keeps you awake on Friday nights, counting the hours until you hit the road."

She sighed deeply and narrowed her eyes. "Did you bring me to a restaurant, so I couldn't evade your questions?"

My eyes lingered on her face. She was right. I was putting her in an uncomfortable position in public. This was no place to talk about it. There were too many prying eyes.

"I'm sorry. I only wish you would talk more about your family."

"What do you want to know?"

"When can I meet your cousin?"

"I don't know, Shane. He doesn't know about us."

Frowning, I asked, "Why not?"

"He's…territorial about me."

"In what way?"

"Well, we are both hybrids. He's half-panther and half-human. After my parents' death, we moved to live with him and his mom. His dad had been killed. He was human. So, you must imagine that, after what happened to my brother, he's been really protective of me."

"There's nothing wrong with protecting you. But you have me now. I'll keep you safe from now on. It's my duty because I'm your mate. I'm now part of your family, whether he likes it or not."

I was being straightforward but, in my defense, felines and werewolves didn't mingle under normal circumstances. We weren't a natural enemy because we were shifters, and we weren't overpowered by our instincts, but felines were awfully territorial about their blood relationships.

In their natural order of things, if Anna had been a pure panther shifter, it would be expected that she would find a mate amongst her kind. Blood ties meant nothing to supernatural beings as soulmates didn't have DNA restrictions or moral standards like humans. It didn't matter if Anna and Jason were cousins—if they were mates, they would be together and procreate. Since they were hybrids, I had no idea what their families thought about their future.

"Were you promised to him?" I inquired.

That would explain a lot. If they thought they didn't have a soulmate, their family might have arranged some sort of union between them. Her cousin could be under the impression that Annabel belonged to him. Maybe she was afraid to tell me that. Afraid of starting a war.

"Of course not. My parents wouldn't do something as old-fashioned and stupid as that. They wanted me to find my place in the world, even if they were led to believe that hybrids didn't have a soulmate."

Arranged marriages were extremely far-fetched in a world where soulmates were designed by the gods. But there were reported cases of that happening. Only soulmates were able to procreate. Yet, I had no idea if hybrids were naturally fertile like human women. Consequently, the soulmate rule wouldn't apply to them.

"Is he in love with you?" I asked.

I wanted to know what was awaiting me when I met her cousin.

"Jason is a Casanova. He loves no one. He likes to fool around and have a new girlfriend each week, sometimes each night."

"That doesn't mean he's not in love with you," I pointed out.

His erratic behavior wasn't a sign that he didn't want Annabel. If anything, it was the elusive behavior of a boy having fun or substituting girl after girl because he couldn't be with the one he wanted in the first place.

"The fact that you haven't told him about us means that you know he would be upset about it."

Anna fiddled in her seat. "You're being paranoid. I didn't tell him about us because he doesn't believe that hybrids can have soulmates. And he has nothing to do with my private life."

"Anna…"

She leaned closer and whispered with a sad expression, "Shane, if I tell him about us, he'll want me to leave this place and never come back."

I stood in silence, analyzing her reaction. She was telling the truth. Maybe she had no idea if Jason was in love with her or not, but Jason's opinion was important to her.

"I don't want him to ruin our happiness," she mumbled after sipping her wine.

"Your place is here with me now," I stated, rattled by the fact that her cousin thought that he could make decisions about her life.

She put down the glass and folded her arms, looking at me sideways.

"Men are all hard-headed idiots when it comes to protecting those they view as a responsibility. I'm capable of deciding for myself where I belong or where I don't."

"So why are you so afraid of telling him that you are with me?"

"Because I don't want you to be his enemy, nor do I want him to be mad at me. I'm trying to find the best time to talk to him. Now isn't the right time. There are too many things at stake, and Jason is on a critical mission." She closed her mouth with an audible click and looked away. I imagined she'd said more than she'd intended to.

She put three fingers on her temple as if experiencing a headache. "I thought this was a date, not an interrogation."

"So, how is school?" I asked, changing the subject and taking a sip of wine.

She frowned, unsure if I was trying to lighten the mood or merely being ironic. I had experience with this type of arguments. I wouldn't keep insisting. Also, I was good at assembling the pieces of her puzzling life. That night, I knew a bit more about her than I'd known the day before.

"I'll try to talk to him this weekend," she said while avoiding my gaze. It made me happy but also upset because I knew I had made her sad.

"Have you decided about what movie you want to watch after dinner?" I asked, putting my hand on the table to ask for hers. She placed her hand in mine, and I grabbed it, caressing her palm with my thumb.

"I didn't give it much thought, but my students were talking about a new superhero movie. It seems to be really good."

"I hope it's better than the last one we saw."

"If I recall correctly, you fell asleep. I hope you don't fall asleep in this one."

"Of course not. I have a lot of things I want to do tonight," I said with a mischievous smirk and husky voice, leaning down to kiss her hand. "Have I told you how gorgeous you look tonight?"

"Twice," she said, smiling and loosening up again. "But I don't mind you repeating yourself."

"Aren't you missing our kitchen right now?" I teased.

She giggled as her cheeks became slightly red. We never finished our meal when we teased each other like that.

"Yesterday was pretty fun, too," she teased back, reminding

me of our afternoon in the woods.

We had gone for a walk and ended up leaving the trail to run through the forest. She needed to get familiar with those woods. Therefore, the following week, I was planning to teach her new tracks and places where people could hide, and where it was more dangerous to go at night. My wolf could use the run, and her vampire form was the most enticing and captivating thing to watch as I enjoyed the sunlight.

"You're the most gorgeous thing in the world, no matter what shape you take," I whispered, high on her scent and my love for her.

"You're a bad influence on me," she stated with a playful smile, her eyes almost glowing.

"Are you talking about skinny dipping in the river?" I asked, beaming as I remembered how exciting it had been to make love to her in the middle of the forest, surrounded by birds and wild animals.

"It would have been embarrassing if someone caught us there."

"No one goes there unless they are tracking someone or something. Besides, you needed to hunt and, after, we needed to clean ourselves from the blood."

"It was fun."

"What was fun? The hunting or the bathing?"

"Both," she answered.

"I was happily surprised. You had hunted before, and you don't seem to need as much blood as other vampires."

"My vampire form hasn't become bloodthirsty yet. I've never bitten a person. I normally drink from hospital bags or animals," she explained, and I nodded.

I had no idea how things worked for hybrids. I knew pureblood vampires would mature at a certain age, becoming dependent on blood, and would then stop eating human food. Shifters like me needed to hunt to survive and eat raw meat from time to time. However, hybrids were probably different. They were still trying to figure out where they fit into our world.

I voiced my thoughts, "There are a lot more hybrids in the world. We should probably look for information about it."

"There aren't many panther and vampire hybrids," she declared. I had to agree with that. "But I'm okay. Don't worry about it."

"I know you can take care of yourself. But I love you, so it's hard for me not to worry about you."

She smiled and leaned closer to offer her lips to me. I leaned forward and kissed her. Displaying that level of affection in a public place wasn't the most appropriate thing to do, but I couldn't care less about what others thought.

"How is your appetizer?" she wondered, watching me play with the food.

"Edible, but too sweet."

"I can buy you a burger after this," she joked.

"I don't know. I'm more inclined to drink champagne and eat strawberries in a Jacuzzi," I said, watching her reaction.

"We don't have a Jacuzzi," she said, distracted by her food.

"The hotel does. I might have booked us a room."

She raised her eyes to watch me. "I'm getting worried about this. You seem to have a well-planned night for us."

I frowned. "And why would you be worried?"

"You might want to convince me to stay with you this weekend."

"I might, but maybe I just want to take advantage of you while you are here since I'm doomed to spend the weekend alone."

"I'm all in favor of you taking advantage of me," she teased back, ignoring my manipulative words.

I smirked and tried again. "Maybe you can spend the next weekend with me. Or maybe we can go somewhere else, together."

"I promise I'll think about it. Is that good enough for you?"

"Yes, it will do for now." I drank my wine, pleased by her words.

It might take a while, but she would eventually open up to me. I would then find out why she was so secretive about her life and family. One thing was certain, Annabel could have a lot of secrets, but she had the kindest soul and the gentlest heart. I was delighted about that.

CHAPTER TWENTY

ANNABEL

TIME FLIES when we are happy. That was never more accurate to me than now. Three weeks went by in a flash.

After my parents' death, happiness was the last thing I thought I would experience again. But even if finding my mate was exulting, at the same time, I was feeling guilty for postponing my other life and quest in order to stay here with Shane. Guilty because I thought I could be doing something else to help my brother.

Jason and the rest of my crew were trying to find a pureblood vampire. But their search was turning out to be as futile as mine. Jessica kept me updated; Jason insisted that I leave and get back home. But I was still hoping that the answer to my problems was there. That, or I was reluctant to leave Shane, hoping that he would understand why I couldn't live in that town with him.

My time was running out. The school would be over in a week, and I had to report back to my superiors and explain to Jason how my time there was a dead end. I had no idea where the vampire's lair was. I had no idea who the king of these lands was, and I didn't believe that there were evil people hiding here anymore. Shane was anything but evil. Everybody else seemed nice and friendly. I was an active member of the community, even if I hadn't had my face-to-face with the king and pledged my allegiance to him. I was still on probation, and between my schoolwork, the patrolling, and Shane, I had little time to myself.

"You were slower today," Shane mumbled, caressing my hair. "Are you feeling okay?"

We had gone for a run in the woods and were seated near a tree, watching the sunset and resting. The place where he lived was amazing. I had fallen in love with it, and I wished I could stay there with him. He was amazing, and I couldn't see my life without him anymore. He was obliterating all my defenses, even without the marking.

"I'm okay," I whispered, opening my eyes while caressing his face.

I noticed how his eyes were still shining with his wolf. I loved his wolf; he had a beautiful gray and white coat. He liked to cuddle me after running in the open air, with me following behind him in my vampire form. We stared at each other for hours after the long walks in the forest. We also had a lot of fun patrolling. When he taught me the shortcuts, he showed me the waterfalls and the hidden caves. Being me had never been as fun! I'd never felt so free and in sync with the universe, with the mysteries of life.

"It's amazing how much you like to stay under the sun," he whispered, smiling at me. "You are the oddest vampire I've ever met."

"I'm not odd. I just like the sun. Blame my panther side. Felines like the sun."

"True," he agreed, caressing the hair away from my face. "You're also the most beautiful vampire I've ever seen."

"No, I'm not," I said, covering my face and trying to relax so my fangs hid and my eyes became normal again.

"Don't do that. I like to look at you like that. Don't be shy—I love your vampire form."

"You're the one being weird."

"Because I'm a werewolf who's in love with a vampire?"

"No, because you get aroused by my fangs," I whispered, teasing him by showing my teeth and leaving the tip of my tongue over my right fang.

He tensed. I felt his hard muscles against my lap. His eyes

turned amber, and I chuckled. Even if I was laughing, I loved the fact that he would get aroused by it.

"You can't blame me for that. I've already told you that I love you in any shape. Besides, your eyes and hair are beautiful when they are purple. Do you know why they are purple and not black?"

I nodded. "Because I've never fed from the source."

Feeding from the source meant drinking from a vein. All the blood I drank was served either in a glass, inside a hospital bag, or from animals. Though, as much as I didn't like to think about the bloodlust, I was aware that my lack of strength the past few days was because I was changing and needed blood. I was being stubborn since I didn't want to drink too much blood. I used to be able to survive by drinking blood once a week. It was becoming a daily obsession, however, and I was trying to control my urges and tame my thirst. The consequence was my lack of stamina to keep up with Shane and the others.

"Have you ever seen a black-eyed vampire?" Shane questioned.

"Yes. I've encountered several vampires before. There are a lot of black eyes in this community."

"As long as they don't kill humans and the humans are willing to donate their blood, we don't interfere in their business."

I nodded, my thoughts slipping to the image of Alaric's red eyes. Red eyes were a sign of madness. Vampires with red eyes weren't sane or safe to be around. In ancient times, they were put to death. Other vampires would go around and kill the sick vampire, or the vampire would eventually kill himself. But an insane vampire had more probability of decimating an entire village, leaving behind a vast number of bodies. Every self-conscious vampire knew that insanity was the same as a true death. However, Alaric had managed to survive, to thrive on his madness and spread death and hate amongst the supernatural community.

"Where did you just go?" Shane touched my chin with his hand.

I looked down at him, trying to chase away the bad thoughts. "I don't want to lose my purple eyes."

"You won't. But are you feeling...different? You know, hungry for blood? Do you want to hunt?"

"I'm just tired. It has been a long week."

We had hunted the other day. I didn't want him to get worried.

His next words reminded me that the week was almost over. "You could stay and rest over the weekend."

I averted my gaze. I didn't want to talk about the fact that we weren't going to spend another weekend together. He had asked me the day before if I was going to stay. I had informed him that I couldn't. He was insisting again. But I had other things to take care of, important things concerning my brother and me. Over the past few days, I'd had a hard time controlling my fangs. I was feeling tired and drained. I was becoming more vampire than a panther. My DNA was mutating. I needed to run more exams on my blood, but the last ones that I'd done said that my DNA was mutating to vampire and would eventually lose my ability to shift to a panther. It was a painful process, and I didn't normally shift, but the idea of losing my shifting ability was making me sad.

"I may lose my ability to shift to a panther," I whispered, unable to keep it inside me any longer.

"How do you know that?"

"I'm having trouble connecting with my feline side, and it's getting more painful to shift."

"Would you rather be a panther than a vampire?"

"I love both," I answered truthfully. "I'm not saying that all

vampires are evil. I understand that blood is a part of our diet.
But if I lose my ability to shift to a panther, will I lose a part of
me? Like the part of me that loves the sun, that likes to jump and
climb trees and gets satisfied by drinking animal blood instead of
human blood? I don't know what that will do to my personality."

Shane remained silent for a while. I didn't want to worry him,
but I had to share this with him. He was my soulmate. If he
didn't understand me, who would?

"It seems to me that you're maturing. Werewolves also
mature. There comes a time when we merge our animal
personality with our humanity, taming the shifting and the feral
instincts. Maybe hybrid DNA battles to find a dominant form,
and you aren't losing a part of you, only evolving to your original
self."

I pondered his words. "We also need to understand how
mating works between us."

"What do you mean? I think it works rather well."

I rolled my eyes. "I'm not talking about sex."

"Then what are you talking about?"

"Hybrids weren't supposed to procreate because we don't
have a soulmate. But since we actually do have a soulmate and we
have sex, it came to my mind that I can get pregnant with your
baby."

"Oh!" He opened his eyes, putting two and two together, and
smirked. "Babies—I want four or six."

"Sure you do," I joked, pushing him out of my lap. "I'm too
young to think about having babies."

"Do you want to see a doctor about that? Were you taking
precautions?"

"It's not like I have to worry about STDs since I'm half
shifter, half vampire, and you are a werewolf. Only humans get
sick with those."

Shane sat next to me with attentive eyes and a serious face. "Are you pregnant?"

"No, of course not," I said, panicking at his question. "I'm not in heat season, and…" I bit the inside of my cheek. "I've tested it, just in case. It was negative."

"We need to work harder for it then," he teased.

I pushed back his shoulder. "Stop joking about that."

"I can't help it. I'm already imagining all the cute babies we both could make."

"I don't even know if we can have babies," I mumbled in a sad voice, trapped in his arms. He was smiling, but he lost his smile and hugged me tight against him.

"You are too young. You're right. And we have plenty of time to talk about that. I only want you to be okay. When the time is right, we'll look for a doctor to test us. Besides, there are plenty of orphan kids in the world."

I nodded, feeling a lot better with his words. Then the oddity of the conversation hit me. We were making plans for the future as if I could have a future, have a family, and be happy.

"What's wrong, baby?" he asked, sensing the tension in my body.

"I've realized that…" I silenced myself, leaning back to watch his face. Shane was a part of my life and someone I wanted to have in my future. "I can't see myself living without you."

"That's a good thing because I can't see myself living without you, either."

"But…my life is messed up."

He chuckled, apparently amused by my confession. However, he had no idea how true that was.

"Just let me mark you, and everything will fall into place," he said.

"You don't know that," I argued, feeling helpless and evading the contact of his lips. I liked how sweet he was, but I was fully aware that he tried to manipulate me with words and kisses. He knew how much I loved him. I couldn't blame him. I was relying on his love for me to be patient.

In my defense, I had a good excuse for delaying the marking. Pureblood vampires have special powers to see their victims' memories when they are drinking from them. The only warm blood I had inside of me was from animals. It worked differently to human blood. I had no idea if I had that power. Besides, what would I see in Shane's head when I did bite him? Would I see his previous lovers? Would I see his kills, his fears, and his dark side?

Marking each other would open a telepathic link between us. We would share memories and thoughts. I was scared of that. How couldn't I be? He would see all my demons, my bad memories, and my fears.

I knew Shane struggled with that, too. He also had his demons, his bad dreams. So, even if he asked often, the lack of pressure was a hint that he was delaying it as much as I was. But my time was running out. It was almost prom night, which meant my contract was finishing, and school was almost over. I would have to accept a new contract there or leave, maybe live between places. Marking would increase my need for Shane and my inability to stay away from him.

"You're the most beautiful thing in the world," he whispered, staring at my purple eyes and touching my lips with his fingertips. "You have the most amazing red lips." He moved closer to kiss me. I leaned down, molding my lips to his and trying not to cut him with my fangs. I loved that he saw me as if I were the most perfect thing and not a simple blood-thirsty monster.

"When are you going to let me mark you and bite me?" he asked, leaving space between us, so he could look into my eyes and analyze my reaction. He was insisting again.

"Maybe next week," I whispered, wanting to delay it but knowing that I didn't have much time left.

"We have patrol tonight. After it, we'll go to Sam's Bar, if you don't mind. Or do you want to skip this patrol and go to bed earlier?"

"Are you coming to bed with me?" I asked.

"I can't skip the patrolling."

"Then I'll go with you. I don't like it when you're doing it alone at night."

"Duncan and Samuel will join me tonight."

"I would rather go on patrols with you than stay at home alone," I said, caressing his face.

"We'll probably just find couples making out in the woods or other kids playing tricks on their friends. It's hot, and the days are longer. Everybody is excited about the summer holidays. Dangerous stuff hardly ever happens here."

"I know, but I still want to go with you."

"Okay," he said, kissing me softly on the lips. "I'd rather have you by my side than one of the boys."

"Someone needs to take care of you." I smirked against his lips.

"Cocky, are we?"

"I totally kick your men's butts."

"Yes, you do. I knew you were holding back. But I'd rather you didn't hold back with me. We've talked about this. Your dad taught you well. I have to give him credit for that."

"I don't want to harm you. Besides, you also hold back with me."

"Yes, you're right. I can't stand the thought of hurting you, either."

"So, let's agree to not compete to know who's the best."

"I know you're the best with the sword. I don't have any

doubts about that. You're really good at it!"

"I practice a lot. It's my favorite weapon."

"Though...you could practice a lot more in body-to-body combat."

"What do you mean?" I asked, feeling slightly offended. "I'm a pretty decent fighter. Your men are proof of it. At least, their bruises are. You should train them better."

Shane chuckled. "Oh, I wasn't talking about that kind of body combat."

"You're such a pervert!" I joked, pushing him back and trying to get away from his arms.

"I think it's kind of late for you to complain about that. Any kind of perverted thoughts I have are all because of you, my gorgeous, addictive, and sexy mate," he declared, grabbing and putting me under him. "How are you planning to get away from this now?"

"I'm not planning to get away from anywhere. I've got you right where I wanted you." My words made him chuckle before he lowered his face to kiss me.

"You can go wherever you want, as long as you take me with you," he whispered against my lips.

My heart stopped beating for a moment. I simply nodded, kissing him back and hugging him tighter. I fought hard not to start crying. I didn't want to hurt him or leave him. I wanted to find a way to tell him all about me and be part of his life. A future without Shane wasn't something I looked forward to. However, I'd never thought much about my future or having a family outside of my twisted way of life, given the burden that I carried around. I needed to tell Shane everything about me, and I needed to talk to Jason, so I could warn him about it and tell him about Shane's existence.

Shane and Jason needed to meet, and Jason needed to

understand that my life was going to change from now on. Maybe Shane could help me save my brother, Kevin. If he knew everything about what had happened, he could help me find a way to convince a pureblood to donate blood. It was too much to ask, but if Shane cared, if his king was as compassionate and kind as Shane described him, then he could help me.

All I had to do was convince Jason that my decision to trust Shane was right. They were my teammates, and I had no right to talk about them and expose the secret organization I worked for without warning them about it and reasoning with them about the necessity of telling someone else about us.

Shane was my soulmate. If I didn't tell him who I truly was, we would eventually fall apart, and the secrets would ruin our relationship and our love.

CHAPTER TWENTY-ONE
SHANE

I WASN'T PROUD of what I was doing, but I couldn't do anything else. Not after the conversation I had with the prince and the proofs sent by Sasha. She hadn't let go and wanted to hurt my soulmate in any way possible.

Her surveillance had paid off, apparently, since the prince now doubted Annabel's intentions. The pictures taken by a private detective weren't very enlightening but were enough for the prince to question her loyalty and assert that my mate mingled with dangerous people.

Sasha even had the nerve to do a background check on Annabel's life. Anna's identity seemed real, but I realized that there were no records of her being an orphan like she had told me. Not that I had told them anything that Anna had shared with me. Still, something wasn't right, and I had to make sure that Anna wouldn't be falsely accused because Sasha wanted her out of my life.

The prince decided to trust me and allow me to investigate on my own. I had to refute Sasha's claims that Anna was a spy. Therefore, I had to follow my soulmate and discover what she did on the weekends she was away from me.

The first time, she spent her entire day in a private and expensive clinic. I was unable to get any information from the nurses or the receptionist about what Anna was doing there or what floor she was on. However, after the conversation we'd had about babies and her transformation, I was sure she wasn't doing anything wrong. I rather felt thrilled to know that she might be testing to know if we could have a family together.

Still, the pictures of her in a bar frequented by radicals that killed hybrids were troublesome. Did she know the danger she put herself in by being there? Why was she mingling with the enemy? Did Sasha fake the evidence that she gave to her uncle?

The second time I followed Anna, I thought she would spend her entire day in the clinic since she headed there again. However, after a couple of hours of waiting, she left and drove for a long time until she arrived at a property in the middle of nowhere. Despite the lack of surrounding structures or living beings close to the property, it was guarded like a fortress of some sort. It had tall walls with electronic surveillance, electronic motion detectors, and video cameras spread around like weeds.

After parking far away and shifting to my wolf form, I was able to sneak into the property and reach a big modern house. It had cameras and electronic motion detectors around it, too. I wasn't able to get closer, so I shifted back, covered my genitals, and climbed like a clumsy monkey up a tall, robust tree. Then I changed back to my wolf form because it had better vision and enhanced senses. I stood there with a small bag containing my underwear and my phone, watching the house through the large windows.

Even if it looked like a house, it seemed like something more. With a modern design that feature floor to ceiling windows, I could see the bedrooms, the kitchen, and the living room in the front. I wondered which of those bedrooms might belong to my Anna. I could see her bike parked out front. She should be inside the house already, but I couldn't find her anywhere on the first or second floor. Everything was quiet and lifeless, like no one lived there. As night fell peacefully, I could only hear the background sound of the surveillance cameras moving.

Lights came on after an hour of heavy silence. Then people appeared from somewhere in the back of the house; three men, to be more exact, and Anna. The men sat down on the couches in the living room, flipping through TV channels while my mate headed to the kitchen. A tall blond guy followed her as they chatted. She seemed to know him well, and she smiled a lot around him. He acted childish, making her get mad and throw pieces of cucumber at him from the salad she was making.

I was getting jealous—my wolf wanted to growl and attack him—but I had to be less impulsive. I concentrated on their moving lips, and I could clearly distinguish his name—Jason. He was her cousin. That made me less jealous, even if he seemed as if he was flirting with her. My jealousy was perhaps because he was handsome, and I was seeing him as a threat. Still, I had to remember they were cousins and friends. They had the familiarity to act like kids, and the fact that she was smiling was because they were family and loved each other as such.

After Anna made some steaks with fries, rice, and salad, they all sat down in the kitchen and ate. Dinner didn't take long, and, soon enough, Anna went to her bedroom. It was the second room on the right, and I had a nice view of it. I couldn't help but wonder if she was aware that people could see everything inside when she had the lights on. Maybe they didn't worry much about it since they had surveillance and alarms to warn them and had no neighbors. But if I were able to get in undetected, others would be able to, as well.

For a while, Anna wasn't doing anything, just lying on her bed, phone in hand, and moving her legs in a pensive way.

Jason entered her room, and she looked bored by his presence. The blond guy sat down on her bed, and he seemed to be annoying her because she was pouting and sneering at his words. He had his back to me, so I had no idea what he was saying.

After a while, Anna rolled over in her bed and stared at the ceiling, simply ignoring him. He sighed, patted the bed for attention. When she ignored him, he got up and exited her bedroom.

Bouncing her legs, Anna stared at her phone and sighed. The look of sadness on her face made my heart hurt in my chest. Though my mind was filled with questions. I wanted to know who the other two guys were, why they all seemed to live together, why the house had so many electronic security devices, and why she had never talked to me about that. She told me she had a cousin, not that she lived with him and two other guys.

Eventually, Anna got up, moved closer to the glass, and stared outside like she was searching for something. She seemed worried, maybe even missing me. I hoped she was. I was missing her, even if I was staring right at her.

Then my phone rang, and I had the hardest time shifting back when I saw Anna's name on the caller ID. I couldn't answer, so I let it ring until it stopped. Far away, she hung up and stared at her phone, glum. I wanted to call her back, but I couldn't. Being naked on a branch also didn't help my case, and I couldn't make noise, so I texted her, coming up with a lame excuse of being at work in a meeting and not being able to talk to her on the phone.

She replied immediately with three simple words: *I miss you.*

I sent her a reply: *Come home then.*

She texted me next: *Tomorrow, I'll be home.*

I ended by telling her that I loved her, and she texted me the same.

It intrigued me. The next day was Sunday. She would normally come back home in the evening. Maybe she was coming home earlier to be with me.

I hoped so.

The messages made me feel a bit better. She was thinking of me while she was there staring at the void, and she missed me. Now, if only she trusted me enough to tell me the rest about her life and why she had to go home every weekend.

I didn't stay much longer in the tree. Anna went to another part of her room that had no window. When she came back to the bedroom, she was wearing a black outfit and had a racket bag in her hand. Was she planning to go and play tennis at night?

Anna entered a code behind a painting on the wall and took two swords and a pair of guns from the safe. I couldn't see properly inside, but it was definitely an armory. Why did she have an armory in her bedroom? Even if she had showed a high level of skills with swords and martial arts, she told me that she had never shot a gun and didn't like them. Was Sasha right and Anna had been lying? I knew she was holding back, but the house and the weapons led me to believe that she was mixed in something dangerous.

My thoughts were in overdrive and I almost missed the fact that she had left her bedroom and was on her bike, putting the racket bag on her back.

I didn't stick around because I had to jump down and rush to my car, so I could follow her. It wasn't an easy task, since she had a head start, and her scent was hard to track down in a city filled with weird smells, garbage, humans, and pollution.

I found her bike parked in a dark, dangerous alley. She was alone, staring at a door with a red sign that had *STAFF* written on top. I parked and mingled with the crowd, making sure I wasn't seen while hiding where I could see and hear her.

That neighborhood was a known place where supernaturals gathered. There were many bars, restaurants, and nightclubs to hang out and feed on unsuspecting humans. *FANGS*, the nightclub next to the alley, was a hookup joint for supernaturals. Highly frequented by vampires and not a radical meeting point.

What was she doing there? What was she waiting for? Didn't she know how dangerous it was to be there?

It took all in me not to reveal my presence there, grab her arm, and get her out of that place. At least, she had the racket bag on her back and a concealed weapon under her coat. She wasn't there to play, but I truly hoped that she wasn't there to kill anything either.

Something seemed to be bothering her, though. She kept glancing back and rubbing the back of her neck. Maybe she could sense she was being watched. Maybe her instinct was telling her that I was nearby.

I was now sure that Anna was far more complicated than she led me to believe. In fact, she was not as innocent as she'd appeared and definitely not as harmless as I'd first thought. I had to face it: Anna was hiding things from me. She lived with a group of men and had weapons hidden in her bedroom. She was a trained warrior, and I had to find out what side she was on.

I would be torn apart if my soulmate was a spy for the radicals, capable of betraying her own kind. She was mine, I loved her more than my own life, but my king would never forgive her.

What if all she'd told me was a lie? What if she had never loved me? Maybe being a hybrid made her immune to our bond, and she'd played me like a fool.

She couldn't be a spy. She loved me. I couldn't doubt that. She was my mate; I had to trust her. I had to trust my instincts, my wolf, and not make quick judgments without proof. I had to wait patiently and see why she was there.

CHAPTER TWENTY-TWO

ANNA

I PULLED MY BIKE to the back of an alley, next to a couple of paper boxes. The garbage container was full of smelly debris, and the odor nauseated me before I could block my heightened sense of smell.

Sneering, I scratched the back of my neck for the hundredth time that day. Since I left Affinity, I had a recurrent itch on the nape of my neck and a terrible empty sensation inside my heart. I couldn't stop thinking about Shane. I missed him, and it felt like it had been more than a day that we'd been apart.

Shaking my head to clear my mind, I focused on the reason to be there.

The alley was dark and eery—the type of place where serial killers wait for a victim. Yet, I wasn't an average person, and darkness was never an obstacle. If anything, it was an ally.

Browsing around with my vampire sight, I confirmed that it was vampire-and-people-free—for the time being, anyway. I couldn't forget that I was in the back entrance of a nightclub called FANGS. The name's obviousness meant the place was crawling with vampires looking for blood donors, plus many vampire-wannabes who had no clue what they were getting themselves into.

This lousy excuse for a nightclub was my best friend's favorite place. Jessica had a thing for vampires. Well, it was more than a thing—it was an obsession. Jessica was a hunter. A damn good one, but she loved vampires. She punished the bad ones or, at least, the ones who were too naughty. But she had a serious inclination to hook up with vampires because being sucked turned her on, and it was her darkest sexual fantasy.

As expected, the back door opened, and Jessica showed up

with a vamp in a serious make-out session. They were too busy kissing to even notice me. Things got awkward when the guy pushed her against the wall, caressing her breasts and putting his fangs on her neck. The weirdest part was yet to come. She started to moan and gasp as if she was having an orgasm. Completely turned on, the guy crawled her skirt up her legs to take her right there.

Gosh! She has the most terrible taste in places to have sex!

"Hum! Hum!" I cleared my throat, hoping to get their attention. "Excuse me!" I said a bit louder. "Jessica, could you not…"

Jessica finally opened her eyes. "What the hell!" she cursed, pulling the vampire off her and glaring at me. "Are you stalking me now?"

"Nice to see you, too!" I joked.

"Did you invite a friend to play?" the vampire asked with a raspy voice.

He didn't seem shy, just a bit confused about being pulled away from his erotic feeding. He looked healthy enough, but his eyes were still black from the feeding. Tall, blond, well-built, and beautiful features, he was totally Jessica's style. She had a thing for blonde vamps. Too bad that her best friend was here to ruin her plans and prevent her from making a ten-minute mistake.

If it lasted that long.

"Sorry, but I'm not on the menu. I have to speak to her," I said, pointing at Jessica. "So why don't you run along? The fun is over tonight."

"You're such a buzzkill!" Jessica nagged.

The vamp squinted at me. "If you're not here to play, you better leave. I don't have time to teach you some manners."

"Teach me some manners?" I asked, chuckling at his audacity. Removing the gun from my back, I pointed it at him.

"This is a semi-automatic that shots WS9 bullets. Is this scary enough for you?"

Sneering, the vamp looked at Jessica. "Did you lure me here so your friend could kill me?"

"I lured you here so I could have sex with you and feed from you," Jessica claimed, fixing her blouse and brushing down her messy hair. "She's just a terrible friend with a gun and mad fighting skills."

Showing his fangs, the vampire groaned, "Do you think that I'm…"

The vampire stopped talking as I stepped forward, and my fangs came out as my hair turned to a purple shade.

Waving his hands in denial, he stuttered, "I-I wasn't going to hurt her."

His eyes were wide open as fear began to get the best of him. Lucky for me, he was a coward and wasn't going to try to show me how big and fast he was. I was in no mood to play anyhow, and he hadn't done anything bad. At least, not that I knew of.

"Don't worry. She can take care of herself," I said, looking at Jessica, who giggled. "Just leave," I ordered, and he used his super-speed to vanish.

"Hey! I hadn't finished with him yet! I don't even have his phone number!" Jessica started to complain. "He was hot! Damn, Anna!"

"Jessica, I really hate when you do this," I grumbled as I concealed back my gun.

She shrugged and made a happy face. It always upset me how reckless she was. Her neck was still bleeding from the puncture marks, and I stared at the blood, mesmerized. I had stronger urges for blood lately. The most recent tests showed I was going to have to drink blood regularly. That morning in the clinic, after talking to my comatose brother, I'd spoken with my doctor.

The news wasn't good for me. My aging process had stopped, and my body was rejecting normal food. And Jessica smelled good. I'd never noticed how good she smelled until then.

"Hungry?" she asked, seeming to notice my fixation on her neck.

"No, I'm intrigued by why you always smell so good. Your blood smells sweeter than the blood from normal humans."

"It's the magic," she explained. "Sorry, I'll fix it." She put her glowing hand over her neck and healed it. "I've missed you!" She ran to me and hugged me tight, making me gasp for air. It was unexpected, but she was always a force of nature and enthusiastic about life. "So, are you having fun there? You don't seem to want to come back home! It's been, what, almost three months?"

"All is fine. I took some time off."

"And how is your wolf?" she asked, letting me go and clapping her hands with excitement.

Jessica was my best friend. I missed her a lot, even if I used to call her several times a week to tell her the news. She was the sole person who knew what was going on with Shane and me. I trusted her not to tell anyone.

"So?" she insisted with an eager expression.

I smiled, relaxing. "Shane's fine, Jessie."

"When can I meet him? I'm so curious to know him. He must be something else to tame you!" She chuckled, finding her joke hilarious.

I put my hand on her forehead and pushed her back to annoy her and make her stop laughing.

She hissed and pushed my hand aside. "Someone is touchy today!"

"Just stop saying nonsense. No one tamed me."

"Okay, okay, so when can I meet him?"

"He doesn't know about you and the others yet."

"What do you mean?"

"He doesn't know what I really do."

"I know that! But I can pretend to be normal. I mean a normal hot witch who doesn't have a secret identity. Besides, you said he's your soulmate. And I'm curious. Hybrids weren't supposed to have soulmates. And that brings up a lot of questions. Like, if two hybrids are soulmates, how will they know that? Because it was Shane, who told you. Since he isn't a hybrid but a pure werewolf, he knows how to recognize his soulmate. So, if it's true that hybrids also have soulmates, do all supernatural beings have them, too?"

"Calm down, calm down," I said, overwhelmed by how many questions she had and all the conjectures she was making. I was amazed. She'd taken the time to think about the subject. "I think the purebloods invented that to make us feel bad and to dissuade other races from mingling and creating superior beings. Hybrids were killed while they were still infants. It's not a surprise they invented myths to make us feel even more like outcasts."

"Point taken." Jessica clapped her hands again, making me frown. She was always so happy that it seemed like nothing could make her feel bad, but I knew that wasn't true. "I'm so happy for you!" Her perfect white teeth were showing in her plump red mouth. I missed her joyfulness. "And I want to meet Shane. So, no more excuses!"

"Okay."

She frowned, apparently stunned by my answer. "Hmm! Are you lying to me?"

"Of course not! I'll arrange for you to come and meet him."

Putting her arm over my shoulders, she inquired, "Good! Now, tell me. What did the doctor say?"

"I'm going to live forever," I said in a grumpy tone that made her pout and roll her eyes.

"Yes, now try telling me something I didn't know," she said with sarcasm as we walked back to my bike.

"I'm becoming a true vampire," I shared, sighing deeply. I halted, so she could process my information.

"Did you stop aging?"

"Yes."

"Everything will be all right," she said, hugging me.

I hugged her back.

"I don't want to...feel the hunger and the blood lust," I confessed, my body shivering.

"How long 'til that happens?"

"I don't know. Days, weeks? Food no longer works by itself. I'm scared."

"I know, honey." She stroked my hair and hugged me tighter. "You should feed."

"I don't want to feed on you," I almost screamed when I felt her hand pulling my head to her neck. "You'll get aroused from that!"

She let me go and laughed hysterically. Between her giggles, she added, "Women don't arouse me, silly! You're safe."

Crossing my arms, I grumbled, "No, thanks. I'd rather not drink from the source."

"Picky!"

"Shut up! You know what happens to purebloods. I don't want to go mad with other people's thoughts and memories."

"You don't even know if you inherited the pureblood vampire's gift!" She put her hands on her hips and stared at me as if I was a stubborn kid.

"Kevin did," I mumbled, and she softened her face and breathed deeply.

"Yes, he did. Let's go talk while we eat. We don't need to go home right now. And we have a lot of stuff to catch up on. What do you say, girls' night?"

I agreed happily and walked to my bike. Then I stopped and closed my eyes, smelling the air. I had the strangest impression of smelling Shane close by.

I was getting paranoid!

Shane was miles away, patrolling or hanging out with his friends in the bar. All alone, because I'd left him and gone to see my cousin and best friend. I was also feeling alone. I wanted to put on my helmet and run back to his arms and cry my soul out on his lap. I wanted to tell him everything until all the pain ended, and I felt safe.

"Again with those daydreaming eyes," Jessica complained, snapping me out of my thoughts. "Tomorrow, you can go back to your wolf. Tonight, you're mine."

CHAPTER TWENTY-THREE
SHANE

I FOLLOWED ANNA and her friend to a diner. After they went in and sat at a table, I covered my head with my hood and went in. I sat far enough to not be seen but close enough to be able to listen to them.

I asked for coffee and pie and concentrated on their conversation. Everything I heard and witnessed so far made me believe that Anna wasn't a spy, but she had many secrets. In fact, I learned more about her in the past hour than in all our time together. At least, in what concerned her weekend activities and acquaintances.

I was relieved. I could not deny that. Anna was just looking for a friend, and her visits to the hospital were because of her mutation. She was worried about her final transformation.

The fact that my mate didn't trust me enough to share all those things with me bothered me more than I wanted to.

I could help her and explain anything she needed to know. She didn't need to be worried about the possibility of hurting people or having bloodlust. She would just need to drink from me. But she didn't know that.

I needed to talk to her and wait for her to open up. She was planning to let her friend come and meet me. Therefore, I thought that she was making progress in allowing me into her life.

Then there was the fact of hiding that her father had been a pureblood. My master would have to know about it, and my contacts needed to be informed, so my suspicions would be answered.

If she was who I thought she was, destiny had a twisted sense of humor.

I calmed all my thoughts and tried to listen to their conversation. It was now about Jessica's dreams. They were eating pie and ice cream while sharing worries and thoughts.

"Have you found your vampire yet?" Anna asked as she put a piece of pie in her mouth.

"No, I'm still searching."

"It wasn't that guy?"

"Who?" she asked, raising an eyebrow.

"That blond one back there."

"No. It wasn't. But I was feeling hot enough with him. You just ruined for me a perfectly good night of sex!" she complained.

"You mean five minutes of sex because that was not a night of sex, for sure," Annabel teased her.

She growled and then pouted again. "Five minutes is better than nothing."

"I wouldn't be so sure."

"You're annoying."

"Yes, it must be annoying to have me as your conscience. I guess I was away for far too long, and there was no one left to stop you from doing stupid things like this."

"Sure, Mom," she said, completely ignoring Anna's lecture and eating the ice cream while staring at the void.

Anna chuckled. "'I've missed you, Jessie!'"

"I may have missed you, too, depending on if you are still going to pester me about my choice of sexual partners or not."

"You're a big girl. Just be careful."

"I'm always careful."

"So…why weren't you home with the boys?"

"I couldn't stand Jason complaining all the time. He's being a stuck-up brat since you gave him the keys to the castle," she grumbled, and Anna smiled, amused. "Are they missing me?"

"Only of your cooking," Anna said, making her friend roll

her eyes and mutter something I didn't understand. "How are the headaches?"

"They're okay. I had my shot of vampire blood the other day."

"So, what were you doing in the back alley of the bar?"

"Trying to have sex. A girl has her needs," she informed her with a piercing pair of blue eyes. Jessie was funny. I had to give her credit. "I was expecting you tomorrow. Or did I mess up the days?

"Today is Saturday."

"Already? I haven't slept well for a while."

"Nightmares?" Annabel wondered.

"Erotic dreams."

Annabel almost choked on her ice cream. Her friend Jessie giggled. "Please spare me the details."

"Sure, they are way too hot for you to hear about, anyway." Then she pouted and sighed with gloomy eyes.

Anna must be used to her mood swings because she let her relax, waiting for her to talk about whatever she needed to.

Jessie stroked the blonde hair away from her face and sighed again. "I—I'm losing hope in finding him."

"Maybe it's just a dream."

"It's never just a dream. I know it was real, from a previous life. And I—feel the need to find him. As if...time is running out." She was truly sad by then.

Anna looked at her with a sympathetic face. She knew Jessica was unhappy and feeling lonely like I did. Apparently, her soulmate was somewhere out there, and all she had were pieces of scattered dreams about him. Dreams she thought were past-life memories.

I didn't envy her powers or her dreams. And I knew Anna couldn't help her. She could only keep secret her escapes into vampire bars in search of her tall, blond vampire soulmate. And she could not even come clean with her and tell her that he could no longer exist.

Jessica's dreams, if memories, were old; he had probably already died of old age or been killed. After all, when a soulmate dies, the other grows old and weak and eventually passes away. Eternity ends when a supernatural loses his other half after the bonding.

If I were to lose Annabel, I wouldn't have any other reason to keep living. My grief would weaken me and trigger my aging process. Eventually, I would die of old age or sadness. Dying of a broken heart was real to supernatural beings.

Jessica's dreams were pointless, and I actually felt sorry for her. I could relate to her pain. I had felt it for a long time before finding Anna. And I didn't have the burden of knowing what she would look like or her race; I had no memories of us together in a past life. I could only understand a bit of Jessica's pain, not all of it. It would be torture for her to have those memories and experience those dreams without being able to do anything about them.

Anna put her hand over Jessica's, and I felt my love for Anna beat inside my chest. She had a concerned look on her face. She didn't want her friend to feel miserable. I didn't want Anna to be upset either.

"But enough about me." Jessica's voice woke me from my own thoughts. She amazed me by smiling and chasing her sadness away, and then she made me smile because I heard my name again. "I want to know about Shane. What's he like?"

"I've already told you everything about Shane," Anna complained, scratching her neck again.

I smirked over my coffee cup at that. She was probably feeling a force pulling her to me like I was. Too bad she didn't want to talk about me. I would have loved to hear what she had to say about me to her best friend.

"Humor me, so I can feel a bit more jealous of you," Jessica dared her.

I liked her already. She made my day. I was curious to know what Anna was going to tell her.

"Shane's sexy, gorgeous, sensitive, and funny. He's a great listener. He makes me feel safe and complete. He's also a great fighter, and everybody respects him. Summing up, he's a great person."

Anna had a soft smile on her lips and dreamy eyes while speaking about me. I was drooling like a fool at every word she used to describe me.

"Okay, fine, that's enough. It's like he brainwashed you!"

"What?" Anna asked, the spoon in her mouth.

"That bond stuff is serious mojo! But I'm so jealous! You were not even looking for your mate, and you found him. And me, here all alone, eating ice cream and pie to drown my sorrow and lack of sex."

"Hey! I'm here with you!"

"Pfft! You're here today. Tomorrow, you'll go back in your mate's arms, continuing to have endless sex."

"Jesus! Stop talking about sex. You're getting paranoid!"

"And you just got all red! Guilty much?"

"Of what?" Anna's eyes flew wide open, as though she had no idea what Jessica was accusing her of.

"Of never giving me any details," she explained, lowering her voice.

Anna rolled her eyes, and Jessica pouted.

Anna sighed, grabbed her phone, and stared at the screen.

I hadn't texted her or phoned again that night. I was following her, and she would most probably feel neglected by me.

I had told her I was in a meeting, so she didn't try to call me back, either, even when she stared quietly at the phone like she wanted to.

The only reason why I wasn't continually texting her was that I was there, next to her, listening to her words and deciphering her sighs and long stares at the phone.

"Anna," Jessica called. "Is everything okay?"

"Yes. Everything is…fine."

"How long have you been away from him?"

"Since this morning."

"Wow! That is some scary shit!"

Anna frowned, as though surprised by her language as much as I was. I was also intrigued by her words.

"Mate bond is like a powerful drug," she explained. "I've been reading about it in my ancestors' grimoire. It's a witch book of shadows," she clarified.

"I know what that is. You're my best friend and a witch. I'm bound to know what a grimoire is!"

"Fine, now let me finish. There it says that a mate bond works like a drug. The more you use it, the more you need it. And you've been there, like, forever so—I'm just saying."

"I'm not following you at all," Anna complained, pressing her finger to her forehead.

She was probably feeling a headache coming on. It wasn't normal for her to be like that. She looked pale and distracted.

"Gosh, Anna! You acting weird and sad because you have been away from him for a couple of hours, and you didn't even drink from him. Imagine what will happen when you do! Not to mention what the sex will be like—wow! Fireworks and an out-of-body experience!"

Jessica seemed excited and happy about that, giggling as she stared at Anna with mischievous eyes and a smile.

"It's already like that," Anna declared, pulling the plate of pie to her, eating it alone, and making Jessica complain.

I smiled at her answer, proud of making her feel like that. She made me feel like that, too. It was perfect, even without sharing my blood with her and we hadn't marked each other yet.

"If it's that good, why are you like that?"

"Like what?"

"All grumpy and moody! It's like you aren't getting any!"

"Oh, trust me, I'm getting plenty."

"Five-minutes plenty?"

"No, of course not. More like whole nights and barely having time to rest."

"Oh, that sounds fun! Are you catching up on everything you didn't do while you were a monk?"

"Do you want to keep breathing?" Anna menaced, and I almost chuckled out loud.

Eavesdropping was entertaining, especially for a supernatural with super-hearing. But Anna would kill me if she found out.

"See what I mean? You're touchy and grumpy! You can't handle a joke."

"I can handle a joke just fine. I'm just hungry," she explained, eating pie.

"Do you want to go out and find us some evil vampires to punch?" Jessie proposed with a wicked smile.

Anna snorted. "Don't tempt me. I really need to sleep tonight."

"Oh right, because you aren't sleeping when you're with your mate. Just rub it in my face, will you?"

"I'm almost regretting coming to find you and spending time with you," Anna declared. "You really are in a terrible mood."

Jessica twisted a strand of her blonde hair around her finger. "No, I'm not. I'm just teasing you and trying to get you to tell me the dirty details. Or maybe all that blood loss from the vampire feeding on me left me grumpy and hungry. Do you want to order another ice cream? We could share."

The young woman seemed excited. I had no idea what it was with women and ice cream.

Anna sighed as she rubbed her temples. "Can we go home? I need to rest. I'm feeling tired."

"If you want. It's not as if you seem happy to be here with me."

"Don't be like that. I'm just…feeling different tonight. But we'll have plenty of other nights to go out and have long conversations about our mates."

"Don't try to humor me. I'm delighted you found Shane. For the past month, you've been much happier and calmer. Shane does that to you. I'm sure I'm going to like him a lot and give him a reward for taming you, so—" She didn't finish her sentence because Anna threw a piece of pie at her face. Jessica blew some cream from her mouth and, with the napkin, cleaned the rest of her nose and left eye. "Not funny!"

Anna chuckled and added, "He didn't tame me. I'm going to the bathroom, and then we can leave."

That was my cue to get up, place the money on the table, and leave the diner. I needed to get back to town as soon as possible and talk with my king.

Anna would go back to her fortress home, and I would have to unfold some pending mysteries. For that, I also needed to talk to James. He had something that I needed to show the king.

CHAPTER TWENTY-FOUR

ANNA

SUNDAY MORNING, I woke up early, grabbed my stuff, and went back as fast as I could to Shane's house. I also had to attend the training at three o'clock, so I had to get back there anyway. However, I was missing Shane and feeling miserable because he hadn't phoned or texted me back all night.

When I got back home, Shane wasn't there, and our bed was untouched.

He hadn't slept at home and wasn't answering his phone, either. It went directly to his voicemail. There could be a perfectly plausible explanation for his absence, so I tried not to freak out.

While I waited for his return, I spent my time cleaning and haunting the house like a ghost.

Training hour arrived, and still no word from Shane.

When I arrived at the training ground, my group was already warming up. I joined in and practiced the fighting techniques for a half hour. I was a bit distracted. I should have fed before coming there, but I didn't and was regretting it.

There were some asshole vampires in training. I would typically win without breaking a sweat, but I was weaker that day.

Once we had a break, I talked to the trainers, Duncan and Samuel. They were part of Shane's enforcer team and usually worked out together. Yet, they hadn't seen him all weekend and had no idea of where my mate was.

Shane's absence worried me. But everybody assured me that there we no problems with the other packs. My mate was probably with the Royal Family.

The training proceeded with one on one combat. The vampire I was fighting got mad each time he lost, but I was not expecting him to play dirty after I won again. He didn't take his loss well and, as a result, grabbed some dirt from the floor, blinding me. He took that chance to throw a punch. I fell back with the impact as the ground swirled under me.

With a burning sensation in my eyes and lightheadedness, I gasped when hands surrounded my neck and crushed my head against the ground.

I fought for air as his body pressed on my stomach and his hands squeezed my neck. We were practicing, but this asshole was pushing his luck. The worst was that I was too weak to move him off me. Soon, I felt my hands losing strength and darkness taking over.

The hands left my throat, and his body weight disappeared as a loud blast woke me from my torpor. I sat up and sucked deep breathes.

Opening my watering eyes, I witnessed a few falling trees while Shane grabbed my attacker by the neck—wolf teeth and claws out— and growled at the scared vampire.

"I will bite your neck off the next time you try a stunt like that on my mate," he menaced, making my heart beat faster with love.

New tears welled my eyes, this time not because of the dirt but because Shane protected me.

He would kill anyone who tried to harm me.

I would kill anyone who tried to harm him.

When you're a child, you believe everything you need is your parents. When you grow up, you understand that parents aren't enough. There's a type of loneliness inside your soul that can't be filled with family and friendship. Until you find the one that can either save or destroy you, consume the loneliness, or increase it—your bliss in the shape of a person.

I watched in silenced awe as the other wolves and vampires surrounded Shane, so he would let go of Peter, the vampire who'd played dirty. As far as I was concerned, the idiot deserved to be scolded.

After a bit of shouting and growls, Shane released Peter and walked to me. Lowering down, he grabbed me in his arms and strolled away as I secured my arms around his neck and gazed at him with adoration.

My mate entered one of the cabins that served as a locker room and storage for training material.

Setting me down on some training mattresses, he caressed my face, and I realized that he was back to his human form—no wolf teeth or claws.

My heart almost stopped beating with the look of devotion in his eyes. He had said plenty of times that I was the most precious thing to him in the world. As stubborn as I might be, I knew I felt the same for him.

"Babe, are you okay? Why aren't your bruises healing?" His voice was soft, and his fingers brushed the skin on my neck.

I cringed at his touch and rubbed my eyes. Shane got up, and I watch him find a towel that he wet and used to help me clean my eyes.

Knelt beside me, Shane inquired, "Anna, are you hurt? Can you speak, or did he held you too tight?" He clenched his jaw. "I can't believe the nerve of that guy! I should go back and use him as a punching bag!"

I grabbed his hands and shook my head. Clearing my throat, I tried to speak. "D-don't." I gulped and gazed at my trembling hands.

Shane must have noticed the same thing. "Are you cold or frightened?" He didn't wait for me to reply. Taking my arms, he placed them around his torso and surrounded his jacket around me. "Just warm up against me." He let go just enough to kiss the top of my head before securing me inside his embrace. "I'm afraid that I might kill Pete if you let me go." He breathed in. "I might even punch Duncan and Samuel for letting this happen."

Before I could even say anything, he added, "And don't even say that it was your fault. It wasn't. That idiot has been acting like a jerk for a while now. His male ego can't stand being beaten by a woman. But what he did is not to be taken lightly. He's going to be punished and removed from the training team until he learns some manners."

I nodded, relaxing with the sound of his voice and the warmth of his body.

"Are you thirsty?"

I shook my head and inhaled his scent. Oxygen deprivation must have damaged my head because I had planned to scold him for being unreachable and disappearing on me. Now that he was there with me, nothing else mattered.

Yet, the heart wants what the heart wants.

"Where were you? Why didn't you pick up your phone?" I fisted both hands to the back of his shirt. "Do you know how worried I was because I couldn't reach you? I even came back home earlier." I sniffled. "You didn't sleep at home."

"How worried were you? And does that mean that you can't be apart from me, not even for a day?"

I pouted and tilted my head back to stare at my mate, who seemed to be fetching for compliments and reassuring love confessions. "Do you feel proud of yourself for making me worry about you?"

He shook his head.

I sneered at him. "Where did you sleep?"

"I didn't."

I huffed.

Shane clarified with a mischievous smirk, "I've been at the palace, and my phone ran out of battery. But I'm here now, and you don't need to be upset."

"I'm not upset," I grumbled.

He snickered. "Cute."

I squinted at him. "What's cute?"

"You, when you pout."

"I'm not pouting."

"Is that a jealous attack, then?"

I shook my head. "I trust you, but I was worried."

"I'm fine," he guarantees, lowering down his head and kissing my lips. "I missed you too."

My chest hurt with the vulnerability and love that I felt for him. Tears rushed to my eyes, but I refused to cry.

Why would I cry?

For loving him? For missing him? For being almost choked to death?

My vision blurred, and I think I lost consciousness for a few seconds because Shane was calling my name with a distressed voice and his hand held my face while he shook my head.

I grabbed his hand, so he stopped shaking me. "I'm okay. I'm just tired."

His eyes swept down my face and stopped on my neck. "You're not okay. You look pale, and your bruises aren't healing."

I smirked at his observation. "I was being stubborn and didn't feed."

"You haven't eaten?"

"Blood. I didn't drink it because ..." I gulped and closed my eyes for a few seconds. "It's silly. I know I don't need to kill to feed. But when we come of age, we become more bloodthirsty, and I'm afraid that I might lose my..."

"You're strong-willed and mindful of others. You save small insects from drowning, and you rescue snails and put them back in the yard when you find them in the lettuce."

I gazed at him with a confused expression.

"I know you wouldn't take a life unless it was necessary," he explained.

"No one..." I bit down on my lower lip. "I mean, some people aren't born evil, but they become evil."

"You're not going to become evil."

"Why not?"

"Because you have me."

I chuckled at his bold statement.

He pushed his fingertip against my nose to get my attention. "I'll save you from your darkness, and you'll save me from mine. Deal?"

Fluttering my eyelashes at him, I nodded in understanding.

"Also, there's something you might not know, but werewolf blood is particularly tasty between mates. It's also very nurturing, and you'll just have to drink from me a few times per month to satisfy your craving for blood."

"How do you know that?"

"There have been plenty of cases where vampires and werewolves were fated mates. Even if they were frowned upon and the majority of couples didn't last long, the ones who bonded discovered that their mates' blood made them stronger and satisfied their craving for blood."

"Oh!" I frowned. "Are you sure I won't need to drink from anyone else?"

"No."

"But, won't you get weak if I feed on you frequently?"

"You won't need to feed often. Wolf blood is different. You'll just need small amounts of it." He kissed my forehead. "I'll let you bite me."

"But...but...I shouldn't drink from the source," I explained.

Drinking Shane's blood meant I'd mark him.

I gazed at him and realized that he seemed attentive to my expressions.

"Would it be so bad?" he asked.

I shook my head, realizing that I wanted to mark him and make him mine forever. I was weary of all the secrets between us. Even so, there were parts of me that I wasn't ready to share with him.

Not just that, Shane had no idea that I might be able to tap into his darkest secrets and fears if I drank from him.

"Shane, I want to, but biting you means that I'll…"

"I can shut off all my thoughts from you if you want," Shane said.

"Is that even possible?"

He nodded.

I frowned. "How do you know you'll need to do that with me? Normal vampires and hybrids can't see memories when they feed."

"All mates share a mental link when they mark each other," Shane replied.

I nibbled on the inside of my lip. Gulping, I decided to open up a bit more. "My father was a pureblood. My brother could read people's thoughts when he fed from someone." I averted my eyes. "I never tried, so I don't know if I'm able to or not."

"Even if you don't want to drink from me, you need to feed today. Let's go home."

I grabbed his collar and prevented him from moving. "Do you know all that because you used to date Sasha? Does that mean that she didn't have access to your memories?"

The princess was a pureblood vampire. She could read his mind if she drank from him. He said that some vampires feed on werewolves. The idea of Sasha claiming Shane upset me more than I wanted. Still, I knew I couldn't control his past. I wasn't even born when they were together.

"Anna." His voice ceased my train of thought, and I gave him my full attention.

Shane's furrowed eyebrows made me believe he was going to protest about my sudden jealousy attack. Instead, he explained, "I can assure you that she never had access to my memories. I wasn't her mate, nor was I her blood bag. I'll let you drink from me because you're my mate. I love you, and I want you to be strong and happy."

Tears rolled down my cheeks without permission.

He lowered down his head and pressed his lips against my salty skin. "Will you let me feed you? Or do I have to get you some blood, so you feel better?"

"Is it true?" I asked, feeling extremely happy about his concerned voice and eyes.

"What, honey?"

"That the sex is even better if I bite you?"

"Oh, Anna!" he said with a huge grin, " for me, it's already the best."

My lower stomach exploded with lust. "Will you bite me back?"

"If you want."

"I want."

"We should probably go home then," he whispered with a husky, sexy voice.

"Maybe we should," I whispered, trailing my index down his chest.

I felt the softness of his lips against mine. "This isn't the place to mark you. I'll take you home and take care of you."

He took me in his arms again, and we got out of there.

* * *

I dozed off while he was driving us home. It felt like home, so I was calling it our home.

My body felt the soft contact of a mattress. Opening my eyes, I watched as Shane grinned at me and gave me a gentle peck.

"Did I fell asleep?"

"Yes." He stroked my hair. "Did you sleep anything last night?"

I shook my head. "I wanted to get back home as soon as possible."

He nodded and kissed my forehead. "I'm glad you think this is your home too."

"You're my home."

He grinned. "Are you this clingy because I saved you today or because you realized you can't live without me?"

"Both," I whispered. I thought carefully at his words. "Wait! Did you just call me clingy?"

He covered his mouth as if he had the words slip inadvertently. "My bad. I'm the clingy one. You're the amazing, sexy, and romantic one."

"I wouldn't love you so much if you didn't show me how much you wanted me in your life. I tend to run away when I …"

He pressed two fingers against my lips. "I know."

I shut up my mouth and my thoughts.

His fingers left my mouth, and he straightened up. "I'm going to run a hot bath for you. You need to warm up."

All I could answer was "Okay" in a feeble whisper.

Moments after, I relaxed in bed while listening to Shane in the bathroom.

A warm bath sounded nice if I could keep myself conscious. I was so hungry! Tired and hungry was a terrible combination, especially if I was planning to bite and mark my mate and then have a long and amazing romantic and sexual experience with him.

The mattress caved when Shane sat beside me. "Let's get you out of these clothes."

"You shouldn't take advantage of me when I'm like this," I tried to joke.

I won a smile and a kiss.

I sighed with lust as he lifted me from the bed. I wrapped myself around him, and he carried me to the bathroom. "I love you so much," I said, feeling emotional and more vulnerable than usual, probably because of the hunger.

"I love you, too, honey," he replied. "You'll feel better in a moment. After you bite me."

It was hard to keep my eyes open as Shane did his best to remove my clothes and help me walk to the bathroom.

When my body was submerged in hot water, I shivered on contact. It was then that I finally noticed how cold I was.

Shane joined me inside the bathtub and reached for my body. I bit my lip harder, gulping with the overwhelming sensation of our naked bodies touching. Sadly, I could barely keep my eyes open and move my hands. I was exhausted.

Then I felt his wrist against my mouth, opening my lips and dripping blood inside. It was sweet, and I lost my breath when I felt it go down to my stomach.

Abruptly, a rush of adrenaline hit me.

I opened my eyes wide and stared at Shane's sweet blue eyes. *I was famished.* My fangs came out, and I bit into his flesh. At that point, everything went black, and I fell inside myself like I had just fallen into an abyss. Suddenly, my heart wanted to escape through my mouth; awful cramps took over my stomach. I think my entire body shook, and my limbs went all stiff. *It was scary.* I found myself inside the bar where I've first seen Shane. To my surprise, I watched myself come into the building and heard Shane's thoughts. I realized that I was inside Shane's memories of the night we first met. It was incredible. I was inside his head, his thoughts, and I could experience it all as if I was in a movie, a three-dimensional movie, where I could hear and feel anything he heard and felt on that night. I experienced his thoughts, his awestruck stare, the feelings that burst inside him, the awakening of his wolf that screamed *mate* when he sat next to me and smelled me.

All that was amazing, unreal, and breathtaking. I realized that I had felt most of the things he had. I had understood that something connected us, that he was *special.*

Blackness hit me again when I swirled back from his thoughts and into the bathtub. I opened my eyes and saw that his wrist was no longer against my mouth. Also, Shane looked concerned.

I sighed and licked my lower lip with my tongue, feeling much better and stronger. Actually, I was feeling another kind of hunger. Lust shot across my body, tingling my skin and making me shiver. My fangs grew out again, my eyes shifted to purple, and my skin became paler because I was changing to my vampire form.

"Lust is a side effect," Shane said, caressing my face.

"You let me see your memories."

"Yes, but they were wonderful memories. Are you mad?"

I shook my head. "Can you decide what you want me to see?"

"I can try. I just have to think about it when I'm feeding you or not think of anything, so you don't see my thoughts. Did you experienced how I felt when I first saw you?"

"Yes."

"Good. I wanted you to understand how I knew you were my soulmate."

I probed, "Are you mad?"

"About what?"

"For only telling you today that my father was a pureblood."

"I can partly understand why you kept it a secret. However, mates don't have secrets after they mark each other. Or, at least, they shouldn't."

His words were clear. I needed to come clean.

"Let's not ruin the moment," he whispered, kissing my cheek and drowning his head in the crook of my neck. "There's nothing that you can say that will make me want you less. So...don't worry, okay?"

"I don't like to keep secrets," I whispered in a sad voice, my heart clenching. "I..."

"I wasn't lecturing you. I was trying to explain to you that it's okay. I'm not going to pressure you anymore. We'll have this conversation some other day. Now, all I need to know is if you're feeling better. Are you?"

I nodded. "I'm feeling a lot stronger, and I'm no longer feeling cold."

"Good."

"I...drank from you, so...I sort of marked you, didn't I?"

It was his time to nod. "Do you feel me inside your head?"

I searched inside of me for what he was saying. At first, I wasn't feeling anything different, then I felt him. I saw the memories from the night we had met pulsing in my brain as if they were my own memories. Imprinted in me also was the happiness he felt when he realized I was his mate. It consumed me now. But I also felt his loneliness, the weight of the years he had waited for me, and the fantastic feeling of love after the first fascinating impression of recognition swept along his body and soul. All that was inside me now. Tears welled up in my eyes because it was overwhelming.

"Are you okay?" His voice sounded worried when he talked. He brushed his fingers on my face, leveling my head to stare at him.

I didn't answer; I simply snuggled him closer and laid my head against his shoulder. I closed my eyes and waited for the emotion to calm down.

"Does it bother you?"

"What?" I asked.

"How much...I need you and love you."

"No."

"So why are you sad?"

"I'm not sad. I'm...at a loss for words. There's nothing I can say that shows how happy I am to be your mate and how the loneliness you had to endure makes me wish I had been born sooner."

"I wanted you to understand," he said, caressing my hair and rubbing my back, making my body relax, "that we are meant to be together. And you don't need to be afraid of... Annabel, I'll never leave you, and I'll never hurt you."

"Okay," I whispered, aware that Shane's heart was beating fast, and he was feeling anxious.

"You're special, honey. You were already special to me, but I had no idea of how much more special you were. My heart is overwhelmed by it."

"What are you talking about?" I asked, raising my head to face him.

"I understand why it's so hard for you to trust people. I can't blame you for that. I didn't want your life to be so difficult before we met. I have to thank the gods because you've survived this long, and...you found me. You could have been killed, and then…I would have never met you. I'd have never known how wonderful and amazing it is to love you."

I smiled, tears falling rolling down my face. "You need to stop talking," I whispered, trying to conceal my shaking voice because I wasn't crying in pain; I was crying with love. I shivered, and he wrapped me tighter, pressing our bodies until I almost couldn't breathe. I chuckled, brushing my cheek to his. "Can someone die from an excess of love?"

"I don't know. I hope not," he breathed, kissing my shoulder and softly nibbling my ear.

"Shane, I don't want to ruin this moment with confusing confessions and regrets. I want to taste you again and make love to you."

CHAPTER TWENTY-FIVE

SHANE

HAVING ANNABEL BITE ME was erotic beyond words. We were still in the bathtub, kissing but mostly talking. I needed to bite her and complete the mating bond, but I had time for that. My blood was making her say the most adorable things. Mate blood will do that. It will also make her feel connected and more vulnerable to my questions. I didn't want to use that to get information from her, but I was feeling exceedingly happy since she had agreed to complete our bond by marking each other.

I had that uncontrollable fear of being dumped and forgotten when her time here ended. She wasn't giving any hint about whether she would stay for the next year or leave the school and me in the process, especially because she had a whole different life outside of her teaching career. I doubted that teaching was even her real job. Maybe it was a cover-up job or hobby. So, hearing from her that she wanted to be marked was the best news I'd ever gotten in my life, up to that precise moment. However, I needed her to be sure about it.

"Anna, when I mark you, we'll be connected forever. I'll always know where you are, and you'll be able to talk to me and access my thoughts, memories, and feelings. Are you sure you want this?"

"Yes," she agreed. "I couldn't reach you today. I almost went mad. I want to know where you are, always. I've missed you terribly!"

"I've missed you, too. But you're the one who wants to spend your weekends away from me," I reminded her. "Are you sure that we can merge our minds and souls?"

She averted her gaze and bit her bottom lip. Her hand

caressed my shoulder pensively.

"Well..." She broke the silence after breathing deeply. "I went to talk to my cousin."

I waited patiently for her to continue. That wasn't useful information; more like an excuse.

"I went to tell him," she added. The vibration of her voice gave away her anxiety.

I frowned, curious about what she'd told him. I remembered they were having some kind of discussion, and he wasn't happy about it.

Was the discussion about me? Did she tell him about me?

They seemed—close. Maybe he was against her dating a pureblood werewolf. Maybe he didn't believe we were mates.

The suspense was killing me.

"What did you tell him?"

"I told him that I won't go back. That I want to stay here longer."

"Just longer?" I asked between bliss and sadness.

I wanted her to stay forever and not just "longer." But I would follow her anywhere. I had come to terms with that. I had thought about that a lot the past week. I would not let her leave me or use the excuse of not wanting to stay here with me to go away. I couldn't blame her if life here was not as attractive as in the big cities. She was young and needed to see the world, feel the freedom of traveling, and know new cultures and ways of living.

"Yes, longer. Would you come with me if I asked you to?" she demanded, her eyes shining while she appeared to be holding her breath. "I don't want to be apart from you, but I can't stay here forever. There are things I need to do."

I paused intentionally, just staring into her eyes. She seemed worried by my answer. I was just happy for her to want to include me in her life.

"I'll go wherever you want me to go with you. I won't ever leave you. You're mine, Anna. We belong together."

She breathed out, apparently relieved. I was not so stubborn as to want to force her to do what I wanted or be where I wanted to live. I'd lived in this place for decades. I'd protected and paid my debt to the royal family of vampires a long time ago. I stayed because it was where I had my friends, and they were like my family.

Now, Anna was my family.

From now on, I could actually have a family. She would be my family, my life, my dreams, and my whole world.

"I'm not asking you to leave your pack and your king. I like it here. I feel at home."

Her words made me smile. I loved hearing that she felt at home. She was at home, so much more than she could know.

"But?" I inquired, knowing that there was a 'but'.

"I have stuff to do before—"

I was intrigued by her reluctance to share what that stuff was, but I was getting used to it. "Will you eventually tell me everything?"

"Yes," she said with a long sigh that captured how difficult it was for her to keep secrets from me.

"Is that stuff related to your parents' death?" I inquired.

"Yes." She bit her lip and looked at her hands, eventually breathing deeply.

I paused for a moment, wanting to tell her things, to ask her a million questions, but I didn't. I still needed to make sure the results were correct before I could share them with her. But my heart knew already, and I could only stare at her, overwhelmed and feeling amazed by the weirdness of destiny.

If things did not happen the way they had, she would have never existed. I would have never met her.

"Are you mad at me?" she asked, probably intrigued by my silence.

I wasn't mad, just mystified by all that I had found out. I was also in love with her, even more than before, which was amazingly impressive. I thought I could not love her more than I already did; I guess I was wrong.

I replied to her in a husky voice, "Not mad, Anna. I simply don't want to lose you."

She got pensive for a while. I noticed she was fighting against her rationality to tell me something or share a little about her life, feelings, and secrets.

"When my parents died, I thought my life was over. Everything I knew was broken and destroyed. But then I found a reason to keep existing. It gave me purpose to walk among the living. You see, my parents waited almost one hundred years to have my brother and me," she whispered, clearly emotional. She laid her head on my shoulder and sucked in a breath to calm down. "They waited for the mentalities to change, so we could be safe and not feel like outcasts. And then they gave their lives to protect us."

"What do you mean, Anna?" I asked, troubled by her words.

She had told me that her parents were killed by a racist organization that came inside their house and executed them. She told me that she and her brother weren't at home, so they were lucky to have survived. However, by the way she was talking, it was like she knew exactly what happened.

Had she witnessed the killing?

That would scar her for life.

"My dad was a bit paranoid when it came to safety. He had cameras everywhere. T-they…tortured them trying to find out where we were," she said near tears.

Swallowing hard, I gently brought her face to mine and asked,

"Did you watch the tapes?"

I knew the answer already.

"Yes..." Tears rolled down her cheeks.

I felt like a punch had landed in my stomach. Watching her family get tortured and killed was a feeling I knew way too well. There were no words that could be said to lessen her pain.

Holding her tight, I stroked her wet hair, feeling her sobs against my chest.

"He thinks we are abominations. We had to change our names because he chased us, and he killed the people who helped us hide. He created a serum to kill hybrids," she explained, trying to calm herself down by breathing deeply several times.

My mate was venting, and I wanted her to tell me everything weighing on her soul.

"My brother was hit by the poisoned darts when he used his own body to protect me. The monster that chases us wants to kill all who are like me. I'm not the only one whose life he ruined. And he will want to hurt you, too, because we *shouldn't* be together. This whole town is a capital sin for him. Its mere existence is blasphemy."

"Yes, I know a lot who think like that, too. We are used to defending ourselves. We aren't afraid of people like the ones who killed your family. You'll be safe here," I told her, to calm her down and give her comfort. "Don't you think it's time for you to stop running?"

"I'm not running anymore," she said, raising her head to face me. "I stopped running. Now he's the one that runs from me."

Her words came out sober and dark. She had a certainty in her voice that made me shiver.

"I'll kill him and all who get in my way to stop me from doing that. I got tired of running and being afraid. *He* is the one who should be afraid. When I catch him, I will rip his heart out and then cut his head off after I stare into his eyes and remind him about killing my parents."

"Anna." My voice must have trembled because I could feel her wish for vengeance so deep inside her heart that it made me feel scared. Revenge could be terrible and wouldn't necessarily be satisfied after it was achieved. She could lose her soul in the process, and I could lose her. She would be reckless and driven by the feeling of hate. "Vengeance can make people blind. There is much more to life than that."

"It's not vengeance. It's justice."

"Not if you plan to be the judge, jury, and executioner."

"I plan to stop him from killing others," she said calmly.

Her eyes were static and focused. She wasn't crying anymore. I felt scared for the part of her that carried those feelings of vengeance and hate.

What was done to her and her family wasn't right. Still, now that I had found her, I wasn't ready to let her go and be killed in the name of justice. I wanted to keep her safe and close to me. I wanted to make her forget everything terrible that had happened to her and prevent her from being killed.

She was mine, and I was hers.

Couldn't the love she has for me be enough to keep her living?

Clenching my jaw, I gripped my fingers a bit harder in her flesh. "And if he kills you?"

She sighed and leaned her forehead against mine, closing her eyes in the process. "I'm not planning to die, not now that I found you. I'm...just trying to help others, to make a difference. It's not hate that drives me. It's not," she said, trying to underscore her words, so I would believe her. "Of course, I cannot forgive the person who killed my parents. Neither can I dishonor my parents' sacrifice. They gave their lives, so I could live. It isn't hate. We can't let people spread hate like that, kill others and not face the consequences. Someone must make the difference and help the ones who are weak and powerless. So you don't need to worry because I'm not on a suicide journey."

"Good," I said with relief. She was mature for her age. I couldn't help but be proud of her being my soulmate. But knowing who her father was, I shouldn't have expected less from her. "Because I'm not planning on letting you die. You're the most important thing to me. I'm not going to leave you. And you can trust me to keep your secrets, fears, hopes, and dreams. I love you more than my own life," I whispered near her lips. She still had her eyes closed, but I could feel her calm breath against me.

We were still naked in the bathtub, and I figured we should probably get out before the water got cold. Besides, there was something I needed to finish.

* * *

ANNA

I stared at Shane, overwhelmed by his words. They were sweetly spoken and breathtaking. I'd never known I could want someone as I wanted him or that love could be like that. It was like now my sole reason to live was that he existed. And even if this screwed things up, the world seemed amazingly coherent and perfect.

I didn't have time to reply to him because he took me from the bath, bridal style, and wrapped me in a fluffy towel. I was feeling much better after I'd fed, but I was confused by his actions.

"Weren't you supposed to mark me?" I asked, unsure if he had changed his mind after what I had told and shared with him.

He smiled and brushed my lips with his, sniffing and licking where my shoulder and neck met. It sent a shiver of pleasure across my body and soul. I liked that a lot!

"Yes," he said huskily. "We'll be on dry land for that," he joked, getting a towel to dry himself. "Are you feeling better?"

"Much better." I sighed, stretching my arms up in the air and smiling. He tasted fantastic, and I knew I had a silly smile on my face because it had been amazing to see his memories and talk to him.

He grabbed me, surprising me, and I let out a startled squeal. He took me to bed, where he crawled on top of me. I felt my body relax against the mattress. It was much more comfortable and dry. I smirked at him, noticing how beautiful he looked: wet hair, naughty eyes, gentle smile, and a rough beard. I liked that on him. He was sexy and irresistible. I bit my lower lip, staring at his plump and dreamy lips.

"Are you going to bite me now?" I asked, breathless. I felt impatient and excited. I wanted to be marked. I wanted to be part of him like he was now part of me.

"No, I'm going to make you scream from pleasure before that."

I giggled.

Shane's expression changed to sober as he explained, "I just want to kiss you a bit more. After I bite you, I can get a bit out of control and…savage. I won't be able to control my wolf. So, don't get scared, and feel free to punch me if I get too wild."

"Don't worry, I'll be fine." I pulled him into my arms to kiss and tangle my tongue with his. "I'm still a bit savage myself," I confessed, feeling my body burn with lust.

I longed for him. I needed his hands on me, and our lips locked, gasping for air.

It was a bit of a challenge to get rid of the towels and rub our naked bodies together. He was already aroused, and I was wet and needy enough to open my legs and feel him slide inside me, making me sigh with pleasure and relief. Our lips together, moving at the same pace, our skins burning against each other and our mouths eagerly kissing—nothing seemed more perfect. I was all feverish and ready to come a few moments later. But I didn't because he turned me on my stomach, gave me a slight tap on my butt before spreading my legs, and slid inside from behind.

It felt even better, like my insides were ready to burst into flames and consume me. One of his hands was grabbing my breast, and the other was on my hip, drawing me against his hard, big shaft. Then the hand that was on my hip trailed up my back until it grabbed my hair and pulled it from my left shoulder. He left a trail of kisses on my neck and upper back. And then he made some feral growls, some husky and sensual growls near my skin, making my body shiver in delight and leaving me breathless with lust. Next, his teeth sank in between my neck and shoulder, in my trapezius muscle, making me gasp at first and then come once, twice, three times while he was still plunged inside me, holding his bite.

I could feel his teeth in my flesh, my blood dripping from his mouth, but it was erotic, sensual, and pleasant. I came a fourth time before his hand descended over my pubic area and held me still against his hips. He was jerking, moaning in pleasure. Then his mouth left my skin. He grabbed my shoulders and turned me to face him. I gazed at him, amazed, gulping at his beastly form. His fangs were dripping with blood as he lazily licked his lips. He had glittering amber eyes with black stripes flickering around like special effects. He looked breathtakingly sexy!

I crawled on the bed, trying to make myself comfortable, feeling his mark burn on my back. It felt painful for the first time, and he growled when I tried to touch it. His growl made me stop and stare at him again. He was a bit scary, I had to confess, and I kind of got startled when he moved closer to me, sniffing and giving me an odd-looking smirk. I swear I thought he was going to bite me again, and I held my breath and closed my eyes. But he just started to lick me, and I opened an eye, finding it weird until I opened both eyes and began to giggle, ticklish.

He continued to lick my cheeks then my neck and breasts until he trailed down me with his tongue, transforming my first *oh* in surprise to a different, shivering *oh!* in delight, that then became an *'oh my God!'*, repeatedly, as if I was a devoted believer in higher deities. But I could not find better words to describe it; they seemed to express perfectly the happiness that was breaking throughout my body under Shane's tongue.

Then I heard him inside my thoughts, which made me open my eyes, amazed. The mind link had been established, and I could hear him as if he was using his voice. He was saying: *God has nothing to do with this, honey. This is all me.*

I laughed hysterically. He grabbed my legs and pulled me down the bed, crawling over me and smirking with shiny amber eyes. He kissed me while I heard him growling in my mind and sigh in both pleasure and pain.

He wanted to mark me again, to carve his teeth once again in my flesh and taste my blood. He wanted to get inside me once more, and I was losing control, feeling my fangs come out. Lust was mutual, and I told him mentally to stop fighting his wolf and give in to his urges. He bit me, and I bit him, and we rolled on the bed, ecstatic and utterly high on love and yearning.

CHAPTER TWENTY-SIX

ANNA

WALKING ON CLOUDS couldn't come close to explaining what I felt the day after our final bonding. I loved having him in my head, loved talking to him without speaking, and loved sharing that strong connection that allowed me always to know his location.

I still had to help out at school with the prom arrangements, plus the meetings to decide the final grades. I also had to write college recommendation letters for those leaving high school. So I didn't have all my time free for Shane, nor did he, because he also had to take care of the town's safety since the prom was a huge event and security had to be tight.

Many kids from other villages would come to town; many kids would do stupid things that night because of the alcohol. Safety measures needed to be in place; students had to attend classes to learn about them. Most kids would find it tedious and unnecessary since their youth made them think they were invincible, being supernatural. However, even if they were stronger than humans, they could still get hurt. Rogues or radicals could enter undetected and cause trouble.

It was, without a doubt, a stressful week for Shane and me. We all hoped it would be worth it at the end of the prom night, though.

My marks burned from time to time, making an itchy feeling or sending waves of sexual desire whenever Shane thought about me or told me he missed me. Mentally sharing the ins and outs of our daily jobs was nice. I loved his sense of humor. I knew I walked around daydreaming with a silly smile on my face because we both got lost in conversations taking place inside our heads.

Of course, others didn't mind because many could guess that I had been marked—mostly werewolves and vampires who looked at me and gave me an 'I-know-how-you-feel' smile.

Well, James, the principal and one of Shane's best friends, did not. He began to look at me in a funny way, weirder than before. He still told his jokes and made flirty comments. However, something was definitely bizarre in how he looked at me. He was probably envious of what Shane and I had. Honestly, I couldn't understand James—he was kind of a puzzle. I didn't much care to try, though. I was in my own world of happiness and was going to enjoy it for as long as I could.

* * *

Wednesday, I had a bizarre meeting with James. He informed me that the prince was coming to town to meet me. The prince was the son of the supposed king, who granted protection and ruled the little kingdom.

Well, it was not that little. The town was big enough, and the surrounding woods were large and good enough to protect, making the town less attractive to humans who wanted to move there.

The royal family was also the owner of most of the houses, the school compound, the health facilities, the theater, and the only shopping mall with many fancy stores and a cinema. They also owned the majority of the companies that provided work to the people in town. They had furniture factories and building-industry companies; even the huge grocery store was theirs.

Summing up, the majority of the real estate was theirs. They also sponsored the fire department and, of course, had total control over the police department, putting their men there to protect and take care of their town.

Obviously, they were wealthy, which wasn't a surprise since they were a pureblood vampire family. What was surprising was how everything was well organized, and how everybody lived relaxed and happy was surprising. They even had peaceful affiliations with packs of wolves and covens of witches that lived in nearby towns. Many of the teachers were from neighboring villages. Their citizens also studied in our local school and were made part of the town security force. We had many werewolves from other packs coming to practice with us during the week; they all seemed to get along just fine.

One of the alphas, Sebastien, was the scholastic wrestling coach. The coach took his job seriously. He was younger than many wolves, just twenty-five, but he was responsible and ruled his wrestling team as if they were a SEAL task force. His team was probably better than the SEALS since they were stronger, faster, and supernatural. He would push them to their limits and smile about it.

Sebastien had always been friendly and charming. Since we were almost the same age, we had more in common. At least, we were part of the same generation since the rest of the teachers were older, much older than us. We usually felt disengaged when they talked with each other and remembered the ancient times. It was no wonder that I had bonded faster with the Math and the Gym teacher. The older teachers seemed nostalgic about times when children behaved better and thought about things besides cell phones, Netflix, and Tik Tok and all the shows that influenced their perspective of the world, giving them ideas to get out of town and explore. The older teachers thought it could be dangerous, but they were young and avid about seeing new things and having new experiences. Who could blame them?

"Everybody is excited about the dual meet on Friday evening," Eve, the math teacher with the crush on Sebastien, said. She had been flirting harder with him for the past weeks. Still, he seemed clueless or was simply not interested.

We were in the teacher's lounge talking to Sebastien, who had given his victims a break for once. Evelyn, the blonde vampire, used this opportunity to flirt with him.

Eve was friendly and talkative; she had a warm personality that reminded me a bit of Jessica. Besides, I could understand her crush on Sebastien. The guy was hot! He had striking green eyes and was an Alpha. Alphas reek of attraction and power to females. He had a whole league of fans among the teachers and female students. He was my friend and Shane's, too. He trained with us and was actually one of the fighting teachers. His pack would often come to practice with us, so they could face vampires and hybrids and become more prepared.

Another thing, he was mateless—he had no Luna attached to him yet. I noticed a seeming curiosity in his eyes about my mate bond with Shane, once that was finally completed. I was guessing that he wanted a Luna badly, and I thought it was sweet of him to be so romantic about his soulmate.

"I had no idea that the wrestling team was the pride and joy of the town!" I said, relaxing on the couch. We were finished for the day, but I had time to waste while waiting for Shane to finish his work.

"It's a huge deal after the football team," Sebastien said, putting down the notes he was reading and giving us his attention.

"This dual meet will attract a lot of people coming to watch from other schools. A lot of supernatural beings will be gathered in the same place, and it's always a problem with the security," I said, reminding myself about all the times Shane was dedicating to secure the town because of that event.

Humans' wrestling season would typically occur from

November to March, but the supernatural season was from January to May because it was something that didn't obey human laws. Our team had made the postseason finals.

"Oh, yes, it's a huge deal. We will fight against three of the strongest teams of other werewolves and shifters. Last year's winner is one of the favorites. The boys are feeling a lot of pressure," Sebastien said.

"The girls are all excited, too." Eve's eyes sparkled, her gaze on Sebastien. "All they talk about is their cheering routine and the prom. I had no idea that the wrestling team needed to be cheered."

"In my opinion, the girls are a distraction," Sebastien said, making me chuckle.

"Boys will be boys. Besides, the girls need to practice their routines." Eve waved her hand, ignoring his lack of interest and grumpy observation. "You should be happy we'll all be there cheering for you."

"James forced me to meet with the cheerleaders to explain the rules so they wouldn't cheer when they shouldn't," Sebastien said. "It was a waste of time. They asked me a bunch of stupid questions and were more interested in knowing about my private life than the scoring rules."

"I'm sure they did." Eve giggled. Sebastien had more attention from the females than he wished. "Sebastien, I could use some lessons about that, too," she added with a mischievous grin.

"The dual meet is tomorrow. But I can give you the flyer I made for the girls," Sebastien said, innocently.

The dual meet was scheduled for Friday evening, the day before prom. The teachers had decided that it was better to hold the prom on the weekend to have the entire population help control the teenagers and have more patrolling teams in the woods and borders.

"Are you coming to the dual meet, Annabel?" Eve asked me.

"Oh, definitely. Shane is excited about it, too. Actually, all the guys are excited about it."

Apparently, the wrestling championship was a challenging display between other packs or teams of supernaturals, so it was rather important for each supernatural community's reputation that competed. Wars weren't an option for resolving disputes anymore. Wrestling matches were a more civilized way of showing superiority. So, the men were excited about the show, and the boys felt the pressure because they would be representing the entire community.

Sebastien had a lot of pressure on his back, too. He had been a champion himself when he studied at that school. I had seen the trophies and pictures in the school's Hall of Fame. This was his first year as the wrestling team coach, so he had to prove himself.

"That's cool. I could join you, and we could cheer for Sebastien together," Eve proposed. "I've never been to a fight before."

"Sure, you can keep us company. Shane will be too busy arguing with the referee anyway," I said, amused because he'd spent a lot of his time arguing with the other guys in the bar how, the previous year, their team had been penalized by the referee.

"Cool. I don't know a lot of people here." Eve smiled, a bit shy, and I realized that it was true.

The math teacher kept to herself. Besides her crush on Sebastien, she barely spoke with the others. She was a substitute teacher like me and a vampire. She might be a recent vampire because she doesn't act with the same maturity level as the others.

"Sebastien, are you going to James's party tonight?" Eve asked.

"I need to rest and get focused for tomorrow. Besides, I'm going to patrol the town."

"I thought Shane had that covered for tonight," I said.

"Oh, I'm not patrolling with the guys. I'm making sure the boys aren't partying until late at night. I don't want them drinking before the fights. They can party all they want after it, not before."

"I could help you with that, and then we could go to James's party to see if one of your fighters is there," Eve proposed.

"I don't want to bother you. I'm sure you have better things to do," Sebastien said.

"Not really. The school year is almost over. I'll go back home for a couple of months, and…we might not see each other for a while."

I smiled, staring at my bag. Was Sebastien clueless or trying *to seem* clueless? Either way, I felt like a third wheel. I also felt sorry for Eve. It was clear Sebastien wasn't into her. She shouldn't be so insistent. Maybe she was just feeling lonely.

"What are you doing tonight, Annabel? Are you and Shane going to James's party?" Sebastien asked.

"What? Oh no, Shane and I are going to Sam's Bar to meet our friends. No wild parties for us."

"It's a pity. We could meet there," Eve suggested. "Unless… I would love to go to Sam's Bar, but I don't want to go alone. You could keep me company and buy me a drink, Sebastien."

"Eve, some other night. I wouldn't normally say no to spending time with friends and colleagues, but tonight I really need to rest," Sebastien spoke soberly.

Eve just sighed and nodded.

"It's a pity that no one thought about a going-away party for the teachers. We may not be together next year," Eve reminded us. "Are you going to keep teaching here, Anna? Since Shane and you are mates, and there's an open position for a permanent literature teacher here?"

"I don't know," I said, blushing at the direct question. I guess people were assuming that I was going to live there permanently since I was Shane's mate. James was pressuring me for a decision, but Shane knew better than to pressure me about anything. We had marked each other. It had been a huge step in our relationship. He had been understanding enough to know that I didn't need to live there to be with him. There was an entire world outside the safety of that town, a world that needed me.

"I'm sorry. I didn't mean to pry," Eve mumbled, perceiving my thoughtful gaze.

"It's okay," I said, straightening up when I noticed that someone else was coming our way. Soon enough, the door opened, and James came in with a worried expression. When our eyes met, he sighed in relief and approached us.

Everybody greeted him.

He grumbled some incomprehensible word, making us stare at him, puzzled. He was usually a lot more cheerful and polite than that.

"Did you see a cross and run?" Sebastien asked. He was funny like that, or, at least, he tried to be.

James ignored him completely, talking to me. "I'm glad you're still here. You need to come now. He's here."

"Who?" I asked, intrigued as the other two frowned.

In my mind, I heard Shane questioning me about who was there, too, wondering what was going on that changed my mood. He could be clingy like that when it came to a change in my feelings. I replied that all was fine, that it was just James acting strange again and my mate became less worried.

"Cut the mind link," James ordered like he'd guessed. "The prince is here to see you."

"Oh!" I said, finally understanding his nervous state.

"The prince! Such an honor, Anna!" Sebastien joked in a sarcastic voice.

"Don't be a smart ass and show some respect. He's older than you, and he was a good friend of your father's." James lectured Sebastien like a grandfather disciplining his grandson for disrespectful behavior.

Sebastien pouted and rolled his eyes. "As if I don't call him by his first name," he muttered, annoyed. "Dude, he's my godfather!"

"Wow, you are friends with a royal vampire? Such an honor, Sebastien," I teased back.

"Yes, I'm important like that," he said with a boyish grin. "But I thought he was abroad."

"He arrived today, and he's in a hurry, so please don't make him wait," James said with a serious face.

I couldn't hear anything else that people said because Shane was invading my mind with all sorts of questions. He wanted to know why the prince was there, why I hadn't told him that he was coming, why James had called him there. I had one answer for him: *I don't know.*

When I looked again at everybody, James looked cranky, Sebastien was quiet and bored, and Eve was merely flustered. I was intrigued and gave her a questioning look.

She formed the words with her lips, "The prince is gorgeous!" then sighed dramatically, fangirling over him.

I laughed, which made everybody stare at me as if I were crazy. So, another gorgeous man slash vampire slash immortal—what else was new? They seemed to grow on trees around there.

"Come on, don't keep him waiting. He wants to talk to you." James hurried me along, more impatient than ever, like the world's salvation depended on my meeting with the prince.

I got up, arranged my skirt and jacket, and smiled at Eve and Sebastien, who waved goodbye. Then I followed James to meet the prince.

I've never met a prince before. It was odd even that people called him 'Prince.' I guess they were royalty back in Europe and had decided to keep the titles. It was something to be proud of among vampires, especially purebloods. I was a bit curious to meet him, mainly because I needed his family's help. But I didn't know why the prince wanted to talk to or see me.

We followed the empty corridor, and I noticed bodyguards in every corner, dark glasses over their eyes and communicators in their ears. They looked like the Secret Service and followed our moves as if we were a threat. It was almost too unreal to be true!

It seemed the prince was waiting in the principal's office because that's where we were headed. However, before James could open the door, someone at the top of the corridor opened the school's front doors.

"James, don't even think about it," Shane ordered.

Glimpsing back, I blushed from head to toe. He was only wearing a pair of jeans; nothing more, nothing less. He was barefoot with messed-up hair, walking toward us and growling at the bodyguards who had taken a step toward him. Then, they went back and bowed their head.

I frowned and folded my arms, staring at him as he came closer. *Is he being serious? Has he shifted from his wolf form and came running to the school? Why? What is going on? Why did he seem so worried?*

"He isn't going to be happy," James said, talking to Shane who had arrived next to us.

"And do I look happy to you?" Shane asked James. His eyes were glittering amber, and his fangs were out.

He was not happy at all!

"Go outside, Anna," he ordered as if I were just some other

person in the group, not his mate, probably because I was his mate. We had completed the marking, so maybe he assumed I was now under his orders or whatever sexist stuff was going on in that mind of his. Anyhow, I was getting mad, myself. *What the hell does he think he's doing?*

I didn't move an inch. And that was not unnoticed by Shane, but he didn't growl at me. That would have been interesting to watch: him growling at me and me telling him to go to hell and then giving him my back. *We could be mated, we could be together, but no one would boss me around.* He had to give me a good reason to leave as I was more than curious.

"Please go outside, honey," he pleaded in a sweeter tone that was much better to hear than the previous one. "Or just go home and wait there for me. I have to talk to the prince."

"Come," Sebastien demanded, appearing like magic by my side. "Leave the grown-ups to their business." He was playful, smiling at me.

I smiled at him. He was cute, with an adorable smile. However, Shane didn't like his hands on my shoulders and my smiling back. He growled at Sebastien.

It was fascinating to see Sebastien's eyes change color as the Alpha in him surfaced to snarl back at Shane.

Great, a contest of who would growl louder was all I needed!

"My mate. Keep your hands to yourself," Shane muttered.

Sebastien rolled his eyes and got his wolf under control. At least, they were not going to measure who could growl longer. That was a relief.

"Possessive much, are we?" Sebastien teased. He shouldn't do that, and I shouldn't have laughed, but I did.

"Men," Eve sighed as she appeared by our side.

I didn't notice when she'd arrived but wondered if they had come to get me out of there. Sebastien had probably come because Shane had asked him to. Eve, likely, because she was stalking Sebastien.

Yes, that explanation was more logical to me.

"All of you leave. I have to talk to the prince," Shane ordered as he rested his hand on the doorknob.

James exhaled, waving his hands dramatically. Sebastien pushed me away as Shane watched.

Shane seemed to talk to him in some sort of wolf-mind link. I was sure of it. Therefore, we left, and I noticed out of the corner of my eye as my hunk of a mate entered the principal's office, followed by James. He sure wasn't appropriately dressed to meet a prince, even if they had known each other for a long time.

The door closed, and I looked at Sebastien. He was still pushing me away, but I was not in the mood to leave. If anything, I was curious and wanted to see the prince. I had lost an excellent opportunity to meet a pureblooded vampire, thanks to Shane!

"What just happened?" I asked them, not understanding the fuss about the prince's visit or the reasons Shane had for not letting me meet the royal vampire.

It was beyond bizarre. And he'd looked stressed and worried, but mostly he'd looked mad. Not at me, but at James and the prince.

"I have no clue! Shane reached me on our mind link, out of the blue, and asked me to go and get you and take you out of here," Sebastien clarified.

"And I came after Sebastien," Eve said, shrugging her shoulders, disinterested in what had happened. Well, her stalking Sebastien—I had already figured that out.

My phone vibrated in my pocket and stopped me from thinking or saying anything else. I reached for it and read a text message from Jason.

My cousin wanted to meet him outside the town. *He was*

nearby, and that could not be odder! What could he possibly be doing there?

I tried to reach Shane to tell him that I was going to meet my cousin, but I got no response. Sebastien and Eve were in the middle of the corridor, waiting for me to start walking again.

"Shane is not answering me through my mind link, and I have to go meet someone," I shared with Sebastien.

"He probably blocked everybody out of reaching him so that he could talk to the prince without interruptions. I can tell him for you when he gets out of there."

"Blocking? Can I also block him out?"

"Of course. It goes both ways. You just need to want to. You need to concentrate, clear your mind, and build a wall around your thoughts. It's beneficial since werewolves can go mad with so many voices in their head if the whole pack decides to have a little chit-chat. Some can think they have schizophrenia!"

I stared at him and sighed about his lame attempt at a joke. Anyhow, his information about the blocking was useful. If Shane was blocking me, two could play that game.

"Okay, thank you. Tell him I'll see him at home," I said, going to get my purse, so I could leave to meet my cousin.

Sebastien and Eve remained in the corridor, Eve smiling creepily while he scratched his head. He was going to be left alone with her, and it seemed he was afraid of what she could do to him. That was a bit funny: a grown man slash werewolf Alpha fearful of a sweet stalker and innocent vampire hottie!

CHAPTER TWENTY-SEVEN

ANNA

I MET MY COUSIN in an almost empty diner outside of town, where humans were the only ones we had to worry about seeing us together.

I was feeling anxious and unsure of the reason he was there. I hated to keep secrets from him. I was also still troubled by what had just happened at school. Shane was being secretive and, to make things worse, I had to face Jason and come clean about him. I was hoping to have a bit more time to tell Shane first and then tell my cousin. Shane was happy that I would spend that Saturday with him so that we could go to the prom together. We had to chaperone the students, but there would be lots of time to dance and enjoy ourselves.

Jason seemed impatient and rattled. He wanted to know why I wanted to spend more time there and why I was so keen on defending the people of that town. He knew I was hiding something important. Therefore, I decided to tell him the truth.

I told him about Shane being my soulmate and how I wanted to tell my mate about my real job and to introduce him to my friends and family. I also wanted to tell Shane about Kevin. I thought that Jason would understand and give me the benefit of the doubt, but he became quiet while staring with a dumbfounded and shocked expression.

"You're being ridiculous, Annabel," he accused. I lost my good mood and waited for another mocking remark. "Did you truly fall for it?" he asked. "You have been here for, at least, three months now, and you didn't find out anything about the purebloods who rule over this community. You continue here even when you know we need you elsewhere! When we talked last weekend, you misled me into thinking that you needed a few more days to find out about the royal family that lives here. Now I find out that the real reason you are staying is that you're dating a mutt, and worse than that, you believe the bullshit that he's telling you about being your soulmate! Annabel—we're hybrids. We don't have a soulmate!"

My worst fears came true. Jason didn't believe me. Furthermore, he was being mean about everything I'd told him. It upset me as he wasn't giving me enough credit. He treated me like a naïve girl and talked to me as if I was irresponsible and stupid. Maybe he forgot that it was my life, and I could do whatever I wanted with it, date whomever I wanted.

Moreover, he shouldn't insult my boyfriend by calling him a mutt. And he should keep it down since the other people in the diner were looking at us with intrigued stares. We were shifters ourselves; we knew a lot of werewolves. He should be more respectful and less arrogant in his biased behavior.

"I thought you were going to be happy for me," I grumbled.

"Happy for what? For falling into a trap, the sheriff of this town laid out for you? Do you really believe him and all that crap about soulmates?" he asked, whispering this time. He seemed disappointed. "He's playing you! Wake up!"

"Playing me for what, Jason?"

I found his fears ridiculous. Besides, I was annoyed by his lack of credit to my intelligence. He wasn't inside my heart, able to know that I'd fallen head over heels for Shane. He didn't know Shane to judge him like that!

"Sex, of course."

I almost burst into laughter at his stupid answer. *Now, who is being naïve? Does he think I'm such a prude?*

"If it was for sex, Jason, my darling cousin, he didn't need to tell me he loved me and that I was his soulmate. I was happy sleeping with him with no strings attached!"

Jason stood, livid at my statement that apparently shocked him. It was sexist of him! Just because I was a woman, couldn't I have casual sex with someone who pleased me sexually, as he did?

"For information, then," he said, making me sigh.

He was doing his best to make me doubt Shane. He knew I was paranoid and very suspicious, but what he didn't realize was that my gut told me Shane was real and loyal. Not just my gut: my heart and soul recognized Shane. He was a part of me as much as I was a part of him.

There was nothing Jason could say to make me doubt my love for Shane and his love for me.

"Jason—why aren't you happy for me?"

"Because we need you. You can't hang your swords and stop doing what we do!" He seemed upset. "You belong with us and not here, trapped in this weird supernatural community teaching literature to kids and marrying some sheriff wolf! You are not marriage material."

"Thank you for that," I snapped, angered by his last observation. "What am I then? One-night-stand material?"

"I didn't mean it like that," he said. "You were born for the life we are living. You are our leader. You are the best we have! Can you see yourself living the life that the sheriff guy wants for you? Even if he's your soulmate, can you see yourself ignoring all the people who suffer at the hands of supernatural beings that have no respect for the rules and for humans?"

"I didn't say I was going to stop doing what I do," I said, understanding what was troubling him.

I'd had those questions, too, before accepting Shane and our bond. But no, I knew that I had to consolidate my secret life with my life with Shane. I had to tell Shane everything, even if I'd postponed doing it. I was sure that Shane would understand. He wanted the best for me. He was the first to tell me he would go anywhere with me.

Now that Jason was there, it was time to get over the secrets and tell Shane why I couldn't stay and continue to teach there, that I had to leave from time to time. We could find a solution to make our relationship work.

"Does your beloved wolf know about your secret life? Or does he think you are just a hot, sexy, innocent teacher?" Jason was being mean again.

"He doesn't know about my real job. But he knows that I'm everything but innocent and helpless. You don't know anything about Shane—you can't judge him like that."

"Trust me, I know plenty. I've been doing my homework, too," he said with enigmatic eyes that left me surprised and curious.

It seemed he had found some big secret but didn't want to share. I was puzzled.

"You had to date the sheriff. Couldn't you have chosen someone else? Or maybe he chose you—have you thought about that?"

I didn't comprehend Jason's rant. There was something he wasn't telling me.

"Jason, what are you really doing here? Did something happen to Kevin? No one called me. Last time I visited, they said he was stable."

"I'm glad that you remember him."

"Of course I remember!"

"Anna, have you stopped to think that maybe you've been too distracted by your supposed soulmate to realize what's going on right under your nose?"

"You're being paranoid! These are good people. I've already

told you this. I've been part of this community, and there isn't anything fishy going on here. Affinity is a nice place to live. They accept people like us. They protect their own. Have you ever found somewhere like this before?"

"They brainwashed you," he muttered, baffled. "I don't recognize you anymore. You used to be a lot smarter and mistrusting of people. How can you trust a guy you've just met?"

"Shane isn't a random guy. He's my soulmate," I reminded him, annoyed. "He's part of my life now, so you better get used to it and stop trying to rule over my life!"

"I'm trying to protect you!" Jason claimed, making his eyes shine golden. "I see that my opinion doesn't matter anymore. I'm your family and—you've kept this from me! Why? Because maybe, just maybe, you were also being paranoid and wanted to hide this from me, so I wouldn't call you to reason and make you understand that you are pushing your luck by staying here and, apparently, by letting a wolf into your life and head!"

"I've kept this from you because I knew you wouldn't comprehend."

"Well, you were right. I don't. We are a team, a family, and you are leaving us because of a dude."

"I'm not leaving you." I sighed, trying to keep calm. "I'm trying to live my life and be happy."

"Really? So tell me, in all of this, where does Kevin fit? Because, last time I checked, he was still in a coma, waiting for the blood cure. Are you forgetting about him, too?"

"Don't be stupid, Jason. I would never abandon my brother. Being in love doesn't interfere with my quest. I've even found an interesting opportunity to cure Kevin finally. But we are not talking about that here, in the middle of a diner, where everyone is starting to stare at us," I whispered, glaring at his stubborn blue eyes.

He was such a baby sometimes! He was also being cruelly manipulative, using my brother to make me feel guilty. I was already feeling enough guilt.

"Jason, why can't you understand me? I have found my soulmate. I'm in love."

"Hearing you say that…" He paused, intentionally, disapproving.

It had been hard for me to believe that, someday, I would say that to him. I had never thought I would have a soulmate and would be in love like that. But I was in love, so Jason had to suck it up and stop being an idiot. It wasn't like I was asking for the impossible. I wanted to stay longer with my soulmate. I wanted to find a pureblood to cure my brother and tell Shane about me and my origins. There was a pureblood right here, in town, wanting to talk to me! I had my opportunity to be face to face with a pureblood, someone who Shane knew. I had to tell Shane and hope for the pureblood's kindness and good heart.

"I know, but I am in love. And you, of all people, should be happy for me. Jessica is."

"Jessica knows?" Now he seemed pissed that I'd told her while hiding it from him. "Of course, she does!" He rolled his eyes dramatically, offended. "I want to meet the guy," he said with a serious voice as if he was my dad and needed to approve Shane.

Now it was my turn to roll my eyes. *At least, he wanted to meet Shane. That was good.*

"I have to see with my own eyes if he's the real thing and that he's not playing you."

"Jesus, Jason! I'm not a teen. I don't need your approval to hang out with a guy. Besides, Shane is much more than my boyfriend." I blushed because his eyes were glued to my neck as if he had x-rays and could see the mark.

He narrowed his eyes, pondering, and then seemed to chase away his thoughts and focus on what he was going to tell me. "I'm a man. I know men better than you. I will know if he's the real thing or not. The last thing I want is for some douchebag to break my beautiful cousin's heart."

I smiled, pleased by his concern. He had the right to be like that. He didn't know Shane, but I was sure that Shane would win him over. On the other hand, they could kill each other. I was hoping that Shane was more mature than Jason. Hopefully, Jason wouldn't act like a jerk to Shane. I grew pale with the idea of having the two meet. "Okay, Jason. You can come with me to meet him right now."

"I have stuff to do. I can meet you and your mate later."

"Oh," I said, intrigued about what he could possibly have planned. "Then you can meet us at Sam's Bar. It's the only bar around there, you can't miss it. We normally hang out there at night, after nine. I'll warn Shane that you are here visiting us, and you can stay with us. We have an extra room."

Jason raised his eyebrows as though troubled, blinking several times to focus. His mouth almost dropped open. "An extra room... Are you staying with him?"

"Yes..." I blushed at that answer because I felt embarrassed by the look on his face as if he didn't know me anymore. Maybe he didn't. I had changed, I admit.

"You've lost your mind!"

"He's my soulmate." I tried to reason with him but was hurt by his words; my answers sounded more like an excuse than an explanation. "Stop judging me without meeting him. I'm getting upset with you!"

"Well, let's hope that my worst fear won't come true. I must leave now. I'll meet you and your boyfriend mutt after nine."

Jason got up, leaving a bill to pay for his food. I stared at him, intrigued but worried about his stubbornness. I hoped Jason would be nicer after meeting Shane. I wanted them to be friends, but I had to prepare myself for the worst-case scenario, and I would smack his face if he were rude to Shane.

CHAPTER TWENTY-EIGHT

ANNA

WHEN I ARRIVED HOME, Shane wasn't there yet. For some reason, I felt worried about his absence. My meeting with Jason also left me with the peculiar sensation that my cousin was up to no good.

I was in the shower when I heard the front door open with a loud noise, which startled me and brought me out of my thoughts. Shane called for me, and it eased my fears. I was used to feeling safe in that house, but noises like those threw me into a defensive alert mode.

The urgency in my mate's voice reached the bathroom where he found me. I just had time to turn off the water when he arrived.

Turning around, I held my breath with the sight of him. Wearing only a pair of jeans and barefoot, his skin was dirty with mud and scartches, and he seemed breathless.

Before I could ask why he didn't use the car to get home, he reached out and hugged my naked body against his sweaty, dirty one.

"Don't ever do that to me again," he gasped.

"What?" I asked, unsure of what I had done to him. My arms were folded against my breasts, imprisoned against his chest. "Did you shift and ran home? You have cuts and bruises. I smell blood on you…"

"I'm fine. Don't ever block me out completely. I couldn't reach you with our mind link, and I thought something bad happened to you."

"Oh!" I had forgotten about that. My mind had been so caught up in my conversation with my cousin that blocking him out hadn't been a bad thing. "You also blocked me out," I reminded him.

He gazed at me with regretful eyes. "I'm glad you are safe."

"Why shouldn't I be safe? And why are you all dirty and bruised? Who hurt you?"

"This is nothing. I'm fine. I've just gone for a run in the woods. I forgot about the time, and then I couldn't reach you and got worried."

I narrowed my eyes with pursed lips, not buying his story.

Releasing me, Shane breathed deeply.

My body complained about the lack of touch as I inhaled his scent. He smelled like forest and sweat, like the earth after the rain, all that mixed with his blood. I tensed with the scent of his blood. It was a turn-on for me.

Shane stroked my wet hair. He had devotion and concern in his eyes like he always did when he was thinking about how to explain something to me. I was more concerned about who had given him those bruises and almost-healed scars.

He shrugged. "Eric and I had a little disagreement."

I raised an eyebrow. *Am I supposed to know who Eric was?*

His gaze wandered down my body, distracting him. Shane smirked with eyes turning amber. "I think you need another shower."

My body jerked back before he could grab me. If he believed he could distract me, he was wrong. "Who's Eric?"

He leaned forward, and I evaded his mouth. "Are you still mad at me?" he asked. All he managed to do was kiss my cheek and then my neck.

I almost surrendered as his mouth trailed kisses on my neck and his tongue licked my earlobe.

Shane spoke softly in my ear. "I wasn't trying to boss you around at the school. I didn't mean to use my Alpha voice on you."

"Why did you block your thoughts from me, then?" I used my childish voice to complain.

He leaned his forehead against mine, and our eyes locked. "Because it's protocol. Before you speak to a royal family member, you need to block your thoughts from others—the whole pack—so no one knows where we are. There are spies, probably even among our allies and community. The lives of the royal family are in constant peril."

"Then Eric is the prince?" I asked, putting two and two together.

Shane nodded, kissed my shoulder, and held me tighter. I moaned, feeling his arousal against my stomach.

He teased in my ear, "Make-up sex?"

I burst out laughing as he nibbled my earlobe slowly.

I snapped my eyes open as I realized something. Stepping back, I glared at him. "Are you stupid? You picked a fight with a pureblood vampire!"

"I had a good reason to pick a fight," he assured, offering his hands to hold. His lips tugged into a smile, and his playful attitude surfaced again. "Eric is one of my best friends. He'd never seriously hurt me. Besides, we're all good now. You don't need to worry."

"But you're bruised, and you smell like blood, your blood. You bled! And you're probably sore and hurt." I proved my point by poking my finger at his bruises. He moaned in pain, and I regretted my action. "I'm sorry!"

"He's also in bad shape," he said as he frowned in pain.

I breathed deeply and grumbled, "I'm worried about you, not some vampire prince. Vampires heal faster." Holding up my arm, I bit my wrist. As if it was the most natural thing to do, I put my wrist to his mouth for him to drink my blood.

Though my action surprised him, he eventually drank and surrendered to it with lustful eyes. It only took a few moments for him to be completely healed, and the side effects of my blood in him soon came to the surface…

If we could call increasing desire a side effect.

Shane's eyes shifted to amber, and he smirked at me, showing his canines. "Cute little vampire mate," he whispered in a husky voice, coming closer and sweeping me off my feet in a tight hug as he gave me a hungry kiss.

I growled against his lips. The nerve of his wolf calling me *little*! I knew I was cute. But little? I could so kick his ass. *Who is he calling little?*

I felt the smile on his lips as they caressed mine.

His breath brushed my lips. "Come on, honey. Calling you little isn't an insult. We both like you as you are, so we can wrap our arms around you and carry you everywhere." He helped me curl my legs around his waist and tightened his fingers on my hips.

I kissed him back because of his adorable reasoning.

Shane rested my back against the shower wall, and his stiff body pushed against mine. I was trapped, but I wasn't looking for a way out. Giving in to his mouth, I let him do whatever he wanted. He was hungry and savage. I was still smiling about his excuse for calling me little.

Jason was an idiot if he thought that Shane wasn't in love with me.

If what we feel for one another isn't love, then what the hell is it?

Shane couldn't be more perfect for me than he already was.

I still needed to know what Shane and the prince had fought about. I had the unpleasant feeling that it was because of me. However, I could obsess about that later and ask Shane what was going on. I had other stuff to deal with at the moment.

My hand reached for the shower tap, and water poured down on us. He needed a shower, and I was offering myself as his human sponge.

My mate didn't complain. He kept kissing me, using one of his hands to open his pants and strip away any clothes that stopped our bodies from melting together.

* * *

Before dinner, I had a chance to talk to Shane about my cousin's sudden arrival in town. We went to Sam's Bar, even though Shane was reluctant to leave the house that night. He seemed anxious, more distracted and pensive than usual. Or maybe I was projecting on him. I definitely felt nervous about the conversation I needed to have with him.

It was ten o'clock, and Jason hadn't yet shown his face. I was beyond impatient by then. I had called him several times, but his phone was off. Jason disappointed me. Still, his reluctance to show up didn't change the fact that I was going to confide in Shane about who I truly was and what I did for a living.

"I don't think your cousin's coming," Shane said after getting up to grab a beer.

"I think you're right."

He sat down and put the beer on the table. "We should go back home."

"Are you sure you don't want to play pool with the guys?" I asked. That was the third time he had suggested that we go home.

Putting his hand on mine over the table, he confessed, "You're worried that Jason may do something stupid. I'm...nervous, too. I want to talk to you about Eric and a lot of other matters that concern us. This isn't the best place to talk. Besides, if Jason does come here, he can always call you, and we'll tell him how to meet us at home."

"His phone may have run out of battery."

"He's a big boy. He can take care of himself. Let's just go home."

"I guess we should be in a place more private to talk," I agreed, getting up.

Rushing to my side, he placed an arm around my waist as he smiled.

I frowned at him. "Why are you looking at me like that?"

"You're the most amazing thing in the world," he said, pecking my lips.

I leaned back in his arms, watching his face.

"Relax, baby. I can open us a bottle of wine when we get home, and we can sit on the balcony, gazing up at the stars, and cuddle."

"I would love that." I laced my arms around his neck. "Tell me more."

"We could listen to the songs you downloaded."

"Or we could talk."

"Yes, we can talk. Anna…if he's mad, let him cool down. He'll eventually accept that you've moved on with your life."

I breathed heavily. "He doesn't believe that I'm your soulmate."

His fingers caressed a loose strand of hair behind my ear. "It doesn't matter what he believes."

Someone called, "Sheriff, are you here?"

My mate let me go as he stared at the door. Turning around, I saw Brad, one of Shane's officers, rush into the Bar with a haunted expression.

"Sheriff Shane!" Brad caught his breath. "I'm glad I've found you. We need you at the police station." The rush of adrenaline made his vampire form surface. He immediately put his hand over his mouth, looking around in search of humans who might have witnessed his transformation. Luckily for him, there were no outsiders around.

"What's happening?" Shane asked, tensing at the urgency in Brad's voice.

"The police station was robbed," he explained.

"What?" Shane's face became pale.

"No one noticed until now when they went into your office to use your computer. You know how the one in the lobby is always breaking down?"

"Yes, tell me what they stole," Shane demanded.

"We aren't sure," Brad said, scratching his head. "You need to get back there and see for yourself."

Shane grabbed his jacket from his seat. "Have you seen the surveillance tapes?"

"The Sergeant told me to call you as soon as we found out. You weren't answering your phone, Sheriff."

Shane searched for his phone in his pockets. "I left it in the car." He gritted his teeth before speaking again. "Officer Brad. I'll be right there. But I need to talk to my mate and send her home."

"I'm not going home. I'm coming with you," I said, sensing his panic when Brad talked about his office being robbed. There was something important to Shane in that room. *I'm going with you*, I clarified inside his mind, so he wouldn't find an excuse to leave me behind.

"Let's go then," Shane said, taking my hand tightly as if the end of the world was coming.

During the entire ride to town, Shane's heart was beating fast. He was breathing heavily and not answering any of my questions. He just wanted to get to the police station and understand what had been taken. He made plans to find clues about who could be the perpetrator.

Minutes later, we rushed into his office, and Shane saw his vault opened and the files, like Brad had said, missing.

I thought his heart stopped when he realized what had been taken. There was a lot of money there and plenty of other files and random papers, but it seemed that whoever went there was interested in those documents and nothing else.

Shane grabbed his head between his hands as his pupils grew bigger. I didn't know what the files were about. Maybe it was something confidential about the royal family. I'd never seen him so anxious!

He paced around his office for a while, thinking about what he was going to do. He had previously spent his time yelling at his deputies for letting something like that happen and then only noticing it much later. I stood quietly, not interfering in the way he treated his men. He knew what he was doing, and they should be more attentive. I would have done the same to my men if they had let something be stolen from under their noses.

I looked around his office, trying to figure out how the perpetrator had entered the room, taken what he'd wanted, and gotten away. Let's face it, the place was crawling with werewolves and vampires with super hearing and super strength. Yet none of the men had noticed anyone or anything.

No one had a clue as to what time the files had been taken. Shane had left the police station when the prince arrived at school and then left to go to the woods. Therefore, the time between the robbery and the discovery of the event was long. To make things worse, the cameras had not picked up anything, at least, the ones that were working. Someone had put them on loop, making it look like no one had been there by repeating the same image. Whoever did this break-in was a professional.

Not finding any clues, Shane grew impatient. He was also staring at me more, touching and holding me against him as if I might vanish at any second. Then, after holding my face, kissing my forehead, and telling me for the hundredth time that everything was going to be okay, a light seemed to pop on inside his head. It looked like he had a possible suspect, so he dragged me out of the police station, put me in his car, and drove to some unknown location.

We took a road I had never taken before. We went deep into the woods, passing a few houses until we were surrounded by nothing but trees.

Moments later, he parked the car in front of a big, old house. It was all lit up and noisy, as though someone was having a party. I could hear laughter, loud music, and a mixed smell of humans, werewolves, and vampires inside. It reminded me of those fraternity parties back in college, where everybody got drunk and crazy. I had no idea that those types of parties happened around here, in such a calm, conservative town.

Shane had the unfortunate idea to ask me to stay in the car. My reply was to open the door and get out. He was out of his mind if he thought I was going to let him go inside without me. There were a lot of vampires and werewolves there. They could hurt him if he tried to accuse someone and take him away. I didn't even know where we were or who owned that house, but I knew a party like that was not a good place to enter alone.

I followed him closely as we entered the house. I studied the place, watching the people inside. There were many whom I didn't know, but others were familiar. Most of them were a part of the community and attended the same practices as I did. Some were even part of the school staff and the town's elite force. I was beginning to realize that this wild party house belonged to James.

Shane didn't stop to greet anyone, and he seemed to know his way around the house. He climbed the stairs and followed a long corridor where I could see what appeared to be several bedrooms. A couple of them were closed, and by the sounds coming through, I didn't have to guess what was happening on the other side.

At the end of the corridor, we paused in front of a white wooden door. Shane didn't knock or anything. He pushed it open and entered, growling, in search of his victim.

It didn't take long for Shane to check out the room and see what I saw: James having fun with two young women who were offering their bodies and blood to him. I almost covered my eyes so I didn't have to witness what was going on. I was glad he was not entirely naked, or I would have a hard time looking at him as my superior at work again.

Shane jumped on James and took him by the neck, dragging him out of bed and holding him against the wall. James looked terrified and confused while Shane growled at him as if he was about to bite his head off. His wolf wasn't playing around. He was pissed!

James's playmates screamed hysterically, warning others that something was wrong. Soon enough, two big gorilla-like vampires came our way, probably to protect James from Shane.

Meanwhile, the girls grabbed their few clothes and ran out of the room.

Quickly analyzing the door behind me and the guys, I ran to them, using my fast movements to knock them out cold with little effort on my part, then closing the door and locking it. It seemed to be a standard wooden door from the other side, but inside the room, we noticed that it was iron-reinforced, constructed to be hard to open or take down by supernatural beings. It would keep out unwanted guests for a while until I could figure out why Shane was acting like this and why he was holding James by the neck.

They are friends, aren't they? So why is he ready to kill him?

Shane noticed what I did and stared at me in his beast form for a moment. I shrugged my shoulders, not knowing what to say or what was going on, but I had his back anytime.

He brought his attention back to James, who was attempting to free himself from his grasp. He tried to speak but wasn't able to and was having difficulties breathing, too. I started to feel sorry for him.

"I told you to leave Annabel alone," Shane growled, loosening his grip a bit so that James could breathe.

James inhaled deeply and looked at me as if he didn't have any idea what Shane was talking about. "I left her alone. What did she tell you?"

"Don't even dare to look at her," he threatened, which made James turn pale and focus on Shane. "You were the only one to know about her, besides Eric. He didn't say a thing to anyone. So why in the hell did you break into my office and steal the files?"

"What?" James stammered as his eyes widened further.

What could those files have related to me. *Why is my name coming up?*

"Don't play innocent. I know it was you!"

"I—didn't—do it," he said, voice trembling as Shane held him tighter, not letting him move.

My mate was strong! He had an old vampire in his hands, and the guy wasn't even able to make Shane move an inch. He could probably snap James's neck whenever he wanted but delayed it to gather information.

My thoughts were interrupted by someone shaking the door, trying to break it down. Because the door was reinforced, it would take a lot of strength and probably two or three strong vampires or wolves to crack it open. Taking a good look at the room, I shrugged at how tacky and sleazy it was! Like James had seen some weird version of a Playboy mansion bedroom and copied it, so his bedroom looked like a sexy lair to lure his victims and do whatever he was doing to them when we'd arrived.

However, he was also obsessed with security. The room had no windows despite all of its red drapes and the velvet hanging around the walls. There were many red and white silk cushions scattered around the bed and on the black velvet loveseats. The only thing nice about the room was the cute loveseats, which had diamond tufting and posh crystal bottoms in the backrest. Even the bed looked sleazy, at least to me. I didn't want to imagine what he had done there with all the women he wooed to bed.

The room smelled like sex, alcohol, and weed. If the situation weren't so bad between James and Shane, I would have been laughing at his lousy taste.

The bouncing noise against the door reminded me that someone was still trying to break in.

I miss my swords.

"I swear, Shane. I didn't do what you think I did. I've been here all night. Ask anyone," James said.

I noticed that Shane seemed tempted to believe him. James's eyes were black and his fangs were out, while his mouth still had blood dripping from the feeding we'd interrupted. "We're friends. I would never betray you."

"Not even to Sasha?" Shane asked as the banging on the door got louder. I guessed there were probably two strong ones bouncing against the door at that moment.

"I have nothing to do with that whore anymore," he groaned, upset, as though Shane had offended him.

I rolled my eyes at his choice of words. It was sexist of him, mainly since he was also a man-whore himself. Yet the mention of Sasha's name did make me curious. I had already forgotten about that stuck-up vampire who thought Shane was her property.

Shane seemed to believe him. He let him go, and, to my surprise, James didn't react and jumped on Shane's neck.

I was ready to take him down if he did.

James cleared his throat, adjusted his clothes, and yelled, "Everything is fine. Go away!"

The noise stopped, and the door became still.

"What the hell, Shane!" James cursed, sounding hurt. "We're like brothers. I'd never betray you and your soulmate."

"You were the only one besides Eric who knew about Anna! And Eric wouldn't need to steal the files!" Shane accused.

"Id' never sold you out. Affinity is my town, and I despise the purists as much as you do."

Shane growled as he fisted his hands. "There are important details that can't be leaked on those files."

"It wasn't me," James reiterated. "Someone else must have known or found out about your little investigation!"

"What is going on?" I enquired, aware that Shane still had a panicked look on his face, and it all seemed to lead back to me. "What the hell is in those files that were stolen from your office?"

Shane didn't answer me. He stared with guilt in his eyes.

James, on the other hand, smirked mischievously and fixed his blond hair. "Things about you, darling. You've been a naughty girl."

I became pale and rigid. *Shane had a file on me.* My stomach cramped, and my heart hurt as if it had been stabbed.

"Shane has been poking around your past," James clarified as if it wasn't already apparent.

My head spun, and the sky fell over me. I looked at Shane after catching my breath, noticing how guilty and ashamed he looked. I felt betrayed and wanted to run out of there.

He had a file on me. He was investigating my life behind my back. How could I be so stupid and trust him?

"I guess he does have a thing for princesses," James added, giggling like a fool.

His words seemed to be a private joke between them. I clenched my jaw, not slightly amused.

Shane's head snapped in James's direction, and he snarled loudly. His fangs showed, and his eyes turned amber. I thought he was going to jump on him again.

"Nice doggy," James held his hands up, stepping back as though scared by what Shane could do to him. Calling him *doggy* wasn't the best way to calm him down. It would infuriate Shane's wolf further!

I stepped between them and held Shane back. I needed James to tell me more. My hand pushed against Shane's chest to stop him from snarling at the vampire.

Squinting my eyes, I questioned James, "What do you mean by Shane having a thing for princesses?" I added, "You better answer me truthfully because I won't be as nice as Shane. I've been dying to slap that stupid smile off your face."

James lost his cocky grin, and Shane chuckled.

I snapped my head at Shane and snarled, "You better have a good excuse. I'm not happy with you, either." His smile quickly slipped from his face. "Shut up," I ordered before he could open his mouth. "It isn't your time to speak."

Shoving James back, I ordered, "Start talking."

James blinked fast as he gulped. "Didn't your father tell you?"

My frown deepened. "What should my father have told me? Did you know him?"

"Seriously, you didn't know who your father was? Who *you* are?" He seemed shocked but also amused by my apparent ignorance.

"Shut up," Shane commanded James.

I looked at Shane. My throat was dry, and my heart was hammering in my chest. The ability to stand was leaving my body because I was panicking with all the secrets. My mate was investigating my life when he had said he trusted me and would wait for me to tell him everything.

When I looked at James, he had heeded Shane's warning to keep quiet. He put his hand on his throat, clearly remembering Shane's grip.

"I'll leave you two lovebirds alone to talk." The vampire exited the room before I could stop him.

Before I could follow James, Shane held my wrist, and James closed the door behind him.

My body shuddered as I tried to release my arm. Having him touching me was the last thing I wanted. I pushed harder, and he let go as I stepped away from him.

I should have left with James. Still, I hoped Shane had a good excuse for what he had done. If he didn't, my heart would experience the most excruciating pain I'd ever felt. I was already feeling sick with disappointment. My mouth was dry; my body felt weak. My thoughts were running wild and crazy. Millions of questions were overloading my brain.

But there was only one I couldn't stop from escaping.

"Was everything a lie?" I asked, feeling overwhelmed by my feelings. I was almost in tears, which was illogical because I should have been angry. Plus, I was not the crying type.

I was beginning to question all the words, everything that had happened between Shane and me. My cousin's words couldn't be washed from my mind. I was becoming my former paranoid self, the person who doubted her own shadow.

I wanted to look at Shane, but I felt scared about what I might see in his eyes.

Would I see his true self for the first time? Was all this a trap to catch me?

Why?

I didn't have time to catch my breath. The next thing I felt was his hands grabbing me under my arms and lifting me off the ground. I wasn't able to scream. I was stiff as a board and totally out of breath.

CHAPTER TWENTY-NINE

ANNA

SHANE CAUGHT ME IN HIS ARMS and pressed me against the wall. For a moment, I thought he was going to hurt me, but he just stared at me with the saddest eyes, making my heart hurt inside my chest.

"What was a lie?" he asked, almost out of breath. He looked as if I had punched him in the gut and marched over his heart. "You can't possibly think that I lied about us being soulmates, about my love for you!" Disappointment and pain floated through his once sexy, deep voice. "Why don't you rip my heart out of my chest instead?"

His words made me feel guilty. The uncontrollable need to cry still stung my eyes. I felt my body tremble again, and my limbs hurt, but it wasn't because of Shane. It was like a secondary effect of the nerves and pain I was feeling. I was still mad at him, however.

"I trusted you. How could you go behind my back and have a file on me?"

"Annabel." He sighed, pulling me closer to his chest, maybe because I was so close to bursting into tears. His hand caressed my right cheek, and he looked deep into my eyes. I swallowed hard, losing my breath when he kissed me, and I let him. It was illogical. It was a possessive kiss. We were arguing: he shouldn't kiss me, and I shouldn't let him, not when he had broken my heart.

So why didn't I push him away and start screaming at him?

He broke the kiss and stared at me. "I love you. I couldn't ever hurt you. Mates don't do that to each other. So, even if for a moment you still believe that I lied to you about us being soulmates, then pull away, hit me, or kill me. I really don't care. If you leave me and stop trusting me, I will eventually die of heartbreak and sadness."

He waited for me to speak, but I couldn't. My throat was obstructed, and the words couldn't get out.

What he said saddened me. I didn't want to hurt him. I wanted to know why he had a file on me and if he planned to use it to hurt my friends. Maybe he couldn't hurt me or didn't want me to get hurt because we were connected. However, that didn't mean he couldn't harm my friends and make their actions public.

"Anna, do you want to hurt me?" he asked, brushing his lips on my ear. My body reacted to his touch as my thoughts came to a halt.

I swallowed, trying to figure out if I truly knew him. Doubt troubled me. *Is he going to hurt my friends?*

"Are you going to make me want to hurt you?" I asked with a hoarse voice, plucking up the courage to face him and make him realize that maybe we were soulmates, perhaps we were meant to be, but I would never be with him if he did something to hurt my only family … my only friends.

He furrowed his brow at my question. His finger caressed my lower lip, and he sighed. "I would never do anything to hurt you. My loyalty is with you. I've already told you that. I've already told you that I would go with you to hell and back if you asked me to. W-would you hurt me?"

"I couldn't stay with you if you hurt my family and friends," I answered honestly.

"No one will do anything to you or your friends. That is the last thing we want."

"So why do you have a file on me?" I asked, intrigued by his use of the word 'we'. *Who is we? Someone else knows? Oh, yes, the prince.* I remembered him telling that to James. And James also knew. It was a conspiracy, apparently.

Tears ran down my face, which I only noticed when I felt Shane's lips catching them.

"Stop using physical attraction to make me feel weak like this," I ranted.

"I'm sorry. It isn't intentional. I'm afraid you will run away, and I can't—I don't want to be away from you, either. I need you to listen to what I have to say."

"So explain yourself," I demanded, bothered by the delay.

"Unblock me. Stop blocking my thoughts. It'll be so much easier if you let me show you."

"Why would I let you come inside my mind again? Don't you know everything you needed to know about me? Don't you have a file on me?"

"Don't be like that, Anna," he pleaded, apparently hurt by my sarcasm.

"Did you know who I was when you first saw me?" I asked, realizing he could have always known who I was. He could have used me to find out things about my organization.

My paranoid self was returning in full force, together with my sarcasm and disillusion.

"Don't be silly, honey. You're being paranoid. Everything will make perfect sense after you let me explain. Plus, I could ask you the same. Did you know who I was? Was that why you went out with me?"

"Of course not!" I protested. "I didn't even want to meet you, remember?"

"So, why did you come here, specifically?"

"Do not turn the table and make this an interrogation about me. I was the one who was deceived by you. I trusted you, and you went and put a file together about me behind my back. You and I have nothing to do with my organization or my job. I stayed here because of you, nothing more. Because I fell in love with you."

I was mad, and he was smiling. Mate bond or not, I wanted to slap him right then and there.

"Well, if it makes you happier, I didn't know that the file I had gathered all these years was about you."

Those words were all but understandable. "What do you mean?"

"Actually, there were two files. Two files on two people who became the same person. I had a file about your organization and their members, the leader included. And I had a file of someone else important to my king, who turned out to be you."

I understood even less by the minute. Shane must have read that on my face.

"It's hard to explain. But you must know that we don't want to harm you or your friends. My king is not against what your organization does. In fact, we are doing the same thing here. We eradicate the ones who disobey our rules or come here to destroy our peace. We're on the same side. No one here hates hybrids or tries to kill them. You know that. You have seen that."

I nodded, agreeing. For all I had seen, nothing would make me believe that they were not what they seemed to be—a peacefully mixed-breed community, protecting each other, and strong and kind. "And the other file you mentioned?"

"Well, here's what you may find difficult to believe if you don't let me show you my thoughts. I was also taken aback by the wonderful coincidence. Anika Isobel," he whispered my real name, the name I'd had to change.

My body froze, and my eyes widened, amazed and terrified at the same time.

"The other file was about Anika, about you."

"Why did you have a file on me? And how do you know my

former name?"

"You see, honey, your father was a well-known vampire before he disappeared with your mom due to their forbidden love. And I knew him well," he explained, and my heart stopped. "Anika!" he exclaimed, sounding worried.

"My name is Anna now. It has been for a long time." I breathed in to get control over my emotions. "Anika is dead. Stop calling me that."

"Actually, you just mixed Anika and Isobel together. Anna is a pet name for Anika. Isobel was the name of your dad's mom. I do like Annabel better," he said, grinning.

"Dad would always call me Anna anyway, and Mom called me Belle. But why did you have a file on me? Why would I interest you?"

"I was looking for you. Your family has been searching for you and your brother ever since the attack that claimed your parents' lives."

"Family? What family?"

"Your father was a vampire prince. The king of these lands is your grandfather."

I squinted my eyes at his farfetched words. For a moment, I thought he was joking. Yet he didn't even flinch, and his face was solemn. Besides the aristocratic title and everything else that rushed to my mind, one other thought overwhelmed my heart.

I smiled, almost crying. "I have more family! I have a grandfather!" My tears fell down my cheeks despite my happiness.

I gulped as my mind began to gather all the pieces. By having a family, a pureblooded vampire family, I would be able to save my brother!

Kevin would be shocked when he woke up. If my grandfather was looking for us, he wouldn't let my brother die.

At least, I hoped he wouldn't.

"Your father renounced the throne to marry your mom. He was the next in line." Shane cleaned my tears away with his thumbs.

His statement puzzled me. "But why? Why did my dad go away and turn his back on his family? Didn't they approve of his marriage? How are you sure that I'm the one you are looking for? When did you begin suspecting that I could be the king's granddaughter?"

"Calm down, honey. I'll explain everything."

"My dad never talked about his past. At least, not his family. He said his family was gone and that we were his family. When I was old enough to understand, he explained what I was and what he and Mom were. He taught me how to defend myself, how to be proud of my legacy. He also taught me not to be afraid. My mom's family was all the other family I had known. So why are they looking for me?"

I was still a bit taken aback and wondered what they could possibly want with my brother and me since my dad had had to go away and reject his family to marry my mom.

"To take care of you, of course. Your grandfather tried to reconnect with your dad. He tried to convince George that he had changed and that his marriage and kids would be accepted amongst our community. Then, all that tragedy happened to George. For a while, everybody believed that you and your brother had also perished. Then we got the news that Alaric was pursuing George's kids. Once again, we tried to get you to safety, but whoever was hiding you two was good at covering their tracks. Neither we nor Alaric were able to find you."

"Wait," I whispered, understanding something. "Alaric. The way you say that name. That's the name of the vampire who killed my parents. My father knew him. I'm sure he did. And you say his name as if you also know him well."

"That's because I do. You see, honey, we have a lot in common, more than you realize. But we'll talk about that later."

"You say you knew my father," I mumbled, sucking in the information that Shane was spilling onto me. "How are you so sure that the kids you are looking for are my brother and me?"

"I had no idea it was you until you told me how your parents died. Your age, the fact that your father was a pureblooded vampire, and your mom a panther were too many coincidences. So, we did a DNA test. The results arrived today. That was why Eric was in such a hurry to meet you."

"Eric," I whispered, opening my eyes wide. "He's my uncle, isn't he? That's why he wanted to see me. To tell me he was my uncle. But…then, why didn't you let him?"

"Yes, but I had to talk to you first. To explain to you what was going on. Eric had no right to do that to me. This news would have blindsided you. I was going to tell you tonight, but you got all stressed by the arrival of your cousin," he tried to explain as best he could. "I was going to tell you at home. I swear I was, Annabel."

The world was spinning under my feet as never before. All those new facts about my life were buzzing inside my mind. Even if Shane didn't want to hurt me, the truth was that he hadn't trusted me. Shane had been investigating my life behind my back. Besides, he'd never shared his suspicions with me.

"You can trust me, Anna. Didn't your father ever talk about his family? About me? I was his best friend before he disappeared with your mom."

I shook my head.

"Are you still mad at me?" he asked.

Shrugging, I didn't know what to answer him. I was more numb than alive. My grandfather was a Vampire King. Shane had been my father's friend, and James teased him about having a thing for princesses. *I guess I'm a princess.* If Sasha's also a princess...

"Is Sasha my aunt?" I enquired with narrowed eyes.

"No, Sasha is your cousin. Your aunt is June who lives in London. She's Sasha's mother. You have another cousin who is Sasha's brother. But he's still a teenager."

"Cousin... Does she know?" I smirked.

"Not yet. She'll find out once you talk to the king and the prince. Anna..." He hesitated. "Are we okay?"

"We need to talk to the king," I realized. Before I could explain why my phone vibrated in my pocket. I had received a message.

I pushed Shane back and looked at the screen. It was Jason. He was asking me to meet him right away. He had critical information to share and insisted it was rather urgent.

After purposely ignoring Shane's question, I faced him. "I need to go."

Shane stepped in front of me, and his gaze showed he was sad. "Anna, don't be like this."

Refusing to look at him, I folded my arms and stepped away from him.

"Honey, I still need to find out who stole your file. Please don't leave. Not while you're mad at me."

Pursing my lips, I faced his begging face. I gulped for air before I asked, "You followed me, didn't you?"

My phone vibrated again, and I stared at the screen. Jason was urging me to call him, so he knew I was okay. He was also asking if my wolf had locked me up, so I couldn't escape.

That's a weird question.

"I had to," Shane replied to my question. "I had to prove..."

Once again, my phone vibrated with my cousin's call. *He must be worried, texting, and then calling.* Still, I had been concerned before, and he hadn't even bothered to answer his phone or text me back. Jason could wait.

"What you had to prove?" I asked Shane.

"That you weren't an enemy sent by Alaric."

"How many times did you follow me, and why would you suspect me?"

"Sasha…" Shane pursed his lips. "She sent someone following you first. I had to prove your innocence."

My body relaxed with his explanation, even if I still felt betrayed. "What if I was the enemy? Would you kill me?"

He shook his head. "You would have a valid reason to be a spy and working with the purists that despise what you are. I'd help you escape them."

My anger melted with his reasoning, but I couldn't give in so quickly and put aside what he did.

"Anna, tell me you forgive me."

Putting my phone in my pocket, I endured his pleading gaze. "We'll talk about this some other time. Now, I need you to take me to my grandfather so I can save my brother."

He looked even more miserable than before, but I didn't even blink.

He frowned. "You said your brother was *gone.* Is he still alive?"

"I've been keeping him alive with my blood, but he's fading fast. He was hit by a dart infected with the killing-hybrid serum. Because he had pure vampire blood, he didn't die immediately. His body tried to fight the virus, but he eventually slipped into a deep coma. I've been donating my blood weekly to keep him alive, but only pure vampire blood can cure him."

"I'll talk to Eric immediately," Shane assured, taking his phone from his pocket and dialing a number. "You should have trusted me with that information sooner. We could have saved Kevin."

"You better not go there," I warned, feeling my phone vibrate for the third time.

"I promise you, I'll get those files back, but you should warn your friends and tell them to get out of the house. Their lives are in danger if the information I gathered falls into the wrong hands," Shane advised as he waited for someone to pick up on the other side.

I finally understood why Shane was so worried about finding the files. The information in there could harm my organization and me.

"I have to talk with Jason." I turned my back on him and answered my cousin's call.

I had to warn Jason about what was happening. Yet, somehow, I suspected that Jason's arrival to town had something to do with the files getting stolen.

I would put Shane at ease *after* I checked out my suspicions.

CHAPTER THIRTY

ANNA

THE MISSING FILES became a solved problem after talking to Jason. Shane could relax now.

My organization had found out about the investigation Shane and my birth family were pursuing. The hacking into our servers didn't go undetected and, in fact, helped us find out information about the people who were trying to hack us.

We had Liam to thank for that. Our computer genius can put to shame most of the supercomputers and geniuses in the world. Liam can hack anything.

Our leader had sent Jason to steal the files from Shane's office, and that was why my cousin had been so paranoid that afternoon and suspected my mate.

Once Jason read the file's contents, he was eager to tell me that I still had family and they were searching for me.

That was old news, so after calming him and telling him to call the clinic to prepare the doctors and the scientists for my guests' arrival, Jason was reassured. He planned to join me later at the clinic to keep me company and wait for Kevin's awakening. At least, we *hoped* my brother would wake up and get well.

So, with the problem of the files solved, it was time to leave, visit my newfound family, and ask for their help.

As soon as we left James's bedroom, Shane and I saw a crowd in the corridor waiting for us near the stairs.

Have they heard everything we'd said? The room had seemed to be soundproof. *Why are they gathered here?*

I walked further down the corridor, looking at the mix of some familiar faces and some I'd never seen before in my life.

Step by step, people bowed to me.

Apparently, everybody already knew that I was an almighty princess.

The idea was disturbing, as were the bows and the surprised looks on people's faces. It was as if I was a rare animal on display.

I continued to walk, aiming for the exit to enter the car and stop being the center of attention. However, my plans didn't work quite as well as I'd wanted.

As I prepared myself to go down the stairs and face another crowd of curious people, I froze.

Below, facing me, was a tall blond man. He had penetrating blue eyes, a well-built figure, and an anxious face. He could have been beautiful—a heavenly sight—if he didn't look so much like the man who had killed my father and my mom!

I thought I would be unmerciful and attack him once I faced him. But I was frozen in place, watching the vampire slowly climb the stairs toward me.

I needed to move, but I couldn't.

Shane should do something. I need him to do something. Why isn't he reacting?

Squinting and tilting my head, I looked at the vampire closely.

He was a few inches from me, piercing me with his gaze. His eyes were sweet and kind. Weirdly kind. He should hate me since he wanted my kind and I dead.

Something was wrong. *Why does he look so much like my father?* Now that he was closer to me, the similarities were daunting.

This man wasn't Alaric.

Had I imagined it? Am I going crazy? First, I'd thought he was Alaric, and now that I could see his eyes and kind face, I thought he looked like Dad! He was a slimmer, younger version of Dad with the same blue eyes. Alaric's eyes weren't blue. They were red when he was turned and green when he was concealing his vampire form. Alaric's eyes didn't have that happiness and kindness in them, either. Besides, Alaric was smaller than the man in front of me. His nose was also different, and his lips were plumper. This vampire's lips were like my dad's lips. He had my dad's traits.

He was my dad's brother.

This was Eric.

"Uncle?" I asked, out of breath, to make sure I wasn't losing my mind.

He nodded with a warm smile. Then, he pulled me into a bear hug, catching me off guard. I was squeezed inside his arms and was about to ask for help when he let me go and stared at my face again.

God, he's tall and strong! He also had a friendly smile with perfect white teeth. Kevin had eyes and eyebrows like him because my brother was the one who resembled Dad the most. He was blond and handsome. I had my mother's black hair and slim figure.

I was almost crying at the thoughts and memories that rushed back into my head.

"You are so beautiful! You look a lot like my mom, and you have your father's eyes," he said, his voice soft yet masculine. "For a moment there, I thought you saw a ghost and that you were going to run away from me!"

He laughed.

I was still too shaken to laugh. The resemblance was puzzling. *Why had I never noticed that Dad resembled Alaric?* If Eric looked like Alaric and my dad looked like Eric, then...

I was trying not to verbalize my scary conclusion.

"Are you okay, sweetie?" my uncle asked.

"What's wrong, Anna?" Shane questioned, placing his hand on my shoulder.

My mate. Those were the words that my heart and soul

repeated to my reason, over and over again.

Yet, somehow, I felt he betrayed my trust. I was still mad at him, even if he followed me around to clear my name. Still, I was sure that he hadn't told me the complete truth. He knew Alaric's true identity and was keeping that from me.

My mate knew that Alaric was my uncle. My twisted, evil uncle who killed my parents in cold blood.

Straightening myself and breathing deeply, I motioned Shane that I was okay and added, "I just need a bit of time to process all this. Please, give me some space."

He stepped back with puppy sad eyes, which made it hard for me to stay mad at him. Nevertheless, I had an important task ahead.

Looking at my uncle, I said, "I need to talk to grandfather."

"You sound worried," Eric declared, losing his cheerful face. "What's wrong?"

"It's best to speak somewhere private," I explained.

I should be happy with the new revelations. But I had to tell them about my brother's situation.

"Follow me, sweetie. We can talk in my car."

My uncle's arm wrapped around my shoulders, and I followed him down the stairs as my mind went in overdrive.

Shane should have told me sooner about who I was and his suspicions. I kept secrets from him. I know I did. Yet the secrets weren't just mine to keep. My friends' lives were at stake.

I hadn't used him to find out more about the Royal Family. I waited until I was sure that I could trust him. In fact, I was going to ask for his help that night once we got home.

Now I wondered for how long had he mistrusted my intentions and followed me around. What did the princess found out that lead him to believe that I might have been a spy? Had she lied to him and planted false evidence? Should I be happy that Shane didn't believe her and wanted to prove her wrong?

Maybe, I should.

As mad as I was, I believed that Shane and I were mates and our love was strong.

Yet, why is my heart feeling so heavy?

Eric's question snapped me out of my thoughts. "Are you okay? You're shaking."

"I'm just anxious," I mumbled as I leaned closer to him. I'm not a hugging person, but I missed my dad, and Eric was the closest I've been to Dad for a long time.

My eyes teared up with the memories, and I clumsily squashed them with my fingers.

Eric squeezed my shoulder with a gentle smile. "It's okay, sweetie. We found you, and you're home."

I smiled at him. "I know… I just miss Dad."

"Me too."

I felt the emotion and suffering in his answer. Clenching my teeth, I cleaned a rogue tear and focused on reaching the exit, ignoring everybody around us who bowed and whispered.

Stepping outside, Eric and I entered a fancy car flanked by two other cars with his bodyguards inside. He was well protected. Someone could look at him and think he was the president of the country or, at least, the governor of some state.

Numbness and sadness were clouding my reactions. With the car already in motion, I looked around, and there was no sign of Shane.

I felt lonelier than before. His absence made my body cold. "Where's Shane?"

I know I asked for space, but I didn't send him away, did I?

"He's following us in his car. He knows the way, don't worry."

Eric's reply made me feel less anxious.

I focused on my uncle. His smile was reassuring, and he was extremely handsome. I took note of the similarities and differences between him and my dad.

"I'm delighted to meet you. I know Dad will also love you. You're gorgeous," he said, holding my hand. "You don't need to be afraid of us. We don't want any harm to come to you. We've looked for you for so long! I'm glad you survived. And I'm also happy for Shane and you being mates. Your dad would be pleased, too. He would be more than pleased. He and Shane were good friends. He would probably want to beat up Shane first, but he would be glad for the two of you being together."

That statement made me chuckle. Daddy would most definitely kick Shane's ass first. Not that I would let him do that, but he was protective when he was alive. He had warned away other boys from school when he knew I had a crush on them or when they'd wanted to be more than my friends.

However, I was a big girl now. I could take care of myself, and I could … I was just glad to know that Dad would approve of Shane.

"So, how are you coping with all this?" he asked, snapping me out of my thoughts.

"I don't know. When Shane told me, I was shocked. I had no clue that Shane knew my father or that my family lived here," I said, trying to smile at him, to reassure him that I was not afraid and trusted them. They had no reason to harm me.

"It was a delightful coincidence. Shane was one of his friends who supported his determination to leave and be happy with his soulmate. At the time, my father was not pleased with the idea of my brother leaving and giving the crown away. However, George couldn't be king if he was married to another species. Mentalities were different then."

"I know," I whispered.

"Shane's like a brother to me. Grandpa is thrilled, and I'm also happy that Shane is your mate. So, don't worry about it. No one will be against you two loving each other." Eric smiled, trying to get a smile from me. "You shouldn't be mad at him."

"I can't help but feel disappointed in him. He should have told me his suspicions about knowing my father and that I had family here."

"We were waiting for the DNA results. Shane shared with us his suspicions last Sunday. We didn't even know that you were alive until he told us his findings. He didn't want to share you with anyone! He didn't even tell us that you were a hunter. He was protecting you and did not want to betray you. He would never do that to his soulmate. To him, you are the most precious thing in the world. He even kicked my ass this afternoon for wanting to meet you after I got the results."

"Yes, I know." I smiled after hearing that. It also helped to know that Shane had kept my secret safe until he knew it was safe to tell them. I had overreacted.

"Don't be so hard on him. He didn't have an easy life. Did he tell you how he met your father and came to live with us?"

"We haven't talked much about our pasts," I said, nibbling on my lip with curiosity.

"You will have a lot of time to do that," Eric assured. "But I can tell you some details that will make you comprehend why he understands your pain and your loss perfectly."

I nodded, dying to know.

Eric indulged my curiosity with his sweet, calming voice. "You see, it was your dad who saved Shane from slavery. He was still a pup. He's a bit older than me, about two years or so. Shane's family was killed, and he was taken prisoner by mercenaries along with the surviving members of his pack and his dad. In the past, some vampire lords enslaved werewolves to work in the mines and build their towns."

"Slaves?" I asked, unable to conceal my shock and disgust at such barbaric acts.

"Yes, it was common. Vampires were greedy and searching for riches. Many packs that came here looking for a new place to live were dismembered and the survivors sold for labor work. He was only thirteen when his whole life was torn apart by the mercenaries who slaughtered and raided his father's pack. Most of the women were raped and killed or taken to be sold as sex slaves. A lot of them took their own lives rather than be taken and abused."

I gasped in horror.

Eric nodded with empathy, understanding that it was not a pretty description, but it was the sad truth. "His younger brothers were killed. They were not strong enough to work. His father's other surviving members were taken to be sold. They never got to the market, though. Your father saved them on the road. Not all vampires were bad at the time. You are just like your father. He couldn't stand injustice and the improper use of power. He would have been a wonderful king."

"I know he was a good person. So, Daddy saved Shane's life?"

"Yes. After that day, Shane followed your dad everywhere. Especially because his own father was broken and died shortly after his mate's death. Werewolves break apart when their soulmates perish. Shane was left alone in the world. No direct family that he knew was alive. So, our family took care of him and the rest of the pack," Eric said, sharing parts of Shane's life.

We have a lot in common.

I became emotional, understanding why it was so important for him to protect the king and his family and protect me. I was his only family. Before I met him, I had Kevin and Jason. Shane had no one, and he didn't want to lose me. I didn't want to lose him, either.

There were still a lot of things I needed to know about Shane. There were many sad events that he had faced alone in life. We needed to talk and forgive each other.

"So, you see, Shane thought all this time, while he looked for you and your brother, that he owed your father his life and that he would defend his kids with his own life if he had to. If he loved you before he knew that George was your father, now he probably worships the ground you walk on."

I furrowed my eyebrows and made an unpleasant grimace at my uncle's last words. *Talk about pressure!*

"Oh, come on!" he teased. "You let him mark you—it isn't like you don't feel the same way he does about you."

"I do," I said, feeling a blush on my cheeks.

"Forgive him and forget all of this. No harm was done. No need to stay mad. Also, your grandpa already thinks you are going to marry Shane and give him great-grandchildren."

"What?" I widened my eyes while Eric burst into laughter.

"It's not like any one of us can do it. Sasha is mateless. The pressure is on you and Shane."

I couldn't tell if he was joking or being serious. I was only twenty-three. For an immortal, it was a young age.

"Okay, forget I said that," Eric suggested, still appearing amused. "Let's talk about something else."

"He spied on me," I shared what was hurting me the most about Shane's attitude. "I can't help but feel betrayed."

"He was worried about you because Sasha sent someone to follow you around, and she believed you were a spy."

I nodded. "He said the same thing."

"He wasn't lying," Eric assured. "If he didn't follow you to find out the truth, you'd be locked up and interrogated." He folded his arms. "For all we knew, you could have been sent here to gain our trust and kill the king."

I fluttered my eyelashes as I thought about my uncle's words. "You're right. Even if Shane and I are mates, that doesn't mean I couldn't use him to hurt you and your family."

Eric nodded. "It's your job to infiltrate and kill your enemies. We aren't enemies."

"I know. It's been a while since I know that this town isn't like any other I've been to."

"We are willing to trust you if you're willing to trust us," Eric added.

I nodded. "I trust you, or I wouldn't request this urgent meeting with your father."

"Your grandpa wouldn't want so long to meet you either," Uncle Eric said with a grin. "And he's not that old, either. At least, not in appearance."

"Okay." I mused for a few moments. "How did you know how to find me at James's house?"

"James called. He told me what had happened—the missing files and the invasion of his home, along with Shane accusing him. I got worried, too. Then Shane called me and told me everything. Dad had also called to tell me to pick you up and bring you immediately to talk with him. I'm sorry you had to find out about us like that."

I averted my eyes with an overwhelming awareness of mixed feelings. I wanted to save my brother more than anything at that moment. I had to postpone my talk with Shane. There were important things to tell my grandfather and a young man's life to save. "I'll reassure Shane that I'm no longer mad at him after we save my brother."

Uncle Eric leaned closer. "Your brother? Is he alive? I thought... Shane said... We all thought that there was only you left." He looked astonished, and I felt bad for not telling him sooner. I had told only Shane. I was planning to tell my grandfather and uncle when we were all together.

"Well, it's a long story. I guess Shane didn't tell you on the phone. He told grandfather, though."

"Maybe Dad forgot to mention it to me. He was eager to see you."

"Well, Kevin is barely alive. But I'll explain everything when you and grandfather are together to spare us time."

"Okay, we are almost at the palace, anyway," Eric said, pointing outside where I noticed two large iron gates opening automatically to let the cars in.

Did he say palace?

My eyes widened in awe.

Bathed by the moonlight and golden spotlights pointed at the garden's rocky walls, stood in all its majesty and gothic beauty a majestic palace.

I guess a typical mansion wouldn't suit a king.

CHAPTER THIRTY-ONE

ANNA

WHEN I GOT OUT of the car, the initial shock of seeing the palace was overshadowed by my urgency to see Shane. I wanted to run into his arms and hold him tight.

Everything Uncle had told me about his past rose in me the need to hug and console him. Even if I was still upset about his investigation of my past and following me around, I knew that he had done it to protect me. He had said it himself. Even if I had been a spy, he wouldn't let them catch me. He'd loyal to me.

Yet, I should scream at him for not telling me who my father was to him and that my family lived here.

He even prevented my uncle from seeing me and telling me about my origins.

After standing still with my back to the palace and staring at the driveway past the palace gates, I noticed that there were no signs of Shane arriving. *He wasn't coming.*

Why isn't he coming? Is he mad because I'd ignored him and gotten upset with him? Is he leaving me alone here, with my uncle whom I'd just met, and all those Men in Black look-alike guys?

I bit my lip then my cheek, only to look at my uncle, defeated. He was quiet beside me, also looking down the dark empty road.

"Where is he?" I asked with an exasperated sigh. "You said he was following us."

"He was," Eric reassured me and motioned toward the last car behind us to get the attention of the driver. "David, do you know what happened to Shane?"

The driver exited the car, walked toward us, and bowed respectfully before replying, "He was following us, but when we were reaching the palace, he turned around with the emergency lights on and drove back to town. I heard them calling him on the police radio. A group of teenagers was fighting. It's probably some pack rivalry because of the game this weekend, your majesty."

I sighed in frustration.

Won't the confusion end tonight? And can't Shane send someone else to control the dispute?

I knew he was the sheriff, but I needed him right now. I would feel a lot more secure with him by my side.

I should reach him on our mind link.

I stopped my thoughts and gazed at my uncle. Eric had cleared his throat and gave me a boyish grin when he got my attention. His eyes sparkled every time he smiled. He was gorgeous and seemed more like my brother than my uncle. We looked as though we were the same age. He had a reliable aura and impeccable manners for a two-hundred-year-old vamp. Is his royal title and social position didn't seem to affect his humble personality. He also radiated confidence in how he talked and tilted his head to look down at me. He was rather tall.

Leaning his face closer to mine, he asked, "What's wrong?"

"I find you extremely nice, so I don't understand how you picked up a fight with Shane." I giggled at the face he made when he furrowed his eyebrows and pinched his lips together. "You seem completely healed."

He smirked. "I didn't pick a fight with Shane. He picked a fight with me. His wolf can get possessive when it comes to the things they love."

I felt my cheeks warm up and covered my cheeks.

His voice was soft when he asked, "Are you less mad at him?"

I nodded. "I wouldn't know what to do with my life if I discovered that Shane was my enemy."

"What do you mean?"

"For just a few seconds, I thought that he had tricked me and…" I bit on my lower lip and shook my head. "It takes me a while to trust anyone. I lowered my guard with Shane and allowed me to … need him."

"He's your mate. It's a natural response," Eric assured.

My lips curled up as I gazed at him, and a warm feeling took over my chest. "I still can't believe that I found my dad's family."

"You have no idea how grateful I am to you."

I frowned. "Why?"

"You gave a reason for Dad to keep living for a bit longer," he whispered with shining eyes. His hands fell on my shoulders. "Forgive us for not finding you sooner."

A tear rolled down my cheek, and I rushed to wipe it out with my sleeve. "Sorry. I didn't mean to cry, but you look a lot like Dad and…"

He puckered his lips, shook his head, and patted my head. "Nonsense. I'm so much more handsome than George ever was." I frowned, and he chuckled. "I'm joking. I know we look alike. I don't mind. Do you mind?"

"Not at all."

"Good!" Stepping back and straightening up, he said, "Dad is waiting for us. We shouldn't make him wait. Shane can join us after he takes care of whatever is happening in town, and we can talk more about your dad and what you've been doing some other day."

I nodded, agreeing. I was a big girl; I could handle the meeting with my grandfather, the king.

Uncle Eric added, "When you see him, you can call him grandpa. He'll like that."

"Do you and Dad look like Grandfather?" I wanted to be prepared this time.

Just imagine if my grandpa is the spitting image of that monster Alaric? I'll freak out again!

He shrugged. "I guess."

I exhaled and looked at my cell phone, eager to call Shane. Did he think I didn't want to see him? I might have been angry, but I wasn't mad anymore.

Grandpa was waiting, and Shane had work to do. I'd check on him later and hear his side of what happened.

"Shall we?" Eric asked from the huge, black, gothic front door beneath a small portico. Someone had opened the door for us to go in.

I followed my uncle inside. The sumptuous décor took my breath away. I barely noticed the ceremonial greeting taking place with the tall, serious-looking man dressed as a butler. He was holding the door and bowing to us, gaze on the floor.

My eyes focused on the huge hall and the two curved, cantilevered staircases that rose from the east end of the grand foyer. That was the first thing that I noticed. The first floor had a long corridor with alcoves filled with huge paintings of Roman gods in shiny, baroque, golden frames. The hall was laid out as an oval. An enormous central bronze and crystal chandelier hung from the glass cupola over the entrance and spread tiers of light in flame patterns. The ceiling was as beautiful as the rest of the hall. It had surrounding frescos of what seemed to be nymphs and animalistic shifters that told some tale that I didn't recognize and didn't have time to ask about.

I stepped onto the white and black marble floor, reflecting the chandelier's light, and followed my uncle, who was already climbing the first row of stairs. I didn't have time to fully take in how, near the downstairs landings of each staircase, there were doors that went somewhere else in the palace and that at the middle of the arch beneath the stairs was a huge glass door that gave entrance to a ballroom. I was too mesmerized by the paintings and the velvets that hung on the walls and screamed baroque style. There was a wide variety of styles inside the palace, which made it unique and less pretentious than most palaces I had seen during my visits to Europe with my parents.

"We have to go upstairs. Dad must be in the library. He is often there," Eric explained, stopping for a second, so I could catch up with him.

The house probably didn't amaze him anymore since he lived there. I was just hoping to memorize the way to the library, so I wouldn't get lost if I had to leave alone.

On the first floor, we followed a long corridor illumined by small sconces on the walls; it had doors on both sides and many paintings of landscapes with rivers and mountains. At the end of the corridor, Eric opened a bigger door that gave way to the library.

If the hallway was amazing, the library was huge; it would probably take up an entire building. I noticed it even had some spiral stairs going up to my right. When I entered the room, what hit me was not exactly the decorations and the bookshelves but the smell. It smelled like oak and linen, not musty at all. It smelled like books, but not like old, dusty books.

The library itself was a masterpiece from ceiling to floor. There were frescos on the ceilings surrounding the small crystal chandeliers. The walls had even more works of art, columns, Greek gods statues, and even some contemporary art as decorations.

There were rows of bookshelves, perfectly aligned and categorized by theme and century. Books with leather covers and hard paper ones filled the shelves.

I even spotted stacks of parchments out of the corner of my eye.

It would be a dream come true for any book aficionado or historical researcher. They could spend years inside, overwhelmed by the variety of books and their antiquity.

After traveling through the jungle of bookshelves and their corridors, we arrived at an open space with a twin-pedestal mahogany desk with a rectangular top inset in green tooled leather. It was filled with books and papers and had a modern desktop computer. On the opposite side rested a black velvet armchair. No one was sitting in it, much to my disappointment.

Guess Grandpa hadn't waited for us and perhaps had gone to bed.

Eric didn't seem surprised by the absence of the king like I was. He turned right and smiled as though he knew something I didn't.

I turned to him, frowning, and he pointed at the back of the room. There he was, with his back turned to me, staring at a huge painting of a lady dressed like a queen. The image was big—two times bigger than Eric! It covered half the wall of the library.

"That's my mom," Eric whispered, not wanting to disturb the silence. "Dad likes to stare at her."

I acknowledged his words and gazed at the woman in the painting. She was beautiful, without a doubt. It was an old painting with many influences of the Romantic period because the painting tried to convey both the majestic quality and innocence of the queen. The landscape had a light blue sky with shreds of clouds. The queen had a soft smile on her pretty face and profound brown eyes. She had her hands on her lap and had been painted in a seated position, wearing a white silk dress. Her brown hair was loosely braided and piled on top for a Victorian look.

I was supposed to look like her, but I thought that the resemblances ended with her lips and the shape of her face. And maybe the nose. I had a rather small, upturned nose. I liked it. So, instead of seeing my grandpa, I had my first meeting with my grandma's painting.

My grandfather was the next person I analyzed. He had his hands folded behind his back. He was wearing a white silk banyan, very king-like, with lovely silver brocade and rich gold embroidery on the sleeves and collar. They may be his casual clothes at home, but they were enough to leave me impressed by the mystery around him. He also had a signet gold ring that attracted my attention for its simplicity.

The vampire king seemed to notice that he had company. When he turned to face us, I came face to face with a tall, well-built man in his mid-forties, with a friendly face.

The king didn't look like a dying old man. He was handsome, distinct, and with a full beard. He had some wrinkles around his eyes and forehead, but nothing that would say he was perishing fast or that he had grandchildren my age. He had aged nicely. What made him look older was probably the beard and the old-styled wavy, blond, shoulder-length hair. He had kind blue eyes.

Summing up, he looked older than the rest of us because age had taken possession of his once immortal body. However, aging had given him a distinct and honorable appearance. He was a rather pleasant man to look at and didn't seem like a grandfather at all.

When he saw Eric and me, his attitude, once gloomy and thoughtful, was replaced with a smile as he walked toward us.

I don't know why I did it. I'm not a hugging person, but I walked to him, and when we met halfway, I hugged him.

It wasn't a shy hug, but a firm and warm one like I had known him all my life and had missed him dearly.

That was my father's dad! I could totally see my dad in his smile. He was definitely the one who reminded me the most of him.

"Isobel," my grandfather spoke with an emotional voice.

I smiled wider at hearing my second name. Dad had wanted to honor his mom's memory by naming me, Isobel.

"You grew up so much, darling! I just saw you once when you were two years old. You also hugged me like this."

"I did?"

"You did. You asked me why I looked so much like your dad. I told you that I was your dad's father, and you hugged me. You told me that you were happy that your name was Anika Isobel. Your dad had a mom named Isobel, and Isobel was your favorite name."

"I don't remember that," I whispered, emotional.

"You were too young to remember. But I thought you were adorable, sweet, and cute. I fell in love with you at first sight. I asked your father to bring you here to visit, but things were a bit complicated between him and me. He still resented my unwilling attitude from the past toward letting him go to be happy with your mom. But I knew the world would be cruel to them. But...now that I see you, I know George made the right choice."

"Dad," Eric interrupted, now near us. "Kevin is also alive. Did Shane tell you?"

"Yes, he told me after I'd talked to you."

"I need your help to save him," I explained, remembering that we didn't have time to waste. We could catch up after Kevin was cured.

"Sweetie, you just need to tell me what you need, and it is yours," Grandpa said.

I smiled at him, thankful for his words. It meant a lot for me to meet my family and be welcomed by them like that.

My grandfather was tall like Eric, which made me feel small beside them both. I was still hugging him with my head leaned and my chin on his chest, so I could talk to him. He had strong arms and a wide chest frame. He also smelled nice, a mix of honey and lavender. I liked him already.

I told him the best I could about what had happened and how Kevin was in a coma fighting for his life. I needed their blood to cure him and make him wake up from the deep sleep. They were more than happy to help and leave immediately to the clinic to start donating Eric's blood because he was younger and stronger.

While Eric talked with his chief of security, arranging more cars and bodyguards to keep him and his father safe on the road, I tried to call Shane.

No answer.

After the third call, I grew frustrated.

Is he ignoring my calls?

He had better be busy, or he would be in serious trouble.

I was being immature. Shane was doing his job.

But I needed him to know where he could find us since we were leaving for the clinic, so I decided to reach him using our mind link. I was going to ask him if everything was okay, but all I heard was a loud, painful sound. I flinched, covering my ears in a defensive position. Breaking the mind link, I gasped for air.

What is going on? Why can't I reach Shane? And where is that loud noise coming from?

"What's wrong?" Eric asked when he noticed my pained face.

"I was trying to reach Shane, but all I could hear was a loud and painful sound that made my head hurt, and my ears almost bled!"

"Was it like a sharp noise you hear when you are looking for a radio station?" The chief of security asked me.

He was a werewolf, so I guess he could hear other frequencies that I didn't and understood them better. *But why did I hear that in my head when I tried to reach Shane?* It had never happened before.

I nodded. "But one hundred times louder."

"That isn't good. He might be in trouble. You heard inside Shane's head," the werewolf explained, becoming paler. "We experience that noise and pain when witches are attacking us. Their chanting slows us down and leaves us almost defenseless."

"What?" I asked, panic slowing my heartbeat and freezing my body. *A witch is attacking Shane?*

"We need to send men to find out what's going on," he said, holding his phone to his ear. "No one is answering at the police station."

I was losing my ability to think straight, but I couldn't agree more. Looking at Uncle Eric, I stuttered, "I-I need to go to Shane. I need… H-how do I get out of here? What's the shortest way to town?"

If I'd known where to go, I would already have been gone. I wouldn't be wasting my time waiting for them to send men.

"And Kevin?" Uncle Eric reminded me.

"You and Grandpa go to the clinic. I need to go to Shane first, and then I'll go to the clinic to meet you. They know you're coming. Jason texted me, saying he had called them. They are preparing to receive you. But I need to go, now," I urged, looking at the garden and beyond the trees to see how far I was from town.

In my vampire form, I could get there faster.

"I need a weapon," I remembered after shifting to a vampire.

Eric said something to the chief of security, and the man promptly set a plan. "We have weapons in the car. Aaron will take you to town, and I'm already sending more men there to investigate and help. I can't reach Shane, either, or any other wolf that was supposed to be at the police station today."

Those words only made me more worried. What if they were

dead? And if Shane was…

I could hear static, so he was probably still alive. Hurting, but alive. I couldn't lose any more time.

"I need swords. Do you have any swords?" I asked the young man who came to take me to town.

"In the trunk," he said, opening the trunk of the car to show them.

"Be careful," Eric advised.

I nodded and gave him a quick hug.

I went to the trunk and picked two swords after swinging them in the air, testing their weight. They were not as good as mine, but they would have to do.

"I'll drive," I said to the guy, grabbing the keys from his hand before he could even blink. "You lead the way."

I entered the car and started the engine.

Aaron barely had time to sit and close the door before I sped my way out of there.

I used my mind link again, but this time, to contact Jessica. It was a spell she had done for me to use for emergencies, and this was without a doubt an emergency. I would need her help if witches were involved. The only problem was that Jessica was miles away, and she could only give me advice, not real help.

"I need your help," I said, using my inner voice, trying to get her attention. *"Are you sleeping? Jessie! Wake up! I need you!*

"Calm down, girl!" Jessica replied inside my mind. I could almost imagine her rolling her eyes and complaining at the noise I was making.

"Did I wake you up?"

"No, I wasn't sleeping. So, what's up? Why are you shouting like crazy in my head?"

"I need your help!"

"Couldn't you use a phone?"

I mentally growled as I made my way down the curvy, dangerous road I was driving.

Meanwhile, Aaron held on to his seat with a scared look on his face and was probably also holding his breath. But I was in a hurry. Besides, I had sharper senses that allowed me to drive like this without crashing the car into pieces against a tree.

"Okay, calm down. Tell me what's going on. Weren't you at a family reunion?" Jessica asked.

"Yes, but now—wait, how do you know that?"

"Who do you think helped Jason steal the files?" she inquired, probably pursing her lips, annoyed at Jason for taking the credit.

"Jason? Are you with him? Please, tell me that you two are still in town…" I asked, sounding hopeful. If only I should be so lucky as to have them backing me up.

"Sorry, but no. We're in the car, leaving. But we aren't very far. Why?"

"Great! Turn around and come back to town. I need your help. Something is going on. Someone is attacking the town. I can't contact Shane—a witch is using her power on him. Hey, it isn't you, is it?" I asked, frowning as I considered that fact. Who knew what those two might be doing!

"No, of course not. I only hurt bad people."

"Sorry, I'm going crazy. I really need your help. Witches are…hard to handle. They have all those tricks. Please, turn the car around and come help me."

"Okay, calm down. We've already turned around. We're heading back to Affinity. And be careful. If a witch is powerful enough to interfere with mind links, then you are in deep trouble. Try to keep her occupied until I track your presence and save you."

"I'm almost there. I can already see the buildings," I said, happier. The town was in my reach. My heart was pumping blood fast, and the adrenaline was clouding my actions. *"Just get here fast, to neutralize her powers. I'll kill her if she hurt Shane."*

I almost lost control of the car. I needed to slow down, for I was finally entering the town and had to figure out where the attack was taking place.

CHAPTER THIRTY-TWO

ANNA

I USED MY INSTINCTS to find Shane. After all, we were mates. Even if I couldn't access his thoughts, I could sense his presence and follow it.

I tracked Shane to an industrial area with abandoned buildings and mostly storage facilities. His car was parked in an alley, but there was no one around.

Once I parked, all I had to do was follow the sounds of fighting and struggling. I could sense at least six other people there, whimpering and afraid. I could also smell two different races and a witch.

I used my stealth abilities to approach and scout the area for the attackers. I wanted to spot Shane's location and make sure he was still alive.

I couldn't react harshly, though I was worried sick. I had to figure out how many attackers there were and reach out to Jessica to tell her my location and to request her to hurry up.

My heart almost stopped when I saw what was going on. There were six young wolves and a girl in a corner with a male vampire watching them, so they wouldn't react or move. He had a gun in his hand. Next to them was a male body down on his stomach. His face was not turned to my side, so I didn't know who he was. I could tell that he was still alive, even if his heart was beating slowly and he seemed unconscious.

Meanwhile, I perceived a pile of ash soaked in blood next to the male. A few meters from me, I saw two other males in police clothes. Once seemed to be dead and the other unconscious but bleeding.

Shane was nowhere to be found to my dismay, and my

anxiety skyrocketed once I realized that the police officers on the ground were Shane's deputies.

Something more serious than a group of teenagers fighting had happened there. Shane's presence hadn't faded, so I had arrived in time. Still, I had to do something because I wouldn't allow anyone else that I loved to die.

I was about to leave my hiding spot when a body flew across the street and crashed against the wall behind a canister in the back of the alley.

The clicking sound of shoes echoed as two shadows floated and took shape under the dim light of the chandelier.

Narrowing my eyes, I focused on the pair of woman boots and the muffled sound of male shoes: the woman was a witch, and the male smelled vampire. My senses also told me that Shane was close and that the witch was still mumbling the crippling spell to render my mate defenseless. I focused further and caught the sound of his heavy breathing and moans of pain.

Three enemies would be easy to handle since I was immune to the witch's chantings. I had to deal with the guy with the gun first and then go for the witch before disabling the vampire that was with her.

Yet, my plan came to a halt when the vampire male strode alongside the witch, and the light glowed against his face. That was no ordinary vampire, but Vincent Alaric's evil right-hand man!

We had crossed paths before. I had no idea of how old he was, but he had been turned by Alaric, and they were inseparable.

Is Alaric here? What's going on? What brought Vincent to Affinity?

Vincent seemed to be alone with his goons. I couldn't sense anyone else.

"Tell me who she is," Vincent growled.

Lowering down, he grabbed Shane by his collar and crushed

his body against the wall.

As Vincent stood him up, I had a clear vision of Shane's bruised face. He had blood on the corner of his lips, and his eyes were swollen.

My heart shrunk inside my chest, and I thought it was going to explode with the hurt and pain that took over as I spotted Shane's bleeding eyebrow, lips, and a bullet wound in his shoulder.

My body quivered when Vincent pressed two fingers into Shane's shoulder wound, and my mate howled in pain.

The scum was torturing Shane for information.

"Tell me!"

"Never!" Shane spat as he tried to endure the pain and resist the torture.

"Hit him again," Vincent ordered the witch next to him.

Obeying, she pressed her hand to his forehead and did something that made Shane scream louder as if he was being consumed by the most excruciating agony.

The sharp pain I had experienced must have been the witch torturing Shane. She's not just blocking the mind links. She's also using her powers to inflict extra pain.

Anger built up in me, and I had to dig my nails against the wall to stop myself from attacking them immediately.

I had to be smarter and stick to my plan. Even if Vincent was a skilled warrior, he'd be outnumbered once the backup arrived.

Firstly, take out the vampire guarding the werewolves, and then go for the witch and Vincent's head. I should go for Vincent first. Even if the witch was dangerous, her master was more vicious and cunning.

I had to save the kids, but I couldn't let them

"Tell me who she is! I want to know who the hell the king's

granddaughter is!" Vincent ordered loudly, making my heart beat faster than before.

He was looking for me, and Shane was being tortured because of me. I shrugged in pain and held back my tears.

No time to cry. I had to act.

The other vampire was still walking back and forth, staring at the group of young werewolves and a girl, who one of the boys was holding tightly as if she was precious to him.

The boys looked pretty beat up, too. They had probably tried to defend themselves, but I had no clue what they were doing there. It wasn't a place for teenagers to hang out.

The girl kept sobbing while the guy was trying to calm her down, but she cried more every time she heard Shane screaming.

"What are we going to do?" Aaron asked behind me, startling me.

"What are you doing here? Didn't I tell you to stay in the car?"

"I'm a trained bodyguard," he said in a grumpy voice. "I can help."

I guess I didn't have any other choice. He was the only backup I had. Therefore, I looked around again, trying to see if there were only three invaders.

Vincent didn't usually travel that light.

"What are they doing to the Sheriff?"

"Torturing for information," I whispered. "Be quiet. They might hear us."

Aaron placed his hand on my shoulder. "The prince ordered me to protect you. Stay here, and I'll save Shane."

I grabbed his forearm before he did something stupid. "Just stay put and follow my lead. I have a plan, and as long as you can save the kids from the big bully vampire watching over them, I can deal with Shane's attackers."

Aaron frowned as if not convinced.

"If I'm the prince's niece, I'm your superior," I reminded him.

"Fine," he muttered. "What do you want me to do?"

"Your task is to get the kids free and kill the vampire guarding them. Do you think you can do that?"

"Yes, I think so," Aaron said, taking out his gun.

He was going to speak, but I held my hand to his chest and motioned him to be quiet. The one guarding the kids had stopped and was observing around.

Even with the crying and Shane's screams, he might have spotted our whispering. Which reminded me that I had to act quickly.

I pointed at Aaron's target, but I grabbed Aaron's shoulder and pushed him back when another vampire landed on the ground, coming from the rooftops, and headed to Vincent.

"We need to get moving. They have sent back up," the guy informed Vincent.

The witch stopped the torturing, and Shane slipped down the wall with an exhausted expression.

"Did you find the files in that idiot's house?"

The vampire shook his head. "No. I sent a group to the high school. She might have them there."

Vincent slapped the vampire across the face. "Stupid! I hope you told your men to retrieve all the electronics and flash drives in her home."

The vampire nodded.

"Order your men to survey each entrance and hold back whoever comes," Vincent ordered.

I looked at the rooftops trying to figure out how many others he was talking about.

"I'm going after this new vampire, so he can't deploy his

men. You'll only attack when I come back and go for their leader and the witch. Okay?"

He nodded.

The other vampire, who had talked to Vincent, disappeared again onto the rooftop.

Stepping back, I straightened up, turned around, and ran to the buildings surrounding us. Leaping into the building's rooftop, I followed the vampire in his super-speed mode.

I knew I was faster than him, and he was concentrating on running. Therefore, he didn't notice when I sneaked up on him and sliced his throat open. Holding his body against me, I covered his mouth to muffle any attempt to cry for help. His body convulsed as he choked on his blood.

I couldn't let him live. Therefore, I turned him around, and, with a fast and swift movement, I took his head off. The vampire disappeared in ashes blown away by the wind and carried into the moonlight.

I flinched when I heard Shane scream again. Focusing my super hearing on what was happening far below me, I heard them talk.

"I'll never tell you," Shane declared.

By the sound of his voice, he was weak and fatigued.

"I guess I don't need you alive anymore, do I?" Vincent threatened.

My heart squeezed, and I hurried back to save him.

"Is that supposed to scare me?" Shane asked.

I heard the sound that Vincent's fist made against Shane's face and ran faster before landing on the edge of the rooftop and focus my vision on Shane's bleeding face. I was about to look around to see if I could spot Aaron when Vincent's words caught my attention.

"Tell me who she is! I know she works at the school!"

Vincent growled at him.

"How do you know that?" Shane asked, his voice with an edge of panic.

"We found the files," the witch informed Vincent. It seemed she was communicating through a mind link with someone. "We can leave and figure out the woman's identity at the fortress."

"Alaric won't be happy with us. We lost our leverage here," Vincent said. "Stupid bitch. She didn't need to die."

"We need to leave," the witch urged him.

She was nervous and probably scared. *She should be. I am going to kick her ass for hurting Shane.*

I finally spotted Aaron, who nodded his head when I signaled him. I showed him three fingers so we'd make our move in simultaneous when I got to three.

"What do you want me to do with the kids?" the vamp asked Vincent.

"Kill the fucking hybrid scum and let the wolves live," he instructed. "This one, I will kill myself." He smirked at Shane and removed a silver dagger hidden under his coat.

We had no time to lose. The moment the vampire strolled to the girl with a wicked smile and everybody but the girl's boyfriend whimpered, I moved my hand, so Aaron saved them.

I heard growls and more whimpers, but I was concentrated on the dagger that was aimed at Shane's chest.

Positioning my sword, I jumped down and aimed my blade at Vincent's neck.

My opponent had sharp senses and used the dagger to stop my attack before I could cut his head off. We had fought before, and he was someone to be feared. Yet, there was no way in hell that I would let him hurt Shane.

My attack made Vincent jump back and push the witch aside, which allowed me to waltzed around Vincent and put myself in front of Shane to protect him.

Vincent's dagger glowed as he moved it up and down and clanged against my blade.

For a few seconds, my enemy locked his black eyes with mine. "Kage? What are you doing here?"

"I could ask you the same question, Vincent."

He sneered. "Sightseeing, killing, and tormenting people. The usual."

I rolled my eyes but caught the quick glancing back he did. He was probably looking for the rest of my crew. Too bad that I had no idea how long Jessica and Jason would take to get there and help me.

Allowing him to breathe was a mistake, especially with a witch by his side. I used my strength to force him back while glimpsing at the witch who had fallen on the floor and seemed disoriented.

I kept swinging my sword, and Vicent kept parrying my strikes. I had to drive him away from Shane.

"Tell me, Kage," he demanded, pushing my sword down and stepping back to protect himself better. "How did you find me here?"

It seemed the first shock of seeing me had passed. Now, he was appearing to sound courageous while distracting me with small talk.

From the corner of my eye, I saw Shane holding on to his shoulder and breathing hard. He knew I was there, but he was weak. He could barely open his eyes. Not far from there, Aaron was shooting at the vampire who was running in circles, trying to avoid the deadly bullets.

"Vincent," I mumbled his name with a smirk.

Kage was my codename in my group; it meant shadow in Japanese. My enemies knew me by that name, not my real name.

It was how I had survived all that time, living a double life. Making their lives a living hell.

"How is your hand? Did it grow back?" I deflected to remind him of the pain I had inflicted on him the last time we'd encountered each other.

"It's all good now," he said, showing it to me.

Smirking, I glimpsed forward, watching Aaron being beaten up by the vampire after running out of bullets. I almost sighed with frustration. Then, I saw the werewolf kids jump on the guy, trying to help Aaron. Some were thrown in the air while the others still tried to prevent the vampire from moving and hitting them.

"Is he a friend of yours?" Vincent asked, resting the blade of the dagger against his shoulder.

I frowned, perplexed by his relaxed attitude.

He browsed the rooftops and glimpsed at his witch. He sneered at her, but when he looked at me, he looked amused. "If he's the only backup you have, you're not getting out of here alive."

I huffed at his bold statement. "We had this dance before, and you ended up running away."

Vincent raised his hand, pointed his finger, and made a gesture for her to move closer to him.

Looking at the witch, she seemed calm, considering what was going around her. Yet, I noticed that it was more than serenity. There was an emptiness in her gaze that gave me the chills. Nevertheless, she had urged Vincent to leave, so I knew she wasn't as relaxed as she wanted me to believe.

I hadn't had time to closely watch her before, but now all I could think was how young she looked. She couldn't be more than seventeen.

"I'm in no mood to dance tonight, so I'll let you play with my new pet," Vincent said nonchalantly.

Before I do anything, I was thrown back by an invisible force and crashed against Shane's body.

It took me a moment to understand what had happened and why Shane was behind me.

"Be careful," Shane moaned, his hands grabbing my arms. "She's very powerful."

I moved forward with gritted teeth. Shane was already wounded, and he had become more because he used his body to protect me from crashing against the brick wall.

The invisible protective runes that Jessica had cast on our crew made us immune to the majority of reciting spells. But against witches who could summon any of the five elemental powers and use telekinesis, we were almost defenseless.

Shane's painful moan when he knelt and held to his bleeding shoulder made me look back, but I had to pretend not to be concerned with him. They couldn't know that we knew each other.

"We got ourselves a gentleman here," Vincent mocked. "But you are both useless against Myra." His expression changed to disdain. "You shouldn't have underestimated me and show yourself without your witch friend only to save a bunch of worthless kids and a stubborn werewolf."

"Probably not, but I'm not very keen on letting you kill innocent people," I retorted, noticing how the witch seemed to be interested in looking at me.

"I like what you did with your hair," she mumbled with a smirk. "Is that a spell when you turn or did you dye it?"

I frowned and held my sword tighter. "It comes with the transformation."

"Cool. It matches your eye color."

Vincent held tight to the girl's arm. "Don't talk with your prey. Deal with them and then leave."

I used their interaction to reach Shane through our mind link. *"Whatever you do, don't show affection for me. Don't protect me. Don't even look at me."*

"Why?" Shane asked, probably thinking that I might still be mad at him.

"Honey," I whispered sweetly in his mind. *"They will kill you to hurt me. Please, do what I ask if you love me,"* I said, trying to get control of my feelings.

I couldn't show weakness, and Shane was my weakness.

"Are you that confident that I can't take down your new pet?" I asked Vincent, trying to stall until Jessica got here.

I gazed at the witch with an overconfident grin on my face. "Do you even know how to fight?"

"I don't need to fight. I just need to crush you." She stepped forward, but Vincent stopped her.

"Maybe… I should stay," he said.

She groaned. "I can take her, and you need to leave."

Most of the witches were arrogant like that. Without their stupid spells, though, they were harmless and weak as any other human.

"You can try, little girl," I dared her, tilting my head to look at her from head to toe with disdain.

She didn't just look young but was also dressed like a teen, with heavy gothic black clothes and chains on her pockets and jacket. She had black lips and black nail polish on her nails.

Way too much makeup on her face! It was probably to make her look older. She must think she's some badass black magic follower.

I didn't know what to think since, for all, I knew she might have been forced to work for Alaric, or she was plain evil and enjoyed killing and harming innocent people.

"What are you looking at?" the witch snarled.

She pulled her black hair behind her ear, pursed her lips, and moved her nose with a distasteful sniff. She was not pleased about my scrutinizing stare.

Two more vampires appeared in a flash behind her and Vincent. I wasn't expecting them, but their arrival made the witch smirk at me and arch a cocky brow.

So, she's not alone, big deal! I could take two vampires with no sweat. It was her nasty spells I was worried about.

I rolled my eyes at her, releasing a bored sigh, and smiled wickedly. The first rule in this business: don't ever look scared. Looking fearless makes your opponents doubt themselves.

"Have fun," Vincent said and jumped in the air, flashing away in super speed.

Coward! He's leaving to save his butt, like always.

"Guess it's just us," I said.

I noticed that the werewolves had succeeded in knocking out the vampire. Still, they were just kids; they should run instead of getting in the middle of that fight. I was hoping that Aaron was wise enough to take them out of here.

The witch frowned and stared at one of the vampires behind her. "Make sure to kill the hybrid girl and leave these two to me," she ordered.

Before I could move, the vampire left to attack the boys, and the witch started to recite a spell. Once again, her magic made the wolves start yelling in pain and drop to their knees, holding their ears.

The vampire was going for the girl who screamed in fear. She wasn't affected by the noise, which meant that she was a hybrid like me.

Vampires and hybrids weren't affected by the spell. There

was only Aaron left to protect her.

Aaron tried to stop the vamp, but he was hit hard with several blows to the face and stomach until he knelt, coughing blood.

We needed a miracle.

I growled at her, hearing Shane's groan behind me. Whatever she was doing, I needed to stop her.

Flashing forward, I aimed at her throat so she shut up. But the other vampire stood in front of me. We fought, sword with sword, sending sparks of fire each time our swords collided. He was skilled enough, and he was strong.

After a few blows, I was able to shred his shirt and slice his chest, which bled. It was not too deep, but it was enough to make the witch lose her breath when she noticed I had harmed the vampire.

Before I could press on and end him, she had thrown me in the air with her power. This time, I stabbed my sword in the floor and tried to hold my place, but the sword broke.

I crashed against a canister, rolling on the ground until I hit the wall.

At least, the pain in their heads had stopped, and one werewolf boy was grabbing the vampire's leg to protect the girl. The vampire got mad and held the boy by his neck, choking him. The girl reacted, jumping on the vampire's back, so he would let go of her friend. It was only a matter of time before he would kill both.

Meanwhile, I had to jump and roll again. The witch used her power to throw a canister at me, and I didn't want to be squashed. As I was getting up, I heard a neck snap, and I shivered in sorrow. Someone had just been disabled, hopefully not dead. Werewolves wouldn't die of a broken neck, but it meant the girl had no one to protect her.

"I hope you don't get too upset when I take your vampire lover's head off," I teased the witch, who was concentrating on attacking me again.

Another canister fell on the ground, making a loud noise. My words had some effect on her because it broke her concentration.

I smirked, pleased to find her weak spot. *A witch in love with a vampire—so interesting, especially because it was forbidden in their cult.* No-mixing-races rule.

"Don't threaten my mate," the witch growled, losing her calm attitude and holding a fire orb in her hand.

I didn't have time to be surprised by her new power. It was unusual for witches to control two elements. I barely had time to flip backward before seeing the orb hit the wall and leave a dark stain.

I noticed the shocked look on the vampire's face at her words. He looked back at the other vampire in his group, afraid he might have heard, too.

It was a secret. *Of course, it was.*

Well, he didn't have to worry about it. I grinned when I saw my cousin with the vampire's neck in his hands.

"Did I arrive in time?" he asked, throwing the vampire's body on the floor and helping the girl get up. He had killed the vamp temporarily, just in time to save the girl.

"Perfect timing," I said, relieved to see him.

"We should leave," the vampire said to the witch, looking around. "The master is safe. We can go back home."

"I'll kill her first," the witch said in disagreement. "Friends of yours?" she asked, turning to Jason and using her power to throw him against one wall and then against the opposite wall like he was a ping-pong ball.

I gasped and ran to stop her. Her mate grabbed me. I hit him in the face and turned his arm around, making him scream with pain when I broke it and made him flip forward to hit his back on the floor. I was about to place my foot on his neck and pull his arm to crush him when the witch used her hands to push me from her lover.

Her hands burned on me, making me step back and try to erase the fire she had left on my jacket. At least she dropped my cousin on the floor, unconscious, and stopped beating him up.

"You bitch!" she snarled at me after looking at the damage I had done to her vampire.

She seemed livid.

I unintentionally looked at Shane to see if he was okay. He was weak, breathing with difficulty. He opened his eyes when I stared at him, sensing my concern. He tried to smile to reassure me, but I knew he was losing a lot of blood and had broken bones. Vincent had beaten him several times before I got there.

I heard bones crack. The witch had put the vampire's arm in place. She was also helping him get up. His arm was around her shoulders, and her hand rested on his chest.

"You know," she said softly like she wasn't mad anymore. "It's the second time you looked at him."

I couldn't make a straight face when she said that. I think she saw the fear reflected in my eyes because she held up her hand and conjured a fireball that swirled above her palm.

I hated witches and their sneaky powers. *And where in the hell is Jessica? She is taking her sweet time!*

"Let's go," the vampire begged with a pained voice.

"Let me teach this bitch a lesson." She smirked and pointed her hand at Shane. "I thought so," she said when she heard my gasp of fear and saw my eyes widen in concern. "I saw the bite mark on his neck. He belongs to a vampire—you, I bet." She looked cocky about her reasoning as she made the orb float higher.

Before she could open her mouth again, I jumped on her neck. The vampire fell to the ground, and I held her up by her throat.

"You lowered your guard," I muttered, showing my fangs as she fought for air.

I should have snapped her neck right away and finished her off, but she looked so young and vulnerable! I was about her age when I was orphaned.

She was a child! I couldn't kill a child.

I saw the fear of death in her eyes. The tears were building up as she tried to free herself. I waited for her to fall unconscious from lack of oxygen but was interrupted.

Her mate, weak and hurting, tried to stop me but was held by Shane, who grabbed him and knocked him to the ground. The witch used the distraction to put her two hands on my shoulders and make her fire burn me.

I screamed in pain, letting her fall. It hurt so much I could have cried, but I didn't have time. She was aiming her hands at Shane.

I shouldn't have let emotions cloud my judgments. I should have killed her. But I had no time for regrets.

Jumping in front of Shane, I followed the two orbs coming in our direction and held my breath while I wrapped my arms around Shane's body.

It was going to hurt, and I loathed fire! But I was a damn vampire-panther hybrid. I would survive.

I hoped!

One orb hit something, but it wasn't me. At the last second, it changed its course and crashed against the wall. The other orb just stood there, floating in the air in front of Shane and me.

Until, I understood why.

"Hello! Did I arrive here in time, love?" Jessica asked, walking in her high-heeled boots and bouncing her hips with all the calm in the world. "Why don't you play with someone of your own species?" she asked the witch with a playful smile.

Turning her hand around, Jessica made the witch's fire orb disappear.

My friend knew how to make an entrance! But was I mad at her for being late. Or maybe she'd arrived just in time.

"Where have you been? Why did you take so long to get here?" I snapped as I helped Shane get up.

He was still bleeding from his shoulder. It should have stopped already. I made him sit away from the confusion.

"Hey!" Jessica complained, putting her hands on her hips. "I walk at normal speed, and I'm in high heels! Jason parked far from here!"

"Whatever," I replied to her. "Have fun," I added and made a movement with my hand for her to take care of the intruders.

Jessica could handle the witch. I was worried about Shane.

"Why isn't your wound healing?" I asked him.

"I have shards of silver inside," he explained, pulling the jacket away and showing the ripped shirt with the bleeding scar.

Jessica's voice boomed in the alley. "Let me introduce myself."

"Let's leave, now," the vampire holding the witch urged.

"I'm Jessica," my friend said after clearing her throat to get their attention. "And I'm a witch," she added, stroking her blonde hair back. Jessie must have lost her focus because of the vampire. "Is he your lover? I'm so jealous now. He's so gorgeous!"

I rolled my eyes at Jessica's girly voice as she drooled over a vampire.

Seriously? She couldn't see a hot vampire without commenting.

I swallowed my laughter when the witch roared at her in a possessive way, making sure she understood that he was hers.

Jessica giggled. "Oh, he's your mate?"

"I know who you are," the witch finally said.

I stared at her, hurting Shane in the process as I tried to pull out a shard. I apologized to him. But what did she mean by her claim to know Jessie?

"Have we met before?" Jessica asked. "I don't remember you. What coven are you from?"

"Black Dalia," she answered to my surprise. Witches didn't usually give away their coven's name so willingly.

"Ah," Jessica said, but I knew she had no idea about the girl's coven. She always answered like that when she didn't want to be rude.

"We're related by blood, you idiot," the girl snapped at Jessie.

"Huh." She smiled like the girl hadn't just insulted her.

I had already taken out the shards in Shane's shoulder while trying to be gentle. He was in pain, but he also wanted to know if things were good between us.

"We'll talk about what happened after we're all safe," I whispered, biting my wrist and putting my blood in his mouth before he could say anything else.

Closing his eyes, he drank and then filled his lungs with air.

Growls and the movement of people reached my ears. Backup was coming. The wolves were arriving.

"Don't let them run away," Shane requested in my head with urgency.

I looked at the vampire and the girl who were looking back, noticing the pack of wolves coming to attack them.

"I'm taking you away from here," the vampire whispered in the girl's ear.

She nodded and started to recite the spell that made the

wolves howl and kneel to the ground in pain.

I should have cut her damn tongue off!

I took my wrist from Shane's mouth and held him in my arms. I tried to reach him in his mind. I heard the loud static noise, and I felt his pain. I tried to tell him that everything would be okay, that I was there with him. And then, the noise stopped.

When I looked up, the vampire and the girl had left. Jessica was left standing there, looking at the void.

To my surprise, Jessie had let them run away and done nothing to stop them.

CHAPTER THIRTY-THREE

ANNA

THE PACK OF WOLVES ARRIVED and snarled at Jessica and Jason.

We all looked up when we heard gunshots from the roof. I could see other vampires armed and aiming at some unknown point. I imagined they were aiming at the vampire and the witch who had gotten away.

Backup had taken a long time to appear but had finally arrived. However, the wolves were growling at the wrong people.

"So that's the way you people thank me for helping, is it now?" Jessica asked, seeming disappointed as she spoke to the angry, growling wolves.

"Stand down!" Shane yelled and coughed. "The hybrid and the witch are friends."

I held him, worried. There was still a lot of silver dust in his bloodstream, weakening him. My blood would eventually heal him completely, but until then, he'd be suffering.

The wolves stopped the noise as they scattered around, sniffing the wounded and dead bodies all around. Two unconscious enemy vampires had to be taken to prison. Aaron got to take care of things like he was the boss.

I watched as he dusted off his suit, fixed his tie, and then shouted orders for the helpers to take care of the wounded and arrest the vampires before they woke up. It seemed that Shane had a serious challenger for the job of sheriff.

"I'm already thinking of taking a vacation anyway," Shane whispered.

I looked down at him, resting his head on my lap while tuned into my thoughts.

"I'm going to take some time off to be with you. I could have died tonight."

"Yes, you could have." My voice trembled. It had been terrifying to think about the possibility of losing him. "I'm so mad…"

"Anna, I'm so—" His words were interrupted.

"Somebody help here!" One of the kids gestured to get attention. His group opened to reveal a body behind them. "Alpha, talk to me. Alpha, tell me what to do!"

I looked toward the body and recognized Sebastien.

"Oh my god! What happened to him?" I asked, running to his side, kneeling, and seeing the blood. Meanwhile, one of the wolves howled at the moon next to a policeman's body. There was a casualty. I was hoping Sebastien wouldn't be the next one.

I looked at the boy, who faced me with worried eyes.

"Can you please help him, miss?" the boy asked, knowing me from school. I also recognized him, but he was not my student.

Sebastien was more dead than alive. I had no idea why they had attacked him. I had to assume it was Vincent and his bullies, but why? And how? What was he even doing there?

The medic was not arriving soon enough to treat him. I was shaking, scared for him. The boy was also worried, applying pressure to the wound Sebastien had in his stomach. I had to do something to save him, so I reopened the wound in my wrist and put my blood in Sebastien's mouth.

I wasn't going to let my friend die.

When I looked up, Shane was by my side.

"He was hardly breathing," I explained, not wanting him to be jealous about me using my blood for Sebastien.

"Don't worry about it. You did well. He can't die. He's our ally and friend. It would also be chaos in our town if something happened to him."

I nodded.

"Is he going to be okay?" the boy asked, looking at me full of hope.

I nodded at him, trying to look more reassuring than I felt. The fact was that I didn't know. I had no clue how much of my blood I was able to get inside of him. He wasn't conscious enough to drink, so I had to force it into him.

"I tried to help my Alpha," the boy explained with a sad voice as tears rushed down his cheeks. Embarrassed, he cleared his eyes with the sleeve of his sweater. "But the guy was really strong."

"Who did this to Sebastien?" Shane asked.

I looked up, intrigued by his question. *Didn't he know? Wasn't he here to witness what happened?*

"When I arrived, Sebastien was already on the ground, and the kids were being attacked by vampires. I thought they were rogue vampires. Then my men and I were assaulted by Vincent and his witch. We tried to fight back, but she used her powers on us. Vincent shot my deputies with my own gun…" He stopped talking to take a breather, also emotional about the memory. "And then kept me alive longer to…"

"I know," I said, not wanting him to explain anything else. "I heard that part. I came as soon as I could. I didn't know—I'm sorry."

"It's not your fault," he said sweetly, caressing my cheek and kneeling next to me. "I didn't even expect to see you here. How did you find out? They were blocking our mind link."

"I tried to reach you, and I heard the noise inside your head," I explained. "Don't ever do this to me again." I leaned my forehead against his.

"The Alpha was trying to protect the teacher," the boy explained.

Now it was my time to ask, "What teacher?"

"The pretty blonde vampire teacher from our school," the boy explained. "She was also your friend, miss."

"Evelyn?" I asked, shocked and worried. "Where is she? I didn't see her."

"He killed her. She's gone, miss," the boy stated with sad, apologetic eyes.

My face showed an array of emotions: worry, shock, anger, and finally, sadness. "No! She can't be dead. I talked to her today. She wasn't going…" I remembered that Eve had asked Sebastien to go out with her. He must have said yes after refusing. "You must be mistaken!"

"Sorry, we weren't able to help her," the boy lowered his eyes and fisted his hands.

I calmed down and breathed deeply.

It wasn't his fault. He was just a pup. What could he possibly have done? They had already done a lot, defending the hybrid girl and trying to help their Alpha.

"I tried to help. We all did. My friends and I heard them being attacked. We tried to help the Alpha coach." The boy looked nervous and defeated for not being able to help Sebastien.

"We were called here to break up a fight," Shane added. "We assumed it was just kids having some stupid quarrel with another pack of wolves or among themselves. We saw them fighting the vampires. I didn't see Evelyn anywhere. And I saw Sebastien lying on the ground after Vincent told the witch to put a spell on us."

"That was because the female vampire had already been killed by the evil vampire guy. He was upset with her—he was hurting her and arguing. The Alpha tried to help the teacher, but there were four against him, and he was stabbed with a silver blade. Miss Evelyn screamed at them to stop, and she tried to get the Alpha out of here, but the vampire didn't let her. He grabbed her by her neck, said she was his cub, and he would do whatever he pleased."

"Wait, *what*?" Shane asked, confused by the boy's last words. "He called her his cub?"

"Yes, sir."

Shane was going to say something else when I was startled by Sebastien moving on my lap. He reacted, coughing out blood and gasping for air like he had just come back to life.

Sebastien's hoarse voice got our attention. "Evelyn was a spy."

We all looked down at him with relief. The color was returning to his face.

"What?" I asked, trying to understand what he had said or if he had really said that.

"Evelyn was a spy. She was here, spying on us. I took her home after leaving James's party. She had insisted so much that I finally agreed to go out with her. We were having fun until she received a text message and seemed frightened." He coughed before adding, "She asked me to take her home, claiming that she was sleepy. I did that and decided to go for a quick patrol around town to see if my boys were partying instead of resting." He looked at the boy. "I found their group in the park, drinking without being old enough, and when I was lecturing them, I noticed Eve leave her apartment and go towards a deserted part of town. It intrigued me, so I followed her."

"So what happened here?" Shane asked.

"She met with three vampires and a witch. They were talking secretively. She was giving them some papers—the security measures for the prom. She also told them about the missing granddaughter of the king. She wanted to renegotiate her freedom in exchange for this information. I tried to leave without being noticed, to warn others, but other vamps were hiding. I tried to outrun them, but they were faster and caught me. Then Eve attempted to help me. I didn't expect that! She was killed because she protected me from her master. I think the stronger one was her master. He got upset with her."

"How did the kids end up in this mess?" Shane questioned.

"Alpha called for backup," one of the boys explained. "We share mind links. We were closer, and we rushed to help."

"It was a stupid move. You should have waited for the police," Shane said, holding on to his ribs, still in pain.

"We called the police," the boy explained. "But if we hadn't done anything, they would've killed the Alpha."

"It's true," Sebastien said. "Things got out of hand. Eve's master killed her in cold blood, right before my eyes. Her cover was blown, and he didn't need her anymore. I tried to stop him, but the witch…" His voice failed him, and he moaned in pain. "I think I have a piece of silver inside me. It burns!"

On cue, Jessie arrived from helping the other wounded and knelt next to him.

"Hello, gorgeous! My name is Jessica, and I'll be your doctor for the evening," she said with a happy grin that distracted Sebastien from the pain.

He looked at her with a confused expression.

"Relax and take a big breath." She put one hand on his forehead and another over the wound in his stomach. She pulled the silver out with her kinetic power.

Sebastien let out a small moan of pain as the piece left his flesh.

"All done, love. You'll survive thanks to Anna and me." Then she got up and looked around. "Next!"

"Me," the boy next to Sebastien volunteered.

"Oh! Hello, love," she greeted with her nice accent that made the boy turn red. "What's your name, pup?"

"I'm—I'm Leonard."

"Who is that?" Sebastien asked, as he looked at Shane and me.

"She's my friend and saved our butts," I answered. "Are you feeling better?"

"Yes, are you? I want my mate's lap back!" Shane teased Sebastien.

He stared at the place he was at and where Shane was and smiled. "I really like her lap," he joked, and then he lost his smile and looked away.

"I know." I understood his pain. "Eve being a spy was something I'd never expected. She was nice and friendly at school. In fact, she was one of my closest friends there."

"I wonder how James will react," Shane said, lost in his own thoughts. "We need to change our security measures for the school prom, and I need to find out what names they took to protect the kids."

"I can't believe Eve is gone," Sebastien mumbled, getting up from my lap.

I rose to my feet, helped by Shane. The three of us stood looking at the alley full of people who were talking and taking care of the dead, the captured, and the wounded.

All that was left of Eve was a pile of ashes.

Sebastien stared at it. "I appreciate you saving my life, Anna. I owe you one."

"Don't worry about it. That's what friends are for."

"Bro," Sebastien said, putting his hand on Shane's shoulder, "you, too. Thank you for having my back."

"You have to thank the kids. They were the ones who came to help you and made the noise, so the police arrived on time. They saved your ass," Shane stated, trying to cheer him up.

"Yes, the kids were great. Reckless, but great."

"You are their Alpha, man," Shane reminded him. "They worship you."

"You six," Sebastien shouted at the boys, who were mostly healed, talking to Jessica as they drooled over her like any hormonal teen. "What the hell were you thinking?"

Sebastien lectured them with some tough love about irresponsible attitudes and suicidal behavior in fights against adults and strong beings. It was almost funny. One moment, they were heroes; the other, they were in detention for saving Sebastien's life. It seemed a bad thing to do, but it was necessary. Better being alive than being dead heroes.

Shane held my hand and got my attention. I turned to him, and we both stared at each other quietly. We didn't know what to say. I didn't know, at least. I had been mad before, but now that all those things had happened, I was just relieved that he was okay. His eyes were sad, showing how much he wanted me to forgive him.

"Uncle has already explained to me why you followed me," I told him. "I understand why you did what you did."

"Why do you still look mad then?"

"I'm not mad. I'm annoyed that you almost got yourself killed! What were you thinking? Why didn't you follow us to the palace?"

"They had no one else to back them up. And I didn't think I was going to get myself in the middle of a fight with Alaric's men."

"That's another issue. Why didn't you tell me that Alaric was family? He's my freaking uncle! You knew I hated him, that he had killed my father."

"I was going to tell you everything when we got home. That was why I didn't let Eric see you this afternoon. I knew you would spot the resemblance and freak out. I was trying to protect you and find the best time to tell you."

"Well, how did that turn out for you?" I asked, unable to hold back my sarcasm.

"Not so good..." He looked down at his feet. "But I love you. Everything I did was to protect you."

"I know," I mumbled, knowing perfectly well that Shane never intended to harm me.

"I could never expect that you had such a big secret to protect," Shane mumbled. "At the time, all I cared about was to prove that you weren't a spy."

"What if I was one?"

"You'd have to have strong reasons for it."

I gulped and nodded. "I'm just glad you're okay. I can't afford to lose anyone else that I care."

He moved closer. "Did you meet your grandfather?"

I nodded and nibbled on my lower lip. "You knew Dad."

He reached for me and held me in his arms, caressing my hair. "Do you have any idea of how hard I've searched for you and your brother?"

I shook my head as I held back the tears.

"Now that I've found you, I'm..."

Tuned on his thoughts, I silenced him with my lips on his since I could feel his love for me and all the conflicted emotions swirling in his heart.

I could have lost him, and my life would have been over.

"You scared me to death," I said, my words muffled against his lips.

He knew what I was referring to because he hugged me tight and stroked my hair. I was allowed to feel vulnerable next to him, so I was not going to hold it back. I'd been afraid for him, but also annoyed at him for being so damn reckless.

"I was not reckless, honey. And I love you more than

anything in the world. In fact, I think I just fell in love with you all over again," he whispered in my ear, raising my chin with his finger, so I would look at him. "You are my favorite superhero," he added, making me smile.

A tear rolled down my cheek; he caught it with his thumb. I stared at his lips and closed my eyes. I needed him to kiss me again.

"So…" Jessie spoke next to us and killed the moment.

Shane and I stared at her as she asked, "Aren't you going to introduce us to your wolf?"

"We're kind of busy." I furrowed my eyebrows to make her understand that it was not the best time to interrupt us.

"You two have a lot of time to do that. Now that I've saved your lives," she reminded me, folding her arms. "No need to thank me. Anyway," she said, breathing out, "Jason and I want to meet your mate."

"Fine! Shane, this is Jessie and…" I looked past her and saw my cousin, holding his head with his hand. "That's Jason."

"Hi," he greeted. "I'm Anna's cousin."

"And the guy who stole your files," I added, folding my arms as I glared at him.

"Yes." He chuckled, adding, "And read them."

"Oh!" Shane said.

It intrigued me because he felt shy in his thoughts all of a sudden.

"Yeah, dude, like you have a serious fixation on my cousin. I mean, Kage. You have to read what he wrote about you!"

"What did he write?" I asked, gazing at Shane, who had turned red. "Before or after he knew who I was?"

"Before, much before. He admired you. I guess it's good that you and Kage are the same person, or you'd have serious competition."

"Now I really want to read it." I leaned closer and brushed my lips against his. "So, I'm your superhero, huh?" I smiled, and he smiled back.

"Shouldn't we be going to the clinic?" Jessica reminded us, staring at her watch.

"Yes, we should," I said, holding on to Shane's hands. "We need to get going. Eric should be getting there any time now."

"Who's Eric?" Jason asked.

"My uncle."

"We can go in my car. I can turn on the emergency lights, and we won't be stopped," Shane offered.

"That's a good idea."

"I'd rather go in my car, but I can follow you," Jason said.

As we prepared to leave, Shane gave Aaron total control over the operation.

The captured vampires would be locked away until Shane decided to come back to question them, and the kids would go back to their homes after giving their statements. The dead officer would be transported to the morgue, and his family notified. That was the hardest part. At least, the other one who had been shot was out of danger, thanks to Jessica's healing abilities.

At that moment, I solely wanted to get to the clinic and wait for my brother to wake up. I hoped it wasn't too late for the blood to work. The doctors and researchers all counted on him to recover, so they could make a vaccine that would inoculate hybrids against the serum and stop the silent, deadly chemical weapon from killing other hybrids.

CHAPTER THIRTY-FOUR

BETH LOOKED DOWN at the deadly fall into the ocean from the balcony of her bedroom.

The fortress, as they called it, was situated on a high cliff above an ocean view. Even for her, a pureblood vampire, it would be difficult to survive that fall. However, most of the time, throwing herself into the void sounded more appealing than living there with her kidnappers and abusers. The only thing keeping her alive was her sister. Otherwise, she would have gladly asked for an end to this life.

At least her holder, who had the arrogance to call her his mate, was nowhere to be seen. She had slept alone, without his hateful presence and insatiable appetite for raping her. But she had to face it: he wasn't as evil and insane as his master. Alaric was the epitome of evil. He was her worst nightmare. She was as scared of him as much as she hated and wanted to kill him.

To make things worse, Alaric was her sister's mate. Her real soulmate. They didn't have the fake mate bond that Alaric had imposed between her and his loyal subject, Vincent.

Beth was Alaric's gift to Vincent, a gift Vincent treasured and made sure to treat a bit better than Alaric had treated her. She had gotten out of the dungeons and was living in the main house, in Vincent's bedroom, as Vincent's mate. She hated him a bit less than Alaric, but she couldn't show it. Vincent had a sick obsession with her that he called love. Meanwhile, Alaric still harassed her and made her life miserable.

At least, her sister Marie had started to talk with her again after months of silence.

Beth's life was complicated and meaningless. Why not just jump? All she had to do was climb out and fly to freedom. It would feel like freedom to fall into the deep, deadly waves that crashed against the rocks below, like falling asleep and never waking up again.

She leaned forward, her hair falling over her face and pulled everywhere by the wind. Then she felt arms surrounding her waist that brought her against someone's chest.

"What do you think you are doing?" a hoarse voice asked next to her ear.

It startled her and left her breathless, especially when she understood who was holding her. She shivered with horror, wanting Alaric to let her go immediately, but she said nothing and did nothing to upset him.

Upsetting him was a bad idea. She wouldn't make that mistake again.

Sniffing her hair and trailing his hand from her stomach to one of her breasts, he held it and released a moan of pleasure.

"I missed you. My worst mistake was giving you away. Did you miss me?" he asked with what could be a sensual voice had he not been as sick and twisted as Beth knew him to be.

As much as she hated Vincent, being his kept Alaric away from her. Most of the time. Even Vincent couldn't control Alaric's urges.

Not that Vincent wasn't twisted enough, but not as bad as Alaric. Which she was aware, it sounded like an excuse. Vincent was the less of two evils, but it didn't make him less of an abuser to her.

His voice sounded harsher when he spoke again. "Don't you miss me, Beth?"

He turned her on her feet, forcing her to look at him.

Beth gazed, breathless, at his green, evil eyes that demanded a swift response. She had to lie to make him happy.

"Yes," she whispered, just audible enough for vampires like themselves.

His face softened, and his mouth spread, opening into a terrifying smile that made Beth swallow hard. She hoped he would leave and not try to force himself on her.

"You are such a bad liar, Beth," he sneered at her. "You know I didn't have any other choice but to give you away. You know because you probably asked your sister for that. You bitch!"

Alaric was being psychopathic like always. One moment, he was sweet; the next, he made a one- eighty-degree turn, becoming paranoid and violent.

"I didn't," she whispered a bit louder, putting her hands on his face and trying to make him believe that she cared for him, so he would calm down. He had serious abandonment issues. "She was the one who was jealous."

Her words seemed to have an effect on his mood. Beth had no idea why, but she was the only one who could calm him down. She wasn't even his mate—her sister was. However, Alaric hated her sister. He scorned and abused her. He would beat Marie, even knowing that anything he did to her, he was doing to himself.

They were bonded, not only by a mate bond, but also by a spell that had been cast on him a long time ago by a witch. It was the only thing that kept Beth's sister alive all these years.

Beth had no idea how many years they had been trapped there. There were no TVs or any kind of technological gadgets to keep track of time. It had felt like an eternity.

"You should be my mate, not her. That would make you love me and want me," he said with a boyish voice that sounded almost unnatural on him.

Beth hated when he said things like that. She would most likely cut her head off with a guillotine if he had been her mate. The idea of being forced to love him was the worst torture imaginable.

"Vincent is so lucky to have you," he added, hugging her tightly, almost making her lose her breath. "Don't you miss me, Beth?"

Beth almost sighed out of impatience. They'd had that conversation already. She didn't want to repeat herself to make him happy. She just wanted him to leave her alone with her misery.

"Didn't you?" he asked, irritated this time.

"Yes, I did," Beth lied again.

His hug became less possessive and hurtful. "You aren't saying it right, Beth. Do you want me to punish you?"

"No, master, I don't," she answered, shuddering.

She wanted him to leave. If the gods existed, they would make him leave. It was all she was thinking and begging, trying to hold back her tears. She felt his hands circle her back, trailing his fingers on her spine until he grabbed her butt cheeks. He groaned with pleasure, and it made her shriek in fear.

"You are so beautiful, it hurts," he whispered, smelling her neck again.

"Master, please don't do this," she begged. Showing fear would only make it worse, but she needed him to stay away from her.

He didn't seem to hear her. He was busy pulling the skirt of her dress up her legs and kissing her neck.

"I promise, I'll make you feel good this time," he said in her ear, nibbling her earlobe and whimpering in lust as he reached her inner thighs with his fingers.

Beth suppressed a scream when she heard him say that. She seriously doubted he could make her feel anything but hate and disgust.

"She'll hurt you," she said, trying to change his mind. It was all she could think of, though she doubted that it would make him stop. He liked pain; he wouldn't mind if her sister hurt him.

"When I find the witch to cancel the spell," he said, holding one hand on the top of her dress and ripping off the front, "I'll make you mine."

He gazed at her breasts in her bra and smirked at the sight of her upper body. His eyes turned red, and his fangs grew in his mouth.

Beth squealed in terror, immediately putting her hand to her lips. No screaming, no screaming. He liked it when she screamed and asked him to stop. He liked it when she fought him off. It made him hurt her harder and take longer to satisfy his needs. When she looked at him, he was not smirking anymore. He was still gazing at her face, but he seemed hurt in some weird, twisted way. His fangs disappeared, and his eyes turned green again.

"I said I wouldn't hurt you this time," he hissed menacingly. "So why the fuck do you have that look on your face?" He was yelling now, making her sob.

Tears fell down her face.

"Don't cry, don't cry," he begged, worried as if he actually cared. Twisted and crazy was all Beth could think of him. "Just stop crying," he repeated, seeming to lose his patience again.

Beth did her best to obey. She cleared her tears with one hand and held her damaged dress with the other.

"Good girl, now give me a kiss," he whispered near her mouth, waiting for her to lean forward to touch his lips.

She stared at him, perplexed and gasping for air, praying to the gods to make him go away for good.

"What the fuck is going on in here?" an annoyed woman's voice screamed as if Beth's prayers had been answered.

It was her sister, Marie, Alaric's mate.

"What the fuck did I tell you about getting near her again?"

She sounded pissed with her mate. "Did you think I was joking? Do you think I'm going to allow this to continue to happen? I will fucking kill myself! Do you hear me? I will. I'll fucking do it!"

Marie entered the balcony where Alaric stood with his back turned to her, holding Beth by the waist.

Alaric rolled his eyes with a grimace at the screams of his mate. "We were just talking."

Letting Beth go, he turned to look at his enraged mate—a young woman of average height, with green eyes like his, and long curly brown hair. She looked similar to Beth, but was smaller and seemed much more fragile. She was pretty when she was not screaming like a mad person.

"Do you think I'm that stupid?" she asked, fisting her hands and narrowing her eyes like she was about to jump on him and tear him apart. "Get away from this whore," she ordered, pulling him away from Beth, who was staring at her sister and holding her breath with a pale face.

"And you, fucking jealous bitch, stay away from my mate," she yelled at Beth, slapping her across her face and leaving a red mark on her cheek.

Beth didn't react, but suddenly throwing herself off the balcony was looking a lot better than continuing to live in this place with a bunch of deranged people. Her sister was being territorial about her mate. And Beth was the one who kept getting the blame for Alaric's twisted obsession with her.

"He is mine, whore. You have your own mate. Stop hitting on mine!"

"He's not my mate," Beth spat at Marie, annoyed by her words.

She was to blame for Alaric giving her to Vincent. She was the one who had arranged the whole twisted exchange. Her attitude hurt Beth. It was the only time that Beth had tried to kill herself and leave Marie to her fate. However, the attempt had failed. Hateful Alaric had saved her and made Vincent torture Marie in front of Beth, knowing that it would hurt her more than doing it to herself. He taught her what would happen to Marie if she tried to kill herself again. Seeing Marie's skin peeled like an apple was not a good thing. It haunted her and made her have nightmares for months.

"Well, that is the only one you are going to get," Marie said in a hateful voice that made Beth's heart hurt.

She missed her loving, caring sister. She didn't know the woman in front of her. Marie was nothing like what she used to be. She was evil and hateful and had this crazy idea that Beth wanted Alaric to herself and that she was jealous of Marie for finding her mate first. But Marie couldn't be more wrong. She couldn't be more different than the kind, cheerful person she had been before Alaric appeared in her life.

"And you," she snapped at Alaric while Beth held her breath. "Do I have to remind you what—" She didn't say anything else.

Alaric walked into the bedroom, grabbing Marie's wrist and forcing her to follow him. He had been silenced, but his eyes were changing from green to red.

That wasn't a good sign.

Beth lost her breath when Alaric held his hand high and slapped Marie's face so hard that she was thrown against the chest of drawers and mirror on the other side of the bedroom.

Beth sagged in despair when it happened but couldn't feel any kind of empathy for Marie. She had pushed her luck. She had deserved that slap. It was wrong for her to think that, but Beth couldn't feel anything but rage for Marie after she'd accused her of wanting Alaric.

When Beth looked up at Alaric, he had his eyes on her, ignoring Marie's crying and whimpering sobs. She was hurt for sure, but Beth didn't move to help. She would normally help, which was why Alaric had an arched eyebrow on Beth, waiting for her to respond. When he realized that Beth wasn't going to help his mate, he smirked at her, who looked away from him, feeling like a trapped rat in a cage.

"Why are you protecting the whore?" Marie asked, sobbing while holding on to her wounded arms.

"The only whore here is you, Marie," Alaric retorted, watching how she couldn't pick herself up from the floor and was already crying like a helpless baby.

He hadn't hit her that hard, but she was a whimpering little bitch. Her sister was much stronger and more interesting. Beth should have been his mate, not this helpless, sobbing girl. He was going to fix that when he found that damn witch and forced her to remove the binding spell. Soon enough, the bond that connected him to that stupid, worthless vampire would be gone, and he could kill her for good.

"Do you think I am bluffing?" Marie asked in a weak voice as she bled from the wounds. She gazed up at her mate and saw scars also appearing on his face. The bastard was smiling as he looked at her sister. She took a big piece of the broken mirror and stabbed herself in the stomach to prove her point.

Alaric gasped, bending forward and clutching his stomach. Blood ran between his fingers.

"You crazy little whore," he cursed, snapping his head to Marie and making her a target.

"I am your mate, not her! Do you like pain? I'll give you pain, bastard," she screamed like a crazy woman, stabbing her stomach again and again.

Beth didn't move or blink. She stood on the balcony, listening to the wind blow and dreaming of quiet and oblivion. She dreamed of going somewhere better than this place where she could forget all that had happened to her over the years. Somewhere, where hate didn't exist, and pain was not the only way to make her feel something.

Alaric grabbed Marie's hand to try and stop her. They were fighting each other until he could hold her tight and make her calm down. She sobbed against his chest, asking him why he didn't love her and didn't want her. They were sick and twisted. He lied to calm her down, or maybe he was telling the truth. Beth couldn't understand. He told Marie that he wanted her and that she was acting silly. Then he took her in his arms, bridal style, both with blood on their clothes like they were some sort of serial killers, and walked to the door. Before they could get out, the door opened, and Vincent entered, breathless.

"What the hell?" he asked, finding Alaric and Marie in that state inside his bedroom. "What happened?"

"Marie is overreacting again," Alaric said with Marie sobbing against his shoulder. "What happened to you?" he asked, noticing that Vincent was wounded and seemed rattled.

"We were attacked, but we have great news."

"What news?"

"We also have bad news. I had to kill Evelyn—she was about to betray us, I'm sure. She had fallen in love with a werewolf from that God forsaken town. Her loyalty was compromised."

"What's the good news?" Alaric asked, narrowing his eyes.

"Myra says she found your witch. She showed up after I left with the data you asked for, master. But Myra swears it's her. Her name is Jessica."

"That is good news, indeed," Alaric said, pleased. Marie had stopped sobbing and was now looking at Vincent with murderous eyes.

Both Marie and Beth knew what Vincent meant by "finding the witch." It didn't look good for Marie or for Beth, who certainly didn't want to fill Marie's shoes.

"Did you find the name of my niece? Is it true that my father found George's daughter? Who is she?"

"It's true," Vincent confirmed. "Evelyn didn't want to tell us. We have the school files with the names of the teachers and the hybrid students, though."

"I asked you a simple thing, and you failed!" Alaric shouted, losing his temper. Marie was all that was stopping him from grabbing Vincent by the neck and punching him. Beth had witnessed it thousands of times.

"I tried to question one of the werewolves, but he didn't say a thing. But it's a matter of time before we find out. I have the files, and Evelyn said it was one of the female teachers. We will find out, sir," he said in a trembling voice.

"Beth!" Alaric yelled, making her shiver and focus on his back. "Come!"

Beth followed, not questioning why he was ordering her to go with him. She hoped he didn't plan to continue what he'd been doing when Marie came in.

"Why?" Vincent questioned, shuddering at the bold attitude of questioning as he looked at Beth. He noticed the state of her dress; he didn't have to guess what had happened. His eyes turned black, and his teeth came out. "You said you wouldn't touch her. That she was mine!"

Beth shivered and stared at him, startled by his nerve. *Is he truly facing Alaric because of her? Is he crazy?*

"Shut the fuck up and bow to your king and master!" Alaric ordered, making him lower his head immediately. "You failed me. Beth is coming with me!"

"No, she will not," Marie warned, looking up to his face. They started a staring contest.

Marie must have won because Alaric changed his mind. "She

can stay, but you will not touch her. If you touch her, I'll rip your head off!"

"What?" Vincent asked. "She's my mate!"

"And I'm your master. You obey me. Beth will stay here and attend to your wound, but you will keep your distance from her. Understood?"

"Yes, master," Vincent said, lowering his eyes to prove his loyalty and submission.

Moments after, Alaric left with his mate, and Vincent shut the door with enough strength to make it crack.

Beth shivered, afraid of what he would do to her.

"Did he assault you again?" Vincent asked, standing next to Beth and putting two fingers on her chin to make her look at him. His voice was sweet, and Beth released a sigh and nodded. "Fucking idiot."

It often surprised Beth when he talked poorly about his master. He always looked so obedient and committed to Alaric, but when Beth understood that Vincent was envious and resentful, she used that to her advantage. He was a prick and a murderer, but he had a weird adoration for her and treated her better than Alaric. At least, he was not a masochist or psychopath. He lusted for her, and he wanted her to act with him as if they were real soulmates. Of course, it didn't work like he wanted, and Beth was not even slightly in love with him, but, at least, she was better at pretending that she didn't hate him and that she cared for him.

"Why did you tell him about the witch?" Beth asked, trying to look concerned with his wound. She put her hand on his shoulder and caressed it. "You should take these clothes off and let me clean your wound. It has silver inside."

"I told him about the witch because when we find her, we can finally kill him for good, and I can take his place."

"And Marie?"

"I told you, I will let the witch unbind your sister from him and let her live. Then, we can make the witch kill Alaric and make us true mates."

That was his plan, and Beth, even if she thought it was a primitive plan, hoped that he could free her sister and kill Alaric.

The rest, she could deal with it after. There was no way in hell that she intended to stay bound to him or anyone else, for that matter.

CHAPTER THIRTY-FIVE

ANNA

TWO DAYS WENT BY since Uncle Eric had donated his blood and Kevin was still in a deep coma.

Eventually, they had to call Sasha to help. Of course, she was shocked to find out that I was her cousin. I think she was more than surprised. I could almost feel the irony of it all and laugh at the joke if things weren't that bad for Kevin.

Kevin's heart was beating steadily, and he was breathing on his own, but he hasn't opened his eyes.

Grandpa was in love with my brother. He said he was the image of my dad at his age. I didn't know it, but I had guessed that Kevin was the one who resembled the family more. He was tall, gorgeous, blond, and blue-eyed. Even Sasha seemed to like him more than me, and he was sleeping! I couldn't picture the two of us being best friends in the near future. We were related by blood, so she had to endure my presence and share her family with me. She was no longer the only niece and the only granddaughter. She had serious competition now.

Sasha was jealous. She didn't like to share Eric and grandfather with me; she would always sulk when they hugged and comforted me. However, she seemed more jealous of my relationship with Shane. It showed every time Shane was near me or held my hand. She needed to move on and understand that she and Shane weren't meant to be.

They weren't speaking to each other. At least, Shane was not talking to her. He simply ignored her, and the others seemed to respect his decision. It was fine by me—I didn't want them being all friendly and cozy together, either. I wasn't ordinarily possessive and jealous, but I was when it came to her. She wasn't over Shane.

To make things worse, Jessica had taken off with Jason's car after leaving him at the clinic, claiming that she had some private matters to handle. She'd told him to tell me that she was confident that Kevin would make it and come back from the coma, but she had some business to take care of and would keep in contact. I tried calling her, but she had her phone off. I could only wonder if her business had something to do with the witch who she'd let escape without any apparent reason. It was weird.

All I could hope for was that everything would be fine, and she would come back soon. I needed her beside me, and I'd gotten a bit mad at her for leaving, but I had Shane, Eric, and my grandpa there with me. Even Jason had stuck around, keeping me company while staring off into space. However, after Sasha's arrival, he'd stared at her like she was some kind of mesmerizing sight. My cousin couldn't help hitting on all the girls. *He was such a player!* I guess he found it even more appealing to hit on her when he understood that I didn't like her. He could be annoying most of the time, but Jason was like that whenever he was near an attractive woman. He would act silly and try to do everything in his power to sleep with her, break her heart, and then leave her to her misery.

My cousin, the perfect bad boy with a narcissistic complex!

Of course, Sasha ignored him when he introduced himself to her. She earned some respect points from me for that. However, I realized later that what kept her away from Jason was that she was too chic to get along with hybrids. It would probably ruin her reputation as an ice princess. Too bad she now had two hybrid cousins!

To sum up, the past two days, I had been waiting in Kevin's room for him to open his eyes. Shane hadn't left my side, being supportive and caring. Eric and Grandpa had rented hotel rooms near the clinic and taken turns keeping me company, watching over Kevin. We were pretty much dependent on Kevin's recovery before we could start living again. And I was hoping the gods wouldn't be so mean as to take away from me another member of my family. My sweet and amazing brother deserved a second chance. He deserved to wake up and find his new family members, even meet his stuck-up cousin and, who knew, his soulmate, to love and be loved like I loved Shane and he loved me.

Shane never left my side. He was worried and focused on my thoughts of guilt and anxiety. There was a feeling of helplessness in me for being unable to do anything else to help my brother. Maybe I had taken too long to find him the blood he needed. Maybe, if I had told Shane my secret sooner, everything would have been different. Maybe, if I had been faster than him, he wouldn't have put himself in front of me and gotten hit with the poisoned dart. It was a lot of maybes, but I had a lot of time to think about everything and stress about it.

What if he didn't want to wake up? Wherever he was, was it better than this world?

* * *

After Sasha's donation, one more day went by, and nothing happened.

The doctors were puzzled. Kevin was perfectly fine, at least physically. They had run many tests on him, new blood analysis, and had even scanned his brain. There was no reason for him to remain in an unconscious state. His brain was active; it seemed to be processing information. Nevertheless, he remained asleep.

I was holding back the tears but was sad beyond words. Shane knew it, felt it, and didn't leave my side because of it. I knew he was there, but my eyes remained dry, and I was caught inside my thoughts. There was nothing he could do to cheer me up, and I was relieved that he didn't try. I needed to remain like that, grieving in silence, trapped in my melancholy.

Knowing Shane was next to me helped keep my sanity and not crumble.

By day four, everybody was losing hope. Eric was making plans to take Grandpa back to the palace, Jason had to go back to the headquarters, and Jessica had still not given any kind of sign that she was alive and well.

Because things seemed hopeless, everybody was trying to convince me to leave the clinic and go back to my life. The doctors would call if anything changed. Spending my days there was not good for me. Maybe not, but I was reluctant to leave my baby brother alone—again.

Shane said nothing about it. I looked at him, trying to find out if he had the same opinion as the others. Whatever I'd decided, he would be there to support me. We both looked a mess—we needed a hot shower, a proper meal, and a good night's sleep in a bed. But he wouldn't leave if I didn't. Therefore, I agreed to go back to the hotel and take care of myself for a while if Eric would stay there, keeping Kevin company, so he had someone nearby if he woke up.

After a long hot shower and a full meal, I got in bed and hugged my mate, who cuddled with me and held me tightly. We didn't talk much verbally. There was not much to say anyway. I was sad, he knew I was, and our mind link was active. I was not in the mood to use my voice to communicate, so using the mind link to reassure him and be pampered by his sweet words was all I could handle.

I was tired, really beat up from sleeping on the clinic sofas or staring at the white walls, saying nothing, waiting, sequestered from the world. Yet, I couldn't sleep. My eyes were wide opened, staring at the shadows in the room from outside lights seeping through the curtains. It was a warm summer's night.

Shane's hand stroking my hair was all that kept me relaxed and less miserable. It felt good to have someone to share my sadness and worries with. He'd neglected everything in his life just to be by my side. He didn't even go to interrogate the vampires we had caught. Someone else was doing that.

For the time being, Shane was all mine, but I couldn't be happy about it because Kevin hadn't woken up.

I sighed and lifted my head to see Shane. He opened his eyes to look at me when I moved.

What's wrong? he asked through our mind link, but I could have guessed by the look in his eyes.

"I love you," I whispered, using my voice.

His lips drew into a smile.

"I know, honey. I love you, too," he whispered back in his sexy voice.

"I'm sorry for not being a good company."

"Everything will be fine." He kissed my forehead, and I leaned my head against his chest, sighing. Deep inside, I wanted to believe that things would work out. "You should sleep. Are you hungry?"

"I ate."

"I know, but you haven't fed in a while."

"Oh!" I reassured him, "Eric spiked my drinks."

My uncle had brought me cups of coffee with blood to keep me strong. He was caring and good at persuading me to eat and rest.

"Good, I don't want you to get weak," Shane mumbled, kissing the top of my head.

"Do you know anything about Sebastien?" I asked.

"He's okay. Don't worry."

"He lost Eve," I mumbled as my heart tightened in pain. "*We* lost Eve," I rephrased. She was my friend too.

"She was a spy, honey. She wasn't your friend."

"She tried to protect Sebastien. He said so. And...she liked him and was always nice to me. Truly nice, and not the fake nice some people pretend to be."

"Well, maybe she actually liked you and Sebastien."

"She was Vincent's cub. That means she had to obey him unconditionally. Maybe she wasn't bad, but they forced her to be a spy."

"Maybe. At least, Sebastien is alive and—" He said nothing else.

"And the spy is dead?" I questioned.

"And I'm alive. And you are next to me, and you aren't mad at me anymore. Promise me that you won't ever be mad at me again."

"Do you promise there won't be any more lies or doubts between us?"

"Of course. I don't want to keep anything else from you, and I hope you don't keep anything from me, either."

"I won't."

"Then there won't be any more secrets between us," he assured me, rubbing my back and making me sigh.

I was sore and stiff as a board. I needed a back rub, a foot, and even a head massage. That's how tense I was. He just had to press on my shoulders and my spine a bit, and I would relax and fall asleep like a baby.

I heard him chuckling. He was tuned into my thoughts. He kissed my face and pulled me into his embrace. I melted in surrender while enjoying his hands on my back and shoulders.

Happiness was all those moments of sharing and cuddling

between us. He was my heaven. Sex was so overrated compared to that.

Of course, sex was good, but it wasn't everything in a relationship. It was moments like these when we needed love and support from the person we were with to determine if they would be a good match for us or not.

So far, Shane had gotten the highest scores. He deserved a medal for being the best mate.

"Don't make me feel bad for being aroused by you being on top of me," Shane whispered in my ear, clearly tuned into my thoughts. His words made me giggle as heat warmed my cheeks. "Just relax and sleep. Ignore me. I know you aren't in the mood. But it's good to see you cheer up, even if it's due to something so silly."

"I really want Kevin to meet you. You'll love him. He is…a perfect brother. We always were best friends, even if he's a bit stubborn. But it runs in the family."

"Sooner or later, he'll wake up, and everything will be back on track. You and I will be happy, and the king will spoil you two with gifts and attention. And…Eric will steal you from me more often than I would like. He's happy he found you."

"Yes, I know. He's also happy that you are my mate. Every time you went for coffee, he always says good things about you."

"I'm sure it's just an excuse to talk about the past."

"He misses my dad," I agreed. "But it's great to know more about my father's past. And yours."

"I hope you don't think less of me if he tells you all my embarrassing moments."

I smiled. "Of course not, I love you, and… it was scary… You know."

"I know."

I became silent, staring at him, unable to say anything else that could explain how much I loved him and how I didn't want anything bad to happen to him. I was holding back the tears but thinking that I could have been left alone without him, without my brother, made me feel overly emotional.

"Anna," he mumbled in a weak voice, holding me under my arms and pulling me to meet his face. "Baby, nothing will happen to me. I swear. I will never leave you alone. Kevin will be okay. And…I love you. So, please, don't be sad." He kissed my eyelids, tasting my tears. We hugged tightly while I tried to keep my sobs from erupting. "You should be trying to sleep and not thinking about depressing things."

"I know, but I can't sleep when I'm swarmed by thoughts and doubts. I'm anxious. I want Kevin to wake up and for this nightmare to end. Once he's awake, we can go back home and be happy. Will you let Kevin live with us?"

"If he wants, but I think your grandfather wants Kevin and you to go and live with him for a while."

"I don't want to leave you."

"I will go with you. Don't worry, I'm not planning to let you out of my sight."

I don't know exactly why, but I giggled and thought his words concealed jealousy behind them. "You don't need to worry about anyone else. I love you, and I will always solely love you. And I won't let you out of my sight, either. I don't want you to be beaten up once more by an idiot vampire. I need to protect you since I'm your superhero and stuff…"

He bit my cheek, and I squealed. It hurt!

"Hey, he had a witch on his side. The damn spell took my strength away!"

"I know. I was teasing you," I said, rubbing my cheek and pouting. "That hurt," I whined.

He smiled and kissed my lips. I was about to complain again

when his tongue entered my mouth, and I sighed and surrendered. I'd missed those breathtaking kisses between us. *Hell, I missed all of him.*

A noise got our attention. It was his cell phone ringing.

Breaking our kiss, I left the bed to look for it. The sound was coming from his clothes on the chair opposite the bed.

I rushed to the phone since it could be Uncle Eric calling us about Kevin. With my heart on my throat, I grabbed his pants and shook them, impatient to find the cell and see who was calling.

"It's in my jacket, not in my pants," Shane said, a bit out of breath as he got up fast and grabbed his pants out of my hand.

I stared at him, blinking several times in confusion. My attention was drawn to a small green box that fell from his pants to the floor and then rolled to his feet. His eyes widened as he cursed. Then he sighed and clenched his jaw.

I had his jacket in my hands, but my eyes were on the little box. That box looked so much like...

I bit my lower lip and stared at him again, swallowing hard.

He picked up the box from the floor and grabbed the jacket from my hands. He took the phone and stared at the screen.

"It's one of my deputies. It isn't Eric," he said, rejecting the phone call.

Maybe I was hallucinating or misinterpreting—it was probably nothing.

That couldn't be. Could it?

"Damn it!" he complained, fisting his hand in his hair and staring at me. "This wasn't how I planned to do this."

"You planned what?" I asked, out of breath and feeling my cheeks turn red.

He isn't planning to... Is he?

Staring at the floor, I sucked a deep breath.

"I had almost two hundred years to plan it, and I've had this for, at least, one hundred years," he said.

One moment he was explaining, and the other he was down on one knee, showing me the box.

Frowning, I stepped back as confusion made my heart beat faster. I didn't know what to do with my hands and eventually brushed my hair away from my face as I gazed at the still-closed box. It was a vintage, sea-green box, not like the new and fancy black velvet wedding ring boxes. Maybe it wasn't what I was imagining. Although, his words and gesture told the opposite story.

"I had thought of doing this on prom night in front of all the people there."

My 'are-you-kidding-me' face showed him that wouldn't be his brightest idea.

He smiled as if amused and continued, "Yes, you'd probably have killed me after." He chuckled when I agreed with him with a nod. "Then I thought that I could do a picnic and put the ring inside something. Maybe prepare a romantic dinner at home, drop to my knees, and ask you. Like now." He put the phone on the ground and grabbed my left hand in his.

My heart raced, and I couldn't help but feel a mix of emotions from amazement to excitement to fear and happiness.

"I was actually planning to propose to you on the night all the confusion happened. I had it all prepared at home. And then you said your cousin was in town and that he would stay with us, so I canceled and was planning to ask you the next day."

I swallowed hard when he opened the box and showed me the antique white gold and sapphire solitaire engagement ring. The precious stone was neither big nor too small. It was centered atop a shank heavily encrusted with pave diamond side stones and milgrain. It was perfect, so perfect that I lost my breath. It matched my eyes, and it was beautiful.

"I know this ring is rather old-fashioned, but I bought it a long time ago," he mumbled. "And I thought it was perfect at the time."

My gaze moved from the ring to him and then back to him. I was enthralled by his words and by the ring. *He was proposing, wasn't he?*

"Yes, I am," he answered, probably noticing that he hadn't said the words. He only showed me the ring. "Sorry, I'm nervous! I'm asking you to marry me. I know we are bonded and marked each other, but I want us to have a ceremony and say our own vows in front of our relatives and friends. I love you. You're my other half, Anna." He paused for a moment, staring at my wide-open eyes and parted lips. My breathing was heavy, and my heartbeat was loud. "Honey, I'm sorry if this isn't romantic and you found out about the ring like this, but—this is yours. It has been for more than one hundred years, and I want you to wear it and to marry me."

Shane waited for my reply, but I was at a loss for words. I kept opening my mouth and closing it without verbalizing any answer. My mind was also void of thoughts though he felt him trying to tune in.

His sudden proposal caught me completely off guard. My heart beat so fast that my ears hurt, and my vision blurred. Still, I knew something, marriage seemed a rushed decision to make without thinking about the pros and cons.

For a long time, marriage wasn't on my plans. It seemed a foreign word that wasn't in my vocabulary because it was synonymous with being caged and restrained from making my own decisions.

For many, marrying meant losing their freedom to have a career and be confined to the role of being a mom. My own mother changed her priorities when she had us. I treasured my independence too much. I had been alone for many years.

Thinking about marriage when we had been together for a few months seemed insane, mates or not.

"It's a natural step to take when someone is in a relationship," Shane stated.

His words made me look at him and notice that his eyes had lost their shine. He seemed hurt by my reluctance to answer his proposal. I didn't want to hurt him.

I fell on my knees and placed my hands over his, concealing the beautiful engagement ring he had brought decades ago. Tears stung my eyes, and I had a lump in my throat. Swallowing hard, I breathed in a few times before being able to put into words all my thoughts.

"I'm not going to lie," I murmured since my voice came out weak. I cleared my throat again. "Marriage has always terrified me."

"Why?" Shane asked, moving his hands so my hands would fall between his.

I felt the sapphire touch my palm. It was perfect. I had never imagined a ring so perfect. Shivers ran down my spine. Emotion blurred my eyes and clenched my heart.

"I could give you a nice feminist speech about why I thought marriage was a way to imprison women and…"

He raised one hand to touch my lips with his fingertips. "I'm sure you can, but I've explained to you why I want to marry you."

"I thought we were already committed. We've marked each other."

"We did, but I want to share our happiness with the others in a ceremony."

"But…" My voice trembled as tears fell down my cheeks. "What if Kevin never wakes up? … if he's gone?"

Shane hugged me when the sobs took over my body. I cried like a helpless, abandoned little girl.

"I wish I had the power to cure him," Shane said, making circles on my back to calm me down. "I'm here, honey. I won't leave you. You aren't alone."

I nodded, restraining my tears and trying to sound rational about what I was going to tell him.

"I'm sorry." I tried to contain the shivers. "I… had never wanted to get married before because I didn't have a lot of family members to invite, and it seemed silly. Besides, I didn't think I could commit so strongly to someone. That I could love someone like I love you." Despite my efforts, my words came out messy. I didn't know if he'd understood anything that I said. His right hand was resting on my back. I could feel the box in his hand. His other hand was caressing my hair while his lips were against my cheek, wet with my salty tears.

"I know this wasn't the best moment to ask you to marry me."

"No, it wasn't." I sniffled. "But it isn't your fault that my life is messed up. And I think the ring is beautiful. It's stunning, Shane. I love it, and I think it's perfect."

His fingers cleaned my cheeks while my hands grabbed his forearms, trying to balance and look him straight in the eye. "I'm here for you. You won't be alone, honey. And Kevin will be fine."

"You don't know that. I appreciate your optimism but…"

"Even if you think we shouldn't get married…or you don't want to get married, the ring is yours." He cut me off before I could finish my sentence. His hands were trembling, and I could feel the vulnerability in his voice.

"I don't mind getting married to you," I whispered, biting my lower lip. "I love you."

He curved his lips into a smile, and his eyes sparkled. "You don't mind marrying me," he echoed.

I nibbled on my lips. "I meant that I can see myself marrying you. Only you. So it doesn't scare me anymore."

His smile widened. "That makes me very happy."

He kissed my lips, making me lose my breath.

"But…" I resumed what I was going to say before. "We're going to take things slow. Kevin isn't recovering, so I need to prepare myself for the worst."

"I'm so sorry, honey," he whispered, holding me tighter.

His hug made me burst into tears again. The idea of losing my brother after all we'd done to find a pureblood, after finding the family I didn't know existed, was excruciating.

"It's all my fault," I cried, feeling the sobs ripple down my spine, tainting my soul and turning my heart to dust. "He's never going to meet you or Eric or Grandpa."

I hid my face against his neck, surrounding Shane's chest with my arms and gripping my fingers on his shoulders. I wanted to be as close to him as I could.

"It's nobody's fault."

"It's Alaric's fault," I disagreed, my voice sounding stronger because of the hate.

"Anna, look at me," he demanded, lifting my chin. "You aren't alone anymore. We are going to be a family, and you have new family members. So, you need to stop blindly pursuing revenge."

"He needs to be stopped. Vincent was going to kill you tonight. And he had spies in your town. Why isn't Grandpa doing something to stop him?"

"He is. We are. Alaric is hard to find."

"Shane," I called out, feeling misunderstood. But before I could say anything else, the phone rang, startling us both. We looked at the screen and saw Eric's name. I was faster than Shane to grab the phone from the floor and answer it.

"Yes?" I asked out of breath.

"He woke up," Eric said with trembling voice, "but then he passed out again. You should come."

"We'll be right there," I assured him and stared at Shane. He had heard the conversation.

"Yes, we should go. We'll talk about this later." He closed the box and put it in his pocket, then turned his back to me.

He was putting his pants on when I straightened up and looked for my clothes. I noticed how sad he looked. It made my heart hurt.

"Shane, you're my mate. I'm not rejecting you, making plans to leave you, or anything like that. I don't want to hurt your feelings. But you can't ask me to forget what Alaric did to my parents and brother, can you?"

"I'm not asking you that," he answered. "All I want is for us to be together…"

"We will," I assured, moving closer to him. "I won't ever leave you, and there aren't any more secrets between us."

"Just to be clear, I asked you to marry me and you said yes… Yes?"

I nodded, feeling the tears fall down my face again. I wiped them away, rejoicing with Shane's smile.

"I'll formally request your grandfather's blessing after things calm down and once Kevin is safe at home and out of danger." Shane kissed me.

"I'm sure he won't be opposed." I smiled, finishing with a theatrical bow to match his formal tone. "Now, we need to move. I want to be there when my brother opens his eyes again."

Kevin had woken up! My brother was reacting to the cure!

Soon enough, he would be out of the clinic and living his life again. And he was going to meet Shane, Eric, and Grandpa.

CHAPTER THIRTY-SIX

ANNA

I VIVIDLY REMEMBERED THE DAY I first met my brother.

We don't normally recall much from when we are little kids. However, I had a strong memory of that particular event. I don't remember events from the time he was inside my mom's belly, but I recall the day after his birth.

It had been a long birth. Kevin didn't want to leave mom's womb, and Dad had been worried sick during the delivery.

The next day after his birth, I stalked my mom's bedroom door. I stood there watching people go in and out—my three-year-old self staring at the grown-ups' legs—holding myself at the door and peeking inside, eagerly ogling what was in the room.

No one seemed to notice or understand that I was worried and curious. I wanted to get in, but I didn't have permission. I was eager to see the baby and my mom, and I was holding in tears of frustration. Everybody was saying that the baby was gorgeous and healthy. I was beyond happy to have a baby brother. Now, if only they would let me see and hold him.

I was peeking inside again, toes on the edge of the bedroom's entry, when a body shadowed my little figure.

I turned around slowly and looked up to the six-foot-tall man who was staring at me with a smile on his lips.

"Daddy!" I jumped up, arms stretched out and hands open, hoping that he would grab me and take me into his arms.

"What are you doing here, Anne?" he asked, lifting me up in the air.

I put my hands on his cheeks and mumbled breathlessly, "I want to see the little baby."

"You want to meet your brother?"

I nodded, and the next thing I knew, I was in my mom's bed, gawking at the baby. I was thinking how tiny and adorable he was. He had a small, round, hairless head and his eyes were still closed. He was holding his fisted hands tight.

He was so cute! I wanted to hold him.

I don't know what I said to convince my parents to let me hold him, but they did. I held and cuddled him contently. I smiled, happy to have him in my family.

My father's words were left imprinted in my head from that day on. "Kevin is now a part of our family, Anne. You have to take care of him and love him unconditionally. Protect him and give him love, like we will do."

And I did.

I did everything my dad asked me to. I took care of him. I protected him from other kids. I tolerated his evil pranks and his stubborn whims.

When our parents died, I took care of him and made sure that hate and pain wouldn't consume him and turn him bitter and mean.

All I've ever wanted was for him to be happy. Maybe, I forgot that Kevin wanted me to be happy too, and that was why he put himself in front of me and protected me. Still, it wasn't fair. I was the eldest—the one who should have been in that bed and not him.

I couldn't wait for him to open his eyes again, so I could hold him, cuddle him, and make sure no one would ever hurt him again.

* * *

I was seated on the couch, staring at the ground, lost in my thoughts. I was holding my breath, praying to divinities in some subconscious part of my mind so that Kevin opened his eyes. The doctors had already examined him from head to toe. He seemed to be sleeping. Even waking up from his coma, he was being lazy.

Shane was on the opposite side of the room, sleeping on one of the couches. He had been quiet since we left the hotel room. I knew he was disappointed because I wanted revenge on Alaric. He thought I was on a suicidal path and that he would lose me. I couldn't blame him, but I needed him to understand that making Alaric pay for what he'd done was important to me. I needed closure to be completely happy with Shane.

As hours went by, I became tired and grumpy. I couldn't think straight anymore. I was feeling impatient and desperate.

Why wouldn't Kevin open his eyes once and for all? Had it been a false alarm? Was Kevin recuperating or falling back into a coma?

I needed to rest, so I laid my head back and closed my eyes. I guess I fell asleep because when I opened my eyes again, it was daytime. Shane was holding me in his arms, and my head was on his shoulder. I was clinging to his shirt, feeling warm and safe, even though I felt as if my whole body had been beaten up several times. When I looked at his face, he was awake and staring at the wall. His eyes met mine, and his lips stretched into a smile as he placed a gentle kiss on my forehead.

"Do you still love me?" I asked with a sleepy voice.

"More than my own life."

"So why the broody stare last night?" I wondered, sitting down by his side and fixing my clothes. I was feeling sore, and my body longed for a proper bed to sleep in.

"I was mad at myself for rushing things," he explained, combing his hair and making it even messier and adorable.

I bit my lip.

"I'm sorry, I didn't want my proposal to be so lame."

"Your proposal was fine. You hadn't the best timing, though," I added and glimpsed at Kevin.

"You saw the box," he excused himself.

I shrugged, putting my hands inside the pockets of my blazer.

"I had a speech prepared for when I would ask you to marry me. I had a list of reasons why you should accept."

"A speech?" I arched an eyebrow at him. "Do tell, I'm curious now," I teased him, grinning.

"It feels silly now."

"I doubt that. You're always good with words and at persuading me."

He puckered his lips and leaned closer to my face. "Do you really want to listen to it?"

I nodded.

"Are you going to laugh?"

"I'd never laughed at something that came from the bottom of your heart," I assured him.

The corner of his lips curled up, and he brushed the hair away from my eyes. He continued to pat my head, and, for a moment, I thought that he wasn't going to say anything else.

"Sweetheart, you're the love of my life. You should know that by now."

I nodded.

"Then, you should also know that I don't want to steal your freedom."

I lowered my eyes and focused on his chest. Shane's fingers brushed my cheek, my chin, and he tilted my head, so I looked at him again. "You can read my thoughts. Does it look as if I'm trying to convince you to give up your former life?"

"I'm not sure." I breathed deeply. "But…"

He shook his head. "In what concerns babies, I want us to be parents. Of course, I do. Still, it doesn't mean that we must do it right away. We'll just do it when you're ready to have them."

"I didn't want to disappoint you," I assured him.

"You didn't."

"I feel as if I did. I feel as if you were expecting me to just settle down and live a normal life. But that's not who I am."

"I know."

"Do you?" I asked, out of breath as my heart pounded faster. "Wouldn't you rather have a submissive mate who would do everything you wanted and never questioned you?"

He smirked. "Where's the fun in that?"

"You're an alpha."

"And you're my superior."

I pushed his hand away. "Just because you found out I'm the granddaughter of your king doesn't make me superior to you."

He shook his head with a smile and cupped my face. "No, silly. You're my mate. So you're my superior." He added, "I should do things to please you."

I pouted. "I want to please you too."

"You please me if you're happy, and you can only be happy if you do the things you want to do."

"I feel selfish if I just do how I please." I breathed deeply. "You can't let me do everything I want just because I might be mad at you."

"Answer me this."

I nodded.

"Do you see yourself living without me in the future?"

I shook my head.

"Are you planning to leave me once your brother is well just because you believe it's the right thing to do to keep me safe or whatever excuse you're telling yourself to validate your actions?"

I shook my head again. "I'd be stupid if I did that."

"You would. Remember that."

"You can take care of yourself. People who love each other shouldn't stay apart. Not even if it's forbidden. Mom and Dad taught me that."

Shane's eyes glowed, and he forced a smile, but tears rolled down his cheeks. "Your mom and dad were brave. I'm proud of you, sweetie. I'm proud of being your mate. Don't ever forget that."

I leaned closer and kissed his lips, tasting his tears. "You're going to make me cry too."

"I… just… miss George," he confessed.

Holding him tight, I felt the pain taking over my emotions. "I miss my parents more than I can explain." Tears rolled down my cheeks. "We shouldn't be crying."

He laughed between his tears. "We shouldn't." Holding me tighter, he added, "Once Kevin is feeling better, we'll talk about how we're going to make our relationship work."

"Okay," I mumbled.

"What matters is that you're not planning to leave me. It would shatter me if you did that."

"It would shatter me too." I cringed since something was poking me on my hip. "Is that box still in your pocket, or are you just happy to have me against you?"

"Both," he answered.

I giggled.

"Does anyone want coffee, or should I come back later?" Eric asked.

Shane and I looked at the door and saw him holding three cups of coffee.

Once I wiped the tears from my face, I ran to grab a cup and brought another to offer to Shane. The coffee smelled great, and

I desperately needed caffeine.

Uncle Eric strolled inside the bedroom and sat on a chair next to my brother's bed. "Did he say anything else after I left?"

I frowned. "What do you mean?"

"He talked in his sleep," Shane explained.

"What did he say?"

"Random things," replied Eric. "Sentences like *I don't want to leave* and what seemed like a name. I'm not sure. It sounded like Bee or Beck or something."

"Why did no one wake me up?" I grumbled.

"You needed to sleep, and Kevin was still sleeping. It wasn't a necessity to wake you up," Eric answered.

I sulked as I drank my hot coffee. Looking at my uncle with glistening eyes, I said, "You put in cinnamon."

"Don't you like it?"

"Dad used to do the same to his coffee."

"Yes, he was the one who taught me."

"Aren't you tired, Uncle?" I asked.

He had suffered the most the last few days. Firstly, he donated a lot of blood, and secondly, he'd been there almost as many days as I. He looked pale and tired.

"I'll rest when Kevin wakes up."

"Good morning," Sasha said, walking in and ruining my day.

What the hell is she doing here?

"Hello, Sasha," Eric greeted her with a big smile as she sat next to him and gave him a kiss.

"I came to see Kevin," she said, talking to Eric, but I knew she was also excusing herself to Shane and me. "I heard he woke up."

"Yes, but he fell asleep again. We're hopeful he might wake up soon enough, though."

"Do you think he will need more of our blood?"

"No, it was enough. He'll just need human blood to gather strength and fully recover. Let's hope he doesn't have any brain damage and remembers who he is and his life."

"Okay." She smiled and looked at the bed with a hopeful stare that intrigued me. It was as if she cared about Kevin and whether he woke up or not. Maybe she was not that heartless. *One could hope!*

An awkward silence fell, and Shane and I focused on each other, drinking our coffee and sharing ideas about Sasha's reasons for being there.

Moments later, she watched us as if she knew we were talking about her. When we looked at her, she smiled and held Eric's hand.

"Is Kevin staying with us at the palace when he can finally leave this place?" Sasha asked.

Eric smiled and nodded. "Of course. We are planning to spend some time together. Anna is joining us, too. Aren't you, Anna?"

"Yes." I placed my cup down on a little table next to the couch. *So, she's planning to spend some time at the palace. That's not good news for me.*

"Good morning," said Jason, coming in with a huge smile. He stared directly at Sasha. "Good morning, gorgeous."

Sasha blinked and rolled her eyes. "It was!"

I couldn't help but giggle at the face that Jason made with Sasha's sarcasm.

Jason moved closer to Shane and me and leaned against the wall. "Is there any news?"

I had texted him about Kevin's slightly improvement.

"He's still asleep."

"As lazy as ever," Jason grumbled.

Yes, Kevin's laziness was well-known among our family.

"I heard that, you dog!" a weak and barely audible voice came from Kevin's bed.

Is Kevin awake? It's s him talking, isn't it?

Everybody jumped to their feet and ran to the side of his bed.

Kevin blinked his eyes. "Wow, so many people swirling around me!"

"Kevin?" I asked as he stared right at me.

"Annie," he mumbled and tried to give me a faint smile. "Where am I?"

"You're in a clinic. Don't you remember what happened?"

"It's all unclear. I was having the weirdest dream! With a girl...and..."

"What else is new?" Jason interrupted with a mischievous grin, touching him on his arm.

"Ouch," Kevin complained and trembled in bed. "It burns, it burns!" he kept complaining as we looked at him, unsure about what to do.

"What hurts?" Eric asked.

"Dad?" Kevin asked, his eyes wide open. "Dad, is that you?"

"No, Kevin. This is Eric. He's our uncle," I explained.

He frowned in pain, moving his right arm to hold his other arm.

"It's burning," he moaned, pulling the sheet off and showing us his left forearm where a tattoo was being imprinted with flaming lines.

Something was being drawn on his forearm—some kind of bird tattoo.

"*Call the nurses! Call the doctors!*" I yelled, but Eric was already doing that while everyone else stared at his forearm, amazed.

Moments later, the burning had stopped, and the doctor examined Kevin's arm. My brother was fully awake, looking at everybody in the room. He was still digesting the introductions and that we had more relatives we didn't know about. He was also fascinated with Eric and happy to speak to Sasha, who was friendly to him.

The burning on his arm left an intriguing tattoo in black. It seemed like a bird of some sort. I had taken a picture of it and sent it to Jessica's phone since she was not picking up the calls. Maybe she knew what that tattoo meant. I sure didn't. It could only be magic at work. What for and why were the questions we wanted answers to.

"The king will arrive in a few moments to see you, Kevin," Eric said after ending the call and looking at my brother with a smile. "How are you feeling?"

"It healed," Kevin answered.

His voice was dry even after giving him water—he could only swallow tiny amounts of it.

"It's kind of cool," Jason said.

"Yes," Kevin said, showing off his arm. "I feel like I should know why it's there."

I was going to say something, but my phone vibrated. When I checked the screen, I sighed with relief. It was my personal witch, Jessica.

"It's about time you gave us a call," I grumbled, not even bothering to say hi.

"Sorry about that, love," she said on the other end. "But I had some business to take care of."

"Where are you? We were all worried sick here!"

"I'm in Italy now. I had to pay a visit to a vampire king."

I frowned. "What vampire king?"

"His name is Francesco. He's the vampire king who protects that young witch's coven. The one who attacked us. Do you remember?"

"Of course, I remember. But did you have to leave without

saying a word and leaving us here to worry?"

"Well, I was in a hurry. Besides, you're all adults, and I needed to arrive here quickly. But I'm not calling you because of that. I saw the picture you sent me."

"And?"

"It's a phoenix's symbol. However, I don't have a clue as to why it's on Kevin's arm."

"A phoenix's symbol... How intriguing! Was it a witch who cursed Kevin? Is it going to harm him?" I asked, worried and paranoid.

"I don't know. I'm assuming it's a phoenix's symbol because it looks like one, but I have no idea what it means or even if it was a witch who cast a spell on Kevin. He was in a deep coma. Maybe it's a weird and artistic side effect of the healing."

"Can't you find out more about it?"

"I'll do what I can to find out more, but now I have to take care of some business with the king. He agreed to grant me an audience. Have you got any idea how hard it is to have a meeting with King Francesco? The vampire's paranoid! I'll be back there whenever I finish my business here. Don't worry. Kevin will be fine. The symbol hasn't affected him in any other way, has it?"

"What other way?"

"I don't know. Has he spoken any foreign language or had convulsions?"

"No, he's fine. Just hungry and complaining that he can't get out of bed before the doctors run some other tests on his blood."

"If he's complaining, then he's fine. Tell him I send him a kiss, and I'll be seeing him soon enough. Don't be paranoid and enjoy your attractive wolf. He's gorgeous, by the way! I'm so jealous of you right now!"

"Just get back here and stop keeping secrets from us!" I nagged.

Jessica giggled. "I love you too, love. See you soon."

Once she hung up, I looked at my brother and Jason, who were listening to the conversation.

"Is she okay?" Jason asked.

I nodded. "It seems she's doing well."

Jason waved in dismissal. "Good. Don't worry, she always does what she wants. She'll get back soon enough."

Eric strolled to my side and rubbed my shoulder. "If not even your witch friend knows what the tattoo means, we should just make sure that it doesn't affect Kevin in any way."

I sighed deeply. "She'll tell us if she finds out anything else about it."

He nodded. "At least, it's not hurting him anymore."

"You all look as if I'm going to die when I just woke up from a coma," Kevin complained. "It's just a tattoo. I don't feel as if it will harm me. Maybe, it's even a protection."

I nodded at him and forced a smile. "Either way, Liam is running a search on the Web, trying to find out more about symbols that look like that one. He will eventually find something."

Jason nodded in confirmation.

We had sent the picture to Liam—our computer genius. He'd tell us if anything showed up.

"That can be a protective rune," Sasha dared to say, and we looked at her. She seemed to rethink carefully what she was going to say next. If she knew anything about that drawing on my brother's arm, I wanted to know. "I have seen it before. Witches with great powers mark their betrothed."

"What you mean by betrothed?" Kevin asked, a bit hysterical. "I've been here, in a coma, how can I—? How can a witch…? My mate is a witch?"

"I don't know." Sasha shrugged and touched Kevin's hand to

calm him down. "But you didn't need to do anything, Kevin. Once a witch completes eighteen years, she and her soulmate will be marked by her family's protective emblem. It's a way to make themselves recognizable because they can't sense their mates like vampires and shifters do. Your witch, Jessica, should have thought about that. Maybe she didn't think that it could be an emblem since she didn't recognize the symbol. But it is the only plausible explanation that occurs to me."

"I didn't know about that," I mumbled, grabbing the phone and texting Jessica immediately. The message was on hold. Jessica had once again disconnected her phone.

"It's a good hypothesis," Eric said. "It's a big secret among witches. If Jessica didn't think about that possibility, maybe the witch's coven is old or thought to be extinct."

"Yes, Sasha is smart," Jason drooled.

I rolled my eyes at him and almost laughed at his smoothness. Could he be more obvious?

Kevin cleared his throat. "So—I'm mated to a witch?"

"It seems so, little brother. She branded you," I teased.

He frowned before grinning. "I wonder if she is hot."

I sighed and folded my arms as the other men inside the bedroom laughed in unison.

Men and their limited thoughts.

CHAPTER THIRTY-SEVEN

ANNA

SASHA LEFT THE HOSPITAL ROOM with Jason on her trail.

My cousin seemed weirdly obsessed with her. It wasn't just because I didn't like her much. I had my valid reasons. Knowing she was my cousin also didn't help me to like her more. Besides, she was stuck-up. She acted like a VIP who couldn't give a crap about others. Her lack of emotion was concerning.

I had no idea what Jason saw in her to be so damned enchanted and follow her like a puppy. She was beautiful, and she looked kind of fragile, but she was not his type. He liked shallow, blonde girls with big breasts and lush lips. She couldn't have been farther from that. She was skinny, and even if she had some curves, she had no breasts. She was slim and tall with a doll face. Her eyes were hazel, and she had a small nose and mouth with thin lips. Fragile like a fairy.

I watched them in the corridor. Jason was following her as she walked out of the clinic. She didn't like to be there as it was too depressing. He looked like a silly clown, asking her a bunch of questions that she seemed eager to answer. She didn't appear interested in him, and he didn't normally chase girls like that!

"So, have dinner with me?" Jason asked, smiling.

"I do not eat dinner," Sasha replied in her monotone voice with a British accent. She didn't even grant him a look, as if he was an inconvenience.

"You are right. We can skip dinner, and you can just have a drink at my place. It isn't far from here," he said mischievously.

He wasn't giving up easily. Though, he was not being resourceful, either. That was a cheesy pick-up line. Maybe I shouldn't have used my enhanced hearing to listen to their conversation, but I couldn't help myself.

"That is not going to happen," Sasha assured.

I sighed in relief.

At least, she wasn't that easy, or maybe she wasn't attracted to hybrids. She had a derogatory look on her face when she first found out that she had hybrid cousins and again when Jason first approached her. She clearly didn't think we were on the same level as her blue-blood line.

"Breakfast then? I'm sure you can find some time to go out with me."

"And why would I do that?"

"Because I'm funny and single. And we are practically family. We should all get along."

Sasha stopped at the end of the corridor, where there was an intersection. She looked at Jason for the first time. He was taller than her and stronger. She looked fragile and petite next to him. "We are not practically family. You are Anna's cousin on her mother's side. We are far from being related. We are not even playing in the same league," she cockily explained to Jason.

"Just because you're a princess?" he asked, raising his eyebrow.

"That, and because I don't date *werecats*."

"You dated a werewolf," he pointed out.

"And that's where I drew the line."

"You don't know what you're missing then," he retorted with a cocky smile.

I almost burst into laughter. *That wasn't a great comeback.*

Sasha faced him, measuring him from top to bottom. "I'm not impressed."

Meanwhile, a couple of nurses passed by them and stared at Jason, giggling between themselves. Sasha's eyes squinted as she watched them. They must have said something about Jason because I could see irritation fill her eyes.

He was a hot guy, and he would normally get that kind of attention from the opposite sex. Even if Sasha wasn't impressed, it didn't mean that others wouldn't be.

"Why don't you go and ask one of them? They seem to be interested."

Jason lost his smile and looked hopeless. He thought he could have any girl he wanted. Sasha not being impressed served him as a lesson. Being rejected would do him some good.

"I'm not interested in them," he said with a sexy smirk.

I wanted to slap my forehead and roll my eyes. *Doesn't he give up? Why is he humiliating himself?*

Next, Sasha did something that neither Jason nor I was expecting. She grabbed Jason's collar and brought his lips to hers.

I almost choked! Then, with super-speed, they stepped back and disappeared down the right side of the corridor.

I hoped that crazy vampire wouldn't hurt him or feed on him! Worried, I sped to the end of the corridor.

When I arrived there, Jason was pinned to the wall with Sasha in his arms in a make-out session. She was kissing him hard, and he had his eyes closed doing the same.

Seriously?

I scratched my head, trying to look away, thinking they were both insane.

When I was walking away, Sasha broke the kiss and mumbled near his lips, "I'm still not impressed."

She let him go and sped her way out of there, leaving Jason in some sort of trance against the wall.

I walked his way, furrowing my eyebrows at him. He acted as if their kiss had been something out of this world.

"Your cousin is freaking hot," he finally said with a witty

smile, like she hadn't dismissed him entirely and made a fool out of him.

"Are you okay?" I asked, not sure if she had damaged his head more than it already was.

"Couldn't be better."

I noticed the tent in his pants and blushed as I quickly looked the other way. He must have noticed my reaction and laughed at my embarrassment.

He lusted for her! That's so wrong in so many possible ways!

Besides being a conceited princess, Sasha had an obsession with my mate.

"Seriously? Sasha? My evil cousin? Are you nuts?"

"She wants me really bad!"

"She just said no to going out with you, and you didn't impress her that much," I reminded him, imitating Sasha's British accent.

"She'll change her mind."

"She left!"

"I'll find her again. It's not like you don't know where she lives," he reminded me.

"Oh, God! I'm not going to get mixed up in your crazy flirtations with girls. I have no intention of talking to Sasha on your behalf."

"What's going on?" Shane asked, arriving next to us.

"How is Kevin?" I asked, reminded that I had left him in the room with the rest of the family.

"He's fine. The king and Eric are with him. They are talking. Kevin seems happy. He's a nice kid."

"Kevin is a sweetheart," I said, glad that my brother was accepting our newfound family.

"He still needs to recover for a few more days before he can go home with us," Shane said.

"Home?" Jason asked, folding his arms and furrowing his brows.

"To the palace. The king wants his grandson and granddaughter," he said, throwing me a look, "closer to spend some time with them."

"I'm going, too," Jason said immediately. "There is no way in hell that I'm letting my cousins stay alone in that vampire lair."

"They are their family. They will not harm them. I wouldn't let my mate near them if I thought they would harm her," Shane reminded him.

"I'm not leaving them," Jason warned with a stubborn face.

"Fine," I said, interrupting their macho staring contest and pulling them apart. "You can come, too, Jason, and stalk Sasha," I added.

He looked at me as if I had read his mind and discovered his real intentions.

Shane had a smirk on his face when I looked at him, and then he laughed. "She's going to eat you alive, boy."

Jason actually growled at him.

"Keep your opinion to yourself, wolf!"

Jason being jealous was like dragons—a pure myth.

"What the hell, Jason? Don't be rude," I complained, pulling Shane away. His wolf would not tolerate another growl from Jason. I could sense that from him.

"I still don't trust your mate, and you are being naïve in believing your family's good intentions. After all, it was your uncle who killed your parents and is chasing you. They didn't want your parents to be together in the first place!" Jason accused.

Shane growled at him.

"Jason, everything was already explained. I trust my mate. You need to suck it up and deal with it!" I told him.

I saw Shane smirk at Jason out of the corner of my eye.

"I'm sorry," Jason said, breathing out.

I put my hand on his shoulder. "Jason, we all need to be friends. We're family now."

"Fine," Jason whispered, rolling his eyes up and folding his arms. "But what happens between Sasha and me is my problem, not yours."

"Sasha is crazy. Forget about her," Shane advised with a serious tone.

I couldn't have agreed more.

"I happen to like crazy girls, and I'm a big boy. I can handle her."

Shane and I sighed simultaneously, probably thinking the same thing, and then we looked at each other and chuckled.

"I'm the one who gets crazy around you two!" Jason said with an exasperated voice.

"Why?" I asked.

He walked away, shrugging. "I'll leave you two lovebirds alone. I'm going to check on Kevin."

I stared at Shane, and a chill ran down my spine. He had a playful smile on his lips, and I couldn't help but to fall into his arms and melt against him.

"Are you happier, now?" he asked, and I knew he was talking about Kevin waking up.

I had to confess, I'd gotten worried for a moment. I wasn't sure the blood would work. A lot of blood was necessary, more than I'd expected, and I was glad my uncle and even Sasha had contributed so selflessly.

"Everything will be fine now, sweetie," Shane said, sharing my thoughts.

He kissed my forehead and then the tip of my nose. I blushed at what he was thinking. It was not about sex, although it was related. It was about our future together, about all the chubby, cute babies we could have.

I giggled. "We have a lot of time for that. I'm too young!"

"I know, darling. For now, I'm glad I have you."

"You make me really happy," I whispered, totally in love and emotional by his thoughts.

His lips kissed me softly. "So now let's talk about the fact that we need to tell your family that we—"

"No, no. We won't say anything to anyone yet," I said, letting him go and walking down the corridor toward Kevin's room.

"We need to tell them. Your family is old-fashioned like that. The king—"

"Shane, you are old-fashioned like that! Don't blame my family," I said, and he grabbed me by the waist and made me stop. We stood in the middle of the corridor.

"Honey, you said yes, so why can't we tell them?"

"Kevin just woke up. Let's wait a bit longer."

"Okay, but the thing is that the king—and your uncle—are expecting us to get married. He asked me yesterday when the wedding would take place."

"What?" I asked, annoyed by everybody's insistence.

Don't they have anything better to do than interfere in my private life?

"I told you, he is old-fashioned like that. Making the vows is one of the oldest traditions between mates. It is taking the responsibility of spending our lives together. He is expecting us to do it, so our union will be blessed by the gods."

"Huh," I muttered as I furrowed my brow. Then, I pouted. "I still don't think we should rush things."

"Why not? We are meant to be together. We are not rushing, just putting it on paper."

"You want to do that because you are afraid that I won't stay with you," I grumbled.

"For God's sake, Anna, marking was far more important than a ceremony. We are bonded. Besides, you've already said that you would never leave me and that you love me. I'm not worried about that."

I thought carefully about his words and growled at him when I heard his thoughts about Sasha wanting to marry him back in the days when they were a couple.

I could so slap him for being such an annoying mate and trying to make me feel more jealous with that information. As if that would be enough to convince me to marry him right away! The nerve he had!

"I love it so much when you get jealous if Sasha's around us," he mumbled in my ear, tickling me while I tried to get away from him. "Stop, honey. I was only teasing you. I didn't want to be so pushy."

"It's too soon. It's not that I don't want to marry you. I do."

"Good," Shane whispered. "Then we wait one year."

I looked at him sideways. *He is really insistent! I could just bite him!*

He smiled, certainly reading my mind and liking it.

"That would be so wrong to do in a hospital," he said with a wicked smile that made me laugh.

His thoughts focused on the biting and the sex that the bite would bring. A hospital was not a good place to think about that.

"Stop it," I demanded, caught inside his daydream fantasies.

He kissed me possessively and caressed my lower lip with his tongue, making me breathless. "It's not like you weren't thinking the same." His husky voice in my ear made me shiver.

He is so shamelessly right. Still, it didn't mean it was what we were going to do it. "I'm just going to remind you of something. Supernatural hospital and super hearing everywhere."

I smiled as he realized what I meant.

It was a bad idea, and I was glad he agreed. I would die of shame if we got caught or someone heard us.

Then, I realized that I was afraid of getting caught, nothing more and nothing less. I was almost tempted to go with him to find a place to make out. It was appealing, and I sure was missing him. We had been there for several days with no privacy.

"Yes, that would be wrong of us, making everybody horny around here with the delicious moans you make."

He ran away because he knew he was in serious trouble if I caught him.

He's so going to pay for saying something like that! How dare he?

I was not the only one to moan when making love! And it wasn't like I screamed out loud when we were doing it.

At least... I mean... I didn't think I did. Did I?

Shane escaped to my brother's room, where my grandfather and uncle stared at me and signaled for me to be quiet, pointing at the '*Quiet Please*' sign on the wall.

I would catch Shane and make him pay, regardless. I would make him pay a lot of times. I was getting kinky again. I needed to go home and have some time alone with him.

Shane sat down on the empty chair, trying to swallow his laughter, while I sat next to him.

"Just wait until we get home," I menaced and looked away to make my point prevail.

"We can go home right now," he said in a hopeful voice.

I laughed, winning a new hush from my grandfather.

Staying mad at my soulmate was nearly impossible since he was charming and drop-dead gorgeous.

He frowned, knowing exactly what I was thinking. He got annoyed when I thought he was adorable and cute, but I knew he liked to hear it. He was playing hard to get.

"I'm not hard to get," he whispered, making me snort. "You

need some rest."

"How would that be resting?" I wondered, and he offered me a sexy, wicked smirk.

"Let's go home, and I promise I'll let you rest," he conveyed through our mind link, trying to convince me. *"I will run you a hot bath, and you can feed. It's been too long since you last fed properly. And I can even make you pancakes. Sweet and hot pancakes with delicious black chocolate filling and caramel topping."*

Gosh! That was such an unfair proposal.

"I should have put the ring inside a pancake and covered it with chocolate," he joked, tuned into my thoughts.

His idea made me smile. That would have been original—a ring in a pancake and then my having to go to the hospital to take it out of my stomach!

He laughed at my thoughts. I mentally rolled my eyes as he smiled and shrugged. His hand was in his pocket, and he was playing with the box.

Blood rushed to my cheeks as I recalled how beautiful the ring was.

He leaned closer and whispered in my ear, "Let me put it on your finger."

"When we get home. Then we can tell everybody over a family dinner."

"That's a great idea," he said. "Are you happy?"

"Yes."

"Kevin's awake. We can go home," he said in a sweet and caring voice. His eyes were shining like the blue sky on a summer's day. I could spend an entire day staring at his eyes. "You need to rest and eat," he insisted.

I brushed his face with my fingertips, delighted by how much he cared about me. His existence filled a hole inside my heart that I didn't know I had. I was also proud of having him as my soulmate. Still, going home so he felt less worried wasn't in my plans.

"I…can't. I can't leave him alone."

Shane nodded in understanding.

My place was beside my brother. I had to keep him company and make him feel safe and loved. I was all he had. Well, I used to be. Currently, we had a lot more family members.

I stared at my newfound uncle and grandpa, thrilled to have found them. They were friendly and seemed delighted about finding us.

Eric was talking to Kevin, and I felt emotional by the captivated gaze Kevin had on him. Eric looked so much like Dad that my brother's fascination was understandable. Besides, Eric was a wonderful uncle, and he had more resemblances to my dad than just the physical ones. Eric was kind and had a paternal gaze when he looked at us. It was unfortunate that he hadn't found his soulmate yet, so he could have his own kids. He would make a wonderful father.

Shane's hand touched mine, holding it and making me feel safe. My hand met Shane's lips. He always acted like a gentleman around my family. It was interesting to watch. On the other hand, I acted more affectionately than Shane, and my grandfather typically made some remarks about it. He was old-fashioned and didn't approve the excessive public display of affection.

I imagined that Shane's extra care was due to my need to cry again. I wasn't crying with sadness, though. My life couldn't have been more perfect. I had found my soulmate, my family, and I'd saved my brother. The only thing that was missing was my parents being alive. There was nothing I could do to make that happen. I had to be content with no longer being alone. I had Shane, and I would have my own family.

"We're *already* a family," he whispered in my ear, holding my hand against his chest.

I nodded in agreement and leaned in to brush my lips against his. The kiss didn't last long since we were hit by a pillow. We looked at the bed where Kevin, Jason, Eric, and grandfather were laughing as they looked back at us.

Did Kevin throw the pillow? Is he strong enough to do that? How funny of them!

"Didn't I tell you that she doesn't care about us anymore?" Jason asked Kevin.

My brother winked at me. He was still pale, and his lips were dehydrated, but at least he was awake. I couldn't wait for him to get out of that bed as he became his happy self again.

"Maybe now she will stop treating me like she's my mom," Kevin joked, looking at Jason, who nodded.

"Yes, keep dreaming." I tossed the pillow back at them, hitting Jason's face.

Perfect throw! Right on the mark!

EPILOGUE

TWO DAYS PASSED before Kevin left the hospital. My life started to get back on its normal track. If I could ever describe my life as normal.

Shane and I were having the time of our lives. We couldn't have been better or happier together. Kevin fully recovered and came to live in our new family's home. Or should I say, palace?

Shane and I lived between Grandpa's palace and our home.

I found out that my grandfather had brought his family palace, stone by stone, from the Netherlands, where they were originally from. They'd moved to the United States more than two hundred years ago when Europe was no longer safe for their kind and when wars had erupted everywhere. Many new ideas about freedom and new types of governments helped their decision to leave on a quest for a new, peaceful place to exist, away from commotion and extermination.

In other news, Jason resumed following Sasha everywhere like a puppy, which was hilarious because he was half panther, half-human!

Sasha couldn't care less about him, or, at least, it looked that way. She would sometimes throw him a bone, letting him babble about stuff, places, and things that might make him seem attractive to her. Sometimes, I had caught them having some steamy make-out sessions. But they weren't a couple.

My crazy vampire cousin didn't seem to want to be a couple with Jason. I think she was playing him for a bit until she got bored.

Smart girl! I loved my cousin, but he was a player! He took nothing seriously. So, I guess he found his match.

Ironic, I know.

My uncle was the nicest person ever! He became like a father to me even after only knowing him for a couple of weeks. He was beyond intelligent and told us a lot of things about my dad. It was nice to talk about my dad again. I used to feel like talking about him was a big secret I had to keep to myself.

My grandfather was an enigma wrapped in a puzzle. He was fascinating, wise, and overall paternalistic toward Kevin and me.

We grew to love him dearly.

He had nice, caring eyes, even if he spent most of his time sleeping. Yes, sleeping. Go figure! It seemed that vampires could fall into a deep sleep and manipulate their dream world to make them relive their memories.

So my grandfather was able to live for many centuries after my grandmother's death because he spent his time reliving the moments of happiness he had with his wife.

I had mixed feelings about that. I didn't know if I found that nostalgic or him being a hopeless romantic. I guess it was both.

Meanwhile, I saw more paintings of my grandmother. Isobel was beautiful. I did resemble her, and that may be why my grandpa had a soft spot for me. We talked a lot when he was awake.

Yet, I couldn't help but think that my grandfather wouldn't be there for much longer. It made me sad, but his mate had died, his older son had died, another son had turned out to be a hateful, crazy demon, and he had found his grandchildren. His life had become kind of aimless and without purpose.

Maybe Grandma was waiting for him to join her on the other side. Living in his dreams was not as good as living in reality, but what did I know? I couldn't picture my life without Shane, and we'd been together for less than four months, so I couldn't begin to imagine the pain my grandpa felt after living with Isobel for centuries.

Things between Shane and I couldn't have been better. We

did have some ups and downs because he wanted me to put the ring on my finger, and I thought it was still early. Then he sulked for an entire day, and I realized I was being an idiot.

I finally put the beautiful ring on my finger, and we announced to everybody that we were engaged.

My grandfather was thrilled about a wedding in our future plans and babies to cheer up the palace.

I was happy as I had never been before. I couldn't take my eyes off my ring! I felt like a fool, but I actually blushed with love every time I stared at the sculptural piece and thought about how Shane had bought it more than one century ago before meeting me. Before I even existed.

He'd kept it for all those years to put on my finger. And it looked good on my finger! It looked like it was made for it. And I will probably never take it off while I exist, and if I die, I want it to be buried with me. Creepy—I know!

I loved Shane so much it hurt!

Have you ever loved someone so much that you thought you would die if he ever went away?

I would die if something happened to Shane. I finally understood Catherine in Wuthering Heights when she said, "He's more myself than I am. Whatever our souls are made of, his and mine are the same."

Tacky, I know. I was becoming a serious sucker for romantic gestures and poems.

But I believed that Shane was inside me like part of my thoughts, and I was inside him, as part of his being. I could never love him less, and it seemed that each day I loved him more. Yes, I would die without him, and I would die for him just the way I knew he would die for me. I loved being tacky like that!

The strangest thing was that all my short life, I'd thought that I would spend eternity alone or would have some lovers to keep me warm at night and satisfy my needs. I'd imagined that I would always be incomplete. I hadn't been able to imagine that someday someone would deserve to have my love and my respect. I had never thought that I would find someone who understood me, who completed me and made me believe that the whole world was perfect and that the birds sang in the morning to make us smile.

Sometimes, I watched the horizon through the break of the morning and reminisced on everything that had happened in my life—all the moments, sad and happy—and I'd smile in wonder and awe.

Everything looked so random. Yet destiny seemed to have its own agenda and had brought me here to Shane's arms. I guess the gods are not that bad, after all.

I was lucky. I knew I was. I had found my purpose to live, and I just had to wait twenty-three years. A lot of other immortals weren't so lucky. My uncle was still waiting for his mate, so he could start living. My grandfather had lost his, and he was waiting for death to join his wife in the afterlife. My brother was overwhelmed by the changes, and he was fascinated by the fact that he might also have a soulmate—a witch, based on our guess.

Regarding him, I was highly intrigued by the tattoo that had appeared on his forearm after he woke up. Jessica couldn't explain that, either. She didn't know if it was a witch's emblem. She knew that powerful witches could mark their soulmates, but it was not a sure thing. Maybe it was not a mating mark since the phoenix was a well-known symbol of rebirth and fire. In a way, my brother had been reborn and had been graced with a new life.

But why did the symbol appear on his arm? Did it have some concealed meaning? Was it some sort of prophecy?

Kevin seemed fine and looked normal, in a normal hybrid sort of way. Jessica had promised me to investigate its meaning. I just had to be patient. Like I was being patient and not running in pursuit of Alaric.

Alaric being my uncle, still haunted my dreams and thoughts. He had lost his soul and was no longer the person he once was. With no feelings, no morals, or empathy, he was simply a twisted, hateful, and pitiful vampire with a crazy quest to exterminate others as if he was a god. All the drinking from the source had turned him into that. It was a reminder to my other relatives not to drink from the source, to keep their souls pure of other people's imprints, dreams, fears, and memories. It scared the hell out of me!

I knew deep down that peace had not arrived permanently in my life. I knew that, sooner or later, even if I hoped it would be later, Alaric would make his appearance, and I would find him. But I would not waste my life in pursuit of revenge when I could spend it with my newfound family and my breathtaking mate.

After all, I had already lost my parents to Alaric's hate. I had been given a new opportunity, and I could either spend my existence hating or being happy.

Shane was my happiness, my safe harbor, and everything I needed to feel that I belonged to this time and place.

Not to mention, I had others to help me go after Alaric: my soulmate, my family, and my friends. We were ready for him. His reign of terror was going to stop, but I was not going to let him ruin anything else in my life.

In the meantime, all my energies were focused on living happily with Shane and the people I loved in a place that I called my home.

Hi, dear reader! ◎

This book is over, but book 2, following Jessica, is already available and there's a preview to give you a taste.

Also, if you enjoyed this story, please a **REVIEW**. Even if you don't enjoy writing reviews, you can rate it.

Reviews are essential for Indie Authors. They help us decide if we should continue to write a series of books or move on to the next one.

If you are enjoying this book and are eager to know more about this family, consider leaving a review and asking for more.

You can also join my Newsletter and know more about my reading suggestions, my new releases, giveaways, and new worlds.

Subscribe <u>HERE.</u>

https://landing.mailerlite.com/webforms/landing/o0z8p3

THE WITCH AND THE VAMPIRE KING—PREVIEW
Chapter One—Burn
JESSICA

THE RIDE TO ANNA'S current house didn't take long. I had woken up at the best part of my dream. It was unfair…I hadn't dreamed about him for a whole week, then I fell asleep on the way to my best friend's house, and there it comes: my vivid dream, my most erotic and intense sexual fantasy. *Only to wake up right in the middle of it!* Livid doesn't begin to describe how I felt at that moment. But I was also surprisingly happy. I always enjoyed dreaming of my mate.

The taxi driver cleared his throat to informed me that we had arrived at my destination.

Taking my bags out of the car, he drove off and left me in front of a cabin in the middle of nowhere. It would have been pretty eerie if the cabin hadn't had a welcoming tendril of smoke rising out of the chimney. There were people I knew inside—Anna and Shane—at least, that's what I hoped for.

I still felt annoyed and somewhat anxious as I carried my small bag up to the porch and knocked on the door. The driver was long gone; I had fantasized for a while before climbing the stairs, and I didn't know what Anna's reaction would be to my sudden arrival. I had not alerted her that I was coming nor did I ask her if I could stay. But she was my best friend, and I needed her help. Surely, she would take me in and help protect me.

I had a hard time keeping my mind on the present. I couldn't stop thinking of that hot dream about my mate that left me with deep yearning. I did feel like I could remember more this time than before, but I could never remember his face. It was always a blur. I remembered inner thoughts, some smells, and some actions between us. Yes, I was able to remember the intimate kisses and his hands roaming my body. In fact, I usually woke up aroused and needy, especially when waking before the actual end of the dream. However, a word echoed in my mind—a word that I had never thought about before. The new word was *king*. My soulmate from another life had been or still was a king. That would explain the feeling I always had of being inside a luxurious castle. He was a vampire king.

That would narrow it down to a mere one thousand kingdoms… But it was useful information. And then, there was the fact that I was sure the castle was not in America. My mate was a European king. And I had just arrived from Europe—*damn!* I'm even running away from a king. *Coincidence?* Probably.

I knocked again and held my breath. I was growing distressed and uneasy. I peered around the darkness and slightly trembled in fear. It was creepy out here. And I felt watched, paranoia perhaps, but I still tried to listen to my surroundings as I prayed for Anna to open the damn door.

I knocked impatiently, tempted to use my powers to open it, so I could get inside, close it behind me, and glue my back against the door while catching my breath. I felt like the main character of a lame horror movie, waiting to become dinner to some wild animal or serial killer. I wanted and needed to get in, and I also needed to stop being so afraid. I wasn't being myself lately. I wasn't a coward, nor was I generally paranoid. However, I didn't make a habit of running away from vampire kings who wanted my head. Topping it all off, I was tired and my magical powers were low.

Finally, someone unlocked the door and opened it slightly to peek outside. It was Shane. *God*, Anna had won the lottery! Her gorgeous mate stared at me, shirtless and in a nice pair of pants, he looked perplexed trying to figure out who I was.

"I'm Jessica. Anna's friend," I reminded him, a bit confused by his blank expression. I had only been gone for three weeks. And I'm kind of gorgeous and unforgettable. I guessed I hadn't made a strong impression on him after all.

"I know who you are," he answered with a drowsy voice.

Okay, I guess I did leave an impression. Well, in fact, I kind of saved his ass. I let out a sigh of relief and was going to ask him something when a crazy woman ran at me from inside and jumped, wrapping her arms around my neck.

"Jessica!" Anna screamed in my ear, causing a ringing sensation to go through my head. I guess she'd missed me. "Where were you? What are you doing here in the middle of the night? And why couldn't we contact you for weeks?"

The interrogation had begun. She acted like my mother. Actually, no, she acted like my best friend who cared more about me than my mother ever did when she was alive. By nature, witches are impulsive and tend to do whatever they please. I guess it was all the dancing naked in the woods that gave us a feeling of freedom and an unwillingness to be restricted by moral standards and 'normal lives'. We are anything but normal. We are magical beings and were adored like goddesses back in the beginning of time. Too bad that tradition was not becoming fashionable again. I would like to be worshiped and paid homage to by humans.

I smiled at Anna and pretended to be playful. I didn't want her to realize that I was frightened. It would make her even more alarmed. Besides, I had escaped, I was here safe and sound, so everything was going to be all right. There was no need to divulge everything about the trouble I'd left behind me.

"I'm here to visit you. Aren't you going to ask me to come in? It's freezing outside, I didn't know the nights could be so chilly here."

"Of course, where are my manners, please come in."

I hesitated. "Can Shane bring my bags in?" I pointed outside to the three suitcases.

Shane frowned slightly, and I smiled and batted my lashes at him.

"Trust me, she is traveling light," Anna said as Shane strolled to my luggage and brought it effortlessly into their home. He was a werewolf and a strong one; three suitcases were no challenge for him.

Anna led me inside her home, asking, "Is everything okay?"

I nodded while looking around at the cozy house that Shane had built for himself. It was charming and rustic. It had an inviting fireplace and next to it was a comfortable couch covered with a blanket and two mugs on the coffee table. I may have interrupted some romantic affair and, suddenly, I felt a bit morose for not having someone to do those sorts of activities with. However, I was more than ecstatic that Anna had found her mate--a gorgeous and powerful mate. Come on, it was hard for me to take my eyes off him. *He should put on a shirt.*

Anna must have thought the same because she threw him his shirt as she gave me a look. I smiled, my cheeks turning red as they warmed up near the fireplace. Staring at the fire, I became mesmerized by it until I heard Shane lock the door. I let out a huge sigh of relief. I was safe at last. I was among friends and next to Anna, whom I'd missed and prayed to have beside me when I was in danger. Above all, I was alive.

Anna cleared her throat. "So, are you staying with us for a while?"

"Only if you're okay with it," I answered, glancing at Shane to see his reaction.

He shrugged his shoulders. It seemed like he didn't mind, so I liked him even more.

"We would love it," Anna said with a happy voice. "We have

an extra bedroom. Shane will put your luggage there. You can rest, but, first, you have to tell me what the hell you have been doing these past few weeks!"

"Sightseeing," I said.

Anna rolled her eyes. She never liked it when I answered her flippantly and didn't take her seriously. So I sat on the couch, clasped my hands together, to keep them from trembling, and let out a long sigh.

"Can we talk tomorrow? I'm tired and sore from my journey. It has been such a long day."

"I've missed you," she said, sitting next to me as she put her arm around my shoulders and pulled me close to her. "You're in some kind of trouble, aren't you?"

I was the witch and, yet, she was the one who could always sense when bad things happened to me. That was creepy, but she was also my best friend. "Yes, you know me. I'm always getting myself into predicaments."

"Is it serious?"

"Nothing I can't handle."

I was lying. I needed help. That was why I was interrupting Anna's time with her newfound mate. I was shamelessly moving into their home, so I could have her protection. Being in her family's territory and them being powerful vampires wouldn't hurt, either. I knew I would be safe here. My anxiety diminished with that thought.

"I'm going to put her bags in the guest room and make the bed," Shane announced.

Anna nodded and pursed her lips before lecturing me, "You left without an explanation. Well, at least, not a credible one. We tried to call you several times, but you were always vague with your answers, or you didn't answer. Kevin needs your help."

Kevin was Anna's younger brother. Although Anna looked

worried, I knew that there was no need for her unease. "He's not going to die. His witch marked him, that's it."

"That's what we are hoping for, but if it's something far worse? Some kind of curse?"

I got up and stood in front of the fireplace, my gaze lingering on the orange and blue flames. "I'm here now. And Kevin is doing great since he woke up from his coma. You're happy with your mate." I glanced over my shoulder, watching Shane who was busy carrying sheets inside what I assumed to be my new bedroom. "Now that I'm here, I'll do everything in my power to find out what the tattoo that appeared on Kevin's forearm means."

I turned around to give her a reassuring smile. Things had worked out okay in the past month. After six months of looking for a pureblood vampire to wake her brother from a deep coma, Anna found her long lost pureblood vampire relatives, and her uncle and cousin had donated the blood necessary to cure Kevin. He recovered and woke up, but a strange mark appeared on his forearm. Despite that, Anna's brother was in good health and his blood had been crucial in creating a vaccine against the serum that was killing hybrids. The world had become a less scary place, and I had to leave to take care of my own issues.

I woke from my thoughts when she said, "You look tired."

"I haven't gotten a lot of sleep lately."

"Did you find what you were looking for?"

I rubbed my sore neck. "I found a lot more than what I was looking for. I know I have been a bad friend. I shouldn't keep secrets from you. But I was on a mission, and now I need your help."

"The perimeter has been breached," Shane warned, appearing in the living room. He startled me to the point a deep shiver went through my body. He had shouldered Anna's swords and was putting his gun belt around his waist. "The sentinels say that there are, at least, eight intruders coming at high speed in our direction."

I bit my lip. They were coming for me. They had followed me here. I thought they had been fooled and that I had lost them, but I was wrong.

"It's my fault," I whispered, immobile as Anna grasped her weapons. "They are coming for me."

"What do they want?" she asked.

"How long before they get here?" I asked Shane.

"Seconds. They are fast. Faster than my men. We'll have to hold them off until backup arrives."

"Fine," I said, breathing deeply. I rolled my shoulders and walked to Shane. "I forgot to give you this the last time."

Putting my hand on his neck, I burned a protection rune on his flesh. It stung, and he complained a little about the pain. Anna didn't move. She knew what it was. She had one. It was a rune to make him immune to spells. It would come in handy, especially if there were some witches among the new bunch of trackers who were coming for me.

"Jessica, what do they want with you?" Anna questioned while Shane touched his mark with his fingers.

"You will be immune to enchantments. Witches can no longer harm you," I explained.

He went to look at the rune in the mirror. In a couple of minutes, it would disappear from his neck, camouflaged by his skin.

"They want me because I took something they had no right to have in their possession," I explained to Anna.

"And what did you steal?" she asked, looking out the windows of the cabin. "They are here," she whispered then flashed over to the front door.

Shane went after her and both of them slipped out into the night. I didn't know what dangers were waiting for them outside. I just knew I wouldn't let them face the trackers alone. So, at my normal speed, I cat-walked to the door.

*　*　*

The silver moon illuminated the entrance of the house, showing me the scene that played out in front the cabin. Shane and Anna stood side by side, staring at the eight dark figures before them in a line, holding swords and daggers. They looked like ninjas. Their eyes were the only thing visible under their masks. But, judging by the shapes of their bodies, they were all unmistakably women. The elaborate suits, the covered faces, signified the vampire king's personal death squad. He had called out the big guns for me.

Anna swung the swords in her hands and threw one of them to Shane. He would need it. The gun by itself wouldn't be enough. I also needed to protect myself.

"You are trespassing," Shane said after a prolonged silence while everyone appeared to be sizing their opponents up, as though measuring their strengths and making strategies.

"Just give us the rogue witch," one of the masked girls said, the one in the middle, probably the leader.

"Rogue my ass," I protested, putting my hands on my hips.

Who are they calling rogue? I could be flying solo and not having a coven or a king to lick his boots and give my services to a master, but I was no rogue witch. I was my own person, and I lived my own life. Making my own choices, freedom of choice—that was what those medieval kings needed to learn.

"You are trespassing," Shane repeated. "You will not be warned again. If you do not leave, we will make you."

"We will not leave without the witch," the girl announced, and, to make her point, she sped to Shane and attacked him with a dagger.

Shane defended himself easily. It was almost surreal the way he predicted her movements. He moved around the assassin like he was humoring her, then disarmed the girl and made her backflip and fall hard on the ground.

Anna didn't move an inch, she completely trusted his abilities. Those two were acting like a team. I was so proud of them! Who would have ever thought Anna would trust someone like she obviously did Shane. I would have clapped if the other seven intruders didn't rush to help their leader and attack my friends.

The sound of steel clashed and echoed in the night as the fight progressed.

They were too fast for me to understand what the hell was going on. I could hear the snarls and the pained cries. I occasionally caught bodies moving fast, attacking each other, but I was a witch. The powers I had were of the magical kind. But the abilities of super-speed or to follow fast movements with my vision weren't one of them. Though, I could easily differentiate Anna and Shane from the dark, red-masked girls. They defended themselves fairly well. The girls were vampires, probably turned and not the original kind. They shouldn't be a problem for Anna and Shane, or even for me, but I was tired and had used my magic too much lately.

Suddenly, Anna rolled on the ground, and Shane was kicked back. The girls were using their teamwork to break their tactical defense.

Two of the girls lunged to try and grab me. Anna jumped up and flashed in front of me. She swung her sword and shoved them, pushing them back. Shane was back beside her, snarling, and I saw how his muscles flexed as if he was about to shift into a wolf and shred the enemies to pieces.

I was tired but not dead. I moved my neck in circles, opened my hands, stretched out, and called upon my magical powers. Breathing deeply, I released my fire from my wrists and made fire whips that slithered on my hands like living snakes. It was unique magic I used. I liked to be original that way. Any witch could make flame orbs and throw them randomly. Me, I would rather have fire whips and use them to beat and burn my opponents.

Channeling the magical power I still had, I pushed forward a wall of kinetic power that launched the girls through the air, landing them hard on the dusty road. Then, I moved to the middle of my pursuers and swirled the whips around, burning them and forcing a retreat. They screamed and growled as they fell back.

"Go back to the house. I got this," I said to Anna, who gave me a look like she was unsure what I was planning. "Get Shane inside!"

She knew when I was serious and when I was not. I was not playing. I wanted this day to end so I could go to sleep and dream of my mate again. I needed to feel safe. I needed to punish that arrogant and deceitful king. I needed to show them that I was not kidding, that I was dangerous and would burn them to ashes.

Anna pushed Shane to safety. I didn't want to hurt them with my powers. Meanwhile, my eyes didn't leave my opponents as we walked in circles. They were angry and wanted to drain and punish me for killing the others the king had sent before them, probably their friends. I couldn't have cared less.

"See you all in hell," I said as I called forth my ancestral witch legacy, a powerful magic that was a challenge even for vampiric assassins.

My hair danced in the air as if gravity had ceased to exist. My hands formed beams of fire as if, around me, the air was pushed out. The pressure made the attackers fall and hit the ground, making a painful noise. I was ready to burst into flames and take those vampires on a one-way trip to hell. But then I saw *him*: the tall blond man. He was not far from us. Backing him up were a group of werewolves and Kevin. Anna's brother was there, staring at me with widened eyes. He had never seen me use my full power before. Maybe he had just never seen me this mad before. And next to him was the tall, blue-eyed man. He had a surprised look on his face and seemed fascinated by my actions.

He looked so—*familiar*. He looked…

The screams woke me up from my thoughts and I stared at the girls, who were trying to run away from my glowing fire shield as it grew, almost reaching their side. It would burn like pure liquid silver on their flesh. Some had already been touched, which explained why they were screaming. *And did I mention that this fire is also magnetic?* They couldn't run far or fast enough, even if they'd wanted to. The shield pulled them into it, ready to make them burst into small pieces of flying ash as they succumbed to the flames.

"Jessica! Stand down!" Anna screamed.

I could understand that a whirlwind had taken form. The wind was all around us, making a lot of noise, but I was able to hear Anna yelling and warning me about the danger. *I need to stand down.* Calm the flames. Reduce my raw power. Easier said than done. Staring at the tall blond man, however, did help to calm my powers down.

Everything finally stopped. The girls were grabbed by the werewolves, and I felt like I was floating as I tried to walk to the man who was walking toward me. My vision tended to blur when I exhibited this amount of power, but he reminded me a lot of my king…

"Who are you?" he asked as he drew near me.

I just had time to smile at him and ask, "Are you my mate?" And then I fainted.

MORE ABOUT THE AUTHOR

Anna Santos is a USA Today Bestselling and an International Bestselling Author. She likes to write about shifters, vampires, angels, mermaids, fae, and occasionally humans.

Anna always keeps her readers on their toes with adrenaline-fueled adventures, genuine characters, strong female leads, and romantic plots.

When she's not writing, she's probably reading or spending too watching TV shows. As an introvert, home is her safe harbor. Yet, she's known for leaving the house from time to time and having her family throw a party because they haven't seen her for days. Then they ask her how many books she wrote while gone, assuming that writing must be super easy.

Anna guarantees that it's not, but she never wanted to be anything else. Unless there's a possibility of being a powerful supernatural being in an awesome world where unicorns and fairies are real. Then, she would probably go there and never come back.

Meanwhile, there's more to come, and if you'd like to know about it, you can join her at:

http://www.annasantosauthor.com
https://www.facebook.com/AnnaSantosAuthor
https://twitter.com/AnneSaint90
https://instagram.com/annasantosauthor
You can sign-up for her newsletter here:
https://app.mailerlite.com/webforms/landing/w4r0o1